Still Close To Heaven

KATHLEEN KANE

St. Martin's Paperbacks

STILL CLOSE TO HEAVEN

Copyright © 1997 by Kathleen Kane.

ISBN: 0-312-96268-1

Printed in the United States of America

St. Martin's Paperbacks edition/August 1997

St. Martin's Paperbacks are published by St. Martin's Press, 175 Fifth Avenue, New York, NY 10010.

10 9 8 7 6 5 4 3 2

To my son, Jason Child, for Little League summers and terrifying driving lessons, for first dates and first loves, for long hair and goatees, for Monty Python and Reel Big Fish, for bear hugs and, most especially, the laughter. Being your mother has always been an E-ticket ride, and through it all, there's been my pride in you. I love you.

Chapter ☆ One

For one taste of whiskey, he'd even be willing to die again.

But if he did that, Jackson Tate told himself, he'd be in the same fix he was in now.

Being dead sure wasn't all it was cracked up to be.

Scowling, Jackson stomped around the crowded saloon. He walked through the card tables, marched through the out-of-tune piano and finally stopped at the bar. There, he dropped one arm around Dolly, a fire-headed female with a body bold enough to make a grown man cry. She didn't feel his presence, even when his fingertips stroked her magnificent bosom.

"Should have listened closer when the preachers warned me about Hell and eternal suffering," he muttered.

Then again, even if he'd paid attention during those mind-numbing Sunday sermons, he wouldn't have been prepared for this miserable afterlife.

He snorted a choked laugh and pretended to lean one elbow on the bar top. Who would have thought his Bible-thumping mother was right about a saloon being the gateway to Hell? Nearly right, he amended. As it turned ou this tumbledown saloon in Washington Territory hadn't been a gateway to anywhere.

This *was* Hell.

"Not quite," a voice said from somewhere close by.

Jackson spun around, raking his sharp-eyed gaze over every corner of the saloon he'd come to know so well in the last few months.

"Who's talking?" he demanded, but he really didn't expect an answer. After three months of talking to himself, was it really so surprising that he had finally started arguing with himself, too?

"My name is," the voice went on, "or rather *was,* Lesley Smythe-White."

The saloon's half doors crashed inward, and every head in the place turned to stare at . . . emptiness.

"What the hell was that?" someone muttered.

"Just the wind is all," another voice said.

"I didn't feel no wind," the first man countered.

Slowly the cluster of people returned to their business, obviously willing to ignore the unexplainable. Jackson, though, stared warily at the being taking shape in the slice of sunlight spearing through the open doorway.

The first person to speak to him directly since the day he'd died had a slight build and a long, angular face, crowned by a beak of a nose that arched higher than a cat's back and curved under at the tip. Her lips were full and twisted into a grimace of distaste. She had curly, white hair that lay like sausages above her ears and she wore funny looking, gaudy knee britches with a matching jacket of pale yellow silk. Jackson's eyebrows lifted as he noticed her shoes with shining silver buckles and too high heels. Her face and wrists were framed with yards of lace.

For all of her fancy gewgaws, she was the ugliest female Jackson had ever seen.

Then the stranger started moving toward him. Like Jackson, she passed directly through the card tables and the gamblers hunched over their hands. Unlike Jackson, as this strange being crossed the room, cards fluttered off the tables and the sawdust-covered floor shifted in her wake.

A pang of uneasiness began to uncurl in Jackson's belly. As usual, he fought down his own nervousness with a burst of temper.

"Who the hell are you, lady?"

Pale green eyes widened, then narrowed into slits. The being tilted her head back until a sharp, contempt-filled gaze was directed along the length of that formidable nose.

"I am *not* a female."

Jackson's eyebrows shot up again. "Are you sure?"

The nose quivered. "Of course, I'm sure. Oh, I knew this was a mistake."

"What?" Jackson asked as he drew his head back to study the newcomer. Now that he knew what he was looking at, he realized it *was* a man. A mighty small, peculiar man. But a man nonetheless.

The smaller man tugged a lace-edged handkerchief from one of his cuffs and dabbed at his nose. Jackson thought the smidgen of fabric was sadly inadequate for the task.

Rather than answering the question, the smaller man sighed heavily and walked a slow circle around Jackson. When he'd completed his route and was once again looking disdainfully at him, he asked, "Haven't you given the slightest amount of thought as to why you have been trapped in this abysmal place?"

Tipping his hat back farther on his head, Jackson stared down at the fellow. Maybe having somebody to talk to wasn't such a good thing after all. "Sure I did," he said. "At first. Then I just figured this here was Hell and I might as well get used to it."

"Amazing."

"What's that supposed to mean?" He had a feeling he'd just been insulted.

"Nothing." The white-wigged head shook slowly. Then,

muttering to himself, he added, "It's hopeless. Didn't I warn them? Didn't I say that it was pointless?"

"Mister," Jackson said, straightening up to his full imposing height of six feet-three inches. "I may be dead, but that doesn't mean I have to stand here and listen to you."

"Of course it does. Where can you go?"

Hmm. The little fella had a point. Off and on for the last three months, Jackson had tried to leave the saloon where he had died in a crooked card game. At first, he'd simply headed through the front door, only to be stopped by a wall of icy cold. He'd been able to see through it, hear through it, hell, once or twice, he'd even thought he could smell the outside air through it. But he hadn't been able to push so much as one finger past that invisible barrier.

Later, he had tried all of the windows with the same result. He had gone into the cellar, but the ice had blocked the tiny windows below, too. Same for the roof. No, he was caught, plain and simple. Like a rat in a trap.

"All right," he snapped. "Say your piece and move on."

The little man sighed. "Fine. It's time for you to begin earning your way out of this . . . ," he glanced around at his surroundings. *"Salon."*

"Saloon." Jackson corrected.

He shuddered. "Of course."

"You mean there's a way I can get out of here?"

"Naturally. If there weren't, don't you suppose there would be more than just *your* ghost haunting this disreputable establishment?"

Ghost?

Jackson took a step back. Reaching up, he rubbed one hand across the back of his neck and swallowed heavily.

Jesus.

He was a ghost.

A haunt.

A spook.

Oh, he'd accepted the fact that he was dead. But, somehow, discovering that he was a ghost took a bit more getting used to.

Why the hell did these things always happen to him?

"Mister Tate," the man said impatiently. "Are you ready to listen to me or not?"

"Uh, yeah. Sure thing, little fella."

He winced. "You may address me as Lesley."

"Lesley. Isn't that a woman's name?"

The smaller man ignored him. "Your assignment is a simple one."

"Glad to hear it."

"I rather thought you might be."

He frowned. Another insult? The way the fella talked, it was hard to tell.

"There is a girl—"

Jackson brightened.

Lesley scowled. "A *child*," he corrected and reached into his silk coat. He pulled out a small tablet and checked something written there. Glancing up, he continued. "She's lost. Alone. Ten years old."

"A kid?" Hell. He'd never liked kids much.

"Her family was killed in a wagon accident," Lesley said. "She's miles from safety and will not survive without intervention."

Hard to feel sorry for some unknown kid when he had plenty of problems of his own. "So?"

Lesley snapped his notebook closed and tucked it away again. "*So*, Mister Tate, it is your assignment to take this child to a safe harbor. She *must* survive."

"How do I help her if I can't get the hell out of this saloon?"

"You will be permitted to leave."

"For good?"

"That will be decided at a later time."

It wasn't as if he had a choice, he told himself. After

three months in the same damn building, he was willing to do whatever was necessary to get out. But first, he had a question or two of his own.

"What happens to me after I get this kid taken care of?" he asked. "Do I go to Heaven?"

Lesley choked.

"Hell?" A little worried now, Jackson waited. Frankly, he'd never really been interested in the preachers' idea of Heaven. Wearing white robes and playing golden harps all day didn't sound like his idea of a good time. On the other hand, he didn't relish the notion of spending eternity with the smell of sulphur and brimstone in his nose, either.

"Frankly, Mister Tate," Lesley said at last, "you're neither good enough for Heaven nor bad enough for Hell."

"So where does that leave me?"

"With countless others like yourself."

Well, that didn't tell him a damn thing.

"Are you willing to begin your first assignment?"

He'd already figured out that he was in no position to argue. "All right, I'll do it."

Lesley nodded abruptly. "See that there are no mistakes," he said. "Oh, and once she's safe, remember to wipe her memory of you."

"How do I do that?" This damned *assignment* was getting more complicated every minute.

"Just think about what you want done, and it will be done."

"If it's *that* easy, why don't I just *think* her to safety?"

Lesley sighed.

"All right, all right. It was just an idea."

"You had best get busy, Mister Tate," Lesley told him just before vanishing.

"Hey, wait a minute," Jackson shouted to thin air. "Where is this kid? How do I find her?"

In an instant, he found himself standing at the bottom of a ravine. He felt the rocky ground beneath his boots. Felt the cool sweetness of a breeze as it brushed across him.

Stunned, he held his breath.

His *breath*.

Jackson grinned, bent down, and snatched up a clump of spring grass. He worked it around in his fingers, delighting in the fact that he could once again, touch. Feel. He wasn't sure *why* this was happening. Or how long it would last. But he sure as hell intended to make the most of it. Dropping the handful of grass to the dirt, he glanced around, trying to figure out exactly where he was.

Steep canyon walls rose on either side of him. The jagged stone bluffs looked as though they'd been clawed from the earth by impatient fingers. Green dotted the surface of the ridge where clumps of brush lay clinging to the rocks like survivors off a sinking ship. Brilliant sunlight danced on the rippling water in a nearby creek and overhead, a hawk, startled by his sudden presence, streaked upward.

Jesus. Who would have thought he'd ever be so glad to get *out* of a saloon?

"Are you my angel?" a soft, wavering voice asked.

He stiffened, then turned around slowly.

Twenty feet away, a small blond girl knelt beside the broken, twisted remains of a wagon. Her face was dirty, bits of grass dotted her long, honey-colored braids, and her faded red dress was torn. But it was the bruised look in her sky blue eyes that touched him.

He'd never had much use for kids, but dammit, no child should have to have eyes as old and tired as this girl's.

"I prayed and prayed for an angel to come and help me," she said, a bit louder than before. "Are you him? Are you my angel?"

A flicker of shame swept through him, and he wanted to look away from those blue eyes. He didn't want to have to tell the girl that the Heaven she'd been praying to hadn't sent her an angel—only a carpenter and part-time cowhand too dumb to spot a cheat without getting himself killed.

Then again, he told himself, she didn't have to know who he was. Just who he wasn't.

"I'm no angel, kid," Jackson replied. "But I am here to help you."

One corner of her mouth threatened to lift in a half smile, then quit before getting started. "Thank you," she whispered, then fainted clean away.

He stirred the fire and watched as sparks drifted upward to be swallowed in the surrounding darkness. Setting the battered tin coffeepot on a rock close to the flames, Jackson sat down in the dirt, drew his knees up, and wrapped his arms around them. He stared across the fire at the sleeping girl, then shifted his gaze to the encroaching night.

The kid had been asleep for hours. Long enough for him to bury her folks and rummage around in what was left of their outfit for supplies. Naturally, he had tried to find their horses first. But when the trace broke, allowing the wagon to smash over the cliff, the dumb animals must have just kept running. No telling where they were now.

But, with the bacon, flour, and coffee he'd pulled from the wreckage, they had more than enough to last them on the two day walk to the town of Stillwater.

How the hell he knew where to take her—and just how far away the place was—was a mystery to him. Just as it was odd how the girl had managed to survive a wreck that had killed the rest of her family. But then, most of this ghost business was a puzzle.

"You're still here."

His gaze shot to hers. "I'm not going anywhere just yet," he said.

He didn't look happy about that, Rachel thought and pushed herself into a sitting position. As she moved a bit closer to the fire, she said softly, "What's your name, Mister Angel?"

He frowned at her and reached for the coffeepot. "I told you kid, I'm no angel."

"My name's Rachel Morgan."

"Jackson Tate."

She watched him pour a cup of thick, black coffee. The familiar scent was comforting, and she inhaled deeply. Just two days ago her parents had been drinking coffee and talking about the land they would claim outside Seattle. In her memory, she could hear her younger sister, Mattie, whining as their mother pulled a comb through her long curls. Rachel remembered holding her baby brother on her lap and wishing that she didn't have to because he always wet himself and she was wearing her best dress.

She ducked her head and blinked away a sheen of tears. What she wouldn't give right now to be holding little Robbie. But he was gone. Along with her parents and her sister Mattie.

Everyone had gone to Heaven without her.

They'd left her alone. And she didn't like alone. It was too quiet. The nighttime was too dark.

"You all right, kid?"

She lifted her head and looked at the man opposite her. He said he wasn't an angel, but she knew he was. Mama had always told her that angels were beautiful and strong and kind. She'd said that if you really needed help and prayed very, very hard, an angel would come to your aid.

And Jackson Tate was all of that.

His long black hair curled around his shirt collar, and his shiny green eyes sparkled with light cast from the fire. He didn't smile much, but he was very pretty. Strong, too. She hadn't really been asleep when he had buried her family. She'd only pretended to be because she hadn't wanted to watch them all go into the ground. But through slitted eyes she had watched Jackson lift her family from the wagon bed one by one. And he had carried her father as easily as he had little Robbie.

Strong and beautiful.

And he'd come to her when she'd prayed for help.

The only thing left to be was kind.

She fingered the blanket he'd draped over her as she'd slept. That had been kind, hadn't it?

"Kid?" He leaned toward her, his nice green eyes narrowing slightly as he stared at her. "You all right?"

"Yessir," she said softly.

"You don't have to 'sir,' me."

"Yes, Mister Angel."

He inhaled sharply and blew it out with a rush. Then he reached up and tipped his hat brim low over his eyes. "I told you, I'm no angel. You just . . . call me Jackson, huh?"

"Yes, Jackson." She liked the sound of his name. She liked the feel of it as it rolled around her tongue. "Jackson?" She smiled.

"Yeah?"

"What's going to happen to me now?" Her fingers plucked at a loose thread.

He took a long sip of coffee, then grimaced and spit it out into the dirt. Staring at the cup as though he'd just been poisoned, he deliberately poured the remains of the coffee into the fire. The flames hissed and spat at him, then conquered the thin stream of liquid to blaze even brighter.

"My coffee still stinks," he muttered.

"I'll make it for you in the morning," she offered.

One dark eyebrow lifted.

"I used to make it for my pa all the time. He said I made better coffee even than my mama did."

He rubbed his jaw and cocked his head to look at her thoughtfully. "Can you cook, too?"

Pleased and proud that she could be of help to the beautiful angel who had saved her, Rachel came up on both knees and nodded vigorously. "Mama taught me. I can make biscuits and bacon and potatoes and stew and all kinds of things."

"Hmmm . . ."

"You'll see, Mister Ang—Jackson. You'll be happy to have me around. I can sew, too." Her sharp gaze raked over him in an instant. "I bet I can find a button in mama's things that would replace that missing one on your shirt."

Jackson shifted uneasily. "Look, kid. You don't have to do all that. Just the coffee. And maybe breakfast, if you want to."

"Oh, I do. Honest." Her hands clasped together in her lap, and her fingers squeezed tightly. She would show her angel just how grateful she was. She would prove to him how useful she could be. Then, maybe, he wouldn't leave her.

Somewhere deep inside her, Rachel knew that she didn't want to be alone again. But it was more than that. She wanted to be with the angel who had appeared out of nowhere to rescue her.

"You better get some sleep now, kid. We got a long walk, starting tomorrow."

"To where?"

"A place called Stillwater," he said gruffly and stretched out on the dirt. Flat on his back, he crossed his feet at the ankles, tipped his hat down over his eyes, and folded his hands over his chest. "Now go to sleep."

"What happens when we get there?"

"I'm going to find some nice folks for you to live with."

A pang of worry squirmed around in her chest as she stared at her hero, opposite. "But, couldn't I stay with you?"

He tipped that hat up and shot her one long look from the corner of his eye. "Kid, where I'm probably headed, you don't want to be."

Rachel held her tongue as he settled down to sleep. A moment later, she curled into her blanket, drawing her knees up to her chest. With her head pillowed on her forearm, she looked past the flickering firelight to the man she'd known only a few hours.

Her family was gone.

The only person left to her was Jackson Tate.

Her own personal angel.

And despite what he thought now, she wasn't going to lose him, too.

Chapter ☆ Two

"It's not right," Imogene Walters declared for the fourth time. "A woman like yourself should know better."

Rachel Morgan frowned at the column of figures she had been totalling and spared one quick glance at her best customer. Imogene's faded blue eyes looked huge behind her spectacles, and her nose was fairly twitching with her indignation. Her long, boney fingers clutched at her drawstring purse, and Rachel could only hope there was nothing breakable inside.

"Imogene, you're getting yourself all worked up over nothing."

"Nothing?" The smaller woman straightened so abruptly, it was as though she was a marionette and an unseen puppetteer had jerked her strings. "This is a scandal, Rachel. A scandal!"

Rachel ducked her head, just managing to hide a smile. Heaven knows she couldn't afford to offend Imogene. The mother of eight spent more money in Rachel's store than half of the men in town combined. But the very notion that she had created a scandal with the meeting she had called the night before was ludicrous.

How could a handful of maiden ladies, coming together to enjoy a relaxing evening of chatting and parlor games, be called a scandal?

"Why, my own dear husband, Mister Walters, was horrified, I tell you."

Hard to imagine Hank Walters being horrified by anything. The quiet, easygoing man was the exact opposite of his wife. Hank liked to say that Imogene was wound up tighter than an eight-day clock. Of course, when his little wife was out of earshot, Hank always added, "an eight-day *cuckoo* clock."

"It was one meeting, Imogene," Rachel soothed and deliberately looked back to the column of figures. The sooner she had Imogene's bill totalled, the sooner the woman would leave.

"One meeting is one too many," Imogene shot back.

The bell over the front door jumped and clanged out a welcome as another customer sidled into the Mercantile. Rachel looked up in time to see a well dressed man take one look at Imogene Walters and hastily back out of the store again.

She sighed and redoubled her efforts on the bill.

"The very idea!" Imogene went on, oblivious to the fact that Rachel was barely listening anymore. "A bunch of maiden ladies getting together to celebrate the fact that they don't have menfolk!"

Rachel gritted her teeth and quickly wrote down the total. Lifting her gaze to the other woman's, she said, "That's fifteen-dollars and thirty-seven cents, Imogene."

Dutifully, the small woman tugged her bag open and stuffed one hand inside. Withdrawing a handful of bills, she began slowly and carefully counting the correct amount out onto the counter.

Rachel bit her tongue until sixteen dollars lay within reach. She grabbed it up and made change. As she handed the coins over, though, she finally allowed herself to say,

"The Stillwater Spinster Society is *not* scandalous."

"It is by its very existence."

"Imogene, we *are* spinsters."

"You don't have to be. In a town filled with lumbermen, no woman need remain unmarried."

"What if we're not in love with any of the men?"

"Faddle!" Imogene dropped the coins into her bag and closed it again with a yank of the strings. Wagging one finger at Rachel, she said, "Love is fairy tale foolishness. What you need is a good, solid man who'll bring home his pay every week and give you a baby every other year. That would keep you so busy you wouldn't have time to dwell on this love nonsense."

"Is that why you married Hank?" Rachel asked, already knowing the answer to her question.

Imogene sputtered a moment or two, flushed a deep pink up to the roots of her gray-streaked brown hair, then sniffed determinedly. "I didn't say that love *never* happens," she conceded.

Smiling softly, Rachel leaned her forearms on the polished oak countertop and said, "You fell in love with Hank when you were twelve years old, Imogene. You've told me the story yourself, dozens of times."

Imogene lifted her chin slightly and pursed her lips.

Rachel went on. "When two older boys teased you after school and took your hair ribbon, you said that Hank flew into them like a windmill in a hurricane. You said even though those boys were bigger than him, Hank bested them both, then walked you home."

"Yes, but . . ."

"*And,*" Rachel added, "you said that Hank asked permission to keep that hair ribbon, and you gave it to him. Folks say that Hank still has that ribbon. Keeps that small bit of frayed childhood on his watch fob."

Imogene flushed and ducked her head.

"Now that seems like *love* to me."

A long moment passed before the other woman lifted her head again. When she did, the fighting gleam in her eye had faded a bit. "All right, Rachel. Love *does* happen."

Ah, vindication. One thing could be said for Imogene. She wasn't afraid to admit when she was wrong. Rachel looked at the woman who had been her schoolteacher and asked quietly, "I firmly believe that there is one man meant to be with one woman. All they have to do is find each other. So why should a spinster give up her independence, her very life, in order to marry a man she doesn't love?"

"Love could grow."

"So could misery."

"What if you never find that *one* man?"

Rachel stiffened slightly. A fifteen-year-old ache sputtered into life in her chest, and she felt it blossom, squeezing her heart until the pain became one with her heartbeat—constant and steady.

How could she explain all that to Imogene? How could she tell her friend that she had already met that man? That he'd rescued her when she was a frightened ten year old and won her heart with his awkward kindnesses. How could she admit that her one true love had never returned for her, despite his hastily given promise? There was simply no way to explain that another man couldn't claim the heart she had already given to her guardian angel—Jackson Tate.

"Rachel?" the other woman asked. "Are you all right?"

"Yes," she said, deliberately forcing air into her lungs. "I'm fine." Nodding abruptly, as if to reassure herself, she went on. "As to your question, Imogene . . . if I really believed that I would find that one man, would I have founded the Stillwater Spinster Society?"

"No, I suppose not."

"And aren't the four of us ladies doing quite nicely? Without a man in our lives?"

Imogene paused, took a deep breath, then shook her head slowly. "You always were a hardheaded girl."

Rachel grinned. "You're only saying that because I didn't pay attention in your class when I first came to town."

"And still don't, though I don't know why that surprises me. You didn't listen then, don't know why you'd start now." Shaking her head, Imogene reached up to straighten her already perfectly straight hat, then turned for the door. "I'll send one of my boys over later to pick up my order."

When the door closed behind her, Rachel breathed a sigh of relief. It wasn't that she didn't appreciate Imogene's concerns, it was simply that at least seven other people that morning had stopped by the store to share their "horror" over the newly formed Society.

Why a group of four maiden ladies coming together for an evening should upset everyone in town, Rachel had no idea. But the ladies were scandalized, and the men seemed to take it as a personal afront. As though the Spinster Society was pointing fingers at unworthy men.

She sighed, straightened up, and walked along the length of the counter until she came to the gated opening. Stepping through, she walked slowly around the store, tidying up. Ever since her adopted father, Albert Heinz, had left her the place at his death two years before, Rachel had taken great pride in running the cleanest, most well stocked Mercantile this side of Seattle.

Her hands paused in their busywork as she silently admitted that Albert wouldn't have been pleased with her success. But then, she thought, dismissing old hurts from her mind, he hadn't been pleased with much of anything. Still, he *had* left her the store, surprising as that had been, and she was grateful. Rachel turned in a slow circle, letting her gaze sweep over the neatly arranged merchandise.

Floor to ceiling shelving lined one whole wall and in the tidy cubicles, everything from woolen blankets to books to hair ribbons and hunting knives rested in their proper places. In one end of the store, she had standing racks where ready-made dresses and suit coats hung, just waiting for the right customer. In the corner, she even had a screened-off section where clothes might be tried on before purchase.

In the opposite end of the store was a mountain of tools. Everything a man might need, he could find at Rachel's Mercantile. And if she didn't have it, she would get it. Her gaze quickly swept over the axes, saws, hammers, and bins of nails before moving to the last wall where she stocked guns and ammunition.

Weak sunlight poked from between the clouds and scuttled in through the wide front windows to sneak around the store. Springtime in Washington meant rain. And mud.

As her thoughts strayed to the weather, it occurred to her to go to the storeroom and unpack her order of knee-high boots. Before the next storm broke, she wanted to be ready.

Jackson sat perched on the edge of the boardwalk and watched the comings and goings around him. A bark of laughter, the chink of coins, and the scrape of chair legs on wood sounded out from the saloon behind him, and he threw a disgusted look toward the building.

Fifteen years.

Dead for fifteen years and he was *still* in this miserable little town.

What in hell did a ghost have to do? Over the years, he'd completed whatever tasks Lesley had given him and even at that, he'd only earned his way out of the saloon two years ago. Sure, he could leave the building, but that icy cold wall now surrounded the town where he had died.

Of course, there had been a few more ghosts littering the place during the last fifteen years. But even before he'd had a chance to become accustomed to having company, they had worked their way out of this mess and disappeared. Which left Jackson on his own, but for the occasional visit from Lesley. Visits he was even beginning to look forward to.

"You are in sad shape, son," he told himself. "When ol' Les starts looking good to you, you've been dead too long."

"Very amusing, I'm sure."

Jackson jumped up and turned around. Damn, he hated how the little fella just appeared and disappeared without warning.

"So, Les, what am I supposed to be doing now?"

"It's *Lesley*, if you please."

"Lesley."

Jackson nodded and frowned as a drunken customer was tossed out the batwing doors, sailing right through his person. Glowering at the drunk, lying in the dirt, Lesley muttered, "How you tolerate this . . . *village*, I do not understand."

Jackson straightened his shoulders and lifted his chin. He'd almost become accustomed to the man's personal insults. But when he started in on America, calling it a land of cretins and bullies, Jackson had all he could do to keep from leaping at him.

"I guess you didn't have drunks in jolly ol' England, huh, Les?"

Lesley shot him a scathing glare, but didn't accept the challenge.

"There is no time today, I'm afraid, for one of your little speeches about democracy and free will."

Jackson's eyebrows lifted. "Must be important."

"It is."

"Shoot."

Lesley's eyes closed briefly, and Jackson thought he heard the little man murmur, "If only I could," but then decided he was mistaken.

"The problem is Rachel Morgan."

"Who?" A quick race through memories didn't bring him any answers.

"Rachel. The girl who was your first assignment?"

"Oh, yeah." Not a bad kid, as he recalled, except for her annoying habit of calling him "Mister Angel." "What kind of trouble did she get into now?"

"One entirely of your making."

"Me?" He slapped one phantom hand to his nearly invisible chest. "What'd *I* do?"

"It's what you didn't do." Lesley stepped down off the boardwalk, floated through the now up and staggering drunk and faced Jackson. "You didn't wipe her memory of you when your assignment was completed."

A stab of worry sliced at him, but Jackson argued anyway. "Sure I did."

Lesley's eyes narrowed and his already thin lips flattened into a slash across his unforgiving features. Turning abruptly, he marched to a nearby horse trough, waved one, lace-hidden hand over the surface of the dirty water and said, "Watch."

Hesitantly, Jackson stepped up beside the other man and looked down at the scene beginning to form.

Outside the general store, Jackson glanced at the faces of the elderly couple who had offered to take Rachel in. The man looked like a hard case, but his wife's eyes shined every time her eyes lit on the little girl. For his first assignment, he figured he had done a pretty good job. The girl was safe. A childless couple had a daughter. Everybody was happy. Now it was time to head on back and find out what kind of reward his good job had earned him.

"Don't leave, Mister Angel," the small voice tugged at him and against his better judgment, he looked down into blue eyes swimming with tears.

Going down on one knee, he whispered, "I told you. I'm no angel. And I have to go, Rachel. You'll be fine here. The Heinzes will take good care of you."

The older woman dropped a proprietary hand on the child's shoulder as if afraid that he would take the girl away after all. She needn't have worried.

"Will you come back?" *Rachel asked.*

He didn't know, but he sure as shooting hoped not. Surely there was something better waiting for him, somewhere. "Maybe," *he said, figuring that it was the easiest answer he could give her.*

"I'll wait for you," *she promised, and one tear escaped to roll down her smooth cheek.* "And when I grow up, I'll marry you."

His brows shot high on his forehead. Hell, even when he was alive, he hadn't wanted to get married. And she was just a kid, for God's sake! This was all getting out of hand. "Rachel, you'll feel different when you grow up."

"No I won't." *She stepped free of the restraining, yet gentle, hand on her shoulder and threw herself at Jackson. Squeezing his neck tightly, she closed her eyes and whispered,* "Promise me you'll come back, or I won't stay here. I'll follow you."

He frowned, disgusted with the turn things had taken. The old man in the doorway was giving him a look that would peel paint, and the man's wife looked about to burst into tears herself.

He had to get out of there. Quick. No matter what it took. "Okay kid, I'll come back."

"You promise?" *Rachel drew her head back to look at him, and Jackson avoided meeting that teary gaze.*

"Yeah. I promise."

At his words, she tightened her hold on his neck and landed a glancing kiss to his cheekbone. "I love you, Mister Angel."

Enough was enough. Gently, Jackson pried her arms loose, stood up, and took a step back from her. "You be good for the Heinzes, you hear?"

"Yessir."

"Don't you worry," the woman said. *"She'll be fine."*

Worry? Jackson was already putting the problem of Rachel Morgan out of his mind altogether. He'd done what was expected of him. That was all he needed to know. As he turned and walked away, he heard Rachel's determined little voice call out to him.

"I'll be waiting, Mister Angel. I'll be right here when you come for me."

He lifted one hand, but didn't look back.

Lesley dragged one fingertip through the water and the scene rippled, shifted, then disappeared.

"Well?"

"Well what?"

"Angel indeed! Imagine, allowing that child to think you're a messenger of God."

"I kept telling her I wasn't an angel." Jackson paced back and forth in front of the trough. Who would have thought that even dead, you could still feel anger? And guilt. "She didn't listen."

"You didn't wipe her memory though, did you?"

Fifteen years was a long time. Even for a ghost. He cast back, trying to recall. About all he came up with was this—leaving the girl as fast as he could. He had been hoping that the successful end to his assignment would be enough to ensure his release from the place where he had died.

A quick glance around the town brought a humorless smirk to his face. So much for high hopes.

Jackson rubbed his jaw slowly and tried to stall. Who knew what could happen to a ghost who mucked things up? "I would have bet hard money that I had."

"But then, you usually lost while gambling, didn't you?"

Jackson flicked a quick, hot look at him. "There's no call to be nasty. It was just one little mistake."

"Because of your 'little mistake,' Rachel Morgan's destiny is in jeopardy."

"Huh?"

He sighed. "When you allowed Rachel to remember you, that memory affected each of her decisions and actions since."

Jackson turned his head and stared off down the short, unimpressive main street. His gaze moved over the loaded freight wagons, their drivers shouting and cursing at the draft horses hitched to the traces. He noticed the merchants, the cowhands in for a day on the town, and one or two of the bar girls out for a stroll.

He focused on the small things. The old yellow dog curled up under a porch, snoozing in the shade. The woman in an upstairs window shaking the dust out of a rug that had seen better days. Two boys flipping pocket knives off their fingertips into the dirt. Anything. Anything to keep from thinking about what Lesley was telling him.

Dammit, how was he ever going to cut himself free of this haunting business if people were forever holding his mistakes up to him?

Lesley sighed heavily. "Rachel should be married by now."

"So she's not hitched. Lots of people don't get married."

"Rachel is supposed to give birth to four children."

Jackson risked a glance at the other man. "Then marriage *would* be a good idea."

"This is not a joking matter. It is *imperative* that she marry and become a mother."

"Back to kids again."

"One of Rachel's children is destined to become Washington's first female doctor. That child *must* be born."

"A *woman?* Becoming a doctor?"

Lesley ignored him. "You are to return to Stillwater and find a way to repair the damage you've caused."

"Why is this my fault?" At a glance from Lesley, he admitted, "All right, fine, I didn't wipe her memory. But just because she hasn't trapped some poor fool into marrying her—that doesn't make this mess my fault."

"Of course it's your fault," Lesley snapped. "She is laboring under the misapprehension that there is one special someone for everyone."

"So?"

Lesley's eyes shimmered with an unearthly fire. "*So,* for some unfathomable reason, Rachel Morgan believes *you* to be her destined soul mate."

Jackson took a quick step back, as if distancing himself from the man would do the same for the man's idea. "Why would she think something so foolish?" he muttered.

"Sadly, even when I was alive, I didn't understand the female heart," Lesley acknowledged. "In the afterlife, I have found no insights, either."

Jackson started pacing again, his brain galloping ahead like a horse with its tail on fire. "Suppose you just send the man who really *is* her match to her. Then she'll forget all about me."

"There is no such thing," Lesley snapped, clearly out of patience. "If there were truly one man meant for one woman, can you imagine the problems it would cause?"

"Well, no."

"I don't have the time to explain it to you." He slipped his fingers into the inside pocket of his coat and pulled out the notebook Jackson had become all too familiar with over the years. Flipping it open, he ran the tip of one finger down a single page, then looked up at Jackson again.

"As I feared, Rachel's first daughter is scheduled to arrive early next spring."

"How's that gonna happen without a man?"

"Precisely."

"Oh."

"By my calculations, you will have approximately six weeks to convince Rachel to marry."

"And if I can't?"

Lesley shuddered delicately. "That doesn't bear thinking about."

Jackson winced, then braced himself. Lifting his chin, he asked, "It doesn't matter *who* she marries?"

The other man checked his notes again and frowned. "That is unclear for some reason. But this is an emergency. Get that woman married. I don't care to whom. Her daughter *must* be born."

"Seems like a lot of fuss over a female doctor. It's not like she'd have any men for patients."

"That is not your concern, Mister Tate." Lesley stuffed the notebook back into his coat and tugged at the yellow silk lapels officiously. "Your duty is to simply follow instructions."

Though the thought of being alive again—for six whole weeks—was a pleasant one, Jackson had to know something else, too. "If I pull this off, get her married, I mean?"

"Yesss . . ."

"Will I finally be able to get out of this town?"

"I don't know. I don't make those decisions."

"Who the hell does?"

Lesley flinched. "Someone who is not in the least impressed by profanity, I assure you."

Hmmm. Maybe he had a point. Lowering his voice, in case there were others listening in on this conversation, Jackson said, "Look Les, *Lesley,*" he corrected at a glare from the other man, "It ain't that I'm complaining, mind you, but this not really alive and not really dead thing is beginning to wear on me."

"I can imagine."

"I just want a decision," Jackson said firmly. "One way or the other. Up or . . ." He looked toward the ground. "*Not up.* Anything would be better than this ghost business."

Lesley looked at him long and hard before nodding. "I'll see what I can do."

Jackson brightened.

"But you must succeed at this if you want any hope at all of ending your present existence."

"Don't you worry," Jackson promised. "Inside a month, I'll have Rachel hog-tied and happy."

Lesley didn't look convinced, but Jackson refused to let the man's lack of faith affect him. At last, he was within spitting distance of leaving this ghostly life behind him.

The smaller man held one hand out, palm up. As Jackson watched, six gold coins appeared, gleaming in the afternoon sunlight.

"What're those for?" he asked, then caught himself. "Oh, sure. I'll need money, won't I?"

"These are not to spend, Mister Tate. They will help you in accomplishing your goal."

"How's that?"

"Simply hold one of them tightly and say out loud what you want to occur."

"Ahhh . . . *magic.*"

Lesley's eyes rolled as he poured the coins into Jackson's upturned hand. Slowly, he bounced them on his palm, testing their weight. The coins shifted and clinked together, making an altogether satisfying sound. Nothing else in the world had the same solid feel as gold.

"Les," he said, as a time-saving idea occurred to him.

"What is it?"

"If these things'll do the trick with Rachel, why don't I just use one of them and wipe her memory now?"

"It doesn't work that way."

"Why not?" Jackson's fingers curled around the coins, and he shoved them into his pants pocket.

"Because, as I've already explained, that memory of you has affected the course of her life. She's made decisions, taken actions, all stemming from those few days with you." Lesley shook his head, then reached up and straightened the silly looking white wig he still wore. "Her memory of that time is intertwined with the memories of her life over the last fifteen years. They are inseparable.''

"Oh."

The sharp report of a gun being fired echoed from somewhere down the street. A woman screamed. The sleeping dog woke up long enough to howl, and the kids raced off in the direction of the trouble.

Lesley shuddered. ''If you want to get out of this place as desperately as you say . . . don't fail, Mister Tate.''

Chapter ☆ *Three*

Jackson glanced over his shoulder toward the dark street, making sure no one was about. But the only signs of life were from half a block away, at the Stillwater saloon. His mouth watered at the thought of having a real drink again. And as soon as he'd had a look at a grown up Rachel, he'd be doing just that.

At least there were no lights burning in the living rooms over Rachel's store. It would have been a lot harder to climb those rickety stairs with any kind of quiet.

Carefully, he stepped over a tidy row of well tended daisies and leaned toward one of the ground floor windows. The murmur of female voices drew him closer. Keeping his body to one side, he peered in through the shining glass pane to the brightly lit Mercantile.

"Ain't bad enough being a ghost," he muttered thickly. "No, I get to be a peeping Tom ghost, too."

His gaze swept across the four women occupying chairs drawn into a circle. A plump woman with brown hair and spectacles reached for a cookie. The blond next to her chewed hungrily at her fingernails. Another brown-haired woman with red, chapped hands laughed and turned to the woman who could only be Rachel Morgan.

Jackson looked her over quickly. She had grown up

pretty well. Even sitting down, she looked to be tall. She held herself ramrod straight, though she was a bit too skinny for his taste. He had always admired women with some meat on their bones. Especially up top. But otherwise, she was certainly pretty enough to have caught a man long ago and spared him this nonsense.

She suddenly turned toward the window and almost seemed to be staring right at him. Jackson's breath caught in his chest. For a heartbeat of time, he held perfectly still, allowing only his gaze to move as it swept over her features. Small, straight nose, full lips, dark blond hair pulled back from her face into a knot on top of her head. Finely arched brows lifted high over those same bruised-looking, blue eyes.

"Rachel?" One of the women said softly. "What's wrong?"

Reluctantly, it seemed, she turned away from the window to face her friends. Jackson's breath slowly sighed from his lungs.

"Nothing," she replied. "Nothing at all."

Jackson eased away from the window, backed over the daisies, and cursed gently when he accidentally flattened one or two of them. Bending down, he straightened them, only to watch them fall over again on their broken stems. Hell. He didn't want her to know he'd been standing in the dirt peeking at her. Frowning, he snapped the fragile stems with his fingers and stuffed the already wilting flowers into his coat pocket.

Glass shattered; Jackson's head snapped around toward the sound. Voices—shouts—lifted in the stillness. Had to be from the saloon. Grinning, he started walking. With any luck, not only could he have a drink, he'd get in on the fight, too.

"I think our second official meeting of the Stillwater Spinster Society went very well," Rachel said, letting her gaze sweep over the three other women seated in her tiny front parlor. "Don't you?"

Mavis Honeysett stood up, then bent quickly, snatched up the one remaining cookie from the serving tray, and popped it into her mouth. As she chewed, she nodded enthusiastically to Rachel, who noted that the little dressmaker's shirtwaist was getting too tight again.

Hester Sutton slid out of her chair and held her coat to her chest like a knight's shield. She nibbled on one fingernail and gave Rachel a shy, half smile.

"It was a nice visit, Rachel," Sally Wiley said and rubbed her work-reddened hands together. "But it would have been a hell of a lot more fun with a man or two."

Rachel grinned. She could always count on the town laundress to say exactly what she was thinking.

"Still," Sally went on as she stood up and slipped on her coat, "if any of us had a man, we wouldn't be holding these meetings, now would we?"

"It's never too late," Mavis said dreamily.

Sally cocked her head and stared at her as though the woman had just sprouted another head. "Mavis Honeysett, you're twenty-seven years old! When are you going to unpack that hope chest?"

Mavis smoothed her plump fingers down the front of her stylish skirt. "My hope chest is none of your concern, *Salome* Wiley."

The other woman shuddered, stiffened, and lifted her chin for battle. "I told you not to call me that."

"Then I'll thank you to keep your nose out of my hope chest."

"Hope*less* chest, you mean."

"At least I stand a chance of actually meeting a nice man some day. There are any number of men who stop by the dress shop every day."

"Yes, to buy things for their wives or lady friends."

Hester backed away from the two women circling each other like prize fighters in a ring.

"At least," Mavis snapped, "when men come into *my* place of business, they're *clean.*"

"Well!" Sally planted both reddened hands on her hips and leaned in toward one of her oldest friends. "My customers might arrive in dirty clothes, but by thunder, they leave clean."

"And come to my store," Mavis finished.

"Oh, dear," Hester murmured and scuttled for the door like a mouse with a cat hot on its heels.

"Ladies, ladies," Rachel shouted, trying to be heard.

"Why don't you have another cookie and calm down," Sally said.

"What's *that* supposed to mean?" Mavis sucked in a breath and lifted her only slightly doubled chin.

"Exactly what you think it means."

Hester hovered at the door, shifting from foot to foot, clearly uneasy with the sniping, but unwilling to leave.

"*Ladies*—" Rachel stepped between them and held her breath. It never failed. Every time the four of them got together, Mavis and Sally would eventually end up at each other's throats. To look at them, a stranger would never guess that they were dear friends.

When she felt she had their attention, Rachel inhaled sharply, then looked from one to the other of them. "You really should stop picking at each other so. What will you do when I have the new house built and we all move in together?"

Sally's dark blond eyebrows shot up high on her forehead, and Mavis scowled.

"Remember the reason we formed this society?" Rachel prodded.

"The reason *you* formed it, you mean?" Sally muttered and scratched at her raw skin.

"So that the four of us could band together as a family," Mavis admitted sullenly.

"Exactly," Rachel crowed like a proud parent. "And if we turn on one another, what then?"

Still shifting from foot to foot, Sally avoided Rachel's gaze. Mavis tilted her head back and stared at the ceiling in profound concentration.

"So, you'll both be here next Tuesday night?"

The two women nodded.

"Hester?" She turned to look at the tiny, uncomfortable woman.

"Yes."

"Good!"

Recognizing that the evening's battle was over, Rachel stepped back and headed for the front door in time to watch Hester scurrying into the darkness.

"See you next week," Rachel called and was almost certain she saw the little schoolteacher lift one hand in response. Behind her, the others drew closer.

"Sally, your hands are bleeding."

"That lye soap just eats into my skin," the laundress admitted. "One day, I expect to look down and see nothing but bones sticking out of my sleeves."

"What about the cream I made up for you last month?" Mavis asked.

"All gone," Sally said and rubbed at her cracked and bleeding hands. "I swear, my skin soaked it right up like the desert does rain."

"You come right over to my house," Mavis insisted and took her friend's arm. "I have another batch almost finished."

"Good night," Rachel called as the two women sailed past her.

Mavis waved, but didn't stop talking to Sally. "This time I scented the cream with lavendar."

"Thank God." Sally shuddered. "The last stuff you

made for me smelled foul enough to choke a horse."

"Well, that's gratitude, I must say."

"You want gratitude? Make me smell like a drawing room, not a stable."

Rachel smiled and closed the door.

Jackson rubbed his aching jaw and kicked at a rock lying in the dirt. Well, he'd managed to throw himself into the fight, but by the time it was over, the saloon was so smashed up that the bartender closed up for the night. *Before* Jackson had gotten the drink he'd been imagining for most of the last fifteen years.

Strange, he thought, he didn't recall a fist to the mouth being this painful. Disgusted, he stalked along the boardwalk, back toward Rachel's place. There was no point putting it off any longer. If her friends were gone, he'd just go on inside and set her straight about this whole marriage business.

He tripped over something in the dark, but caught himself before he fell.

"Dammit," he muttered. "Can't a man walk in peace?"

"Shorry, mishter," a slurred voice floated up to him. "Din't shee ya."

Boot heels scraped on wood as the drunk pulled his legs back out of the way.

A sharp stab of envy sliced through Jackson as the distinctive, musky odor of whiskey surrounded him. He hadn't had one damned drink. And this man had had way too many.

He took a single step. Life just wasn't fair.

"Have a drink?"

He paused, glanced back at the drunk and had an idea.

"You got enough to spare?" he asked.

The man in the shadows hiccuped. "Yep. Got a half empty one here and 'nother one I ain't even opened yet."

Jackson's mouth watered. He bent down and stared into

the darkness until he could see the man's face clearly. Tired eyes, a week's worth of whiskers, and the hardscrabble clothing of a prospector. "How about I take that full one off your hands?"

The drunk's arms curled around his bottles protectively. "You gonna steal it?"

"Hell no. I'm not a thief." Of course, the only other way would be to buy it from him. And Jackson didn't have any money. Except for . . . Before he could think better of it, he dug his hand into his pants pocket and pulled out one of the gold coins Lesley had given him.

What harm could it do? After all, he had six of them, and surely it wouldn't take more than one to find Rachel a man. The longer he thought about it, the better it sounded. Why, he'd actually be doing this poor drunk a favor. He'd already had too much to drink. He didn't need that extra bottle. And maybe that magic coin would do somebody some good. His thumb and forefinger smoothed over the cold, golden surface as he struggled with the decision.

The drunk miner lifted his half full bottle to his lips, took a long drink, and sighed in satisfaction. Whiskey-scented breath wafted over Jackson. Decision made, he said, "I'll give you this coin for the full bottle."

Even in the dark, Jackson saw the other man's eyes widen then narrow suspiciously. "Thish ain't twenty dollar whishkey," the man pointed out. "What elsh do ya want?"

"Nothin'."

Carefully, the miner handed over the full bottle, then snatched the coin from Jackson's fingers. The dull sheen of gold disappeared into one of the man's pockets.

Hand curled around the neck of the bottle, Jackson stood up. He pulled the cork out, tossed it aside, then took a long, thirsty drink. Fire blossomed along the course of the liquor. Heat burned through his throat, down his chest, and settled in the pit of his stomach. His eyes watered, and his voice trembled as he acknowledged, "Good whiskey."

"It'll kill ya or cure ya," the other man agreed.

Jackson tipped his hat to the drunk and murmured, "Thanks, friend." He took a step or two along the boardwalk, intending to find a nice, quiet spot to enjoy the hellishly bad liquor. Instead, he stopped again, almost immediately. Turning back to the prospector, he dropped to one knee and leaned in close.

The man pulled away until he was pressed against a wall. "You can't have your money back," he said tonelessly.

"I don't want it back," Jackson assured him. Hell, he'd only just gotten his hands on a bottle he'd waited fifteen years for. He wasn't about to give it up. But he also couldn't leave, knowing he'd given a coin, with who knew what kind of magic powers, to an unsuspecting drunk. How to warn him, though? "Look," he said slowly. "That gold piece is kind of a good luck coin."

"Huh?"

Jackson scowled into the other man's bleary eyes. Chances were, the man wouldn't even remember this warning once he sobered up. But dammit, he had to try.

"Kinda like magic, you know?"

"Magic?"

"Yeah." He glanced over his shoulder to make sure that the street was still deserted. Turning back to the prospector, he went on. "If you hold it in your hand and make a wish, it'll come true."

A snort of laughter dissolved into a coughing fit that shook the drunk's body like a broken doll in the hands of a vicious child.

"All right," Jackson snapped. "You don't have to believe me. Just remember."

The laughter faded, and red-rimmed eyes stared at him.

"When you're holding that coin . . . be careful to only wish for *good* things."

"Like finding the mother lode?" A dreamy expression settled on his worn features.

Jackson shook his head and smiled briefly. "That'd do, mister. I guess that'd do." Pushing himself to his feet, he looked down at the man and said again, softer this time, "Remember."

"Remember . . . ," the slurred voice repeated dully.

Bothered by the small curl of worry and guilt beginning to form in his belly, Jackson took another long drink to drown it. Fire leaped into his bloodstream as he turned his back on the prospector and walked down the boardwalk. All he needed was the time to finish his drink in peace. Then he would deal with Rachel.

She sat straight up in bed. Cocking her head to one side, Rachel listened, searching for the sound that had awakened her. But there was nothing. Her gaze moved around the small bedroom she'd inhabited since the day her angel had dropped her on the Heinz' doorstep of Albert and Martha Heinz.

Moonlight whispered between the folds of the curtains and stretched out across the polished floorboards like silver ribbons. The shadows and shapes surrounding her were familiar ones. Her wardrobe. The chair pulled up neatly to her dressing table and mirror. The dress form in the corner. The cold hearth and the solitary easy chair in front of it.

Everything was as it should be.

She pulled in a deep breath and settled back against her pillows. Her eyes drifted closed as she deliberately tried to return to her dream.

This time when the sound came, she was awake enough to identify it. Someone downstairs, pounding on the door. The soft tinkle of glass breaking told her that whoever it was, they'd already broken one of the leaded panes in the door panel. She'd have to hurry if she wanted to prevent any more destruction. Swinging her legs off the bed, she stood up, grabbed her wrapper from the foot of the mattress, stepped into calfskin slippers, and snatched the gnarled, heavy oak walking stick she kept close by the bed. Then she flew into the hall and down the stairs.

Her slippered feet made a whisper of sound as she hurried across the plank floor. She didn't need a light. She knew the store and its contents well enough to find her way blindfolded, let alone in the soft shimmer of moonlight.

"Rachel!" Someone shouted before pounding an impatient fist against her back door.

She blinked and skidded to a stop, her fingers curled tightly around the stick.

A drunk.

Scowling, she took a moment to tie the ribbon at the neck of her robe, then wrapped the belt tightly around her waist. If she had to deal with a drunken lumberjack, she wanted to be covered as decently as possible.

"*So bang the drum slowly . . .*"

Rachel flicked an impatient glare at the door. Whoever her visitor was, he had a terrible singing voice. She hurried across the room.

"*And play the fife lowly . . .*"

She closed her eyes and shook her head. Not only a drunk. A maudlin one. Kicking the largest jagged shards of glass to one side, she glared at her broken window pane.

First thing in the morning, she promised herself, she would go to the lumber camps outside of town and have *another* talk with the timber bosses. A person would think that they would be able to control the men who worked for them!

"*I spied a poor cowboy all wrapped in white linen . . .*"

She frowned at the door again. He wasn't even singing the song *right*.

Rachel's fingers tightened around the stick even as she firmly hoped she wouldn't have to use it. Fixing a stern expression on her face, she flipped the latch, turned the brass knob, and yanked the door open.

Obviously, he'd been sitting down, leaning against the

door. Without its support, he fell into the store, smacking his head on the floor.

She winced in sympathy.

Flat on his back, he lay there, arms outstretched, staring up at her.

The stench of whiskey hung between them like a thick cloud. A lopsided grin flashed across his familiar features. The stick in her hand fell from suddenly nerveless fingers and clattered noisily onto the floor.

He hiccuped.

Rachel gasped.

"Mister Angel?"

Chapter ☆ Four

"Shhh . . ." Jackson waved his index finger in front of his pursed lips and only vaguely wondered why he couldn't seem to bring it any closer. Then he dismissed the idea altogether and allowed his hand to slap down onto the surprisingly comfortable floor. "I tol' you before, kid. I'm no angel."

"You're drunk."

"Jus' a little." He shook his head briefly, then thought better of it as the store began to swirl around him in wild patterns of color and motion.

"It's really you." She pushed his legs out of the way of the door and when he was clear, closed and locked it. Sinking to the floor herself, she braced her back against the wall and stared at him blankly. "And you're really here."

He hiccuped. "Came to tell you somethin' . . ." his voice faded off as he desperately tried to make his mind work. "What?" His eyes screwed up as he tried to gather his scattered thoughts. "Somethin' impord..imporn..*big*," he finished on a different word since his tongue didn't seem to be cooperating.

"What?"

Her voice came as if from far away. His brain snatched

at it and missed, like a child grabbing at a balloon's dancing string.

"Somethin' about a kid?" he wondered aloud. He blinked, then narrowed his gaze, trying to bring her into focus. Grinning, he hiccuped again and said, "Nope. Can't be it. You're not a kid anymore."

He admired the fall of her long, blond hair as it lay about her shoulders. He watched as she impatiently pushed it behind her ears and wanted to tell her not to do that—that it looked prettier the other way. But he couldn't make the words come.

Didn't matter, he told himself as a warm, fuzzy feeling crept over him.

"What did you have to tell me?" she repeated. When he didn't answer right away, she started muttering to herself.

He glared at her through tired, aching eyes. "You still ask too many questions."

Rachel pinched herself, winced at the pain, then did it again. But it was no use. He really was lying there, in her store, drunk as a lord.

Moonlight streamed through the windows and washed across him. He chuckled softly, whispered something she couldn't quite catch, then actually started *snoring*.

Slowly, carefully, she pushed herself to her feet and looked down at him. Fear, disbelief, and anger warred within her. He looked exactly the same as he had the first time she'd seen him. Fifteen years, she'd carried the memory of his face. Each night before falling asleep, she'd make herself remember everything about him, from the timbre of his voice to the tiny wrinkles at the corners of his eyes. She'd waited so long, sure that he would come back—believing the promise he'd given her all those years ago.

At least she had believed until about five years ago, when she'd at last given up on him. Or rather, she thought, she'd given up on her dreams. Because she had convinced herself that that's all he really had been. A dream man she'd concocted to bring her comfort, much as fairy tales of handsome princes had done for other little girls.

Now that he was actually here, though, what was she to think?

As she watched him, he shifted, muttered something in his sleep, then rolled onto his side, cradling his head on his drawn up forearm.

Shouldn't she be frightened? Shouldn't she be at least a bit concerned for her sanity? No. She wasn't scared. She wasn't crazy. What she was, was furious.

"Why did you come back *now?*" she demanded and got only another snore for an answer. "Why now, when my life is just the way I want it?" Taking her slipper off, she pulled one bare foot back and kicked his booted ankle. He felt nothing, but shimmers of pain swirled up from her injured toes. Unwanted tears flooded her eyes briefly, but she blinked them back.

"I won't cry. Not over you." She shook her head firmly. "Not again." Rachel took three steps away, then whirled around and came right back.

One corner of his mouth lifted, and he smiled at something in his sleep. Apparently, their "reunion" hadn't upset him in the slightest.

She inhaled sharply, then blew it out again.

"Fifteen years," she said as she looked down on her rumpled, drunken knight in shining armor. "Fifteen years of questions with no answers."

He snorted, sighed, and shifted to make himself more comfortable.

"And now that you've finally come back, I'm *still* waiting for those answers."

Disgusted, she turned her back on him and angrily crossed the floor toward the stairs and her room. She left him where he was and only glanced back once at her fallen hero, passed out in a puddle of moonlight.

*   *   *

A woodpecker.

Jackson winced, screwed his eyes tighter shut against the growing light, and wished that blasted bird straight to hell.

Tap-tap-tap-tap.

On and on it went, like spikes being driven through his forehead. Couldn't somebody shoot that damned bird so he could have some peace?

"Wake up."

He groaned.

"Wake up," the voice came again and carried right over the tapping that still beat at his already aching head.

Cautiously, he opened one eye. Sunlight stabbed through that eye into his brain, and pain rocketed throughout his body. Jesus! He didn't remember a hangover being this damned painful. Blearily, he forced his vision to focus and the first thing he saw was a woman's shiny black shoe, just inches from his face, the toe slapping furiously against the floorboards.

Not a bird, then.

"Awake?"

That one word carried enough venom to force an immediate reaction. With both eyes opened, he rolled over onto his back to face his torturer.

A tall, well-built blond with murder in her eye glared at him.

"What the hell do you want?" he muttered thickly around the cotton in his mouth.

"Answers, Mister Angel," she countered quickly.

At the ridiculous title, memories flooded him. Squeezing his eyes closed again, he licked dry lips and said, "Quit calling me that, will you? Shit, I thought we had that name thing settled fifteen years ago. The name's Tate. Jackson Tate."

"Fine, Mister Tate."

"Jackson."

"Mister Tate."

He groaned again. Nothing worse than a hardheaded woman when a man had a hangover.

"I want to know what you're doing here. Now."

"It's a long story."

"I'm sure."

He pushed himself to a sitting position. Ignoring for a moment the hideous pain lancing through his brain, he braced himself up with his palms flat on the floor. Tilting his head to look at her, he dismissed the pounding behind his eyes. "You got any coffee?"

For a moment, she looked as though she might refuse him. Then apparently, she decided that she'd get more out of him if he were conscious, thank God. Without another word, she marched across the store to a shining black potbellied stove in the corner.

Every step she took hammered at his head. Her heels clicked against the wood in an angry dance that seemed determined to punish him. Damned if she wasn't succeeding.

By the time she returned, he'd pushed himself to his feet. When he survived standing, Jackson was pretty sure he was going to make it. But to be on the safe side, he took the blue china cup she offered him and gulped down his first taste of coffee in far too long.

Hot, black, and strong enough to jump out of its own pot and climb into a cup by itself, the coffee was perfect. Just like he remembered it. He allowed himself a small, satisfied smile and a moment to inhale the familiar, comforting scent.

Then the tapping started up again, and Jackson swiveled his head for a good, long look at his assignment. In her starched, sunshine yellow dress, with buttons neatly done up to her neck, she looked more formidable than she had the night before. At least, he thought so. His memory was hazy, due, of course, to the bottle of whiskey. But he seemed to recall flowing white fabric, lots of wavy hair, and a softness in her eyes that wasn't there now.

Just as well, he told himself. Those adoring gazes she'd directed at him when she was a child had been hard to deal with. Coming from a woman full grown, it'd be downright impossible.

"It's been fifteen years," she demanded. "Why didn't you come back before?"

"Wasn't any need." He shrugged and took another sip, hoping the coffee would smooth away the last of the cobwebs stuffed in his mind.

"No need?" She folded her arms across her chest defensively. "You promised you would come back."

If she'd known him when he had been alive, she'd have had less faith in his promises. Lord knows, he'd never made his mark as a dependable man. But he didn't say so out loud. Instead, he said only, "I'm here now."

"Yes," she snapped and let her arms fall to her sides. Turning her back on him, she walked to the stove again, poured herself a cup of coffee, and looked at him from across the room. "And I want to know why. Why now?"

"I was sent here."

"By who?"

He shrugged again. "Nobody you'd know."

"You'll have to do better than that, Mister Tate."

He choked and spit a mouthful of coffee onto the floor. When the coughing spasm passed, he wiped his sleeve across his lips and shot her a wicked glare. "Jesus, you've got a razor for a tongue! No wonder you're a spinster!"

She snatched up a towel off a nearby shelf, then marched across the floor to stop beside him. Dropping the towel onto the coffee spill, she looked at him. "Has it occurred to you that I am a spinster because I prefer it that way?"

"Nope."

Standing up, Rachel inhaled sharply and set both hands at her hips.

"You grew up into a fine looking woman, Rachel," he admitted, letting his gaze rake her up and down. "But with a tongue like that, you'll never catch a man."

"I am not trying to catch—"

"Probably got half the men in town scared to death of you."

"They are not."

He smirked knowingly at her.

Clearly exasperated, she bent down, wiped the mess dry, picked up the towel, and clutched it tightly in both hands. "You look exactly the same as you did fifteen years ago. How is that possible? Just who . . . or *what* are you?"

He opened his mouth, but she cut him off.

"Why haven't you aged? Why are you wearing the same clothes?"

"Jesus, woman," he lifted one hand to rub his eyes. "Can't you let a man wake up before yammering away at him like that?"

She sniffed, and her well shaped lips thinned into a line sharp enough to draw blood. Those eyes of hers were snapping with anger looking for a target, and he figured that he was going to be it.

"Fine," she said and looked as though it was anything but. "One question then. What are you?"

That was better. Throw these things at him one at a time, and he would do all right. Now if she just wouldn't talk so loud.

"That's easy," he said quickly. "I'm a ghost."

Her face paled. Jackson hid a smile behind another sip of coffee. Well, now he knew how to shut her up.

She took a step back, her gaze fixed on him. She looked him up and down, raised one hand to her throat, and repeated, "A ghost?"

"Yeah."

He had to hand it to her, he thought. All in all, she was taking it mighty well. Even as he thought it though, she shook her head, stepped up closer to him, and laid one hand on his arm. Her fingers clenched around his forearm, squeezing, testing.

She shot him a sideways glance, and he caught the triumphant gleam shining in her eyes.

"There are no such things as ghosts," she whispered. "And even if there were, you're much too solid to be one."

He snorted a laugh. "Should have seen me yesterday. And the day before that."

"I did see you yesterday," she said and both eyebrows lifted. "Last night as a matter of fact. When you fell into my store and passed out at my feet."

He frowned. "I was tired."

"Drunk."

Now that was the honest truth. And a shameful one at that. When he was alive, one bottle never would have knocked him end over end. It seemed, though, that once a man was out of practice, he lost his touch.

Horrified suddenly, he wondered if it were the same for other things as well. He had hoped to find himself a woman while he was solid.

"I'm not a little girl any longer, Mister Tate," she said and took a step back from him. "I don't believe in angels, or ghosts, or heroic princes riding to the rescue."

"Huh?"

"There is a rational explanation for your appearance," she continued. "And I want to hear it."

"I already told you."

"Don't bother repeating it."

"Fine." He shrugged and drained the last of his coffee.

"Tell me the truth, or leave my store."

"I *did* tell you the truth," he countered and looked into the empty cup dolefully. "And I'm not going anywhere. At least, not yet."

"This is ridiculous," she whirled around and paced a bit before turning back and retracing her steps. "It's 1880! I'm an adult. You can't expect me to believe in silly stories that you would tell a child at bedtime.''

"I'm not asking you to believe anything, Rachel. I only answered your question.''

"Prove it.''

"Prove what?''

"That you're a ghost.''

"How'm I supposed to do that?''

"I don't know . . .'' She threw her hands up in the air. "Do something ghostly. Shake chains, howl, become a specter.''

Oh, Lord, his head hurt, and she wasn't doing a damn thing to help, either. Why hadn't Lesley told him how hard this was going to be?

"I don't have a chain to shake. I'm too sober to howl.'' He frowned then and admitted, "And I'm not even sure what a specter *is.* ''

"Then how can I believe you're a ghost?'' She shook her head and gave him a grim smile. "No, I'm sorry. I don't believe you. I don't want you here. And I most certainly don't *need* you.''

He *needed* coffee. Gallons of it. Jesus, just to keep up with her, a man had to be cold sober and on his toes at all times. What had happened to her in the last fifteen years?

Reaching back across the years, he recalled the child she had been. The wide-eyed, trusting little girl who had nearly driven him to distraction with her countless questions. He remembered her laughter and her sunny disposition. Shamefully, he also recalled the sound of her heartbreak when he had hurried away from her. At the time, he had been too interested in collecting his "reward" for an assignment completed satisfactorily to worry about it. Now, though, when faced with the woman his charge had become, he had to wonder.

What had happened to her that had changed her so completely?

Three sharp raps on the front door had Jackson wincing again and holding his forehead as if he expected his head to split in two.

Disgusted, Rachel threw a quick look at the door and saw Tessa Horn through the glass. The older woman had her hand cupped around her sharp eyes as she peered into the store. Looking from her impatient customer to the man who still hadn't explained his presence, Rachel didn't know which of them frustrated her more.

With Tessa in the store, she wouldn't be able to pry any more information out of Jackson Tate. And with Jackson in the store, Tessa would be like a hunting dog on the scent, as she sniffed out gossip.

"Here is the perfect opportunity to prove to me you are what you claim to be," she whispered in a rush.

"What are you talking about?"

"Disappear," she told him quietly.

"Huh?"

"Disappear," Rachel repeated and lifted one hand to wave at the woman rattling the doorknob.

"I can't do that."

She turned her head to stare at him. "What do you mean you can't? You said you were a ghost."

"I am."

"Well, if you can't disappear, what kind of a ghost are you?"

"A hungover one," Jackson said on a soft sigh.

"I'm not interested in your well deserved penances," Rachel muttered and reached over to unneccessarily straighten a few items on the counter. "I just want you to fade away now. Dissolve or whatever it is ghosts do."

He curled his fingers around the china cup, sighed, then admitted, "I don't know how."

"You don't know how to disappear?"

"That's right."

"*Can* you fade?" Her hands stilled as she looked up at him.

"Don't know. Never tried."

"Well, *try.*"

The older woman knocked again, an impatient burst of raps that demanded her attention. Once more, Rachel waved to her. "One minute, Tessa."

"All right, but I don't think it's going to work," Jackson said amiably. He straightened up, closed his eyes, and waited.

Nothing.

"You're still here," Rachel prodded.

His eyes opened, and he looked down at her with a smile. "Sorry."

He didn't look the least bit sorry.

"I've never heard of a solid ghost. Or one who drinks coffee. Or gets drunk."

One corner of his mouth lifted. "It's not like that all the time, believe me." His smile drained away as he told her, "Whenever Lesley sends me somewhere, I'm solid. That's all I know."

"*Leslie?*" Unwillingly, a short, sharp stab of jealousy ripped at her. Fifteen years. She hadn't seen him in fifteen years. For ten of those long, lonely years, she had waited for him, prayed for his return, *dreamt* about him, for goodness sake! And he had been spending his time with some woman named Leslie?

Ghosts don't have lady friends, she told herself, then immediately discounted that statement, as well. There were no ghosts.

In the next instant, though, she brushed those thoughts aside. They had nothing to do with anything. Jackson Tate didn't matter to her anymore. She'd long since given up on the notion of him returning to rescue her again. She didn't *need* rescuing this time. What she needed was for him to go back where he came from and leave her to the life she'd made for herself.

"If you can't disappear, just go away."

"Nope," he said softly. "Can't do it."

"This is *my* store, and I don't want you here."

"You don't have a say in this." He frowned slightly. "Neither do I."

"I can't have a man staying here. In my home. What would people say?"

His frown disappeared, and a surprisingly wicked grin lifted one corner of his mouth. "You're safe enough, believe me. If I want a woman while I'm here, I'll find one not quite so prickly, thanks."

A small slight that shouldn't have bothered her, but it did.

"What am I supposed to tell people about you?"

He grinned again, and she wanted to kick him. Blast him anyway, she thought, and hurried across the store to the door. He was too big for her to throw out bodily. And even if he wasn't, she didn't have time. Maybe, a wild voice in her brain said hopefully, he really *is* a ghost. If that were true, then perhaps she was the only one who could see him.

In the next instant, she laughed at her own thoughts. A ghost, indeed.

Oh, she didn't believe one word of his nonsense. He was no ghost. He was simply a man who had popped back into her life for some reason of his own. What that reason was, she would have to find out later.

And if he didn't explain himself fully, she would have the sheriff arrest him.

Fixing a welcoming smile on her face, Rachel turned the latch and opened the door to the first of the day's customers.

"According to my clock," the woman said with a telling glance at the brooch pinned to her abundant bosom, "you're five minutes late, Rachel."

"I'm sorry, Tessa," she said. "But my morning has been a bit . . . unusual."

The woman's sharp gaze slipped from the broken window to Jackson, who grinned and tipped his hat to her. "So I see," she muttered.

Rachel threw a look at him and tried to see him as her customer did. Lord. Whisker stubble on his cheeks, clothes rumpled, his eyes looked as though he were still half asleep.

In fact, he looked as though he had spent the night.

Right there.

With her.

Great days! Her carefully earned reputation was about to be shattered.

"And just who is this young man?" Tessa asked, already moving closer to her prey.

They spoke together.

"A carpenter," Jackson offered.

"A cousin," Rachel said.

Jackson grinned and stepped up to the two women. Laying one arm around Rachel's shoulders, he bent down and planted a quick kiss on her temple.

She stiffened until she thought her spine would snap and still, he was too close.

"It's a pleasure to meet you ma'am," Jackson said, charm oozing into the room. "Actually, I'm only Rachel's third cousin—twice removed," he paused, gave her shoulders a squeeze and asked, "Or was that three times removed, cousin?" Without waiting for an answer, he sailed on, clearly enjoying the entire situation. "I've come to build my little cousin's house for her."

Rachel gasped. She snapped her gaze up to his and only just remembered to close her mouth. How had he known about the new house?

"Really?" Tessa looked from his face to Rachel's. Instinctively, Rachel forced a smile.

"But Rachel dear," the woman said meaningfully,

"you're an orphan. How in heaven did you happen to locate a member of your family?"

Her mind went blank. Not a single idea presented itself. She hadn't had time to consider the consequences of her lie. Of course everyone in town knew that she had been orphaned at ten.

"Well now," her "relative" spoke up before the silence could stretch out any farther. "That was just a bit of luck, wasn't it cousin?" He looked down at her and smiled, daring her to contradict him.

"Yes, indeed it was."

"Tell me, do," Tessa urged unnecessarily.

"Well, a man came by our place in Oregon several weeks back and happened to mention shopping in Rachel's store. Talked her up a good bit," he winked at the woman. "Sounded like he was sweet on her, to me."

Tessa simpered.

"Anyhow, when he mentioned her name, why, the folks and I got real excited. So I came up here to see if Rachel was our long lost cousin." He hugged her tightly to him. "I'm pleased to say she is indeed our little Rachel. I can't tell you how much this is going to mean to my folks."

"How very nice for you, Rachel, dear," the woman reached out one hand to pat her arm. "To find family at this late stage of your life."

"Yes, isn't it?" Though she hated the lie he was spinning, one corner of Rachel's heart couldn't help wishing it was all true. Wouldn't it have been a miracle to discover that she actually *did* have family? A family who would love her?

"So then," Tessa's voice interrupted her thoughts, "you'll be staying on to build Rachel's new house?"

"Oh yes," Jackson winked at the older woman. "Why, where I come from, family sticks together, ma'am."

"Very commendable."

Inhale, exhale. Inhale, exhale. Rachel repeated the instructions silently, over and over. Any hope she had had of getting him to leave was now dashed. By the middle of the afternoon, Tessa would have spread Jackson Tate's story from one end of town to the other.

"There's no family resemblance at all," Tessa pointed out.

"Lucky for Rachel, eh?" Again, he winked at the woman. "She comes from the pretty side of the family, that's for damn sure."

Tessa blinked, not really shocked at the profanity, but after all, she couldn't pretend she hadn't heard it.

He seemed to understand.

"My apologies for my loose tongue, ma'am," he said. "I've been living too long among heathens, I guess. But no doubt Rachel will straighten me right out."

If he squeezed her shoulders one more time, she told herself, she would . . . what?

"Pretty as a picture, isn't she?" Jackson asked, tipping one finger under her chin until her face was tilted up to his.

Rachel flushed. Ridiculous. The whole situation was ridiculous. And yet . . . she couldn't quite deny the jolt of pleasure that she felt hearing herself described as "pretty."

"Oh my, yes," Tessa agreed. "I've always thought so."

"Now you take my side of the family?" Jackson said. "Mud fence homely, the best of them. And the rest . . . well, they're not allowed out in daylight. Neighbors claim they frighten their cows dry."

Rachel stared at him while Tessa twittered like a schoolgirl under his attentions. Idly, she listened to her supposedly ghostly visitor launch into a wild, sometimes lurid tale as to how exactly they were related. Uneasily, she noted that Tessa Horn, nobody's fool, was completely captivated by the man.

Whatever his real reason for being there, she told herself, she sensed big trouble coming.

She hadn't noticed when she was a girl. But this *ghost* of hers was a very good liar.

Chapter ☆ Five

The late afternoon sun did its best to poke through the layer of clouds that had drifted in off the ocean, only a few miles away. A damp chill in the air had Jackson wishing for his old sheepskin jacket. The few other assignments he had completed for Lesley over the years had been finished so quickly that he had barely had time to notice that he was solid—let alone, take an interest in the weather.

He shivered again, then told himself it had been so long since he'd been either hot *or* cold, maybe he should just enjoy the sensations.

Slowly, he bent over, picked up a milled two-by-four and turned it carefully in his hands as he straightened. It had been too long for this, too. The feel of the raw wood beneath his fingers brought a smile to his face. He inhaled the fresh, clean scent of it and admired its crisp, straight lines.

His thumb moved over the wood as he shifted his gaze to encompass the rest of the unfinished house. Just a shell stood on the foundation. A wooden skeleton, stark and bare, marked the spaces where walls would be. Rooms, halls, and the beginnings of a staircase were laid out in what looked like a haphazard fashion.

Frowning, he realized that the builder in him was offended by the obvious lack of knowledge Rachel's previous workmen had possessed. If she wasn't careful, she was going to end up owning a house that would fall down in the first good storm that passed.

Although she did have a nice spot for the place, he thought, and stared out toward the road at the edge of the two-acre property at the tail end of town. The house sat at the back of the lot, with more than two dozen trees between it and the road. Noise from Stillwater was muffled, and every breeze that shifted across the lot carried the sweet scent of pine. Somewhere close by, a bird called to its mate, and Jackson smiled.

"Pretty place," he said, taking another quick look around at what would one day be her house.

"Thank you," Rachel replied.

His fingers smoothed over the raw timber in his hands, and his palms itched to pick up a hammer and go to work. First off, he would rip out the support beams and re-set them at the proper angle. Then, he'd . . . Odd, he thought with a wry smile, he didn't remember being so fond of carpentry when he was alive. Oh, he had been good at it. Damn good. But the truth was, in those days, he had been much more interested in finding a good saloon at the end of the day than actually putting in a full day's work.

And just look where that had gotten him.

"Are you really a carpenter?"

He slanted Rachel a glance. "Used to be."

She nodded, met his gaze, and asked, "Back at the store? You told Tessa you were here to build my house."

"Yeah?"

"How did you know I was building one?"

Jackson smiled, looked away from her, and stared out toward the road again. Shrugging, he said, "I just knew. I don't know how. All of a sudden, it was there. In my mind." After a moment, he asked, "Why'd you tell her I was your cousin?"

She walked toward the front wall, leaned her palms on what would one day be a window sill, and admitted, "I couldn't think of anything else."

"Well, it worked out fine," he said and tossed the timber to the littered floor before joining her. "Now I can stay at your place and the neighbors won't talk."

"Nothing's changed, Mister Tate."

He cocked his head at her. "Call me Jackson, will ya? I never could answer to 'Mister' real easy."

She inhaled slowly, deeply, and seemed to think it over for a long minute. Then she started talking again.

"Fine. *Jackson,*" she corrected. "I still don't want you here."

"You still don't have a say in it."

"I most certainly have a say in who stays at my house or not."

"Suppose so," he agreed and turned around. Perching on the edge of the sill, he stretched his jean clad legs in front of him and crossed his feet at the ankles. "But, you might ask yourself what those neighbors are going to think of a woman who'd turn her own cousin out into the street."

She scowled at him, but Jackson wasn't worried. She could get as mad as she wanted to. He wasn't going anywhere. Not for a while, yet.

"Blast it," she snapped. "Who *are* you? What do you want from me?"

"I told you, I'm a—"

"Don't try to tell me you're a ghost again," she interrupted. "Not unless you can prove it."

"Now how the hell does a man prove a thing like that?"

"A man can't. A *ghost* could."

"Woman," he said, "you are not making this any easier for me."

"*That* is not my concern," she told him and turned her back on him. "My problem is getting this house built so my friends and I can move in."

Straightening up, he walked across the floor until he stood beside her. "Now why would a bunch of females want to share a house? More than one woman in any place is bound to cause trouble. Why don't you just find yourselves some men?"

Rachel looked up at him briefly. "Believe it or not, Jackson, some women are quite happy not being married."

He didn't know about that, but he was damn sure that most men would prefer living their lives unshackled. But somehow, the poor fools always seemed to wind up hogtied to a woman who spent the rest of her life trying to change the man she claimed to love just the way he was.

"Rachel," he tried a smile on her and saw right away that she wasn't impressed. That was a bit worrying. In the good old days, his charm had been well known for keeping him from being lonely. A shame indeed, he thought. Not only couldn't he handle his liquor any more, apparently, he couldn't dazzle the ladies, either.

So, he told himself, he'd have to try to reach her tender heart. *All* women had tender hearts. Especially for babies.

"Don't all women want to be mothers?" he asked.

Her features softened slightly before taking on that stubborn look with which he was becoming far too well acquainted.

"Most of us do, I think," she said quietly, but firmly. "Unfortunately, you don't always get what you want."

"You could though, Rachel," he insisted and bent his head. Whispering in her ear, he went on. "And that's the pure truth. You're a fine looking woman. You'd be a great mother. Probably have smart kids, too. Maybe even turn out a doctor or two."

Her eyes took on a faraway shine as if she were drawing up a mental image of his words. Her lips softened, and her breathing slowed. Maybe, he thought with an inward smile, this wouldn't be so hard after all. Clearly, she had a real strong bent toward motherhood. All she really needed was a push in the right direction. Point out to her how good it would be. Maybe show her the possibilities.

Quickly, he began drawing her word pictures of a possible future.

"Think about it, Rachel," he went on, his breath hushing against her ear. "You could have a daughter as pretty and smart as you. She maybe might be a doctor." Though privately, despite what Lesley had said, Jackson doubted that *any* woman would make a good sawbones. Heck, everybody knew that a woman was too delicate to deal with blood and such. No female would be able to dig out a bullet . . . or set a busted leg.

Not to mention the fact that no man in his right mind would let a woman go poking and prodding at him. At least not in a doctor's office.

But obviously Rachel didn't have the slightest problem imagining a female doctor. Her eyes shone and glistened. He could almost think she was tearing up.

"My daughter," she whispered to herself. "A doctor."

"Why not?" he asked, keeping his voice soft, urgent. He inhaled deeply and unwittingly drew the soft scent of her light, floral perfume into his lungs. Lordy, she smelled good. Shaking his head, he told himself to get back to business. "Then maybe you could have a boy or two, just for good measure. Why, Rachel, there's likely all kinds of fellas who would just love to be those children's daddy."

Well, there could be, he thought. If she'd learn to hold onto her temper and try to keep from sharpening that tongue of hers.

The light in her eyes slowly dimmed. Swiveling her head until she was facing him, she said, "No, Jackson. I'm through with dreams and idle speculation. There aren't going to be any daughters or sons. Not for me."

Disappointment rose up in him like an incoming tide. Slowly, steadily, it lifted until it had drowned every one of his hopes for a quick end to this assignment.

"Dammit Rachel, you're just not trying!"

She stepped back and glared him into silence. "What possible difference can it make to you either way? I haven't seen you in fifteen years. You don't even know me."

"The hell I don't." He snorted and shoved both hands into his pockets. "I saved your life, didn't I?"

"When I was a child," she reminded him. "But I'm all grown up now, Jackson. And I don't need an angel, or a ghost or—for all I know, a *lunatic,* telling me how to live my life."

He blinked. Lunatic? "You think I'm crazy?"

"It's certainly one explanation."

"Not the right one." Dammit all, it was one thing, arguing with him about every little thing. But it was damned insulting for her to think of him as a drooling loon. "I'm not crazy, Rachel. I'm just a ghost sent here to help you fix your life."

"By getting drunk and passing out on my floor? Or by endangering my reputation until the only thing that can save it is a lie?" She shook her head. "No, thank you. Besides, as I have already said a dozen times, I don't need your help with *my* life."

"Seems to me you haven't been doing any great shakes on your own," he pointed out.

"Is that so?"

"You're not married. You got no kids. No family." He waved one hand at her. "Hell, Rachel, look at yourself. You go all cold and frosty just talking about a man. What kind of life is that?"

"*Mine.*"

"If you ask me, it's nothin' to be proud of."

"I didn't ask you, if you'll remember."

"Yeah, but—"

"And I think it *is* something to be proud of." She lifted her chin and poked him in the chest with the tip of her index finger. "I live my own life, the way I want to. I answer to no one. I have my store and my friends. I'm a part of the community.''

''But nothing else.''

''What else is there?''

''There's love, Rachel.''

She looked as if he'd slapped her. He didn't even know what had made him say it. It wasn't as though he'd been a big believer in love when he had been alive. At least where it concerned him. But dammit, even *he* knew it existed.

What she had said about her life was all true. Rachel had the things around her that most folks clamored over. But she didn't have somebody to talk to and laugh with. She didn't have somebody to warm her feet against on a cold winter night. And blast it all to hell and back, if she didn't get herself a goddamn man and find herself pregnant, he was going to be in a sore amount of trouble.

''Love?'' She chuckled to herself, but the sound wasn't a pleasant one. Grabbing hold of one of the tall timbers nearest her, she leaned against it. ''I used to want that.'' She sent him a long, slow look over her shoulder. ''I always believed that there was someone for everyone in this world. One special someone. I even thought that I had found him and all I had to do was wait for him to come back to me.''

He ducked his head to avoid her eyes.

''But then,'' she went on, turning back to look out across the land, ''I grew up. Love belongs in fairy tales, Jackson.'' She sent him a hard, quick glare. ''I don't believe in fairy tales anymore. I don't believe in angels. Or ghosts.'' She pushed away from the beam and started walking toward the back of the house. ''In short, Jackson,'' she said calmly, ''I don't believe in you.''

Oh, she wanted to. There was nothing Rachel would like more than to believe again. To believe in all the magic she had once blindly trusted.

She heard his footsteps as he followed her to what would

one day be her back porch. Briefly, she allowed herself to
remember the girl she had been. Memories drifted in and
out of her mind like the faded fragrance of a dying rose.
She'd been so sure, then. So positive that he was the one
she was meant to love. All she had to do was grow up.

And even after living with the Heinzes she had still believed. She had had to believe that he would come back.
That he would rescue her. Again. Rachel had continued to
look for him, to wait for him, and to dream about him long
after she should have given up.

Because she had had to.

She shuddered. That was all past though, now. She didn't
need his help anymore. It was too late to rescue the crushed
dreams of a little girl who had loved an angel. The same
little girl who had discovered that people were not always
what they seemed. It was a hard lesson, but she had learned,
the first time her foster father had taken a strap to her, then
locked her in a closet.

Inhaling sharply, she curled her fingers around the fabric
of her skirt and squeezed.

"I thought of something that might convince you," Jackson said as he stepped up beside her.

"Please don't start that again."

"Can't help it. It'll be easier all the way around once
you believe me."

"I believed you once before," she said and walked past
him, down the steps onto the grass. "When you said you
would be back."

"Here I stand," he countered.

She glanced at him over her shoulder and shook her
head. "Years too late."

"Look." He took the steps then crossed the grass until
he was standing beside her. He gripped her elbow and
turned her to face him. "I didn't come back earlier because
I couldn't. I'm *dead.* I don't get a choice in what I do or
don't do."

She pulled her arm free and looked up at him. "For a dead man, you seem fairly lively." Before he could argue, she held up one hand to stop him. "And if you're going to tell me your ghost stories again, don't bother. Unless you're willing to prove they're true."

"I think I can," he said, shoving one hand into his pants pocket. "But first, let me ask you something."

"What?"

"You said yourself that I looked the same as I did the last time you saw me."

"Yes?" She knew where this question was leading and wasn't at all sure how to answer him.

"If I'm *not* a ghost, how do you explain it?"

That question had been bothering her, too. The simple truth was she didn't have an explanation. But that didn't mean there wasn't one. After all, the last time she'd seen him, she had been a frightened little girl. Memory was a tricky thing at best. "I can't," she said at last. As she saw a victorious gleam light in his eyes, she added quickly, "But I don't have to explain it. For all I know, you come from a long line of people who simply age well."

He smirked at her. "That's the best you can do?"

"As I said, I don't have to explain it."

"Fine," he grumbled. "Hardheaded, stubborn female." He pulled his hand out of his pocket. Uncurling his fingers, he held a single gold coin on the flat of his palm. "Then look at this. Maybe *then* you'll believe me."

"A twenty dollar gold piece?" She lifted her eyes to his. "That's supposed to prove that you're a ghost?"

"Look closer," he insisted, placing the coin in her palm.

As he watched and waited, she turned the gold coin over and over in her hand.

Even before she held it close to her eyes, Rachel knew this was no ordinary coin. Its edges were irregular, not round. The surface of the gold gleamed and shone like nothing she had ever seen before. And most telling of all, she thought with a start, there was none of the ordinary Mint imprinting on either side of the coin. No *E Pluribus Unum.* No eagle. No dead president. No date.

Instead, one side of the coin held an image of a five-pointed star and the other, a sculpted quarter moon.

Something inside her turned over. Her throat tightened, and a ribbon of worry snaked its way through her bloodstream. Still, it wasn't proof. For all she knew, he might have filed down the normal imprinting and had this made up just to frighten her. Squeezing the coin between her thumb and forefinger, she noticed something else. Something more disturbing than the coin's appearance.

The gold was warm. Not the kind of warmth one would expect from a coin that had been recently handled. But a heat that seemed to come from the metal itself. An indistinct energy of sorts hummed along her palm and simmered up the length of her arm.

"Where did you get this?"

"Lesley."

"Leslie who?"

"I don't know what his last name is," Jackson snapped. "Or I've forgotten."

Lesley, she corrected mentally. A man. Why that should make her feel better, she didn't know. But it did. Her thumb smoothed over the gold surface, and she could have sworn invisible sparks of heat jumped from the coin.

Her fingers curled around the gold tightly, and she looked up at him. "What are you supposed to do with these coins?"

"Hell if I know." He tipped his hat back farther on his head. "Lesley gave me six of them, told me that if I needed to, I could use them to help me out."

"Help you do what? And how?"

"You're probably not supposed to know this," he muttered, more to himself than to her, "but hell, if I don't convince you to believe me, I'm going to need more than coins to get this job done.''

''What job?''

''Never mind.'' He pointed at her closed fist and the coin within. ''Lesley said that all you have to do is hold that coin and say out loud what it is you want.''

''You're telling me these are *magic* coins.'' Sarcasm dripped from every word.

''I guess magic's as good a word as any.''

She laughed shortly. Magic. Ghosts. Gold coins that felt hot and humming with energy. How could any sane person believe any of this? And yet, the coin in her palm continued to radiate heat.

''Six magic coins. Sounds like the name of a bedtime story.''

''Well,'' he said, ''only five, now.'' He shifted his gaze from hers as if he didn't want to talk about the missing coin. Rachel wasn't going to let go that easily.

''Five? What happened to the other one?''

He scratched his jaw, pulled in a deep breath, and spoke. ''Shames me to admit it, but I might as well get it all out. I traded it to a man last night.''

''Traded it? For what?''

He glanced at her guiltily, then looked away again. ''A bottle of whiskey.''

''Whiskey!''

He grimaced at the memory.

''Who did you give this magic coin to?''

''I don't know his name.'' He shrugged as if sluffing his actions off his shoulders. ''Just some prospector.'' In his own defense, he added, ''But I warned him about the coin. Told him to go carefully with what he said.''

''Your story gets more complicated and less believable every moment.''

''Why would I make up a story like this?''

''I don't know,'' she said thoughtfully. ''But there's really only one way to test what you're saying."

"Huh?"

"It's very simple really," Rachel went on. "And then I'll know for sure if you're telling the truth or not."

He looked at her sharply, then, reading her intention in her eyes, he said, "Don't do it, Rachel. I've only got five of those left and I might need—"

She squeezed the coin tightly, closed her eyes, and said clearly: "I want Jackson Tate to disappear."

"Shit!"

Rachel opened her eyes an instant later, and he was gone.

Startled, she took a half step forward, then stopped and turned in a fast circle, letting her gaze sweep across her surroundings. But he was nowhere nearby. He hadn't had time to run. There were no hiding places close to the house. Eyes wide, she shook her head and looked down at her palm. As she watched, the coin shimmered, glowed brightly, then faded completely away.

It was gone.

Just like Jackson.

"Oh, my God." She staggered backward a step or two, then fell to the ground, landing on her rump with a solid jolt that rattled her teeth. "He *was* telling the truth. He really was a ghost."

"Well," a familiar voice said, as if from a great distance, "Glory Hallelujah!"

"Jackson?" she breathed.

Directly in front of her, the air seemed to thicken. Throat tight, eyes wide, her heart hammering in her chest, Rachel watched as Jackson Tate slowly began to take shape. At first, he was no more substantial than a shadow. But as the seconds ticked past, he began to solidify, until finally, he looked exactly as he had just before she'd made her hasty wish.

He looked down at himself, patted his thighs, then his chest, as if making sure he was completely back. Lastly, he reached up to shove his hat down more firmly on his head. "Dammit, Rachel, I told you not to do that. I might need those coins, you know."

"It's all true," she whispered, and shook her head in denial even as she said it. "All true. You *are* a ghost."

Her heartbeat skipped, staggered, then went on beating as if nothing had just happened. But it had. She looked up at him and let the wonder of the moment sink into her brain.

"Isn't that what I've been telling you all along?"

"But, why?"

"Because I died."

"No." She swallowed past the knot in her throat. "Not why are you a ghost . . . why are you here?"

"I told you that, too." He hunkered down on one knee. "I was sent."

"By Lesley."

"There you go."

"Why?"

"To help you, Rachel."

"This is impossible."

"I think," he pointed out unnecessarily, "we've already taken care of proving *that.*"

True. She had seen it with her own eyes. There was no denying it any longer. Jackson Tate was a ghost. *Had* been a ghost fifteen years ago when he'd come to her rescue.

She had spent most of her life in love with a dead man.

"Oh, Lord." She rubbed a spot between her eyes tiredly. Her head ached, and her heart still felt as though it would beat hard enough to fly through her chest. After several deep, calming breaths, she finally risked another question. "How did you come back?" she wanted to know. "I wished for you to disappear."

"Yeah," he said and dropped to the ground beside her. Shooting her a wry look, he pulled a handful of grass up and began to twirl it in his fingers. "Pretty sneaky."

She reached out one hand and laid it on his forearm,

touching him to reassure herself that he was, indeed, back. Real.

"I'm solid again."

"How?"

One dark brow arched. "You only said you wanted me to disappear."

"Yes?"

"You *didn't* say forever."

She nodded thoughtfully. "Silly of me."

"Although," Jackson went on and slowly let go of the handful of grass, one dark green blade at a time, "I have a feeling that even if you had said 'forever,' I would have been back."

"Because of this job you have to do?"

"Yeah." He braced his forearms on his upraised knees and squinted into the distance.

"Are you going to tell me what that job is?" she asked hesitantly, not really sure if she wanted to know or not.

"You won't like it."

"Now I definitely want to know what it is."

Slowly, he swiveled his head until he was looking directly at her again. Their gazes locked and for one heart-stopping moment, Rachel felt herself drawn into the depths of those green eyes she remembered so well. Then he spoke, and the moment was shattered.

"I'm here to get you married, Rachel. And I'm not leaving until I do."

Chapter ☆ *Six*

M arried?

Her heartbeat quickened, her stomach churned, and even drawing breath seemed suddenly too difficult a task. This is why, she told herself. Why Jackson had talked so much about marriage. He'd only been softening her up in hopes of marrying her off to someone.

Rachel hurried her steps, trying to outdistance the man running to catch up with her.

She didn't even remember jumping to her feet and heading for town. She had just known that she had to move. To walk. To escape the ghost with the knowing green eyes.

"Rachel," he called out from well behind her.

No. She wouldn't stop. She wouldn't talk to him. Wouldn't listen to him.

"Dammit, Rachel," he yelled again and his voice was closer. "Wait just a dang minute."

"We have nothing to say to each other," she called back over her shoulder and gasped when she saw him gaining on her. Blasted skirts and petticoats. She yanked the yards of fabric out of her way. Holding the mass up above her long stockings, she started running.

But it was too little, too late.

Jackson caught her after only a few more steps. Grabbing

her upper arm, he turned her around to face him.

"What in the hell came over you?"

"Nothing." She dropped her skirts again and tried to regain some of her usual composure. But it didn't work. She heard the quaver in her voice when she finished, "I simply have to get back to town."

He cocked his head to one side and eyed her warily.

She licked dry lips and willed her voice to steadiness. "I told Hester that we would only be gone a short while, and I'm sure she's more than ready to go home by now."

"Rachel . . ."

"No." She shook her head fiercely. "I don't want to talk about something that *isn't* going to happen, Jackson."

"Rachel, I said I was here to get you married—not sent off to prison!"

"Marriage without love would *be* a prison, Jackson." She turned her back on him so he wouldn't see how deeply all of this had shaken her. Married. The man she had fallen in love with as a child had come to see her married to someone else. Well, it wasn't going to happen. He couldn't *force* her into a marriage. And she certainly wasn't going to enter into one willingly.

"Hell." He released her, and she turned toward town again. This time, she walked more slowly, despite the urge to run.

As they neared the road, Rachel's labored breathing finally evened out. Her corset felt too tight, her feet hurt, and strands of her hair now hung limply along her face. Calmly, she tucked them back behind her ears.

She chanced a quick look at the man walking beside her. The disgusted expression on his face didn't cheer her. Her gaze moved quickly over his features and in response, something twisted and tightened in her chest. Despite her efforts to deny it to herself, those old feelings she'd carried for him still existed.

"Jackson," she said and stepped over a fallen tree

branch, "if the only reason you're here is to see me married, you might as well leave now." Please, she added silently, please leave before those old wants and emotions became strong enough to hurt me again.

"Leaving's not up to me."

Rachel felt her hopes drain away.

He tilted his head back to stare up at the gray clouds scuttling in off the ocean. "I didn't come here to hurt you, Rachel."

Maybe not, she thought. But she had a terrible feeling that pain would be the result, anyway. She tore her gaze from him to look straight ahead. "I won't cooperate with you. I won't marry just because you—or someone else—wants me to. Without love, there is no reason for marriage."

"Rachel, love can grow over time, you know."

"If the seed is there," she countered. "Without that seed, the only things to grow are resentment and bitterness."

His gaze shifted from the coming storm to the walking storm beside him. She wasn't ready for any of this, Jackson thought. He could tell from the stiffness of her posture. From the way she avoided looking at him.

Well, he'd done a hell of a job so far. He should never have told her why he was there. Why he'd been sent. With that hard head of hers, she'd be fighting him at every turn, now. And with the snarling and snapping going on, how would he ever get some nice young fella to fall in love with her?

He shot a quick, disgusted glance at the sky. Lesley might have given him a few tips on how to go about this job, he thought. But no, he just hands over some magic coins and says, "Go do it." Hell, nobody knew better than Lesley just what a miserable failure Jackson was at this ghosting business. But then, he'd been a failure at most everything when he was alive, too. Frowning, he waited for inspiration. When none came, he started talking again, hoping that he would say the right thing.

"Rachel, remember what you said about that one person for every other person?"

"Yes."

He winced. Her voice sounded tight, strangled. But he couldn't quit now.

"Well, the man who sent me here, Lesley? He says that's hogwash."

"He's wrong," she said quietly.

Jackson ignored her argument. "Lesley says folks can find happiness with lots of other folks."

"I'm already happy."

"But you're not married."

They walked a few more yards before she answered him. "And I'm not going to be, Jackson."

"Rachel, this doesn't have to be so hard."

She laughed shortly. "Hard? Hard was waiting for you for ten long years before I finally gave up. Hard was living with Mister Heinz."

"What do you mean?" Something in her eyes tugged at him.

"Nothing." She waved one hand and shook her head as if dismissing what she'd said. "Just know this, Jackson. I will never marry anyone, unless I'm in love."

"That's what I'm saying," he pulled his hat down lower over his eyes. "We'll find you somebody to love, Rachel."

A sheen of water glistened in her eyes. But if they were tears, she refused to let them fall.

"I don't want to be in love, Jackson. Not again."

He knew what she meant and despite himself, he felt a ripple of shame. But it hadn't been his fault that she had imagined herself in love with him long ago. Hell, she'd been nothing but a kid.

"Rachel, you're all grown up now. That was—"

"Love, Jackson. That's what it was." She cut him off

neatly. "Just because I was a child, that doesn't make the feelings any less strong. Or the disappointment any less brutal."

There went that thread of shame again.

He looked into her clear blue eyes and tried to see the shadow of the child she had been. But he couldn't. That little girl was gone forever. In her place was a pretty, independent woman with eyes that held no welcome for him. Strange, but he almost missed the worshipful gazes she'd sent him when she was a child. Though it had been downright annoying at the time, it was certainly better than the cold, fish-eye look he was getting now.

Still, she'd grown up all right. She held herself arrow straight, her shoulders back, her chin lifted at a defiant angle. Jackson caught himself admiring her. Not just her looks, which went without saying. But there was more to Rachel Morgan than just being pretty.

There was strength. Determination. And the brass to live her own life just the way she wanted to. It didn't seem right that he'd been sent there to take it away from her.

A strange, skittering sensation started low in his belly and traveled downward at the same pace his gaze moved over Rachel. Lordy, she was a fine looking woman, he admitted silently. Too fine for the likes of him, even if he had been in a position to do anything about it. The flicker of desire that leapt into life inside him, he explained away as being the result of too many years without female company. Jesus, you would think that being dead would take care of those kind of feelings. Those wants. Needs.

Jackson dragged his gaze upward until he met hers. As he looked at her, he knew that it had been a mistake, his being sent here. This woman was never going to trust him again. Dammit, if it was so blasted important that she get married to some poor fool, then Lesley should have sent somebody else to deal with the problem.

Somebody she might listen to.

He's supposed to know so much . . . hadn't he known how Rachel would feel about Jackson reappearing in her life?

"I don't suppose my asking you to leave again would do any good?" she whispered.

He sighed and shoved his hands into his pockets. His fingertips brushed the edges of his remaining coins and his resolve strengthened on the spot. "No, it won't."

"Then I won't bother saying it."

"Rachel!"

They both turned to look up the road leading from town. A dark-haired man with saddlebags tossed across his shoulder hurried toward them.

"Who's that?" Jackson muttered.

"Sam Hale," Rachel said with a smile.

He sneaked a quick look at her and noticed the shine in her eyes. Apparently Sam Hale was enough to cheer her right up. Scowling, he turned back to study the man approaching. A few inches shorter than Jackson, the man had brown hair, brown eyes, and skin tanned from long hours in the sun.

"Rachel," he said as he came to a stop in front of her. "The woman at the store told me where to find you."

"Hester," Rachel nodded.

"I wouldn't know," he admitted. "She hardly spoke above a whisper and never did look at me."

"She's a bit shy."

He grinned and glanced at Jackson for the first time. "Hello," he said and held out a hand. "I'm Sam Hale."

Reluctantly, Jackson took the hand and shook it. "Jackson Tate."

Clearly, Sam wasn't interested in talking to him. His gaze shifted immediately back to Rachel. "I was wondering if you still needed someone to work on your new house."

"I certainly do," she said eagerly.

Jackson scowled at the change in her manner. Apparently, she'd already forgotten all about him and their argument. His gaze shot back and forth between the two friends and as he did, he realized that a hard knot of anger had settled in his belly. Stupid, he thought. He should be pleased that she was smiling again. But dammit, it would have been nice if *he* had been the one to chase off her bad temper.

And just who the hell was this Sam Hale, anyway? Why did the man look at Rachel like she was a nice, cold drink after a long, hot day? But most importantly, why was Jackson upset that these two friends seemed to get along so nicely? This was his big chance. Obviously, Rachel already liked this fella. How difficult could it be to ease liking into loving?

Jackson scratched his cheek thoughtfully and ignored the simmering resentment inside him.

"The last man I hired," Rachel was saying, "walked off the job after two weeks. He wasn't nearly as good a worker as you were." She reached out and laid one hand on Sam's forearm.

Jackson flinched. "Are you the one who put in the support beams?" he demanded.

Sam looked over at him in surprise, as if he'd forgotten someone else were there. "No," he answered quietly. "Why?"

"Because whoever did it, didn't know a damned thing about building."

The two men's gazes met and locked. Like two big dogs meeting in the street, they took each other's measure. Rachel looked from one to the other of them and back again. She had no idea why Jackson looked so fierce. Sam, though probably just as confused by the other man's sudden challenge, apparently had no intention of backing down.

Well, she wasn't going to stand by all day and watch the two of them bristle and snarl at one another. But just as importantly, she wasn't going to risk losing Sam's expertise in carpentry over Jackson's unpredictability.

"You're hired, Sam," she said and noted that he barely tore his gaze from Jackson's long enough to nod at her. Her ghost, on the other hand, shot her a look she didn't even want to try to interpret. "Jackson, my uh, *cousin*, will be supervising the job."

"You know anything about carpentry?" Sam asked.

"A sight more than the last fool she had working on the place."

"Oh, for heaven's sake," she murmured. "You two work out the details. I'm going back to town."

If she hadn't been so caught up in worrying about Jackson and his plans to marry her off, Rachel would have seen the man in time to avoid him.

As it was, she nearly bumped into him as she crossed the street and headed toward the store.

"Miss Rachel—" A deep, smooth voice as dark and rich as molasses spilled over her, and she instinctively stiffened.

She lifted her gaze and looked into the almost black eyes of a man she instinctively disliked.

"Hello, Mister Lynch," she replied courteously and tried to step around him.

He moved with her, blocking her escape.

"It's good to see you again, Rachel," he said and reached out to touch her arm.

She shifted.

He noticed the rebuff and let his hand drop to his side.

"Ah," he sighed, "I had hoped that my absence would, as the saying goes, make your heart grow fonder."

Quickly, she countered, "I assume you have also heard the saying, Out of sight, out of mind?"

His features tightened for an instant before relaxing into the genial pose he normally assumed. But it was too late. She'd seen that flash of annoyance.

Rachel's gaze swept over him thoroughly. Dismissively. He wore a beautifully tailored gray suit with a white shirt and a red vest. His black string tie was knotted at a perfect angle, and the shine on his shoes dared dust to land on his feet. He held a black planter's hat with a wide brim in one hand and with the other, dug a gold pocket watch out of his vest. When he popped the gold case open, she heard a slight tinkle of music before he snapped it shut again and slid it home.

He smiled, but the action only affected his lips. There was no trace of good humor anywhere else on his handsome features.

Dark, empty eyes watched her. His neatly trimmed hair, gently sprinkled with gray at the temples, was combed straight back from his forehead. A patrician nose wrinkled as if at a disagreeable odor.

For some reason, he chose to ignore her snub. "It is almost supper time. Would you care to join me in a meal?"

Incredible, she thought. Two men. One alive, one dead, and neither of them paid the slightest bit of attention to anything she said.

"No, thank you," she said quietly and stepped around him again. This time, he allowed it. "If you'll excuse me, Mister Lynch, I left Hester Sutton minding the store for a while and I'm sure she's more than ready to go home by now."

"Of course," he swept her past him with an elegant wave of his arm. "Until later," he added.

Rachel's shoulders stiffened in response. There was something about the handsome gambler that bothered her, she just wasn't sure what it was. She had never been able to pinpoint anything specific that repelled her. Yet at the same time, she hadn't been able to get past the unpleasant feelings he aroused in her.

Ever since moving to Stillwater two years before, Noble Lynch had wormed his way into the town's good graces with benevolent acts of charity. Rachel's fellow citizens at first had been loathe to accept money from a professional gambler. But Noble was also a man of impeccable manners. Somehow, he had convinced the townspeople that he had nothing but goodwill in mind with his donations to the town.

She should have been pleased with the new schoolhouse and the organ he had donated to a church he never attended. Yet, instead, she found herself watching him, wondering when his true nature would reveal itself.

As a child, she'd learned to read expressions very well. Her foster father's anger was quick to flare, and her ability to see it coming had saved her more than a few whippings.

As an adult, she recognized the same quicksilver temper in the elegantly dressed, well spoken gambler.

"I look forward to our next meeting, Rachel," he said and tipped his hat. She nodded, and he stepped back into the crowd of people milling about the street.

Rachel paused for a moment to look after him. Then she shook her head, dismissing Noble Lynch from her mind completely. She had to deal with more than enough trouble already.

Jackson and Sam walked back into town side by side. The noise and bustle of the crowded street surrounded them. A hundred or more yards away, stood the Mercantile and through a break in the mob of people, Jackson spotted Rachel, standing just outside her store.

"Who is that?" he asked Sam, straining to look for the man he'd just seen standing much too closely to Rachel. Something about the fellow had seemed oddly familiar.

"Who are we talking about?" Sam asked.

"There was a man in front of the store. Talking to Rachel."

He shrugged. "She's a pretty woman."

Jackson shot the carpenter a quick look. Soon after Rachel had left them on their own, knowledge of Sam Hale and the kind of man he was had filled Jackson's mind. It was damned unsettling, this all of a sudden *knowing* a person he'd never seen before. But at least he could be assured that Hale was a decent man. Except for his tendency to drift whenever the mood struck him.

But a good wife could cure him of that.

"Yes, she is," he said cautiously. "Makes a body wonder why no man has thrown a loop over her yet."

Sam nodded, then glanced at the man beside him. He laughed, held up one hand and shook his head. "No sir, don't start getting any ideas in that direction."

"What are you talking about?"

"I've seen that look before," the carpenter added, a good natured smile on his face.

"What look?" Blast it, Jackson thought. Too long dead, that was his problem. He'd even forgotten how to bluff.

"That one that says, 'My sister—or in your case, cousin—needs a husband. How about it?'" He started walking again, still shaking that shaggy head of his. "Well, no thank you. Rachel's a fine woman. And if I was lookin' for a wife—which I'm not—she'd be a good choice. If a man was willing to overlook that hard head of hers."

He couldn't very well argue with *that,* Jackson told himself wryly. He'd come up against it real often himself lately.

"But me," Sam went on with a sigh, "I'm a drifter and I like it that way. No ties. No wife and kids. Nothing to hold me into one town longer than I want to stay." He glanced at the man walking beside him. "Sorry, boss. But if that's what you've got in mind, you might as well forget it straight away."

Honest too, Jackson told himself as he and Sam headed for the blacksmith's to see about ordering some metal braces for the support beams at the new house. Yessir, Sam Hale ought to do just fine as a husband for Rachel.

Jackson stuffed one hand into his pocket and touched

one of the golden coins. With a little help from him, ol' Sam would fall right in love with Rachel and sweep her off her feet before she had a chance to fight it.

The two men threaded their way through the late afternoon crowd, and Jackson told himself that everything was going to work out fine. Rachel would have a husband to love her and give her those babies she was supposed to have. Sam would have a home instead of blowing around the countryside like a tumbleweed. And he would get whatever reward it was he had coming to him.

Things were finally coming together.

So why was there a small, niggling sense of doubt tugging at his insides?

By the time he left Sam at the boarding house where the man had taken a room, it was growing dark. Jackson tugged his hat down low and told himself to speak to Rachel about maybe borrowing a coat from the store for the length of his stay. Of course, she probably wasn't in the mood to be doing him any favors, he thought grimly. Disgusted, he kicked at a warped board that jutted up from the walk.

Lamps lit against the coming night spilled islands of soft, golden light into the street. The few people out and about looked to be in a hurry for home and Jackson felt a sharp stab of envy. Fools, he thought. He'd be willing to bet that not a one of them realized how lucky they were.

Not just to be alive. But to have a home to go to. People who cared. Maybe a woman sitting in the parlor, staring at the front door as she waited for her man.

He scowled to himself and rubbed one hand across the back of his neck. Something was wrong, here. He didn't remember wanting any of those things when he was alive.

Why now, when he was dead and gone?

Was it Rachel, doing this to him?

He stopped short.

There's a fine thing, he thought. Getting notions about a

woman who would just as soon spit as say his name. Hell, getting notions about a woman, period. He was a dead man, he reminded himself. And it was high time he got used to it.

A small, mousy woman scurried past him, eyes down, long black shawl drawn tight around her shoulders. He stepped aside to make room for her on the narrow walk, but he wasn't even sure if she noticed. Shaking his head, he continued on toward the store.

Then behind him, a commotion rose up.

A man's shout of laughter.

A woman's shocked gasp.

And the heavy thud of bodies smacking into the dirt.

Jackson spun around in time to see a giant of a man looming over the tiny woman laying in the street. Instinctively, he jumped off the boardwalk and went to help.

"I'm sorry, Miss Hester," the huge man was saying. "I never saw you. Honest, I didn't." He reached out one big hand toward her, but she shrunk back, obviously terrified of the man's size.

Jackson stepped up. "What happened?"

The man shot him a grateful look, then turned a sheepish gaze on the woman. "I didn't see her. A couple of us was having a bit of a tussle, and Nels tossed me through the doorway. Ran right into her, I did, and knocked her flat."

Jackson's eyes widened. He didn't even want to see the size of a man who could toss *this* one through a doorway. The big man, dressed in a lumberman's costume of red checked flannel shirt, worn levis and knee-high leather boots, stood over the woman with a look of pure misery etched in his features.

Instantly, a flood of information about the big man poured into Jackson's brain. He frowned as he tried to mentally sift through it all.

"Miss Hester," the giant said and even his whisper rumbled loudly. "I'm sure sorry. Won't you let me help you out of the street?"

She shook her head slightly and didn't look up.

Jackson stared at the man for a moment and bit back a smile. Couldn't be easy, trying not to scare someone so tiny when you're the size of a draft horse. Still, the man's bone deep gentleness seemed to shimmer in the air around him.

"I'll take care of her," Jackson said, suddenly sorry for the man who looked so damned helpless. "I'll see her home. You go on."

The lumberman eyed him carefully from beneath heavy blond brows. A shock of his pale hair fell across his forehead, and he reached up to push it out of his way. After a long moment, he nodded slowly, but issued a whispered warning before leaving. "You take good care of her, or answer to me. Charlie Miller."

Jackson's brows lifted high on his head at the threat, but he brushed it aside. After all, even a man of Charlie's size couldn't do much damage to a dead man.

When the big man moved off, Jackson stretched out a hand and helped the woman to her feet. Immediately, she let go of him and stepped back.

Skittish female, he thought.

"You're a friend of Rachel Morgan, aren't you?" he asked suddenly as the knowledge slipped into his brain.

She glanced up at him before nodding.

"Well then, you're my friend too." He bent his head and looked into her pale blue eyes. "Jackson Tate, Rachel's cousin."

Those eyes widened a bit.

Deliberately, he took her hand and threaded it through the crook of his arm. "Why don't I walk you on home?"

She hesitated, clearly uncomfortable. But after a quick, covert look at the doorway where Charlie Miller had disappeared, she nodded and started walking, leading him down the street.

Jackson glanced down at the tiny hand on his forearm and noticed that her fingernails were chewed down to the quick. Poor little thing. Miller probably scared the bejesus out of her. As they walked, he tried to tell her that the lumberman hadn't meant any harm.

"Oh," she said in a hush of sound, "I know he wouldn't hurt me. He's a very kind man."

"You know him?"

Her head dipped again, and Jackson wanted to tell her to lift her chin, but he didn't.

"I know of him," she said softly. "But tonight is the first time he's spoken to me directly."

"Ah . . ."

"Of course, why *would* he speak to me?" she said, more to herself than to him. "A fine handsome man like that. Why would he look twice at a shy schoolteacher?"

Jackson smiled to himself. So. She hadn't been terrified of the lumberman. She'd just been too tongue-tied to speak. Well, hell. He wasn't having much luck with Rachel's love life. Maybe it wouldn't hurt to get in a little practice with somebody else.

"You know, Hester . . . you don't mind if I call you Hester?"

"No."

"Well Hester, sometimes I think females expect too much of us men."

"What do you mean?"

Interested, she was actually looking up at him now.

"You take Charlie Miller, for instance," he said thoughtfully. "Big man like that, folks wouldn't guess that he was shy."

"He is?"

Jackson looked into those hope-filled eyes and nodded solemnly. He now knew more about Charlie than anybody had a right to know. The man's awkwardness and innate gentleness were at odds with his big body and made him even more shy around women. And Jackson hadn't needed the flood of information to see the look in Charlie's careful gaze. If he was any judge, the lumberman had a soft spot in his heart for the little schoolteacher.

"Yes ma'am," Jackson went on. "Why, he probably has no idea of how to talk to a fine, educated woman like yourself."

Her spine straightened a bit, and he noted that she was at least two inches taller than he had at first thought.

"Probably scared to death he'll make some mistake in his grammar, and you'll think him a fool."

"I wouldn't, though," she assured him.

"I know that, Hester. But Charlie doesn't. It's a terrible thing to be so afraid to make a mistake that you don't say anything."

"It must be," she said and lifted her chin.

He knew she understood all too well. Even Rachel had said that her friend was a bit shy. Hell, if not for him, Hester and Charlie might never get around to talking to each other.

"You might want to be extra kind to him, Hester," Jackson told her as they came to a stop in front of a tiny, well kept cottage. "Take pity on the man."

She lifted her face to his, and Jackson noted a new shine in her eyes. A small smile curved her mouth as she told him, "I will, Jackson. And thank you for telling me."

"That's what friends are for, Hester."

Chapter ☆ Seven

Two days later, Rachel straightened a stack of fabric bolts until they looked as though they had been aligned with a ruler. Only when they were perfect did she move on to the counter, where a small mountain of stiff, new Levi's waited for her.

Outside the store, rain fell in torrents, smacking into the already waterlogged ground and creating a river of mud and water running the length of the street. No one was out. Everyone in town was, no doubt, huddled next to a stove or fireplace, waiting for a break in the weather to do any shopping.

Rain pelted onto the roof, slashed against the window panes, and seeped beneath the front door to puddle on the hardwood floor.

Keep busy, she told herself. Busy enough to avoid thoughts of Jackson and his humiliating intention to get her married.

Her hands smoothed and folded the jeans, then stacked them neatly on the shelf she'd prepared for them. As she went about the familiar task, her mind, unfortunately, was free to wander.

Naturally, it wandered straight to the man whose very presence was threatening to drive her around the bend.

Married. Couldn't he see how demeaning this all was? Didn't he understand that by his very presence, he was telling her that she was incapable of finding a man?

Blast it, why did it matter to anyone if she was married or not? As that thought careened through her mind, it was followed by another. He hadn't told her why she was supposed to be married. If her marrying was important enough that *someone* had sent a ghost to see that it happened, there had to be a compelling reason for it.

A ghost.

Great heavens, she had a ghost living with her.

And there was no getting rid of him.

Her lips twisted wryly. Lord knew, she'd tried. She had locked him out of the store the night he had made his grand announcement. Determined to keep him as well as his plans for her future at bay, she'd barred the door, hoping to let him know in no uncertain terms that he wasn't welcome.

When she'd come downstairs in the morning, he was inside. Drinking coffee he had made. Waiting for her.

Apparently, locked doors were no challenge for ghosts. He claimed to not be able to disappear, but obviously he had no trouble passing through solid wood.

The front door rattled, then swung open. Rachel glanced up to watch a woman step into the store, then struggle to close the door against a gust of wind-driven rain.

"Mavis!" Thank heavens, she thought. A visitor. Someone to take her mind off Jackson for a while. Rachel hurried around the end of the counter and crossed the room to her friend. Together, the two of them slammed the front door, then leaned against it, dripping wet and grinning at each other.

"What brings you out in this mess?" Rachel asked as she stepped away from the doorway.

Mavis pulled her dark green rain slicker off and watched the water sluice down the material to the floor. "I'm dripping all over everything," she said softly.

"Don't worry, it'll dry." Rachel took the slicker from her friend's cold, wet hands and hung it on a hook beside the entry. "Come on, you're freezing. I'll get you some coffee."

"That does sound good," the shorter, plump woman agreed.

At the stove, Rachel poured two cups of coffee, then added a generous helping of sugar into her friend's cup before handing it to her. Waving her into one of the chairs pulled close to the fire, Rachel sat in the other one and asked, "Why on earth did you come out in such a storm?"

Mavis plucked at the damp fabric stretched across her ample bosom and took a sip of coffee before answering. "In this weather, I don't have any customers, so I thought it would be a good time to recheck your measurements. You know, for the dress you wanted."

Rachel's coffee cup halted a few inches from her mouth. Looking at her friend, she asked, "Which dress is that?"

"The one you asked your cousin to order for you," Mavis said and sank gratefully onto a nearby stool. She plucked a soaking wet strand of wavy, dark brown hair off her face and pushed her rain spattered spectacles higher on her nose. "My," she said and leaned in close, "he *is* a handsome man, your cousin. And so charming."

Charming. That was certainly one word to describe her "cousin." Others were *liar* or *promise breaker. Ghost.* But she could hardly say so to Mavis. The woman would think her completely mad.

"What kind of dress did cousin Jackson order?"

"Oh." Mavis sighed into her cup, and steam from the coffee fogged her spectacles. "It's lovely, Rachel." She reached up and wiped the fog away with her index finger. "I'm sure it will be just the thing for the town social."

The social? Rachel stood up abruptly. She never attended the socials. Instead, she kept her Mercantile open longer hours to accommodate the extra customers who came in from outlying ranches for the day. The one useful thing she had learned from her foster father had been how to run a successful business.

And closing up the store—on a day when dozens more people than usual were in town—was not the way to do it.

"Rachel?" Mavis asked, clearly perplexed. "What is it? Is something wrong?"

Wrong? Everything was wrong. Jackson was insinuating himself with her friends. Sneaking around behind her back. And there didn't seem to be anything she could do about it.

"No," she lied, since she couldn't really talk about any of this, either. "Not a thing. It's just that . . ." She reached for something—anything to say. "I made a batch of your favorite cookies yesterday, Mavis," Rachel finally said. "I just thought I would run upstairs to the kitchen and get some to go with our coffee."

"Oh, that would be lovely." The plump woman leaned back in her chair and brushed at the water spots on her bodice.

"I'll be just a minute," Rachel told her and hurried to the staircase. She wanted—no *needed*—a moment or two alone to get control of her raging emotions. Jackson Tate had his nerve, she thought as she practically ran up the steps. Going behind her back and enlisting her friends into helping him with his plans.

Didn't her wishes matter to him at all? Couldn't he see that he was ruining her life with all of his meddling?

At the top of the stairs, she paused and leaned one hand on the newel post. She stared blankly at the wall opposite her and saw not the clean white paint of her sitting room, but Jackson's face. How could he be so different from the way she had remembered him? For more years than she liked to think about, she'd hugged his memory to her like a shield against loneliness. She'd remembered every little thing he'd said to her.

Could she have been so wrong about him? Had it been wishful thinking by a frightened child that had built him into such a stalwart hero?

She inhaled sharply and banished the mental image of Jackson. This train of thought served no purpose at all. What she had to concentrate on now was the man attempting to dismantle her life.

And how to get rid of him.

"You ought to think about settling down," Jackson said as he and Sam trudged through the muddy swamp that was Main Street.

"I don't see any brands on you," Sam countered with a laugh.

"Well, it's different with me."

"Yeah? How?"

Caught offguard for a moment, Jackson muttered, "It just is, that's all."

Sam laughed and the sound was swallowed up by the rain. We'll see who's laughing soon enough, Jackson thought with calm determination. He had it all figured out.

On a rainy day like this, the store would be empty but for Rachel. It was the perfect opportunity to use one of his coins to see her settled.

Sam seemed like a nice enough fella. He was a good carpenter and didn't drink much, which Jackson had a hard time understanding, but then, people are different, aren't they? All the man needed was a little help from him to see that Rachel would be the perfect wife.

He stuffed his right hand into his pants pocket and pulled out one of the golden coins. Closing it tightly in one fist, he told himself that this was for the best. Rachel would understand once she saw how much Sam loved her. She'd be happy. And he could leave.

His thumb smoothed across the star etching on the coin as he told himself again that this was his job. His mission.

It was none of his business *who* she married—his only concern was *getting* her married, and he'd do well to keep that in mind.

"You might as well forget it, Jackson," Sam said and gave him a friendly shove. "You're not gonna marry me off to that cousin of yours, so you can quit trying so damned hard."

Jackson's head snapped around, and he looked Sam dead in the eye. A lightning-like flash of anger shot through him. "You saying Rachel's not good enough for you?"

"No, 'course not." Sam sighed heavily. "I got no problem with Rachel, the problem's with me."

"How's that?"

He shrugged. "Guess I just like all women too much to fall in love with any *one* of them."

"Oh." That was different. Of course, if the idiot had tried to say that Rachel wasn't worthy somehow . . .

Jackson looked ahead at the store on their right. Inside, Rachel would be warm and dry and pretty. She'd be going about her business with no idea at all that her very life was about to change forever.

"Well," he said as they climbed the step to the boardwalk. "You know what they say. When it comes, love hits you like a rock between the eyes."

Sam ran the flat of his hand down his rain slicker, pushing most of the water off onto the walkway outside the Mercantile. He glanced up at Jackson with a grin on his face.

"I've always been able to dodge that particular rock."

Until now, Jackson thought. Concentrating, he squeezed the coin in his hand even tighter. This was for Rachel's own good, he told himself. Aloud, he said, "I'll be willing to bet that you're so ready for the love of a good woman, Sam, that you'll fall smack in love with the very next woman you see."

The other man laughed and turned the brass knob. Pushing the door wide, he looked at Jackson over his shoulder and said, "I'll take that bet!"

Then he stepped into the room and stopped dead.

Jackson watched the man stiffen, then gulp in a breath like a drowning man coming up for air. Shifting his gaze from the thunderstruck man, he looked down at the gold coin in his hand and watched its lustre slowly dim until, at last, the coin faded completely away.

It was done.

He smiled slightly. The coin had worked its magic, and Sam had fallen deeply in love with the woman waiting inside that store.

He'd actually done it, Jackson thought. He'd completed his assignment successfully. He knew Rachel. Though she claimed to not be interested in marriage, she wouldn't be able to say no to a man so desperately in love with her. In no time at all, Rachel and Sam would be marching down the aisle together. She would have Sam's babies. Live with him. Love with him. And in time, forget all about the ghost who had visited her one spring.

A small twinge of regret nipped at him. When he had died, there had been no one to mourn his passing. No one to remember him fondly. He should have been used to being a forgotten man. The regret bit deeper. Uncomfortable with the feeling, he shrugged it aside.

He'd done his job.

Everything was as it should be, he told himself.

Sam stepped out of the doorway and moved off to his left. His footsteps sounded out on the floorboards and when they stopped, Jackson followed him inside. Smiling, he turned to see for himself Rachel's reaction to Sam's sudden devotion.

A noise on the stairs caught his attention, though, and he shot a quick look in that direction. As Rachel marched down the flight of stairs glaring at him, a sinking sensation crawled through Jackson.

Slowly, he turned around and was in time to see Sam
Hale drop to one knee before a startled, yet clearly very
flattered, Mavis.

"Shit."

Rachel followed his gaze and almost fell down the stairs.
She grabbed hold of the bannister railing to steady herself.
As she watched, Sam yanked his hat off, took one of Ma-
vis's hands in his and clutched it to his chest.

Poor Mavis looked absolutely flummoxed. Hair still dripping wet and stringing about her face, her gown soaked and
dirty, the hem edged with mud, she looked at her sudden
suitor through wide, astonished eyes.

Sam's voice was pitched too low for Rachel to hear what
he was saying. But if the expression on Mavis's face was
anything to judge by, he must have been impressive.

When the man quickly rose to his feet and pulled Mavis
up beside him, Rachel finally found her tongue.

"Mavis?" she asked. "Are you all right?"

"Hmmm?" The woman didn't take her gaze off Sam's
face. "What's that?"

"I asked if you were feeling well."

"Oh. Oh, yes," she whispered. "I feel . . . wonderful."

Sam smiled down at her, draped one arm around her
shoulders, and led her to the front door.

Rachel flicked a quick, annoyed glance at Jackson, then
turned back to the couple preparing to leave. Sam lifted
Mavis's slicker down off the peg and gently helped her into
it before reaching for the doorknob.

"Mavis," Rachel called and hurried down the last few
steps to the floor. "Don't forget about our meeting tonight."

"Hmmm?" The woman had to drag her gaze away from
Sam's face. "Meeting?"

"The Spinster Society?" Rachel prodded.

"Oh, of course." Mavis looked from her friend to Sam
and back again. At last, she smiled weakly. "I'm afraid I

can't make it tonight, Rachel," she said. "Something's . . . come up."

Before Rachel could say another word, the blissful couple had strolled through the doorway and into the stormy afternoon.

The front door had barely closed behind them when she turned on the man across the room from her.

"You did this, didn't you?"

"Rachel . . ."

"You used one of those gold coins on him, didn't you?"

She stared at him, waiting for him to confirm what she already knew. Not long after she'd seen Sam Hale, confirmed bachelor, kneeling in front of Mavis, Rachel had guessed the truth.

"Yeah," he muttered, "for all the good it did me."

Clearly disgusted, he walked to the row of pegs alongside the front door. Stripping out of the rain slicker Rachel had given him, he muttered viciously under his breath as he hung up the dripping coat. Then he yanked his hat off and placed it on a peg next to it.

"How could you do something like that?"

He turned around and glared at her. "You didn't leave me much choice, Rachel."

"So, because I don't want to get married, you're going to marry off my friends, instead?"

He winced. "That wasn't supposed to happen."

Realization dawned on her all at once, and she cursed herself for being foolish enough not to have recognized it immediately. Of course, he had planned on Sam falling in love with *her*. It was purely an accident that it had been Mavis sitting in the store instead.

"You were going to trick me?"

"Not you, Sam."

"It's the same thing."

"No it's not." He stalked to the far side of the room. "It *should* have worked," he muttered thickly. "I had it all worked out. Rainy day. No customers. You alone in the store. Dammit." He threw her a furious look. "Why the hell weren't you where you were supposed to be?"

"You're saying this is *my* fault?" Astonishing, she thought. Simply astonishing.

"Well, if you *had* been here, everything would have been taken care of."

"Making Sam fall in love with me wouldn't have been enough to convince me to marry him." Didn't the man ever listen to her?

"You say that now," Jackson said. "But I knew if Sam fell in love with you, you wouldn't be able to resist him long."

"I've already told you a dozen times, I won't marry anyone unless *I'm* in love."

"You would have been," he retorted. "Eventually."

"Blast you, Jackson," she shouted. "You don't listen. To anyone."

"It's mighty damn hard not to listen when you're screeching, so."

"No," she countered thickly. "You *hear* me, but you don't *listen*. There's a difference."

"Fine," he snapped. "I'm listening."

"Don't you see?" She looked into his eyes briefly, then shifted her gaze away again. "I loved you for years. You didn't care. If it had been me in this store, the same thing would have happened to Sam. He would have loved someone who didn't love him back."

"You don't know that."

Her gaze lifted to his. "I *do* know it," she said quickly. "I wouldn't wish that pain on anyone."

To his credit, he looked uncomfortable.

"Rachel—"

"You have to promise me you won't use that coin on anyone else. Not the way you used it on Sam."

"I can't—"

"Yes, you can. I know I can't make you leave, but Jackson, I want your word on this."

He inhaled sharply, swiveled his head to glare at the darkness hovering just outside the rain spattered window and muttered something under his breath.

"Well?" she prodded.

Scowling, he tossed her a quick glance and nodded briefly.

"You promise, then?"

"Yeah, I promise," he grumbled. "But I'm not happy about it."

Rachel sighed her relief. At least now she wouldn't have to worry about being surprised by suddenly love struck men around every corner. "Thank you."

"You're welcome. But I still don't see why you're so upset," he said, annoyance coloring his voice. "The coin worked for Sam and Mavis."

"But it's not *real*," she said, and walked to his side. "None of it is real. Did you see Mavis's face when they left here?"

"Yeah," he shot back. "She looked happy."

Delirious actually, Rachel corrected mentally. Her rather plain friend had practically floated out of the store on the arm of the man who looked at her as if she were a fairy princess.

And that was precisely the point.

"Of course she's happy," she went on. "But for how long?"

"What?"

"I asked how long it would last." Rachel paced back and forth in front of him, her heels tapping out a harsh, staccato rhythm. "Don't you see? When that spell of yours wears off, Sam won't want her anymore, and that will crush Mavis."

"That's not going to happen, Rachel."

"You can't be sure of that."

A flicker of unease crossed his face.

"See?" she accused, pointing at him. "You're *not* sure at all."

"I'm as sure as I can be," he told her. "When I held that coin, I didn't say 'fall in love for a month.' I was thinking about you. I wanted him to fall in love with you and give you a lifetime of happiness." He shoved one hand through his damp hair. "Dammit, I wanted you to be safe. Loved."

"Married."

"What's wrong with that?" he bellowed.

She met his gaze squarely and ignored the tiny flutter of . . . something in the pit of her stomach. "Nothing, if *I want* to be married. But for you to go out and shanghai a husband for me?"

"All right, it was a stupid idea."

"Yes."

"But there's no harm done, is there? Sam loves Mavis. They'll be happy together."

"Maybe," she conceded, as her temper began to slowly fade. Perhaps it would work out all right. Her friend's sweet face rushed into her mind, and she realized that Mavis had looked happier than she'd ever seen her.

Foolish of Rachel, then, to feel so . . . betrayed. So . . . forgotten.

"What is it now?" he asked.

How could she confess to him what she was feeling? She could hardly admit it to herself. Briskly smoothing her hands up and down her forearms, she tried to rub away the cold beginning to crawl through her body. But it didn't help.

"Rachel?"

Concern tinged his voice and that was somehow harder to deal with than his anger.

She swallowed past the knot that had suddenly lodged in her throat. A sheen of water filled her eyes as she forced herself to look up at him. She would have been fine, if he hadn't started being nice. If he hadn't looked at her with, almost, understanding.

How could he understand what she was thinking, though? What she was feeling?

"Your friendship with her won't change," he said and took a step closer to her.

Her eyes widened. Could he read her mind, too? Good God, wasn't she allowed *any* secrets? It was terrible enough for *her* to have to know that she could begrudge her friend happiness because of her own fears. It was humiliating to have Jackson know it, too.

Is this what she'd come to? In her eagerness to bring her friends together to form the family she'd always wanted, had she overlooked the possibility that her friends might have other needs?

The natural desire for a husband and children?

Rachel covered her mouth with one hand and raced back through her memories. All the times she had convinced Mavis, Hester, and Sally not to attend dances and box suppers. Every time she had advised them to not follow their hearts. To snub whatever man had shown some interest in them.

She remembered clearly the night she had suggested founding the Stillwater Spinster Society. *She* had been the only one of the four to show any enthusiasm.

Lord, had she been so hurt by the fact that Jackson had never returned for her that she had turned her back on the idea of love—not only for herself, but for those she cared about? Had her foster father's heavy hand and lack of warmth so poisoned her that she was incapable of loving someone?

"Ah, Rachel . . ." Jackson stepped up in front of her and slowly drew her into the circle of his arms.

She went stiffly at first. Unwillingly. But as his warmth seeped into her bones, as his hands moved up and down her back in comfort, she leaned into his support, grateful for it. His soothing whisper brushed the air around her, but it was his words that finally made her feel better.

"You're being too hard on yourself, Rachel."

"No, I'm not."

She heard the rumble of his chuckle as it moved through his chest.

"Sure you are. Mavis and the others would be just as put out if you turned up with a beau all of a sudden."

No, they wouldn't, she told herself. They were much nicer than she was. Her friends would have been delighting in her happiness, not wallowing in self-pity.

"Just like when you were a kid," he said, and she drew her head back to look up at him. Smiling, he went on. "Always had to question everything. Never could take my word on something. Had to know how. Why. What."

A hesitant, answering smile touched her lips briefly. So he *did* remember those few days they'd spent together. She couldn't help wondering if he'd thought about them as often as she had over the years. Probably not, a voice inside her whispered. Why would he have? She'd been just a child. But even as a child, she had known that Jackson was the man she wanted to grow up and marry.

She'd felt it from the moment she'd first seen him. Her mother had always told her that there was someone for everyone in this world—and that all she had to do was find him.

When Jackson had suddenly appeared in answer to her prayers, Rachel had known that she had found the one man meant for her. In all the years since, she had never once met a man who had made her question that belief.

Which was why she had had no interest in marriage. When he hadn't returned for her, she'd made up her mind to remain a spinster. Better, she had told herself, to go through life unmarried than married to the wrong man.

If she hadn't been perfectly happy, she thought, at least she had been content.

Until lately.

Wrapping her arms around his waist, she laid her head on his chest and allowed herself to enjoy this one stolen moment. She felt his breath ruffle her hair, felt the strength in his hands, and the solid reassurance of his broad, muscular chest.

Rachel closed her eyes and held her breath, listening for the steady beat of his heart.

But there was nothing.

His heart didn't beat, despite the fact that he was alive and warm and holding her tightly.

He was here, with her.

Yet, this man she had loved so desperately wasn't real.

Chapter ☆ Eight

A familiar tightening in his body told him that he should back off.

Blast it, he couldn't seem to do a damned thing right. All he'd wanted to do was comfort her. Just hold her for a minute or two until she felt better. He hadn't planned on his body's reaction to her closeness.

As she snuggled in even closer, laying her head on his chest and pressing herself tightly to him, Jackson took a deep breath and tried to keep his mind off what his body was doing.

He sensed the change in her immediately. The sudden tension that gripped her, making her spine so rigid beneath his hands that he thought it might snap. He released her, and she took a step back from him.

"What's wrong?" he asked, hoping to hell she hadn't felt his arousal.

"You . . . ," she stared at him, eyes wide.

Blast it anyway. Why didn't his groin realize he was dead and just stay down? Now he'd gone and upset her all over again.

Lightning crashed outside, and thunder rolled through the room.

"Look Rachel," he started, then shifted his gaze from

hers and paused. What was he supposed to say to her? *Sure sorry about bruising your belly when you rubbed against me?* A silent groan echoed around inside him.

"You don't have a heart."

His head snapped around, and his gaze locked with hers. Now that's going pretty far, he thought. Granted he never had been a saint or anything. But dammit, he'd been as good a man as the next fella.

"There's no call to get nasty, Rachel," he told her. "I didn't make Sam fall in love with your friend just to hurt you."

She shook her head vehemently. "Your heart. It isn't beating."

"What?"

She waved one hand at his chest and drew in a gulp of air. "I couldn't hear your heartbeat. There's nothing there."

Startled, he slapped one hand against his chest and waited. Nothing. An eerie feeling crept through him like a thick, gray fog in winter. Coldness swirled around him. He swallowed heavily. It probably shouldn't bother him. It wasn't like he *needed* a heartbeat. After all, nobody knew better than he did that he was dead.

Still . . . he was breathing. Talking. Walking around. Hell, he even got an erection! He glanced down at his chest and scowled. Why the hell *wasn't* his heart beating?

Why hadn't he noticed before this?

But then, why would he have noticed? He would have been willing to bet that nobody ever checked to make sure their heart was thumping away. No need to. If you were up and moving, you could bet your heart was working fine.

Usually.

"Jesus," he muttered and let his hand fall to his side.

"You're actually dead," Rachel whispered.

"Isn't that what I've been telling you?" he snapped, then

cursed himself for barking at her. It wasn't *her* fault that he'd come to this.

"Yes, but you seem so . . ."

"Alive?"

"Well, yes."

Parts of him were apparently more alive than others, he admitted silently and shifted to accommodate the ache in his groin. He inhaled, just because he could, then blew it out in a rush. Pushing his own uneasiness aside, he said, "I guess this is just Lesley's way of reminding me that I'm not here for long."

"Lesley again."

Jackson shrugged.

She rubbed her hands up and down her forearms as if the cold eating away at him had reached out for her somehow.

"Who is this Lesley, anyway?"

"I'm not really sure," he said and walked aimlessly around the room. He looked back to Rachel. "I just know that he shows up every once in awhile to send me off on some errand or other."

"An errand," she repeated dully. "Like me?"

He could have bitten his tongue off, but it would have been too late anyway. Why was it he always seemed to say the wrong thing at the wrong time?

"You said he shows up. Shows up where?"

He looked into her eyes and saw that she was calmer now. And curious. Well, she had a right to be. He wasn't sure how much he was supposed to tell her, but at the moment, he didn't really care about what was forbidden for her to know or not.

"In Pine Ridge, at the saloon where I died."

She blinked, paled a bit, then steadied herself. "You died in a saloon?"

Somehow ashamed to admit it aloud, he ducked his head in a brief nod.

"In Pine Ridge?" she echoed, mostly to herself. "That's only a few days from here." After a long pause, she asked. "How did you die?"

Old resentment bubbled up inside him. His eyes narrowed as he stared into the past, remembering the last moments of his life. A life that had ended too soon. His voice scraped along his throat and came out raw with unresolved anger and pain. "Professional gambler shot me when I caught him cheating."

"Good heavens." One of her hands flew to her throat.

Her blue eyes softened in sorrow, and he cursed himself silently for telling her. He'd had countless years to regret the manner of his death. Frustrated fury at missed chances and a life unlived had simmered inside him for what seemed forever. But dammit, it was too much for him to have to face her sympathy.

Maybe he shouldn't have told her. She didn't need to know that he'd died a useless death. Then again, it was probably better she knew him for what he was. Maybe then she'd stop expecting too much of him.

Rachel took a long, staggering breath and slowly walked across the room to the counter. When she reached it, she leaned her forearms atop it, as if for support. "Why are you still there?" she said, and her voice was almost lost in the next rumble of thunder. "In that saloon? Why didn't you go to . . ." She let the sentence trail off, and Jackson was grateful.

He would rather not be reminded of Heaven or Hell just now. He had a feeling he'd never see one of those places and the other one was beginning to feel too close for comfort.

"I don't know," he said and walked to the far end of the counter. A hollow feeling had opened up inside him. Stepping through the gated portion of the counter, he squatted down and pulled a bottle of whiskey off the bottom shelf.

He glanced at her. She looked from him to the bottle and back again, but didn't say anything. He took her silence for permission. Lord knows, he needed a drink and would have taken one whether she approved or not.

Yanking the cork out of the neck, he lifted the bottle to his lips and took one long pull. The liquor poured down his throat in a stream of liquid fire and filled that hollow, however temporarily. Warmth surged into his veins and with it came the courage to face her.

"I'm just a damned ghost, Rachel. I don't know why I never went anywhere else." He laughed shortly, mockingly. "Hell, I can't even disappear proper." Another drink of whiskey and he wiped his mouth on the sleeve of his shirt. Staring down at the amber bottle in his hands, he went on, more to himself than her. "You lock me out of the store, but somehow I get inside. I look at people and can see what's in their minds. I don't even know how *that* stuff happens. And you want me to tell you why I didn't go to Heaven?"

His fingers tightened on the neck of the bottle. "My best guess is that I'm not good enough. Of course," he added in a disgusted mutter, "I wasn't much good for anything when I was alive, either."

"That's not true," she countered and looked at him until he felt forced to meet her afronted gaze. "You saved me. When I was little, I would have died if not for you."

He snorted and shook his head. "Doesn't count. I was already dead then. Besides, that was Lesley's doing. He sent me."

"But you did it."

"Yeah. A fine job I made of it, too." He took another drink. The whiskey was doing its work already. He felt the blessed numbness spreading through his limbs. Now all he had to do was drink enough to dull his brain and he would be a happy man.

"What do you mean?"

He snorted, shot her a quick look, then turned his gaze back to the depths of the amber bottle in his hands. "Just that I messed things up with you then, too."

"But you saved me."

She might as well know everything, he told himself. Before he lost his nerve, he blurted, "Yeah, but I was supposed to do something else before I left you here," he glanced around the dimly lit building, "with the Heinzes."

"What?"

"You weren't supposed to remember me, Rachel." His eyes lifted to hers, and he watched pain flash across her face with the speed of the lightning still crashing outside. "I was supposed to wipe your memory of me."

"I wasn't supposed to remember you?"

"Nope."

"At all?"

He nodded and took another drink. The whiskey's warmth was fading too quickly. "See? I made a mess back then that you're still payin' for."

"Jackson . . ."

"If you hadn't remembered me, you'd probably be married with a couple of kids already."

She flinched as if he'd struck her.

By thunder, he told himself, he was having a helluva good night.

"I'm glad you made that mistake," she said.

"How can you be glad?" He stood up and faced her. "You don't know what your life might have been like without the memory of me."

"I know what it was *with* your memory."

He shook his head and set the bottle on the counter. Twirling it between his long fingers, he muttered, "You are the hardest headed female I ever met."

"Thank you."

He flicked her a quick look and couldn't help smiling. Figured that she'd take what he said as a compliment.

"You're not how I remembered you," she said.

"You've changed some, yourself," he said and let his gaze slip over her figure. Strange how her too thin, too flat form was beginning to affect him. But then, that was just one of the reasons why he needed that whiskey so badly.

"No, I mean—" Her fingers folded together on the countertop, and she looked at her joined hands as if they held a secret she needed desperately. "I don't remember you drinking."

"Didn't have any whiskey, then."

"Or swearing."

"Didn't say much of anything as I recall."

She acted as though she hadn't heard him. "Why do you seem so different?"

Jackson snatched up the bottle, took a long drink, then slammed it back down onto the counter. He winced when she jumped, startled. "I'm no different than I always was, Rachel. You're just older now. You see things different."

"No . . ."

"I'm not a damned angel," he yelled. "Never was, never will be. I'm just a man—" his voice softened as he finished, "—*ghost* of a man."

"Why are you shouting at me?" she demanded. "I didn't *ask* you to come here. I didn't ask for you to disrupt my life and interfere with everything I know."

He closed his eyes briefly, then opened them again to look at her. There was a soft, fine flush to her cheeks. Her blue eyes glinted with high emotion. Her bosom rose and fell with her rapid breathing, and the knuckles of her clasped hands were white from the squeezing grip she held.

No, she hadn't asked for him to come. He *didn't* have the right to be yelling at her. Christ, none of this was *her* fault. But dammit, how could he explain that it was easier to shout at her than to rail against an anonymous Fate that hadn't listened to him in more than fifteen years?

How could he tell her how tired he was of being neither

dead nor alive? How could he tell her what it was like—existing in some half world where no one heard you, no one cared, and silences stretched on for eternities?

He couldn't, so he took another drink, hoping for peace. He didn't get it.

As if that one, fleeting moment of closeness between them had never happened, she glared at him and said, "I want you to go. To leave me alone. Go back to your saloon."

He gave her a sad smile. She still had to learn that when it came to "wants," the only ones that mattered were Lesley's . . . and his boss's . . . whoever that was.

Rachel must have read the answer in his eyes. She bit down hard on her bottom lip, slapped her palms against the counter in frustration, then turned for the stairs. Hiking her hem up to her shins, she ran up the steps to the second floor. He listened to her as she raced down the hall and into her bedroom. Then the door slammed shut behind her.

A flash of lightning pierced the room, followed by a crash of thunder. The wind howled and moaned like a lost soul. Jackson shuddered and took another long drink.

He was alone.

Again.

Rachel picked up the broom and stepped outside. Squinting into the bright sunlight streaming down onto the soggy mess that was Stillwater, she felt the promise of a hot day in the morning sun. She inhaled the fresh, clean scent of rain-washed air and set the business end of the broom against the plank walkway. Pausing for a moment, she let her gaze stray over the crowded main street.

Her friends and neighbors ignored the mud and slogged on about their business. Here and there, along the boardwalks lining either side of the road, her fellow merchants were busily sweeping away the remnants of the storm and greeting customers.

Her gaze shifted, moving from face to face, looking for Jackson. He'd been gone when she came downstairs that morning. But she knew he hadn't disappeared for good. He was there, somewhere in that crowd.

He was close by. Just as, apparently, he had been for the past fifteen years. He had said that he died in Pine Ridge. A little town only a few days south of Stillwater. Knowing that he had been so close and yet so out of reach was painful and frustrating.

All night long, Rachel had lain awake, thinking of the "mistake" he had made so long ago. What would it have been like without the memories of Jackson to comfort her? Growing up in the house of Albert Heinz, she had *needed* those memories. She'd clung to them like a piece of driftwood, loose in a raging river.

She shuddered to think of the loneliness she would have experienced without them. At least, those memories had given her something to dream on. Without them . . .

Her fingers tightened on the broom handle. What was happening to her? Only a week ago, she'd been happy. Content with her life. Her friends. Resigned to the fact that she would never feel that sense of belonging with one special man.

Now, her life was unraveling.

And she knew exactly what it felt like to be held in the arms of the man she had dreamed of for years.

"Morning, Rachel."

Startled, she jumped and spun around.

Tessa Horn sailed up to her like a brigantine flying a pirate's flag. The woman's bulk was encased in a too tight black dress, and she held a slightly bent parasol out in front of her like a lance. She only carried it on particularly busy days in town and used it deftly to part the people cluttering up the boardwalk.

"Hello, Tessa."

"Where's that handsome cousin of yours?" she asked and shot a quick look into the Mercantile.

"I was just wondering the very same thing," Rachel said.

"This is a fine how do you do," the older woman snapped. "I'm a busy woman, you know."

Rachel smiled, but felt it fade away as Tessa went on.

"The Ladies Guild has decided to ask him to build us a nice dance floor for the social, and I need to speak to him about the details."

"Why Jackson?" she asked. He was beginning to encroach on every aspect of her life now. Even the town ladies were turning to him.

"Well, he is your cousin and he did say he was a good carpenter, didn't he?" A lumberman passed them on the walk and came a bit too close to Tessa. She smacked him with her parasol, glowered at him when he had the nerve to look insulted, then turned back to Rachel. "Now, he'll only have a week or so to get everything ready, so I must speak to him immediately."

"I don't know where he is."

"Hmmph!" She flipped a long, gray sausage curl of hair back over her shoulder. Lifting her brooch watch from where it lay atop one pendulous breast, she frowned at the time. "I can't stand about all day waiting for him. Typical man. Never around when you need him. You send him to me as soon as you see him, will you Rachel?"

Without waiting for a reply, she marched off down the boardwalk, sending grown men jumping out of her way as she passed. Her skills with that parasol were widely known.

"Jackson and the Ladies Guild. Jackson and my house. Jackson and Mavis," Rachel grumbled under her breath as she started sweeping. It appeared that the memory of him was easier to live with than the reality. Long violent strokes of the broom sent debris flying into the street, but didn't seem to make her feel the least bit better.

* * *

Jackson leaned back in the barber's chair and settled in as the man snapped a clean white sheet over his chest and let it float gently into place.

Despite his hangover, Jackson had vowed to begin again with Rachel. Sometime during the long, sleepless night, he had decided that the only way to make things easier for her was to throw himself into his mission, accomplish it, and get out as quickly as possible.

The best way to do all that was to find out all he could about Rachel Morgan and the kind of woman she had become. Especially since he'd promised not to use one of his coins to accomplish the task of getting her married.

"Rachel's a fine girl," the barber said now as he started snipping at Jackson's hair with a pair of lightning quick scissors. "Even when she was a little thing, she was always helpin' folks . . ."

A man waiting his turn for a haircut shook the newspapers he was reading and muttered, "Even to them who didn't deserve it."

Jackson frowned into the mirror. "What do you mean?"

"Now Henry," the barber said. "No need to dig up old dirt."

"No diggin' needed," Henry countered. "Everybody around here remembers that old bastard."

"Who?"

The barber frowned, clipped another section of hair, and muttered, "Albert Heinz."

Oh. Sure. Rachel's foster father. The man Jackson had left her with fifteen years before.

"Meanest son of a bitch ever walked the earth," Henry muttered.

"Mean?" Jackson stared into the glass, willing the other man to put his paper down and get on with it.

"Now Henry," the barber whined. "Albert had his good points."

"Yeah. He didn't talk much and he died early."

Jackson didn't like the sound of *this*. Guilt had him shifting uncomfortably in his seat until the barber grumbled, "Sit still."

"You sayin' he was mean to Rachel?" Jackson prodded, despite the feeling that he really didn't want the answer to his question.

Henry snorted, lowered his paper, and looked like he wanted to spit. But there was no spittoon handy, so he didn't. "I don't know if he ever hit her or anything," he said. "But mind, there's other ways of treatin' a child harsh."

No one knew that better than he did. He'd practically raised himself as a boy. His mother had died when he was young, and his father couldn't be bothered with a "pesty child."

Something cold crawled up his spine. Had Rachel experienced anything like that?

"She never said," Jackson whispered. "I didn't know."

" 'Course not," the barber consoled him. "How could ya? You wasn't here, and Rachel ain't the kind to complain about somethin' that's long since past and best forgotten." He shot Henry a meaningful look.

"Fine, I won't say another word." The barber relaxed until Henry added, "Except this. Albert Heinz worked that girl like a chinaman and never gave her a thing for it. Not so much as a kind word."

Jackson swallowed past the knot of guilt in his throat. Memories of the young Rachel flitted through his mind and disappeared again. Why hadn't he bothered to make sure the girl would be safe before he left her in the care of Heinz and his wife? Why hadn't he taken enough time to find the little girl *good* parents?

He groaned silently and squeezed his eyes shut. Apparently, forgetting to wipe Rachel's memory of him wasn't the only crime he had committed fifteen years ago.

"What about Missus Heinz?" Jackson asked, quietly hoping that Rachel had had *some* kindness.

"Ah well," Henry eased back in his seat and lifted his newspapers again. An easy smile creased his leathery features. "Martha was a saint, pure and simple. Put up with Albert—why I don't know, and fairly doted on that girl."

Jackson released a breath he hadn't known he'd been holding.

"But she died only a year or two after Rachel came to them." Henry's smile shifted into a sneer. "Only mean thing Martha ever did in her life was to die and leave that child alone with the likes of Albert."

"Don't you have somewhere else you could wait?" the barber demanded.

Henry snorted at him, hid behind his newspapers, and slid into silence again.

The barber went about his business, leaving Jackson to his own miserable thoughts. A voice in the back of his mind tried to rationalize his actions. After all, it reminded him, his mission had been to find folks to take care of her. He had. Was it his fault that one of them had turned out to be a bastard? How was he supposed to have known that?

He could have checked, he thought, dismissing the placating voice as a mercy he didn't deserve. Beneath the sheet that covered him, Jackson's hands curled into fists of helpless rage. Who he was more angry at—the late Albert Heinz, or himself—he wasn't sure.

When he left the barbershop, Jackson wandered down Main Street, stopping every few feet to gather more information about Rachel from her friends. At the hotel, he was told what a good neighbor Rachel was. In time of sickness or trouble, she was always close at hand.

The mayor of Stillwater, a short squat man with a nose that looked to have been broken a few times in his younger days, bragged about how Rachel had raised most of the funds to build the town's schoolhouse and hire a fulltime teacher.

A couple of older ladies stopped him to tell him what a fine wife she would make for somebody if Jackson could only talk her out of this Spinster Society nonsense. And the man at the livery stable confided that several of the men in town had tried to court Rachel at one time or another. But she'd turned them all down flat. The other men, he admitted, were probably a little intimidated by such a strong-willed female.

Jackson finally turned toward the store around noon, his head spinning with more information than he knew what to do with. Rachel was certainly admired by the folks in town. But the ladies were mad about the Spinster Society, and most of the men were just plain scared of her.

This job looked to be getting harder and harder every minute.

He shoved his hands into his pockets and his fingertips brushed across his three remaining coins. Tossing a glance skyward, he muttered, "A little help now and again wouldn't be out of line, you know."

He waited hopefully for some sort of answer, but wasn't surprised when none came. In fact, he thought, he wouldn't be surprised to find that Lesley was stretched out somewhere, watching him and laughing his wig off.

As he neared the Mercantile, he spotted Rachel, out front washing down the rain-spattered windows. A moment later, a middle-aged man wearing a well tailored suit over a comfortable belly stopped beside her.

Hmmm. Older, he thought. Settled looking. By the cut of his clothes, he had plenty of money—he could afford a wife. And best of all, Rachel was smiling at the man. Hope blossoming in his chest, Jackson jumped off the boardwalk and hurried toward them.

Chapter ☆ Nine

"Actually, Mr. Sprague," Rachel said, "I'd like to talk about increasing my loan."

The nearly bald man tugged at the vest that strained to contain his formidable stomach, then lifted one hand to smooth the wispy strands of gray hair stretched across his scalp. He seemed to mentally measure each word before speaking. "A loan is not something to be undertaken lightly, Rachel," he pointed out.

Irritation flared up briefly in her chest. Since taking over the Mercantile after her foster father's death, she'd more than doubled the business. She carried more stock, priced her merchandise more reasonably, and kept longer hours. Howard Sprague, though, looked on her success as a stroke of good fortune that could peter out at any moment.

She swallowed her impatience and forced a smile. After all, it wouldn't do to make the one banker in town angry. "I realize that, Mr. Sprague," she said. "But on the other hand, you must admit that I've been a good risk so far. There are several ways I'd like to expand the Mercantile, and there is the new house I'm building."

"Yes." He frowned slightly. "I heard about your . . . Society." His upper lip twitched nervously. "Quite frankly, the ladies in town are most distressed with you and your friends flaunting your unfortunate state of life.''

He made them all sound like lepers. Smile Rachel, smile, her mind coaxed. ''Why Mr. Sprague, I wouldn't think you would be a man to listen to idle gossip.''

'' 'Course not m'dear.'' He cleared his throat, rocked on his heels, and nodded. ''But you must see that I have to be careful. Don't want to offend the citizenry. Seattle's not so far away that some wouldn't be tempted to travel a bit of a distance if they felt put out with my banking establishment.''

''I understand,'' Rachel countered quickly. Far better than he thought, probably. As a matter of fact, she had considered going into the city to deal with a larger bank. But she'd finally decided that she would have a better chance with a bank that already knew her and her business. Although it was difficult at times, dealing with a man who cared more for what his customers thought of him than for making a good business deal.

She was willing to wager none of the business*men* in town had to explain the way they lived their lives in order to secure a loan.

Out of the corner of her eye, she caught sight of a man leaping off the boardwalk on the opposite side of the street.

Jackson.

Instinctively, her heartbeat quickened.

As Mr. Sprague droned on about the seemliness of spinsters setting up house together, Rachel turned her head slightly to watch as Jackson landed directly in the path of an oncoming freight wagon. She gasped as he missed being run down by a hair's breadth, then he moved nimbly out of the way only to step in front of a horse and rider. He jumped backward and bumped into a woman carrying a basket full of vegetables from the Farmers' Vegetable Stand.

One corner of her brain noted that Howard Sprague was still talking, but she wasn't listening. Instead, she watched

Jackson and struggled to keep from laughing.

He picked up the woman's spilled cabbages, brushed off the spattered mud, and replaced them in her basket. The woman shouted something, and he ducked when she swung her knitted purse at his head. Backing carefully away from her, he tripped over a dog and staggered to catch his balance. Finally, muttering under his breath, he loped across the clearing toward her.

"So," Mr. Sprague was saying, "if you'll come by the bank this afternoon, we'll discuss your plans in full."

"Hmmm?" She snapped her head around and smiled at the man. "Oh, thank you. I'll be there. Shall we say two o'clock?"

Jackson leaped up onto the boardwalk. "Morning, Cousin."

She nodded at him briefly, then turned to the banker. "Thanks again, Mister Sprague. I'll see you this afternoon."

"This afternoon?" Jackson echoed and looked from Rachel to the banker. Giving the man a knowing grin and a quick wink, he said, "Sprague, is it? You're a friend of Rachel's?"

The portly man drew himself up to his less than imposing full height and peered along a narrow nose at Jackson.

"I, sir, own the bank."

"Ahh . . ." Jackson nodded. "A well set-up man then. Are you married?"

"Jackson!" Rachel's voice was strangled, horrified.

Mr. Sprague glared at him and huffed like a man running uphill. "Not that it's any of your concern, Mister . . . ?"

"Call me Jackson. I'm Rachel's cousin."

Rachel felt the banker's disgruntlement and shared it. How could Jackson do something so stupid? She grabbed his forearm with one hand and squeezed, hoping to shut him up before it was too late.

"Now," her "cousin" went on, "as to being my business or not, guess it wouldn't be, ordinarily. But I couldn't help noticing how you had your eye on Rachel, here.''

''I *beg* your pardon?''

''No need.'' He paused to look down at her fingers, digging ever deeper into his arm. He shook his head slightly, patted her hand, and turned back to the banker. ''Just between us men, I wanted to let you know that you have my permission to court her.''

''Of all the . . .'' Mr. Sprague shook all over and his shiny pate turned a deep, violent scarlet.

''Good God,'' she muttered and tried to put herself in between the banker and the ghost.

''Why wait 'till this afternoon to get together and . . . *talk*. Why don't the two of you sneak off somewhere quiet and get to know one another?''

''Oh, for heaven's sake,'' Rachel groaned, unable to keep it in.

''Sir,'' the banker countered in a high, shaky voice, ''you insult me!''

Clearly surprised, Jackson's eyes widened as he looked at the other man. ''No such thing,'' he said. ''I only wanted to help you two—''

''And *you!*'' Mister Sprague turned offended hazel eyes on Rachel, who wanted the boardwalk to open up and swallow her whole. ''I'd thought better of you, Miss Morgan!''

''Mister Sprague,'' she started, ''I can assure you—''

''Frankly,'' the banker cut her off rudely, ''I'd imagined it far beneath you—using feminine wiles to sway my business decisions.''

''*Wiles?*'' Rachel snapped a quick glare at Jackson, but he didn't notice. He was already moving up to the banker.

''Hold on a second, mister,'' he said and stopped close enough that the other man took one nervous step backward.

Mr. Sprague's gaze raked him up and down. ''I am appalled. A member of her own *family* conspiring to assist her in her nefarious schemes?'' He pulled a snowy white handkerchief from his coat pocket and blotted the beads of sweat forming on his pate and upper lip. "For shame, my good man! For shame."

"Nefarious?" Jackson asked, obviously puzzled.

"Oh, good heavens!" Rachel muttered.

With one last look at the two of them, Howard Sprague turned on his well polished heel and scuttled off down the boardwalk toward his bank.

"Well?" Rachel demanded a moment later.

Jackson stared off after the man and asked, "What's *nefarious?*"

"That's all you have to say?"

He pulled his gaze away from the retreating banker and shrugged. "I figure I got a right to know if I've been insulted."

She shook her head, then tossed the broom down in disgust. Planting both fists on her hips, she said, "*Nefarious. Corrupt. Criminal. Disgraceful.*"

Jackson frowned thoughtfully. "Just as I thought. I'll just go see that fella and have a little talk with him. Set him straight on a few things."

He took a step, but she grabbed his arm and stopped him in his tracks.

"I think you've talked to him quite enough for one day," she countered. "Just what was that all about?"

"You know darn well what it was about."

"A husband again."

"I told you, I'm here to see you married."

"To Howard Sprague?"

He looked into those wide, amazed blue eyes and conceded, "I admit, he's not much to look at. But he's a banker. Must have plenty of money. Certainly looks like he eats well."

"His *wife* is a very good cook."

"Wife?"

"Yes, wife."

"Oh." Jackson swiveled his head to look for the still retreating figure of the banker. Why, he wondered, hadn't he picked up that piece of information about the man? But he knew why. He hadn't waited for the information to come to him. Instead, he had leapt right into the middle of things.

"Well, how was I supposed to know he was married?"

"Not only is he married," Rachel told him, folding her arms across his chest. "Howard Sprague is the worst prig I've ever met."

"Huh?" He turned back to look at her. The fire in her eyes nearly burned him.

"A prig. He is as straitlaced and prudish as ... as ... I can't even *think* of someone as rigid as Howard Sprague." Her toe started tapping a furious rhythm on the boardwalk. "He'll never give me the loan I wanted now."

"Why wouldn't he?" No one was stupid enough to pass up a good business deal because he, Jackson, had said the wrong thing.

"Because, thanks to you, Howard believes I was trying to seduce him into a loan!" An unbelieving chuckle shot from her throat. "Seduce. Howard." She shook her head slowly. "Now I'll have to go into Seattle and find a banker there."

Jackson rubbed the back of his neck. He'd done it again. Blast it, he seemed to have a real talent for throwing rocks into the lake just before the fish were about to bite.

"I'll go with you," he said.

"No, thank you. I'll do it myself. Some other time."

Jackson scowled thoughtfully. She didn't want his help, and he could hardly blame her.

"What made you do something like this?" she asked.

He inhaled deeply. "Sprague looked like the kind of man who could take good care of you. Give you a good life."

"I can take care of myself."

He shook his head at her. "It's not the same thing."

"Jackson, you can't just storm up to a complete stranger and try to talk him into marrying me."

Fine, he thought. Maybe he hadn't handled that situation as well as he might have. But she wasn't being much help. Fighting him all the time, arguing.

A lumberman passed them on the boardwalk, and Jackson stepped closer to her to let the man by. "Look, Rachel," he said under his breath. "I can't stay here forever, you know. I've got to find you a husband. And I have to do it soon."

"Why?"

"Why what?"

"Why is it so bloody important that I be married?"

He inhaled sharply, drawing her soft, faintly floral scent deep within him. Even as he enjoyed the sensation, he knew it was a mistake. Because noticing one of Rachel's charms only opened the door to becoming aware of the rest. However, then he met her eyes, and the look that met his told him that the sweetness of her scent belied her rising temper.

Rachel glanced around her quickly, making sure they couldn't be overheard before saying in a rush, "You keep insisting I marry—but you don't say why. Why would someone send a ghost to see that an on-the-shelf spinster finds a husband?"

He frowned and scratched his jaw. He'd already told her more than she probably should know. It would only make things worse if he was to start telling her about the children she was supposed to have. Besides, she probably wouldn't even believe him if he told her about one of her daughters being a lady doctor.

Who would?

"It's just important. That's all."

She crossed her arms over her chest and tilted her head back to look up at him. He had to force himself to meet her eyes. "There's something you're not telling me, isn't there?"

"Rachel . . ."

"No." She shook her head, then bent down to pick up the broom. "Never mind. I don't want to know."

Relief swamped him.

"It doesn't matter anyway," she continued, ruining his brief sense of peace. "Because no matter what else you're not telling me, it won't change a thing. I won't marry except for love."

Love. He was getting almighty tired of that word.

His gaze swept over her and not for the first time, he silently admitted what a handsome woman she was. As he looked at her honey-colored hair, Jackson couldn't help wondering just how it would feel in his hands when released from that bun she insisted on wearing. His fingers itched to pull her hairpins free. He wanted to see her hair spilling wild and free around her shoulders. He wanted to thread his fingers through its length.

Caught by surprise at his own imaginings, he blinked away the thoughts and forced himself back to the matter at hand. Now was not the time to let his idle brain stroll down a path that stopped at a dead end.

Love, he reminded himself. That's what this was all about. What did he know about love for God's sake? Rachel wants love, and his mind was busy with lust.

Oh, they made a fine pair.

Still, if she were serious about wanting to find love, it wouldn't hurt her any to cooperate a little. Before he could tell her so, though, he saw her gaze slide past him to stare at something or someone behind him. When her features tightened, something inside him shifted. Was she afraid?

"Come on," she said. "Let's go inside."

"Why?" He turned around and looked down the boardwalk at the milling people. What had she seen? Or rather, who?

"Someone's coming, and I'd rather not have to talk to him if I don't have to."

She didn't sound scared. More like anxious. His eyebrows lifted, and he examined the crowd more thoroughly, determined now to find the source of Rachel's discomfort. If there was a man in this town who could make *her* nervous, Jackson wanted to meet him.

Unfortunately, he didn't have the slightest notion of who he was looking for. His gaze moved over the constantly shifting crowd. Lumbermen, miners, a couple of fancy women from the saloon, and one or two wives with baskets on their arms passed in and out of his line of sight. Old men gathered in little groups and exchanged lies. Wagons and horses pushed through the muddy street.

Then a familiar face flashed briefly through a parting in the mob. Jackson frowned, drew his head to one side, and looked for that face again, sure he was mistaken.

Rachel pulled at his arm, but he didn't move.

He couldn't.

His feet felt as though his boots had been nailed to the planks beneath him. If his heart had been beating, it would have stopped. Seconds crawled by. The sounds from the street disappeared. He held his breath and waited. In moments, his patience was rewarded with another glimpse of the face he was watching for.

There was no mistake.

It was him.

Horo.

Headed right toward Jackson.

"Blast it," Rachel muttered, just before plastering a smile on her face. "Good morning, Mister Lynch."

Jackson shot her a quick, disbelieving look, then snapped his head back to face his past.

The gambler stepped up to them and stopped just a foot or two away. He glanced briefly at Jackson, then dismissed him and concentrated on Rachel. Pulling his hat from his head, he gave her a half bow. "Miss Rachel. Lovely to see you."

Just hearing her name fall from those lips sent chills sweeping over him.

"What do you want?" Jackson grumbled, his eyes narrowed into slits.

Lynch lifted his eyebrows and he slanted Jackson a thoughtful look. Clearly amused, he answered, "Why nothing at all, Mister . . . ?"

"Tate," his voice was tight. "Jackson Tate."

"Of course." Again, that dismissive nod, then he turned a slow smile on Rachel. "May I invite you to share a cup of tea with me?"

Tea?

With *him?*

Jackson surged forward, his fists hard and ready. He was checked by her hand on his arm.

Rachel felt the tension in his muscles. Shimmering waves of tightly leashed anger seemed to hover around him. Fear and worry spiraled together in the pit of her stomach. It was all she could do to keep her voice even, polite.

"Thank you, Mister Lynch, but no. I'm afraid my cousin and I are quite busy at the moment."

Noble Lynch spared Jackson another brief look, but whatever he was thinking didn't register on his features.

"You stay the hell away from her," Jackson said then, and the gambler's sharp gaze narrowed.

She swallowed heavily and forced herself to breathe. Something was terribly wrong.

"Whatever passes between Miss Rachel and myself is hardly your concern."

Rachel shivered. The gambler's voice was light, but she sensed icy fury beneath the words.

"Everything about Rachel is my concern, Lynch."

Stunned by the rage glittering in Jackson's green eyes, she tugged at his forearm, drawing him closer to her. In the few days she and Jackson had been together, she hadn't seen this side of him. His usual affable good humor had disappeared as if it had never been. The sharp planes of his face looked to be carved from solid marble.

Something flip-flopped inside her, and she didn't even question the instinct to protect Jackson. To help him through whatever was tearing him apart. Tugging on his rock hard arm again, she said, "If you'll excuse us . . ."

Her ghost didn't budge. His gaze remained locked on the man opposite him. She wasn't even sure he knew she was there beside him.

"Do I know you?" the gambler asked, taking a slow side step closer to Rachel.

Jackson moved so quickly, she didn't have time to react as he pushed her safely behind him and answered quietly. "We met a long time ago."

A strained, taut silence stretched out for what seemed like forever. Then, from behind Jackson's broad back, she heard the gambler say, "I'm afraid I don't recall."

Rachel took a half step to the side and glanced up into Jackson's features. He looked like he wanted to leap at the other man's throat. Instead, he only said, "I recall enough for both of us."

Lynch's fingers tightened on his hat brim.

Out in the street, a dog barked, someone shouted, and another wagon rolled through the mud. Rachel tugged on Jackson's arm again. A sense of urgency rose up inside her. She wasn't sure why, but she knew that she *had* to separate the two men quickly.

"I'm sorry, Mister Lynch," she said abruptly. "You'll have to excuse us."

"Naturally," he replied, his gaze never leaving Jackson's.

Rachel reached behind her, turned the knob, and shoved the door open. Planting her feet, she pulled at Jackson's arm until he had no choice but to follow her. She didn't relax until the door was closed behind them, shutting out Noble Lynch and everyone else in town.

She leaned back against the door and willed her heart to stop racing. What had just happened? What was there between the two men? And if it were important enough to cause such a reaction in Jackson, how could Lynch not even remember it?

Or was the man lying?

Rachel drew a long, shaky breath and turned her head to look at the man whose memory had been a driving force in her life.

Jackson crossed to the nearest window and stared out into the street. "What's going on between you two?" he said and his voice rasped into the sudden stillness.

"What do you mean?"

Green eyes blazing, he wasn't looking at her, but rather he was following Lynch's progress as the gambler strolled down the boardwalk in the direction of the saloon. "I mean, him. Lynch." He spat the name out like it was a mouthful of mud. "Why is he sniffing around, trying to get you to step out with him?"

"I don't know why," she said without adding that she had asked herself the same question many times. She wouldn't have thought that she was the kind of woman a professional gambler would be interested in. But Noble Lynch certainly was. "He started coming here more often several months ago. He invites me out, and I don't go."

"Good." The word sounded as though it had been squeezed past his throat.

"What's going on, Jackson?" she asked and waited for him to look at her. When he did, she said softly, "You're the one who *wanted* me to spend time with a man."

His eyes narrowed even farther. "Not him."

Tendrils of worry snaked through her stomach, and Rachel laid the flat of her palm against her midsection in a vain effort to calm herself. But how could she be calm when he was in such a state?

"Jackson—"

"I mean it, Rachel." His gaze flicked back to the window then returned to hers. "I don't want you talking to him. I don't even want you in the same town he is in."

A choked, humorless laugh shot from her throat. Uneasiness crawled up and down her spine. Though she'd never really cared for the gambler, Jackson's violent reaction to the man made her own discomfort seem like nothing in comparison. But as much as she hated to admit it, Lynch had as much right to live in Stillwater as anyone else did.

"There's nothing either of us can do about that," she said. "I'm certainly not going to move and I don't believe Mister Lynch has any notions about leaving, either."

"We'll see about that," Jackson muttered darkly and crossed the room to the front door. Throwing it open, he glanced at her over his shoulder. "I'll be back later. Close the store and keep the door locked."

Before she could argue, he stomped off toward the edge of town, his boot heels thundering like drumbeats against the weathered wood.

"Lesley!" Jackson shouted the name and turned in a tight circle, letting his gaze sweep across the sky dotted with clouds. "Lesley, you sonofabitch! Show yourself!"

The air crackled, thickened, and in an instant, Jackson was no longer alone in the meadow.

"May I ask why you are bellowing my name?"

"You bastard." Jackson started for him, and Lesley did a quick skip to one side. "Why didn't you tell me Noble Lynch was going to be *here*. In Stillwater?"

"Your business isn't with Mister Lynch, Jackson. Concern yourself solely with Rachel Morgan."

"Easy enough for you to say," he snapped and angrily stalked off a few feet before whirling around to face his tormentor again. "I'm supposed to just ignore the miserable bastard?"

"Correct."

"Dammit, Lesley!" Jackson marched back to the spot where he'd started. Looming over the smaller man, he forced his guide to tilt his head far back on his neck to meet his gaze. "How am I supposed to do that? Lynch is the one who killed me!"

"I know."

"In a crooked card game in that damned saloon that I've been trapped in for fifteen lousy years," Jackson went on then suddenly stopped. "What do you mean, you know?"

"I *mean* I know who Noble Lynch is." Lesley tugged at the lacy froth spilling from his coat sleeves, then calmly looked up into Jackson's angry stare. "When you accused Mister Lynch of cheating, he drew his weapon and fired. He shot you dead."

Jackson rubbed his jaw with one shaking hand. He winced at the memory of hot lead puncturing his chest. In memory, he felt his chair topple backward, spilling him onto the dirty, sawdust-covered floor. He stared up at the shocked faces of men he'd known for years. He heard the scrape of chair legs, the angry mutters of the men in the room, and the shocked gasp of his best friend. Once again, Jackson lifted his head enough to see the flow of blood trickling from his chest as he lay prone on the floorboards. In memory, he looked up into the cold, dark eyes of the man who had killed him.

In his mind's eye, he watched Noble Lynch tuck his derringer away, then sweep the money off the table and into the crown of his hat. He saw the gambler stop alongside him, look down and smile. He heard the man say, "Thanks for the game," just before he walked out as calm as you please.

Jackson shuddered and looked at the little man opposite him. "If you know all of that, how can you ask me to ignore him?"

"The past is done, Jackson." Lesley steepled his fingers. "What was done to you cannot be undone. Taking vengeance on Noble Lynch will not bring your life back.'' He paused, then added, ''You must trust that all things are addressed, eventually. Mister Lynch will, one day, answer for his crimes.''

Small consolation for a life cut short.

For the fifteen years spent in virtual isolation—not dead, not alive.

''I can't do this job,'' Jackson said suddenly and had the satisfaction of seeing Lesley's features tighten.

''Precisely my opinion.''

''Good. Then get me the hell out of here. Let someone else deal with Rachel.''

''I'm afraid not,'' the shorter man said.

''Why? It can't matter *who* gets her married.''

''Apparently, it does.'' Lesley reached up and straightened his wig. ''The general feeling seems to be, that since you were the inadvertent cause of this situation, that you should be the one to repair it.''

''Blast it all Lesley, I can't stay in this town for weeks, watching Noble Lynch walking around enjoying life!''

''Stay away from him, then.''

Jackson shot him a quick look. ''I can't do that, either. That bastard killed me, Lesley, and he should have to pay for that.''

''He will. Eventually.''

''Not good enough.''

''It will have to be.'' Lesley's form began to fade. ''I advise you to leave petty thoughts of revenge alone and concentrate on the matter of Rachel Morgan.''

''Don't you leave yet,'' Jackson told him sharply. ''I'm not finished with you.''

''But I am finished, Jackson,'' Lesley said, and his voice sounded more like an echo of a voice long silenced. ''And by the way,'' he added just before disappearing entirely, ''Don't think for a minute that we didn't notice you trading a coin for liquor.''

Jackson had to swallow the angry words that rushed into his mouth. His target was gone. There was little satisfaction in shouting at nothingness.

Without seeing, he stared at the open meadow surrounding him. A soft breeze brushed past him, but he didn't feel it. Birds sang in the trees, but he ignored them.

Noble Lynch.

Why hadn't Lesley warned him that he would be meeting up with his murderer?

Or, was this Hell and no one had bothered to tell him?

Chapter ☆ *Ten*

Minutes slipped past. Rachel stood rooted in one spot, staring blankly out through the open doorway. At least, she told herself, Jackson had headed in the opposite direction of the saloon. She sucked in a deep breath and rubbed her upper arms briskly, hoping to dispel the lingering sensation of cold she had experienced a few moments before.

Her mind whirled as too many thoughts at once raced through her brain, each vying for precedence.

In snatches of memory, she saw fury flash in Lynch's dark eyes. She saw pain and raw anger glittering in Jackson's green gaze. And she saw herself, instinctively drawn to help the man she'd waited for most of her life.

It didn't matter that a ghost shouldn't need defending. It didn't even matter that he seemed to want her clear of whatever lay between he and Lynch.

All she knew was what she felt.

As if invisible strings holding her in place suddenly snapped, Rachel ran to the door and through it, slamming it closed behind her.

She had to find Jackson.

The last of the children were running down the steps and into the late morning sunshine almost before the words "Class dismissed" had left her lips.

Hester Sutton smiled sadly. A shame they weren't as eager to arrive. Still, she remembered what it was like to be young and have a sunny day stretching out in front of you. Which was one of the reasons she'd let the children leave early today.

She stacked her books in the center of her uncluttered desk, then picked up the apple Tommy Littlefield had given her that morning.

Undoubtedly, he'd been sure his gift would win him the return of his pen knife. Hester shook her head and patted the drawer front behind which lay the countless *treasures* she'd confiscated since the beginning of the school year. None of the children would get their things back until school closed for the summer break. Tommy knew that as well as anyone, but still had tried bribing her.

On that thought, she shot the shiny apple a wary look. Knowing her pupil, she'd better check that perfect looking piece of fruit for a worm.

Standing up, she smoothed the fall of her dove gray dress, then reached up to pat the dainty lace collar adorning the high neckline. Then she picked up her dark gray bonnet from the edge of her desk and quickly put it on. She tied the black ribbons in what she hoped was a jaunty bow just below her right ear and told herself for the hundredth time since the night before that she was being a fool.

Still, she couldn't quiet the insistent voice inside her. The voice, born of years of loneliness, that urged her to take a risk. Whispers rattled through her mind. Whispers that promised a chance at happiness if she could only find the courage to take one small step.

Nodding to herself, she drew a deep breath, then picked up the stack of books and headed down the center aisle past the empty desks. As she stepped outside and closed the door behind her, she turned around to face Main Street just as another wave of doubts assailed her.

What if Rachel's cousin were wrong?

Her fingers tightened around her books.

Charlie Miller, shy?

Was it possible?

Such a strong, loud, *handsome* man? Could he really be secretly suffering? Did he really fear speaking to her?

She looked to the right. To the crowd of lumbermen standing about outside the small hotel restaurant. Her stomach churned. Her mouth went dry; she had to fight the almost overwhelming urge to run.

Raucous laughter rolled toward her on a short gust of wind, and she shivered in response. In that group of seven or eight men was Charlie Miller. Hester's gaze moved over them and stopped when she spotted his pale blond hair.

Mentally gathering her tattered nerves, she started down the steps before she could change her mind. Keeping her eyes fixed on that blond head, she walked slowly and steadily toward the rowdy group.

"Well, lookee here," someone crowed.

She tensed, but kept walking.

"Little bitty thing, ain't she?" Another voice joined the first.

Wind plucked at her skirts and teased wisps of hair from the knot at the back of her neck. A long, dark blond strand flew across her eyes, and she reached up to push it back into place.

"Say, boys," one man said in a voice as deep as a well, "which one of you made the teacher so mad she's comin' lookin' for him?"

Hester lifted her chin. This was going to be harder than she had thought. There were so *many* of them. And they were all so big. And loud. As she came closer, she saw Charlie move from the back of the group to the front. He stopped at the top of the three short steps leading to the restaurant and watched her approach.

He looked even bigger somehow. Her strength began to slip away, leaving her legs as wobbly as a newborn foal's.

Then he gave her a soft, hesitant smile. Her gaze fixed on his sun-browned features. She noted the tiny crinkles at the corners of his eyes, the strong, cleanly shaven jaw, and the breadth of his shoulders beneath a worn, red flannel shirt.

Turning to his friends, he waved them to silence as she stopped at the foot of the steps.

"Hello, Miss Hester."

Someone laughed, and she felt heat flood her cheeks. Still, she stayed. If what Jackson had said was true, then she owed it to Mr. Miller . . . and herself, to say what she'd come to say. Butterflies swarmed in her stomach. Her hands ached from the death grip she held on her books. A moment or two of silence stretched out, and she didn't know which was worse—the men making noise and laughing with each other, or the intimidating quiet where everyone could hear her speak.

She swallowed back her fear and started. "Mister Miller . . . Charlie . . ."

Another chuckle rippled around them, but he glared the offender into silence.

Say it, she told herself. Just say it and go.

"Last night," she went on, looking only at Charlie, "Mister Tate told me about your . . . problem."

"What problem's that, Miller?" one man managed to ask before dissolving into fits of laughter that the others quickly joined in on. They were all staring at her. She felt their gazes stab at the remnants of her courage until it was all she could do to remain standing.

One of the men slapped Charlie on the back, but he didn't seem to notice. His gaze was locked with hers as he came down the steps and stopped in front of her. He seemed to sense her distress, and the understanding in his pale blue eyes soothed her frayed nerves.

Her breathing steadied as she looked up at him.

She had to say it. She would never forgive herself if she didn't. Indeed, she would spend the rest of her life wondering what might have happened if only she had had the courage—just once—to ask for what she wanted most.

Gripping the books cradled to her chest, she opened her mouth and forced the words past her throat. The words she had lain awake the night before, practicing.

"Jackson has explained that you suffer from shyness," she managed to say. "Just as I do."

"*Shy?*" One man snorted. "Charlie?"

The big blond man in front of her dipped his head slightly.

She winced and went on, determined to finish what she'd come to say. "I wondered if you might escort me to my home?"

Laughter dissolved. Silence dropped over the crowd. The men still stared at her, but now their gazes held traces of wistful envy as they watched her. Hester, though, saw only Charlie. His strong features softened, and a quiet, proud smile curved his mouth. Pale blond hair fell across his forehead, and he reached up to push it back.

"I would be pleased to, Miss Hester," he said and his deep, rich voice caressed her ears.

She released a breath she hadn't known she'd been holding and felt a swirl of bright, lovely colors blossom inside her.

He stepped even closer and offered her his arm. Hesitantly, she laid her small hand on his. The brush of flesh against flesh sent a skittering sensation jolting through her bloodstream. Gently, he smoothed his thumb over the back of her knuckles for a moment before drawing her to his side and tucking her hand into the crook of his elbow. Then, as if touching spun glass, he patted her fingers where they rested on his arm and lifted his gaze to hers.

"Can I carry your books for you?"

"Thank you . . . Charlie." She felt warmed by the light in his eyes. Her heartbeat thundered, and her blood seemed to dance in her veins.

He took the small stack of books from her and held them easily in one huge fist. His great size dwarfed her, but his almost reverent gentleness made her feel safe. Treasured.

Charlie looked at her hand on his arm, then met her gaze for a long, heart-stopping moment. In the pale blue depths of his eyes, Hester saw more than she had ever hoped to see.

"Are you ready, Miss Hester?" he asked quietly.

There was a world of promises and hopes in his simple question, and she heard them all clearly.

"Yes," she said and smiled at the big man beside her. "I *am* ready, Charlie."

They moved off together, oblivious to the startled murmurings of the men they left behind.

Rachel wasn't sure exactly why she'd gone to the site of her unfinished new house. Maybe it was because she could think of nowhere else to look for him.

But the reason didn't matter as soon as she came around the side of the building and spotted him standing in the center of the meadow behind the house.

Relief washed through her, and she drew her first easy breath since the confrontation with Noble Lynch. Telling herself it was beyond foolish to worry about a ghost's safety, she started walking toward him.

Meadow grass brushed against her skirt, and the water-logged earth clung to her shoes, making each step a test. Wildflowers dotted the landscape, marking their spots with brilliant splashes of color and lending their mingled scents to the wind that eased across the open ground.

Jackson stood with his back to her and as she drew closer, she heard him talking.

To no one.

"Don't you leave yet," he said hotly. "I'm not finished with you."

She thought she heard the faint echo of another voice, but she couldn't be sure.

Rachel's steps faltered as she looked around the empty meadow. Uneasiness welled up inside her. Maybe she shouldn't be there. Maybe there were rules about such things, and she was breaking them with her presence. But even as that thought entered her mind, another more insistent one followed. Who was he talking to?

He was quiet again as she walked across the last few feet of space separating them. Hesitantly, she reached out and touched his arm.

Jackson spun around as if he'd been shot.

When he recognized her, the wildness in his eyes faded, and his entire body seemed to slump in reaction. "Jesus, Rachel," he groaned after a moment, "don't sneak up on a man like that."

Birdsong drifted to them from the woods at the edge of the meadow. The wind ruffled his hair and teased her with his scent. A scent she was becoming entirely too used to.

"I didn't mean to startle you," she said.

He shook his head, brushing away her apology. "I should have heard you coming. My own fault."

"Who were you talking to?" she asked.

"Huh?" He frowned, pushed one hand through his hair, and shrugged. "How much did you hear?"

"Not much," she conceded and didn't add that her curiosity was mounting steadily by the minute.

He nodded, and she thought he looked pleased with her admission.

"Who was here?" she asked again.

"Lesley."

Lesley had been there? In the meadow? She looked carefully from side to side as if she expected to see evidence of the ghostly visitor.

"He's gone, now."

"How do you know?" She looked past him.

"I can't see him anymore."

Rachel shivered a bit. Even believing that Jackson truly was a ghost didn't prepare her for things like this. The idea that he could see people no one else could and talk to beings most people were sure didn't even exist was a bit worrisome. But the fact that she *couldn't* see and hear these other beings was worse.

"What does he look like?"

He pulled his head back and looked down at her quizzically. "Is that what you came to ask me? What Lesley looks like?"

"No." She shook her head and tried to ignore her sudden curiosity. "I was worried about you."

"Worried?" Jackson nodded thoughtfully. "It's been a long time since anyone worried about me."

Rachel saw a muscle in his jaw twitch. She wanted to reach out to him. To smooth away the lines in his forehead. To ease the pain she still saw glimmering in his eyes.

Instead, she curled her hands into the folds of her skirt and held on tightly.

"Why'd you come out here, Rachel?" he finally asked quietly. "I wanted you in town. Safe."

"I can't stay behind a locked door, Jackson." Her voice matched the softness of his, but held a thread of steel. "I have a business to run. Customers to take care of."

He shot her a quick look. "So who's watching the store now?"

She inclined her head and admitted, "It's closed right now."

"Ah," he nodded slowly. "So you're willing to close up when it suits you. Just not when I ask you to."

"Jackson," she cut him off. "This isn't about me. This is about you. And Noble Lynch."

His features tightened and, again, she had to force herself to keep from reaching out to him.

Looking past her toward the unfinished house, he said, "The house is starting to take shape."

She sighed as she realized that he was trying to change the subject. A curl of disappointment snaked through her, but she went along with him.

"Yes, it is." In the few days Jackson and Sam had been working on her house, they'd done remarkably good work. More of the framework was in place, and Rachel could almost see the place as it would look when finished.

"You have a nice spot for it," Jackson added and started walking.

"I know," she said and fell into step beside him. Her foot slipped in a wide patch of mud, and his fingers curled around her elbow to steady her. Warmth surged through her, and she felt his heat seep deep into her bones. When he didn't release her, Rachel drew on the strength of his touch and tried again to coax him into talking to her.

"Are you all right, Jackson?"

Bending down, he tugged a long sprig of grass free and tossed it high into the wind. She watched him and knew that he was trying to decide whether to confide in her or not.

"Why did you run out of the store? Why did you come out here to talk to Lesley?"

He glanced at her, and a wry, half smile lifted one corner of his mouth. "Full of questions still, aren't you?"

She knew he was thinking back on when she was a child. When she had peppered him with questions about him, her future, and anything else she could think of. But this was different, she told herself. This was now. She needed to know the truth about what was happening.

"What is it, Jackson?" she asked and reached for his arm. "What is it between you and Noble Lynch?"

He stopped walking, then stared into the distance. Pulling away from her, he shoved both hands into his pants pockets. "Let it go, Rachel."

"I can't." She stepped directly in front of him, willing him to look at her. When he did, she shrugged slightly and repeated, "I can't."

He choked out a strangled laugh. "This'd be a helluva lot easier if you'd just do as I asked and stay away from that gambler without asking questions."

"Jackson, I'm not asking out of idle curiosity." She laid both hands on his forearms and looked deeply into his eyes. An old pain shimmered there, and she wanted to do something to stop its power over him. But without knowledge, she was helpless. "I've been doing my best to stay away from Mister Lynch since he first moved to town." She shook her head gently. "I'm not sure exactly why, but he's always made me uncomfortable."

"You've got good instincts, Rachel."

"Tell me, Jackson. Tell me what it is between you two."

Their gazes locked.

She held her breath.

"Noble Lynch is the man who killed me."

Rachel stumbled backward, shaking her head as she went. One hand lifted to her throat, and she stared at him, waiting for more. Not sure that she wanted to hear it.

Now that he'd started, Jackson couldn't stop. He told her everything.

He squinted, as if looking into the past. Calmly, slowly, he described what had happened on that night fifteen years ago. As he said the words, describing his own death, he felt her sorrow grow. He knew he should be quiet. He didn't want to see pain in her eyes, let alone a pain *he'd* caused. Lord knows he didn't want her pity.

But blast it, if this was the only way of making sure she knew exactly what kind of man Noble Lynch was, then it would be worth it. She had to see that he was a dangerous man and not one for her to take lightly.

When he finished speaking, he waited for what seemed a lifetime for her to say something. Anything. When she finally spoke, though, her words were so unexpected, she caught him completely offguard.

"We have to go see the sheriff."

She hiked her skirt hem up to her knees and started walking.

Dumbfounded, Jackson stared after her for a long moment, then followed after, catching her in three long strides. He grabbed her arm and turned her around to face him. "We can't go to the sheriff."

"Why not?" Lifting her chin, she bunched her skirt into one fist and shook her index finger at him like he was a schoolboy caught pulling the girls' hair. "Noble Lynch is a murderer, Jackson."

"Yeah, I know." A chuckle started building in his chest, and he was amazed at the sensation. He'd expected to feel a lot of things once she heard the truth about him. Laughter wasn't one of them.

"Well, we can't let him get away with this." She reached up and brushed a long strand of hair back behind her ear. "It's . . . it's . . ." she groped for a strong enough word. *"Appalling!"*

Jackson grinned as he looked at her. Indignation stained her cheeks a deep scarlet, her rapid breathing had her chest moving up and down like a bellows, and she fairly danced from foot to foot in her anxiousness to get busy.

Both eyebrows lifted as his gaze rose from her shifting feet to admire the view of her legs. It was quite a view. That long skirt of hers had been covering some mighty shapely legs. Of course, she wore sensible, black cotton stockings, so not an inch of flesh was exposed. Yet, something stirred inside him as he allowed himself to appreciate the curve of her calves, the bend of her knees. His imagination completed the journey.

He sucked in a gulp of air then dragged his gaze away from temptation. An uncomfortable ache began to build within him, and he realized that, unknowingly, Rachel had managed to take his mind off Noble Lynch.

"What are you waiting for, Jackson?" she asked. "Let's get into town and swear out a Complaint."

She took a step and came to an abrupt halt when he grabbed her arm again.

"What are you gonna tell the sheriff, Rachel?"

"Well, that Mister Lynch . . ." Her voice trailed off.

"Yeah? Mister Lynch what?" Jackson shook his head at her and said quietly, "We can't go into town and tell the sheriff that Lynch killed me fifteen years ago."

"Oh."

He wanted to smile at the disappointment on her face. This was a new experience for him. Not once in his whole miserable life—or afterlife for that matter—had *anyone* wanted to defend him. Protect him. A spot of warmth settled in his chest, and Jackson welcomed it like the first day of spring after a long, cold winter.

Gently, he reached out and smoothed his fingertips along the side of her face. Her skin felt soft, softer than anything he'd ever felt before. Looking down at her, he felt his chest tighten and the ache in his groin blossom until the pain was almost blinding.

His fingers curled into the palm of his hand, and he slowly pulled away from her. He didn't have the right to touch her. The right to look into her eyes and lose himself in the pure deep color of them. He didn't have the right to admire her legs or feel pleasure in the fact that she wanted to come to his rescue.

All of this was denied him because he'd been a fool fifteen years ago.

"Jackson?"

"I appreciate what you want to do, Rachel," he said and knew it didn't come close to describing what he really felt. "I really do. Nobody's ever wanted to go out and do battle for me before." He reached for her again, then let his hand drop to his side. "Especially someone I wronged so badly."

She looked at him. "What do you mean?"

It shamed him to bring it up, but he had to tell her how sorry he was. "I talked to a few folks this morning."

"About what?"

"You. The Heinzes."

She glanced away.

"Christ, Rachel, I'm sorry." He shook his head and studied her profile. "I should have been more careful. I should have stuck around long enough to find out if they were good people." Disgusted with himself, he sighed and forced himself to keep looking at her. "I didn't, and you paid the price."

She turned, shifting her gaze to his. "Martha Heinz was a lovely woman."

"Yeah, but she wasn't around long."

"True." Rachel studied him for a long moment before continuing. "Mister Heinz wasn't evil, Jackson."

"Yeah, from what I hear, he was a real charmer."

A half smile lifted one corner of her mouth. "No, I wouldn't go that far. He was strict and believed in using what he liked to call, 'a firm hand' on a child."

"Bastard."

She rubbed her hands up and down her arms. "I think he did his best, Jackson."

"If that was his best, than he was a sore excuse for a man."

"Probably." At least, Rachel had always thought so. But going backward was not the way she wanted to live her life. "Jackson, Mister Heinz isn't important anymore. He hasn't been for a long time."

"He beat you."

She winced as memories flashed before her eyes, then disappeared. "He took a strap to my legs occasionally. Nothing more."

"Ain't that *enough?*" Jackson reached up and shoved both hands through his hair as if he could tear the image of a young girl being whipped from his mind with his bare hands. "Jesus, what I'd give to have that bastard in front of me for a minute or two."

"It wouldn't change anything," she told him quietly. "I survived, that's all that matters."

"No thanks to me."

"You saved my life, Jackson."

"And then didn't bother to make sure that you were safe." He shook his head as air rushed from his lungs. "I should have done better by you, Rachel. You were just a kid."

"The past is over," she said. "Mine and yours. It's what we do now that matters. What are you going to do about Lynch?"

"Nothing." He paused thoughtfully. "For now." Forcing a smile, he nodded at her. "Don't worry, all right?"

"I do, though." She said it simply, quietly.

"Why? You don't even want me here, Rachel. Why would you worry about me?"

She ducked her head briefly, then looked up into his eyes again. "You're important to me, Jackson."

He winced and stuffed his hands into his pockets. A thoughtful look crossed his face, then he nodded to himself, pulled his hands free, and reached for her hand.

Rachel watched as he turned her hand over palm up, then placed a single golden coin in its center. He curled her fingers over it, holding her hand closed with his.

"What are you doing?" Rachel asked. The warmth of the coin settled into her flesh, but was nothing compared to the heat of Jackson's hand on hers.

"I want you to keep this coin, Rachel."

She shook her head and tried to pull away. "You can't give this to me, Jackson. It's not allowed, is it?"

"I don't know," he admitted. "But I don't care, either.

I'll feel a lot easier, knowing you have this gold coin."

"But . . ."

"I still have two left besides this one. It's important to me that you have it."

"Why?"

"Just in case," he said and reluctantly, it seemed, released her.

"In case of what?" She opened her hand and looked from the shining gold piece to him.

His shoulders lifted casually, but his voice was firm and steady. "In case you need help one day, and I'm not around."

Not around.

Something wide and dark opened up inside her, and the echoes of loneliness sounded out in her ears until she wanted to shout, just to drown them out. She didn't want him to leave. She didn't want to even think about the empty years ahead of her when she wouldn't see him. Talk to him. Argue with him.

Rachel stared into his soft green eyes and thought for a moment that she saw like emotions written there. But in an instant, that flash of longing was gone, as if it had never been.

It didn't matter though. Whether Jackson felt the same things she did or not, it couldn't change the truth she was only now admitting to herself.

She recognized the feelings fluttering into life inside her.

When, she wondered, had it happened?

When was the exact moment she had fallen in love with him again?

And why was the one man she was destined to love a ghost?

Chapter ☆ Eleven

Rachel glanced at the man walking beside her. With his gaze fixed on the distance, he took long, slow steps as if he were in no hurry to return to Stillwater. She noted the set of his jaw and the hard, unforgiving glint in his eyes and knew he wrestled with thoughts he wouldn't be sharing with her. He hadn't spoken since they'd left the meadow and, in truth, she'd been grateful for the silence.

She had enough wild thoughts and raging notions flying through her own brain to keep her busy. How had this happened? How had she allowed herself to care for him again?

Or had it simply been a matter of igniting again the spark that she'd felt so long ago?

Dappled shadows stretched across the road, and the pine trees lining the long track whispered to each other in the wind. She shivered slightly and promised herself that whatever happened, this time when Jackson left her, she wouldn't be heartbroken. This time, she wouldn't allow pain to color her life for years.

As they neared town again, the muted hum of activity reached out for them. The subtle intrusion slowed their pace, but they kept walking, their footsteps muffled by the soggy dirt.

Jackson stopped suddenly at the edge of town. Rachel turned to face him.

"What is it?"

"You go on back to the store, Rachel," he said stiffly, his gaze raking over the busy Main Street just ahead of them. "I've got to find Sam—get back to work on the house."

Anger flashed briefly inside her. "You're lying."

He flicked her a quick look, then slid his gaze away again just as quickly.

"You're not looking for Sam. You're going to the saloon, aren't you? To see Noble Lynch."

Jackson inhaled slowly, deeply, and his chest expanded until she thought the straining shirt buttons would pop off the fabric. He braced his legs in a wide stance and crossed his arms over his chest. The soft wind ruffled his night black hair and at the open *v* of his collar, Rachel noticed a slight dusting of the same colored hair against his tanned skin.

He looked so strong. So alive. She wanted to hold him. Feel his arms slide around her. Yet at the same time, she wanted to smack him and shout at him until he listened to her. But even as she watched him, Rachel felt him drift farther away from her.

"I thought you weren't going to do anything about him right now?"

"Who said anything about Lynch?"

"You don't have to say it," she whispered. "I can see the truth in your eyes."

He looked away from her briefly, then turned back. "Go to the store, Rachel."

"Like a good little girl?"

He scowled at her, but she stood her ground.

"Well, I'm not a little girl anymore, Jackson." She took a step closer and poked that broad chest with the tip of her index finger. "You can't just tell me to go and expect me to do it."

"This has nothing to do with you. You'd do well to stay out of it."

"Stay out of it?" Someone in the street behind her shouted, and she lowered her voice at the reminder that they weren't alone. "How can you say that to me?"

"It's for your own good."

"Blast you, Jackson. I'm only *in* this because you appeared out of nowhere, insinuating yourself back into my life." She had to tilt her head back to look into his eyes. "And now that you have, you expect me to just step aside and say nothing about what you're planning to do?"

He chuckled and shook his head. "What do you think it is I'm planning?"

She threw her arms wide, then let them fall to her sides again. "I don't know. It could be anything." Glancing down pointedly at the pockets in his jeans, she said, "For all I know, you're going to use one of those gold coins on Lynch to turn him into a snake."

His eyes widened, and he tipped his head to one side thoughtfully. A moment later, he said, "No. A waste of a coin. He already *is* a snake."

"Jackson, tell me what you're going to do."

"This isn't your business, Rachel."

"You're my business, Jackson."

He shook his head at her slowly, patiently. "No, Rachel. *You* are *my* business."

"So, you can stick your nose into my life, but I have to stay out of yours?"

"I don't have a life," he said tightly. "That ended fifteen years ago."

"Because of Lynch."

"Yeah." His eyes locked with hers.

She read anger and pain in the green depths, but more than that, she saw helplessness, and that tore at her.

"Because of him," he said, his voice raw. "And now Lesley . . . and *you* expect me to ignore him?"

"If you don't ignore him, if you do something to him, what happens to you?"

His features tightened as he shrugged wide, muscular shoulders. He didn't answer, but the truth was obvious to her. He didn't *care* about himself.

This wasn't happening, she told herself in a futile attempt to ease the pain growing within her. She wasn't really standing in town on a busy day, talking to a ghost about the safety of his soul.

Yet, the truth stood before her.

A man unchanged in fifteen years.

Her heartbeat staggered a bit, then steadied itself again. As a child, she'd thought him an angel. As an adult, it was painfully clear that he wasn't a heavenly being. But her feelings for him were stronger than ever. Maybe *because* he wasn't perfect. She didn't know. But then, lately, she didn't seem to *know* anything for sure.

"Jackson, please. Come back to the store with me."

"I can't," he said stiffly.

"Why not?"

"I have to do *something*."

"What, Jackson? What do you have to do?"

"I don't know," he snapped her a hot look, then turned to stare off down the street again. "I don't know," he repeated in an agonized whisper. "But I can't pretend he's not here. *Alive*."

"You could stay away from him, though."

A horse and rider headed toward them, and Jackson pulled her out of the way. She fell against him and braced her palms on his chest. He flinched at her touch. As he looked down into her eyes, Rachel thought for one wild moment that he was going to pull her even closer and lower his lips to hers.

Then a child down the street shouted to his friend, and

that was enough to shatter the spell surrounding them. Holding her upper arms, Jackson set her back a pace. The tick in his jaw was the only outward sign that he had felt anything at all at their closeness.

"Rachel, you can't understand this."

"Yes, I can."

He glanced up, as if to assure himself that no one was near, then drew her to one side of the street for good measure. She hurried her steps to keep up with him and silently cursed her skirts as they tangled around her legs. When they reached the shelter of the back wall of the livery, Jackson slapped one palm on the wood siding, shielding her from view with his body.

She stared up at him. His eyes blazed, his jaw was tight, and it was as if those peaceful moments in the meadow had never happened. She felt his mounting frustration as a wall rising between them.

"Rachel, you can't know what it's like to come face to face with your own killer."

She reached up and covered the hand he'd laid against the wall with one of her own. Looking him squarely in the eye, she agreed. "No, I can't."

He nodded abruptly, but she went on.

"But I *do* know what it's like to face a ghost from your past."

He stiffened and tried to pull away. She tightened her grip on his hand. "And I know what it is to have that ghost disrupt your life—"

He snorted.

"Your *existence*," she corrected. "It's a helpless feeling, Jackson. You get angry. Frustrated."

"It's not the same." He pushed away from the wall and her. Taking a step or two back, he shoved both hands through his black hair.

"Close enough," she said quietly.

A long minute passed, and she held his gaze with hers.

She waited and watched as he thought over what she had just said. Finally, he spoke again.

"All right." He nodded at her. "We've both had our pasts thrown at us. But that's where it ends, Rachel. That's where your understanding of this situation ends."

"Jackson—"

"No," he said quickly and stomped back to her side. "I didn't shoot you and leave you to bleed to death on a dirty floor."

Pain stabbed at her as she imagined the horrible death he had suffered before she had ever met him. True, she didn't know what that felt like. But there was more than one kind of pain in the world.

"I didn't harm you all those years ago, Rachel." His voice was tight, hard. "So you can't understand what I'm feeling."

"Didn't harm me?"

He slanted her a look, alerted by the tone in her voice.

"Granted, you didn't shoot me." She pulled in a deep breath, lifted her chin, and said, "But you made a promise you never intended to keep. You let me love you, knowing I'd never see you again."

He groaned. "Rachel . . ."

"And now you turn up again." She pushed away from the wall and stalked past him, still muttering to herself. "Make me care again. Make me wish for things that can't be . . ."

"Dammit, Rachel," he started after her. She heard his footsteps.

But she was finished talking. At least for the moment. Rachel wanted to lose herself in the crowded street. She wanted to hear noise and people. She didn't want to think anymore. And she definitely didn't want to be alone with Jackson. She hurried her steps and rounded the corner of the livery just as he grabbed her elbow to drag her back into the shadows.

A loud, female voice, though, stopped him cold.

"Just the man I wanted to see."

Rachel nearly groaned when she saw Tessa Horn rushing toward them. She'd forgotten all about the other woman's visit earlier that morning. But then she could hardly be blamed for that, could she? So much had happened in the last few hours, it was a wonder she could remember her own name.

Glancing up at Jackson, she noted his put upon look and shrugged helplessly. It was too late to avoid Tessa and if they turned around and went the other way, not only would it be rude . . . it would be useless. Tessa would only follow and eventually catch them.

The older woman came to an abrupt stop directly in front of them. Her black skirt swished around her ankles, and her heavy breasts swayed beneath the incredibly tight fabric of her dress.

"Jackson," Rachel said, "Tessa wanted to speak to you about building a dance floor for the town social."

He breathed deeply, nodded, and looked at the woman waiting impatiently for his attention. "Yes ma'am, I'd be happy to do what I can."

"Excellent, young man. I do approve of citizens taking an interest in the town's doings."

Rachel listened to the incessant chatter spilling from Tessa's lips and knew she didn't have the patience to deal with the woman at the moment. She glanced up at Jackson and noted wryly that he didn't seem to be having the same trouble. To look at him now, no one would guess that only a minute ago he had been in the middle of an argument. He smiled at Tessa patiently, and only Rachel seemed to be aware of his rigid stance.

She reached up and rubbed her temple with her fingertips. There were too many things to think about, she told herself. Jackson, Noble Lynch, her own lingering feelings for a ghost. Not to mention, she groaned inwardly, the gold coin she still held in her hand.

Taking the coward's way out, she spoke up, interrupting Tessa in midstream. "If you two will excuse me, I really had better get back to work."

Jackson shot her a quick look, but Tessa dismissed her without a glance.

"Of course, of course. Your cousin and I will do quite nicely, my dear."

Rachel stepped off the boardwalk and hurried away. As she went, she felt Jackson's stare boring into her back.

"Really Sam, I shouldn't," Mavis insisted, though with a little less vehemence than a moment before.

Early afternoon sunlight streamed in through the sparkling windowpanes of Mavis's dress shop on Main Street. Outside, hurried footsteps clattered on the boardwalk, and the muffled noise and confusion that usually reigned in town colored the air. But here, in the quiet, there was only the two of them.

"Mavis, darlin'," he countered and slid one arm around her shoulders, "wouldn't you rather take a long walk in the moonlight with me, than go to one of those meetings at Rachel's?"

She tilted her head back to look up at him, and Sam's breath caught in his throat. How had he known her off and on for years and never noticed before now what beautiful eyes she had? Reaching up, he pushed her spectacles higher on her small, straight nose and lost himself in those soft, whiskey colored eyes.

She smiled at him and for the first time, he noted a tiny dimple in her left cheek. There was so much about her that he was only now discovering.

Why had he never taken the time to discover her gentle heart and the way she fit so nicely in the circle of his arms? His hand slid off her shoulder and down along her rib cage.

There were no boney angles on Mavis. No hard, steely bands of a corset to prevent him from feeling her softness.

She shivered as his fingertips drifted too close to a breast he longed to touch, and he dutifully retreated.

Yes, soft was the word to best describe the woman he loved. Her figure was a bit rounder than most men would have preferred, but Sam appreciated the feel of her in his arms. But more than that, her warm, generous spirit offered comfort to a man too long alone.

Her kisses left him breathless, and her eager inexperience fed his desire until the flames of his wild need for her threatened to consume him. His body ached to possess her. His heart and mind wanted nothing more than to be near her.

"Sam?" she whispered and ducked her head, muffling her voice.

He tipped her chin up with his fingertips until their gazes met and held. "What is it, darlin'?"

"I've been thinking about your proposal . . ."

Tension gripped him. She couldn't refuse him. He wouldn't allow himself to even entertain the notion. Since finding Mavis, he couldn't imagine being alone again. "And you've decided to say yes?" he prodded gently as his wandering hand continued to stroke her back and side.

She sucked in a gulp of air greedily and said in a rush, "I want to, Sam. I really do. It's just that everything has happened so quickly. How can we be sure that you really love me?"

"Oh honey," he gratefully felt his fears slide away. She didn't doubt her love for him. Only his for her. That, he would gladly spend the rest of his life proving to her. "I know I'm rushing you. And maybe all of this does seem a little quick."

She nodded and her bottom lip trembled a bit.

He bent his head and planted a slow, chaste kiss to the spot. Then he pulled back again and looked into her eyes, willing his love for her to show on his face. For her to be able to read it in his eyes.

"Mavis darlin', I *do* love you."

She blinked and those wide, amber eyes filled with a sheen of water.

He smiled gently. "Maybe this has been building in me for a lot of years," he said. "That's what it feels like." He had to make her understand something he was only beginning to comprehend himself. "The other night, when I saw you at the store?"

She nodded.

"It was like somebody tore the blinders off my eyes, and I *saw* you for the first time. I mean, *really* saw you."

"But . . ."

"No buts, Mavis." He laid his fingertips across her lips and shook his head again slowly. "I don't know why or how all of this happened so fast. All I know is that I love you. I think I've always loved you, I was just too stupid to see it sooner."

"If I could believe that," she whispered.

"Believe it, sweetheart," he said in a pleading whisper. "Please believe it and love me back."

Mavis reached up and laid her palm against his cheek. He turned his face into her touch and kissed her hand.

"I do love you, Sam. I've loved you forever."

He looked at her in surprise. He'd never known or even suspected how she had felt about him. Momentary regret for years wasted rose up in him, but he immediately pushed it aside. None of that mattered now. All that mattered was that they had finally found each other.

"Then you'll marry me?"

"Yes, Sam."

"When?"

"As soon as you like."

He sighed as he gathered her in close to him. "Then it'll

be real soon, honey. I don't think I'll be able to hold out much longer.''

Mavis smiled knowingly and reached up to pull his head down to hers. ''I know, Sam. I've waited a long time, too.''

His lips came down on hers, and he felt like a man waking up from a long, lonely sleep to find his dreams had become reality.

''Why's the store closed?''

Rachel hurried her steps and smiled an apology at Sally Wiley.

''Are you sick?'' her friend asked.

''No, I was just . . .'' Rachel let her voice trail away into silence because she couldn't think of a single excuse to offer. Saying *no, I've just been off falling in love with a dead man,* didn't seem appropriate. Thankfully, though, Sally didn't seem very interested in explanations.

The woman followed Rachel into the store then immediately headed for the far end of the room. There, she picked up four bars of lye soap and turned around again. ''I ran out,'' she said with a shrug, ''and I'm hip deep in dirty clothes.''

Rachel, glad for the chance to think about someone besides Jackson, or herself, walked to her friend's side. Reaching out, she took one of Sally's reddened, cracked hands in hers. ''That lye is eating your skin right off the bones, Sally.''

The woman glanced down at her hand, shrugged, and pulled it back to cradle the bars of strong, brown soap close to her narrow chest. ''Don't look now, but you're starting to sound like Mavis.''

''Well, she's right.'' Rachel shook her head as the other woman tugged her black crocheted shawl up high enough for her hands to bury themselves in its folds. ''Maybe you should close the laundry for a week or so. Take some time off to let your hands heal a bit.''

Sally nodded solemnly, lifting her dark eyebrows. "My, what a good idea. I'll just go to my summer home in Seattle for a week or two, shall I?"

Rachel smiled wryly.

"Or no," Sally added with a wicked grin, "even better. I'll take a couple of months off and head for France. I hear it's lovely this time of year."

"All right," Rachel said with a resigned chuckle. "I understand."

"I suppose you would. I don't see you closing up shop and taking off for parts unknown."

"Yes, but the store isn't making my hands bleed."

Sally frowned briefly. "They'll heal. Mavis made me some more of that cream of hers."

"But . . ."

"Smells a good deal better than that last batch," she laughed and shook her head. "Remember the stench?"

"Sally . . ."

One sharp look from a pair of dark brown eyes cut Rachel's argument off short. Sally's fierce sense of independence was too much like her own to fight against.

"Now, if you'll just put these on my bill, I'd best get back to work," Sally said with a brightness Rachel knew was forced. "There's a mountain of laundry calling my name."

"Let me guess. Mike O'Hara's been by."

"Yesterday." Sighing, she headed for the door. "I swear to you, Rachel. Sometimes I think that man rolls around in the mud on purpose. No man alive could get that dirty without working on it."

Before Sally could step outside, Rachel asked, "Will you be coming over tonight?"

"Hmm?" She slapped one hand to her forehead. "Oh, the meeting. I'd forgotten all about it."

"That's all right, you're tired." Rachel smiled halfheartedly. Besides, she was willing to bet that Mavis, too, had forgotten about the meeting of the Spinster Society. No doubt, she was too wrapped up in Sam Hale to notice much of anything.

She and Hester alone wouldn't make much of a meeting, she told herself, ignoring the fact that she didn't feel much like celebrating spinsterhood at the moment, either.

"Why don't I just cancel, and we can all meet next week?"

"I do feel like dropping in my tracks," Sally said. "Thanks. Next week though, I promise."

When she was alone again, Rachel opened her clenched hand to look at the coin Jackson had given her. She smoothed the tip of one finger over the deeply etched, five-pointed star and felt a tingle of . . . *something* run up her arm.

The gold glinted in the sunshine and felt warm on her palm. Closing her other hand over the coin, she held it trapped between both her hands as if half expecting it to disappear at any moment.

Magic coins.

Ghosts.

Nodding to herself, she crossed the floor to the long counter. Stepping through the gated section, she walked along the length of the counter until she reached the far end. There, she bent down and reached to the back of a shelf filled with canned goods. In the shadows behind the neatly stacked rows of beans and peaches was a small tin box.

She pulled it out, then plopped down onto the floor.

Opening the box, she barely glanced at the folded loan papers and the deeds to the store and the land where her new house was growing. Instead, she stared at the coin in her hand for a long moment before gently laying it down atop the documents. Then she closed the lid again and held the box tightly in her hands.

Just in case, he'd said.

In case she ever needed help and he wasn't around.

"Jackson," she murmured softly, "the only help I need is to stop loving you." She glanced down at the tin box, then returned it to its nest in the shadows. "And I'm afraid there's not enough magic in the world to accomplish that."

Chapter ☆ Twelve

"We want the dance floor big enough for everyone to have enough room to enjoy themselves, but small enough that we can tuck it away in a barn until next year's social."

"Yes ma'am," Jackson said.

Tessa looked up at him, frowned, then batted his shoulder with her parasol. "Young man, are you listening to me?"

He gave her a sheepish grin. "I sure am, Tessa, and that dance floor will be just right. I promise."

"Good. See that it is, mind." She wagged the tip of her parasol like a teacher waving an index finger at a naughty student. "I'll brook no slapdash jobs, now."

Jackson grinned and nodded, tipped his hat, then started along the street again. Strange, but he was slipping into life in Stillwater like he'd been born there. He nodded hello to the barber and kept walking.

In a few short days, these people had become familiar to him. He was learning the pace of the town and fitting in as he had never belonged anywhere else. All the time he was alive, he didn't remember feeling such a part of a place. But then, when you spent most of your time in saloons, it wasn't easy to meet the solid citizens.

He stepped to one side to allow a woman and her small

son to pass him on the walk. A loose board caught his eye and his first thought was to find a hammer and fix it before someone broke their neck.

Shaking his head, he stepped off the boardwalk into the street. Something else, he told himself. He didn't remember being so eager to work when he was alive, either. Oh, he'd had more than enough jobs to keep him in drinking money. He'd always been good with his hands, and expert carpenters were hard to come by in most towns.

Odd that now he was dead, he could discover the real joy of working with tools to build something. Something that would stand long after he was gone. He snorted a silent laugh at his own thoughts. Hell, he was already gone!

He shot a quick look up the street and down, then trotted across the still muddy expanse to the other side. A boy about nine raced past him, followed by a mangy looking dog. Jackson turned to watch the kid dart in and out of the traffic, calling to his hound. The boy's laughter floated back to him, and he frowned thoughtfully.

He was beginning to get way too attached to living again. These last few days had been the best he could remember. He didn't want his time here to end, despite the fact that he knew it had to. He didn't belong with the living.

He didn't even belong with the dead.

The only place he really belonged anymore was that rat tail saloon at the edge of nowhere. The place where he'd spent the last fifteen years. The place where he would, very probably, spend eternity.

Something turned over inside him as he walked toward Stillwater's one and only saloon. His own footsteps sounded loud to him as he paced off the short distance. People passed him, but he didn't notice, for his gaze was locked on the bar as he approached.

Thirty feet away from the place, he stopped dead and a man behind him was forced to do a quick sidestep around him. Jackson looked at the bright red building. Inside, sat the man who had killed him. The man who had sentenced him to an eternity of nothingness. And he was expected to simply ignore the man's presence.

Jackson scowled and leaned one shoulder against the support beam of the boardwalk's overhang. Crossing his feet at the ankles, he stared at the garishly painted Golden Garter as if he could see through the plank walls to the, no doubt, smokey interior.

What kind of afterlife was this where a man was forced to meet his own killer? Had he done such a miserable job of living that he had to be punished in such a way?

Tinny, out-of-tune piano music spilled from the saloon, calling to him in a language he had always responded to. The songs were always different, but the message remained the same. *Step inside,* it said. *Try your luck. Have a drink and forget about your troubles.*

How many hours had he spent in the shadows of some saloon? How many days had he passed away, shut off from the sunlight? How many chances at life had he ignored in favor of raucous music, ready whiskey, and the warm, willing hands of whatever female was available?

These thoughts and more filled his mind until he was forced to admit that, yes, he had made a mess of his life. But dammit, he was being punished. What about Lynch? Why was he still alive and capable of experiencing everything Jackson had lost?

Abruptly, he straightened up. It wasn't right. It was too much to ask of any man, ghost or not. He couldn't ignore Noble Lynch. And he wouldn't pretend he didn't care that the man was still enjoying a life he'd stolen from Jackson.

His right hand curled into a fist, he took a single step toward the saloon and retribution.

"Hey, boss!"

Jackson stopped and glanced over his shoulder in time to watch Sam Hale approaching.

"I've been looking for you," the other man said as he leaped up onto the boardwalk.

His mind still filled with thoughts of pummelling Noble Lynch into a puddle, Jackson stared at the man blankly.

"Thought we should get back to work," Sam said, his smile fading.

"Yeah. Work."

"You all right, Jackson?" Sam frowned. "You don't look so good."

He uncurled his fist and reached up to rub the back of his neck. Forcing his mind away from thoughts of the gambler, Jackson finally said, "Yeah. Yeah, I'm all right."

For a dead man.

"So, you ready to work on Rachel's house?"

"Sure," he said and looked at the other man carefully. For the first time, he noticed the look of suppressed excitement glittering in his brown eyes. "What's the hurry, though?"

Sam reached out and slapped Jackson's shoulder in a hearty blow. "I'm gonna be needing the money, boss. I'm about to be a married man."

Jackson smiled in spite of the turmoil still bubbling inside him. The coin had worked. Of course, he wasn't really surprised. He'd expected this. He'd even told Rachel that no woman would be able to say no to the force of a man's love for her.

It looked like Mavis had proved him right.

"Can't hardly believe it," Sam was saying. "Imagine, *me* getting married."

"Happens to all of us one time or another," Jackson said and tried to ignore the pinprick of jealousy poking at his insides. Marriage would never happen to *him*. Not now.

Another thing Noble Lynch had taken from him.

"It's the strangest thing, Jackson . . ."

"Hmm?" He looked up. "What is?"

"These feelings I have for Mavis?"

"Yeah?"

"They came on me so sudden." He shook his head slowly. "I mean, I've known her for at least five years. Never really thought about her one way or another."

Jackson frowned briefly. Was it possible that the coin's magic wasn't a permanent kind?

"Now though," Sam said and glanced over his shoulder at the dress shop across the street. "I don't know why I didn't see it sooner."

Coiled tension unwound, and the relief was almost painful. He didn't have to worry about Mavis and Sam. The coin's magic was obviously strong enough to last a lifetime.

"The worst part about this is," Sam went on, "I waited so damned long to open my eyes. Years that I might have spent with her are gone now. Wasted."

Jackson stiffened slightly. That last statement cut too close to the bone. He'd waited too long to notice a lot of things. At least Sam still had time to correct past mistakes.

Jealousy reared its ugly head again, and he had to fight it back down. Desperate for a change in subject, he said, "Well, you're wasting time, now. Let's get to work, huh?"

"Right." Sam nodded and stepped off into the street, with Jackson just behind him.

Noble Lynch stood at the window and peered through the rain-spotted glass at the two men walking toward the other end of town. For a moment, he'd thought Rachel's cousin was headed his way. Not that he was worried. Noble had survived countless boomtowns and any number of gun battles. One hot headed cousin wasn't enough to make him anxious.

Still, the man had looked at him as though he knew him, and *that* bothered Noble. Where did he know him from? There were so many faces littering his memories. Too many towns, too many poor losers. No doubt, this Jackson Tate had lost a pile of money to him in a poker game and was still holding a grudge. Well, he was willing to overlook the man's insults this time. For Rachel's sake.

Soon after arriving in Stillwater, Noble had decided to court Rachel Morgan. After all, he wasn't getting any younger. Besides, he could do worse than a fine looking spinster with a profitable business. She was still a bit skittish, but he had no doubts that he could win her affection, in time.

Her cousin, though, would do well to watch his tongue and keep his back protected. Noble wasn't about to lose his rich spinster because of one annoying relation.

Lifting his glass to his lips, he took a small drink of whiskey and let it slide slowly down his throat, appreciating its fiery wake. From behind him, familiar sounds rose up and settled around him like old friends. Beneath the out-of-tune piano's discordant noise, he heard the slap of cards onto tables, the scrape of chair legs on wood, and an occasional burst of throaty laughter from one of the whores.

He drew strength from the familiarity of it all and told himself that Jackson Tate was nothing more than a bothersome insect. And the best way to deal with insects was to squash them.

"I am sorry, Rachel," Mavis insisted and looked up from where she was kneeling, pinning up the hem of the new dress. "You understand, don't you?"

Rachel bit back her disappointment and smiled. "Of course I understand, Mavis. A woman about to be married wouldn't be interested in a meeting of spinsters."

"Oh," the other woman countered around a mouthful of pins, "I'm not leaving town. We'll see each other all the time."

"I know." Rachel nodded and lifted her head to stare straight at the wall opposite her. Terrible to feel so—abandoned. She should be happy for Mavis. Instead, she was feeling sorry for herself again—and just the tiniest bit jealous.

That was a hard thing to admit, even to herself. She'd thought she'd come to terms with her spinsterhood years ago. But then, she'd made up her mind to remain a spinster because the man she had wanted was out of her reach.

Now he was back and just as far from her as ever.

A ghost.

How in heaven could loving a ghost ever come to a good end?

"I still can hardly believe it," Mavis was saying, and Rachel forced herself to pay attention. "You know, I've had . . . feelings for Sam for the longest time."

"You have?" She looked down into wide, amber eyes. Why had Mavis never said anything? In the next instant, the answer came to her. Because she herself was always preaching the joys of single life, that's why. No wonder her dear friend had hidden the fact that she was in love.

"Oh yes." Mavis sat back on her heels and looked up at Rachel. Her full cheeks were flushed a becoming pink, and even her eyeglasses seemed to sparkle. "But I never once thought that Sam might notice me one day."

"Why not?" Rachel demanded. "You're a beautiful, kind, loving person. He's lucky to have you."

Mavis smiled gently. "That's my friend talking," she said. "But what you're not saying is that I'm blind as a bat without my spectacles, I'm too short, and . . ." She patted her thick waist. "Plump."

"Mavis," Rachel started.

"It doesn't matter," her friend cut her off. "Don't you see? Sam loves me exactly as I am."

Because of a golden coin? Rachel wondered about that. Or was there some truth in his feelings, too? For Mavis's sake, she hoped for the latter.

Looking at her friend, though, Rachel felt another small stab of jealousy, even knowing that Sam's love had been wished for by a desperate ghost. Did it matter how love was born? Or was it more important that two people—the right two people—found each other?

Briefly, she let herself remember the look on Jackson's face as he'd held her that morning. For one, brief instant, she'd been sure he was about to kiss her. She'd read the intention in his eyes. Breath held, she'd waited, only to be disappointed when he set her back from him and acted as though nothing had happened.

She reached up and rubbed her forehead tiredly. Maybe, though, she had been wrong. Perhaps he hadn't been thinking about kissing her at all. After all, she was a spinster. What did she know about reading desire in a man's features?

"Are you feeling well?"

"Hmm?" Rachel shook off her disturbing thoughts and told herself to stop thinking entirely. It did no good at all when you had more questions than answers anyway. "Yes, Mavis. I'm just tired."

The shorter woman pushed herself to her knees, then stood up. "I've finished marking the hem. Why don't you get dressed and go home? Close the store for a while and have a rest."

"That sounds exactly like the advice I gave to Sally this morning."

"Good advice it is, too."

Nodding, Rachel stepped behind the dressing screen, carefully peeled off the unfinished dress, and stepped into her own clothes again. When she was ready, she walked into the main room and handed the gown to Mavis.

"I'll have it finished in time for the social," she promised. "Don't you worry."

The social. A silent groan echoed inside her. She had never felt less sociable in her life.

"Thanks, Mavis," Rachel said. "But shouldn't you be working on your wedding dress, instead?" Hopefully, she added, "You know, I don't *need* a new dress. I wouldn't mind at all if you didn't have the time to complete it."

"I wouldn't dream of not finishing that dress for you," Mavis said softly.

"But . . ."

If possible, Mavis's cheeks pinkened even further as she dipped her head before looking into Rachel's eyes again. "If I tell you something, will you promise not to say a word to anyone?"

"Of course."

"Not even Sally? Or Hester?"

Rachel frowned worriedly. What on earth could Mavis have to hide? "I won't if you ask me not to."

Mavis nodded and leaned in closer. "The truth is, I made my wedding dress four years ago."

"What?"

She laughed delightedly. "It's true. You know the hope chest that Sally's always teasing me about? Well, my dress is safely tucked away inside, just waiting for the right moment."

Impulsively, Rachel reached for her friend and gave her a tight hug. Tears stung the backs of her eyes, but she blinked them back determinedly. How little any of them knew each other, she thought. Mavis had been in love for years, dreaming of the one man she thought she couldn't have.

Now that dream was coming true.

Jackson had given her this, whether he had meant to or not.

Yet, perhaps this was how it was supposed to have worked out all along. Maybe it hadn't been an accident that Sam had seen Mavis instead of Rachel. Maybe Destiny had taken a hand while Jackson's back was turned.

"I'm so happy," Mavis whispered as if afraid to say the words too loudly.

Rachel patted her shoulder, then pulled back a bit to look

at her friend. Fixing a mock stern look on her face, she said, "Well, Sam had better see to it that you *stay* happy. Or he'll have to deal with me."

Mavis grinned at her, and Rachel left the store quickly, before those tears that refused to go away could fall.

Lamplight fell through the Mercantile's windows and lay in soft, golden patches on the boardwalk. In the growing dusk, the store looked warm and welcoming.

"Tomorrow, boss?" Sam asked.

Jackson stopped daydreaming and looked at the other man. "Yeah. Be there early so we can have time to work on that dance floor in the afternoon."

The blond gave him a sharp nod, then loped off in the direction of Mavis's dress shop.

Alone in the twilight, Jackson swiveled his head to stare at the Mercantile again. Inside, Rachel waited, and he hoped to hell she wasn't still in a fighting mood.

He was tired clean down to the bone. All day, he'd worked in a frenzy of activity, taking out his anger and frustration on the wood beams and timbers. Between his fury at finding Noble Lynch in town and his sudden, desperate need for Rachel, he had been like a man possessed. Sam had wanted to quit an hour ago, crying exhaustion, but Jackson had needed to keep going. Working kept him from thinking. That kept him sane.

His entire body ached, but the new house was coming along well. Glancing down at his hands, he noted the new blisters atop ancient calluses and smiled. He flexed his hands gingerly and pulled in a deep breath of the cool, evening air.

Funny, he'd forgotten how good it felt to put in a long day's work. To have something to show for the hours of labor.

The store's front door swung open, and Rachel appeared in the doorway. She wore a deep yellow dress that hugged her figure and made her look as fresh as a summer morning. Her hair, neat as a pin up in that knot she preferred, still tempted him to release it and let it fall across his hands like warm honey. Lamplight shone from the room behind her and made a soft, golden halo around her.

Jackson clenched his jaw and told himself to stop noticing such things. It would be better for both of them if he just did what he'd come to do and disappeared from her life again.

A ghost had no right to be thinking about the living. At least, not the kind of thinking he'd been doing lately.

"Are you coming inside?"

"Not yet," he answered, stalling for time. Taking a step or two closer to the store, he waved one hand at his sweat-stained, dirty shirt and shrugged. "I was thinking about going down to the creek. Having a bath."

"You don't need to do that, Jackson," she said and stepped out onto the porch. "You can use the tub upstairs again."

God, he wished she hadn't mentioned that tub. The thought of getting naked anywhere near her right now was way too dangerous. For both of them. As it was, he didn't think he'd ever be able to stand being in the store when she was bathing upstairs again.

Listening to the splash of the water and her soft, off-key humming would just be too much for him now that he'd allowed himself to start noticing her.

Nope, a nice hot bath wouldn't do him a bit of good tonight. What he needed was *cold* water. Lots of it.

Quick.

"Too much trouble, Rachel." He started walking before she could argue. "I won't be long."

He didn't wait to hear what she would say. He couldn't afford to. One more minute of just looking at her and a cold bath wouldn't be nearly enough to keep his wandering thoughts in line.

Muttering to himself as he walked to the nearby creek, he told himself that he shouldn't have looked into her eyes that morning. He shouldn't have held her, however briefly.

Then, he'd spent the day listening to Sam going on about Mavis. And love. And marriage. It was enough to turn anybody's head.

Especially a ghost who'd been fifteen years without a woman . . . and a lifetime without love.

Chapter ☆ Thirteen

"What's it like?" Rachel asked quietly. "Being a . . . ghost?"

Jackson's hand tightened around his coffee cup as he stared at the woman sitting across the table from him. How, he asked himself, could he explain?

His gaze shifted, slipping about the homey room above the Mercantile. In a glance, he took in the blue and white calico curtains over the windows, two overstuffed chairs drawn close together, with a reading lamp between them, and shelves of books lining the wall just behind. A small fire burned in the stone hearth, contributing the soothing hiss and snap of flame-consuming wood.

Beyond Rachel was a tiny kitchen area and on the far wall of the great room sat a rolledtop desk, neatly closed now, concealing the books and ledgers for the store. He didn't turn to look down the narrow hall behind him, but he already knew it well. Three small bedrooms opened off the passageway and at the far end was a washroom with indoor plumbing.

He had only spent the last few days here and already he felt . . . distanced from the dirty saloon that had been his only home for fifteen years. How could she ever understand?

"Jackson?"

He looked at her and his insides twisted. In the hazy, yellow glow of the lamp, her skin seemed to shimmer with golden light. She chewed at her bottom lip, and his gaze locked on the motion. His groin ached with a pulsing throb that kept time with each tug of her lip.

Jackson swallowed a groan. His hair was still damp from the cold dip he'd taken in the creek, but he suddenly felt as though he was on fire. Apparently an icy bath wasn't a strong enough cure for a fifteen-year fast.

Grumbling to himself, he lowered his gaze to the less captivating, yet safer, depths of his coffee cup.

"If you don't want to talk about it—" she started.

"No," he cut her off quickly, though it was a struggle to keep his voice steady. He had to talk. About anything. To keep his mind busy. Perhaps too, he told himself, talking about his existence as a ghost was just what he needed. A vivid reminder that his time with Rachel would be brief.

He reached for the coffeepot in the center of the table and refilled her cup before pouring more of the brew into his own. Jackson took a long sip, then started talking.

"It's not that I don't want to tell you about it," he said. "It's just that I'm not sure what to say."

She toyed with the handle of her flower sprigged china cup. "You said you live in a saloon."

"I know I didn't say *live,*" he corrected wryly.

She flushed and the pink in her cheeks looked lovely in the lamplight.

"I meant—you know what I meant."

"Yeah, I do." His fingers tightened on the fragile cup handle that was much too small and dainty for a man's grip. "The name of the place is The Black Hound."

Her eyebrows lifted.

He snorted a laugh that held no humor. "Not much of a name for a man's eternal resting place, is it?"

"No."

"But," he went on, leaning back in his chair and feigning a casualness he didn't feel, "there hasn't been much rest for fifteen years, either."

"What do you mean, rest? Sleep?"

"No, although I will admit, it's been good to lay down at night and close my eyes again." He could have done without the occasional dream about her, though.

"I meant the kind of rest the preachers are always going on about."

"Oh."

"You know, peace. Serenity."

"There isn't any?"

He glanced at her and read the worry in her eyes. Damn him for a fool, he told himself. No doubt, she was imagining that her adopted folks and maybe even the real family she'd lost so long ago were stranded somewhere between Heaven and Hell.

Jackson sat up again and hunched over his coffee cup. Sparing her a quick glance, he shook his head. "I don't know about anybody else, Rachel. Just me." Memories teased at the edges of his mind, and he added, "But there've been others."

"What others?"

"Other folks who died in Pine Ridge, too." He swirled the coffee in his cup and watched the brown liquid slosh and dance with his movements. "They were stuck for a while too, then they left."

"Left?" she repeated and leaned in closer to him. "Left for where?"

He shrugged. "Don't know. Just one day they were there, the next, they weren't. I hope they went somewhere better than where they died." A wry smile lifted one corner of his mouth. " 'Course, wherever they went, it couldn't have been much worse."

"If others have died and gone on, Jackson," she asked,

her voice hushed, as if afraid of the coming answer, "why haven't you?"

"Don't know." Shaking his head, he laughed shortly at his own ignorance. "Guess you asked the wrong ghost for information, Rachel. I'm just as stupid dead as I was alive."

"You're not stupid."

The handle of the cup snapped off in his hand, and hot coffee splashed over the rim onto his fingers. "Damn it," he said and glared at the flimsy cup handle laying in his palm. "I'm sorry, I—"

"It's just a cup, Jackson."

"It's *not* just the cup. It's everything." He pushed himself back and up from the table, then stalked across the floor to the wide window overlooking the street.

She didn't say anything, and he was grateful. It gave him an extra minute or two to gather up the thoughts splintering through his mind. After several long moments, he started talking, his voice a whisper, his gaze locked on the blackness hovering just beyond the pane of glass.

"I've messed up nearly everything I ever tried to do," he said and shook his head. "Not just since I died," he quickly pointed out. "Even when I was alive. I've been getting into scrapes ever since I can remember."

"Jackson . . ."

"First it was with my pa." He snorted. "Then teachers and finally, the law."

"You were a criminal?"

This time his short laugh sounded harsh, even to himself.

"No. I never worked hard enough at anything to be a real outlaw. Knew a few of them, though." He nodded to himself, lost in memories he hadn't dredged up in years. "Those boys knew what they were doing. Hell, if they'd worked as hard at real jobs as they did at being outlaws, they'd have all been rich old men dying in their beds instead of dying broke and too damned young at the end of ropes.''

He glanced at her and saw her shiver. Shame rippled through him, but now that he'd started, he was determined to finish. She had a right to know just what kind of a ghost she was dealing with.

Before he could change his mind, he started talking again. ''My problems with the law were usually for fighting and drinking,'' he admitted and felt that shame inside him blossom until it threatened to choke him. Lordy, this wasn't as easy as he'd thought it would be. ''I was a good carpenter once,''

''You still are,'' she said quickly.

''Thanks,'' he replied, smiling at her, then returning his gaze to the night. ''But when I had the chance to do something with my skill, I didn't. Worked enough to eat, played cards enough to lose anything I had left . . .''

''Jackson.''

He heard her get up and started talking faster, wanting to get it all said before she could stop him.

''I wasn't much good, Rachel,'' he said as she walked up to him. ''Heck, my own mother died when I was eight, just to get the hell away from me.'' Surprising that that still hurt. He pulled in a long, shuddering breath. ''I let people down. Even you.'' He shoved one hand through his hair. ''Moved on whenever I started getting close to somebody. Fouled things up, then pulled up stakes so I wouldn't have to clean up my own messes.''

''Jackson, stop it,'' she begged and laid one hand on his arm.

Rushing now, he told her the rest of it. ''You wanted to know what being a ghost is like? What it is to be trapped in a filthy saloon watching other fools like yourself throw their lives away?''

''I'm so sorry,'' she said softly.

"Don't be. I don't deserve your sympathy," he assured her.

Spinning around to face her, he looked into her blue eyes and said, "I made my own Hell, Rachel. Built it fine and strong, all by myself. Stone by stone. Brick by brick."

"Jackson . . ."

"Maybe I was never a *real* bad man. But I sure as shooting could have been a better one." He inhaled deeply. "You wanted to know what it's like? Being a ghost?"

She didn't say anything, so he plunged ahead.

"It's nothingness, Rachel." His throat ached with the agony of forcing the words out. "It's day after day of nothing followed by long nights where the only thing to do is sit in the dark and curse yourself for wasting everything you were given. It's watching others do the same things you did and being unable to warn them. To tell them that they still have time to change."

He dragged in a deep breath, let his head fall back on his neck, and stared unseeing at the ceiling.

"It's listening to the wind and not feeling it. It's standing in the rain and not getting wet. It's hunger that can't be fed and thirst that won't be quenched."

She choked back a sob, and Jackson moved to look down at her. So close to him and yet so damned far away she might as well have been on the other side of the world. Tears spilled from her eyes and rolled down her cheeks. But he didn't want her crying for him. He didn't want her tears. He was too far beyond any help her pity might generate.

He grabbed her upper arms, feeling her, holding her, and accepting the pain that followed as his due. Pain far sharper than anything he'd felt since the night he'd been killed.

"It's touching and not feeling." His thumbs moved over the sunny yellow fabric covering her flesh. "It's talking and not being heard. It's being more tired than you ever thought possible and yet being unable to sleep." His voice broke, caught, then went on in a strained whisper that rose up straight from his soul. "It's an eternity of loneliness.

Her features twisted in grief, and stabbing into whatever was left of his heart.

"I watch each sunrise. Each sunset." He shook his head sadly and gave her a smile meant to dry her tears. "It's a marvel, Rachel. A miracle. *Two* miracles, every day. And I never noticed until it was too late." His gaze swept her up and down, and a deep, unfathomable sadness seeped into him. "There are so *many* things I notice now. When it's too late for any of them."

A sob tore from her throat, and she launched herself at him. He caught her and held her tightly within the circle of his arms. Her breasts flattened against his chest; she tucked her face into the bend of his neck and shoulder. He felt her tears, hot and damp on his skin, and the brush of her breath like a salve to a long open wound.

"It's not too late, Jackson," she whispered and her breath brushed across his throat like a prayer. His arms tightened around her, crushing her to him with an intensity that terrified him. But he was more terrified of letting go. He wanted to believe that she was right. That it wasn't too late. That there still might be a chance, however slight, for him to find a bit of the happiness he'd been denied for too long.

She drew her head back and cupped his jaw with one hand, turning his face to hers until their gazes met and locked. Her blue eyes swam with tears, and it felt as though a giant fist squeezed his chest.

Rachel pulled his head down to hers. When her lips were just a breath away from his, he stopped, listening to the one last, rational thought screaming in the back of his mind. That voice yelled at him to go no further. To walk away from the comfort she offered because it was the right thing to do.

Because he had never done what he should have and now would be a good time to start.

Then she rose up onto her toes and pressed her mouth to his, and the voice was silenced by the thundering of desire pulsing through him.

His lips came down on hers, drawing her sweetness inside him. He tasted her, glorying in the feel of her. The soft, yielding pressure of her mouth, the strength of her hands about his neck. Parting her lips with his tongue, he swept into her warmth, a gentle invasion that stole breath and rocked souls.

She gasped and tightened her hold on him. Her tongue moved along his, inexpertly, yet eagerly. She pressed closer to him until he felt the pebbly hard tips of her nipples as brands searing into his chest.

His hands moved up and down her spine, drawing her tight against him even as his mouth claimed her and his tongue stroked her passions into a fiery blaze.

He tore his lips from hers and raked long, damp kisses along the length of her slender throat. She moaned and tipped her head to one side, silently inviting him to take more of her.

"Jackson," she whispered brokenly, and he felt her pulse point beneath his lips. He lingered there, reveling in the rapid beat of her heart, the hot taste of her skin. He inhaled the faint, flowery scent of her, drawing it deep into his lungs and capturing the memory forever. She shivered in his arms and curled her fingers into his shoulders, holding onto him as if he were the last stable force on earth.

One hand smoothed up her back and around until he cupped one small, perfect breast in his palm. His thumb stroked across the fabric hiding her rigid nipple and she tensed, instinctively arching toward him.

The pain in his groin tripled and tore at him until he wanted nothing more but to bury himself deep inside her and feel her hot, slick body hold him tightly. At that mental image, he groaned her name and returned to claim her mouth once more.

His tongue darted in and out of her heat, in an imitation of the ancient dance he so wanted to share with her. Her hands cupped his face, holding him to her, caressing him until he wanted to shout with the joy of touching and being touched in return.

Rachel gasped again. Lightning-like flashes of something she couldn't name shot through her body. Her toes curled in her shoes, her stomach swarmed with what seemed millions of butterflies, and in one very private place, dampness pooled along with a throbbing, driving ache like she'd never known. She met his tongue stroke for stroke and knew in her heart that this was just the prelude. The beginnings of something more powerful than she'd ever imagined.

Her knees wobbly, she sagged against him, and he caught her up with one strong arm around her back. With his other hand, he continued to stroke her breast with light, gentle touches that only served to make her want a stronger, firmer caress.

Craving air desperately, she pulled her head back from him, shivering in his embrace as need continued to race in her blood.

"Rachel," he groaned her name softly. "Jesus, God, Rachel. You're so sweet. So tempting."

The air she needed refused to come. Her lungs trembled as she fought for breath. His thumb flicked across her nipple, and she groaned aloud, arching her body into his until she felt his rigid body pressing into her abdomen. The damp heat in her center multiplied; her mouth went dry.

She looked into his green eyes and saw that desire had obliterated the pain she'd sought to ease. Everything he'd said, the haunting word pictures he'd painted, had struck a chord inside her. He'd reached her with his pain. His agony of loneliness.

That was something she understood far too well. Something she'd fought against. Something she'd tried to fix by founding her Spinster Society and drawing together friends who suffered the same way. She'd thought she could bury loneliness by creating the family she'd always wanted.

Now, though, she knew that it wouldn't have been enough. There was still Jackson. Without him, she would always be lonely. It was as if he were the other half of her soul. They were interlocking pieces of the same puzzle. Just as her real mother had promised so long ago, *he* was the man she was meant for.

Unless they were together, she knew they would each forever be incomplete.

"Jackson," she managed to whisper and wasn't surprised to hear her voice come low and raw. "I feel so . . ."

"I know, Rachel," he murmured and lifted his hand from her breast to smooth his fingertips along the line of her cheek. "I know."

"I want to feel more. I want to know what it is to be loved."

He ground his teeth together, and the look on his face told her that her words had struck home with the impact of a double-edged knife.

"Rachel," he groaned and eased his hold on her. "We can't. *I* can't."

"Yes you can," she urged him, already afraid she was losing him to cool, reasonable thought. "This was meant, Jackson. From the very beginning, it was meant. All it needed was for me to grow up and be ready."

He smiled at her, but the desire in his eyes had faded to embers. "It was too late for us long ago, Rachel. When we first met, it was too late. When you were a child, I had already been dead for months."

"No," she said, her voice deep with denial. "There was a reason you were sent to me. A reason we met."

His thumb moved gently over her temple. His breathing

had slowed, and she sensed the difference in him. With every moment that passed, he became more in control. And moved farther away from her.

She should never have broken their kiss. She shouldn't have given him time to think.

"Ah, honey, don't start wishing for things that can't be. You'll only be hurt again." His arm dropped from around her waist and she felt its absence keenly. "I don't want to hurt you again, Rachel. Not again."

"Then don't do this," she pleaded and reached up to link her arms around his neck again in a desperate effort to regain what she had already lost. "Don't pull away from me, Jackson. I love you."

He stiffened as if she'd slapped him.

Slowly, gently, he reached up and pulled her arms free. Holding her wrists tenderly, he shook his head. "Don't. Don't love me. Don't want me to stay. Because I won't. And there's nothing either of us can do to change that."

A yawning, black emptiness opened inside her and began to spread. She felt the cold darkness ease into her limbs, crawl through her chest, and blanket her heart with a chill she would never be rid of.

It can't be, she told herself. There had to be a reason they were brought together.

As if he could read her mind, he said, "I'm not the man for you, Rachel." He swallowed heavily, and she felt as well as heard the sorrow in his words. "As much as I might like things to be different, they aren't. I'm only here long enough to see you married."

"You can't still want me to marry someone else?"

His jaw tightened, and a tiny twitch developed at the corner of his eye.

"It has nothing to do with what I want."

"*Or* what I want, apparently."

"It's better this way, Rachel."

"How can *this* be better?" Her voice broke; a sob rose up in her throat.

Weary resignation filled his eyes as he shook his head. "I know you don't want to hear this."

No. No, she did not want to. She wanted to go back. Just five minutes back in time. She would change all of this. She would kiss him hard enough to make him forget their differences. Hard enough to make him believe that he was alive again. That he belonged to her.

"But it's true, nonetheless." He stroked her cheek one last time with the tips of his fingers, then let his hand fall to his side. "If, by some miracle, we *could* stay together, I'd only end up breaking your heart."

The sob tearing at her throat choked off her air.

"I'm gonna take a walk," he said on a heavy sigh. "You go to bed, Rachel. Get some sleep." Reluctantly, he turned away and walked across the room.

She heard him take the steps, and each footfall echoed in the unnaturally loud silence.

He thought he was doing the right thing. He was trying to protect her in some strange, twisted way. She knew that. But what he didn't seem to understand was that he was already breaking her heart.

Two days later, Jackson pounded the last nail into the dance floor, then sat back on his haunches and grinned. It was a damn fine piece of work, if he did say so himself.

"You're really something, boss," Sam said and ran the flat of one hand across the smooth, sanded boards. "How in the heck did you think of those hinges, anyway?"

Jackson shot him a quick look, then glanced to the center of the floor where an almost invisible seam split the floor into two halves. Beneath that seam were three brass hinges. He'd designed the dance floor so that it could be folded in two for easier storage from one year to the next.

Shrugging, he said, "When Tessa told me they wanted

to be able to tuck it away in a barn for next year, I just figured it'd be a lot easier if they could fold it up a bit.''

Sam chuckled. ''You 'just figured.' Nobody else would have thought of it, Jackson.''

''Maybe,'' he said and stood up, taking the time to stretch muscles that ached with fatigue. He'd spent the last couple of days in a frenzy of work, trying to make himself tired enough so he could get to sleep at night.

It hadn't helped.

Even though he'd avoided spending any more time alone with Rachel, memories of those few minutes with her in the dimly lit great room kept him wide awake and tortured. He couldn't forget the feel of her.

The scent of her.

The taste of her.

Hell, he hadn't even been able to think about Lynch and the justice he so wanted to mete out.

Rachel invaded his every thought, and there was no escape.

Actually, there *was* an escape open to him. All he needed to do was find her a man. Then he'd be gone in a heartbeat and have the rest of eternity to concentrate on the agony of not having her with him.

''So,'' Sam asked, interrupting his thoughts, ''you want to get started staining it now?''

Jackson glanced at the cloudy sky above. There were still a couple of hours until nightfall. Plenty of time to get the first coat down. No sense going back to the Mercantile any earlier than he absolutely had to.

''Yeah.'' He nodded to one side. ''The cans and brushes are stacked right over there.''

Sam went to get the supplies, but kept talking as he walked.

''You know, Jackson, I've been thinking.''

He hoped Sam's thoughts were easier to deal with than his own. ''Yeah?''

"I know you said that you wouldn't be staying in Still- water for long."

His chest tightened.

"But I was wondering if maybe you might be willing to change your mind." Sam walked around the new flooring, careful to keep his dirty boots off the surface he'd just finished preparing.

"What are you talking about?" Jackson asked as he took one of the cans and a new paintbrush from the other man.

"Well," Sam said as he pried the lid off his can, picked up a stick and swished it through the dark brown stain slowly. "You know Mavis and I are getting married after church a week from Sunday."

"Since that's all you've talked about for two days, yeah. I know."

Sam grinned at him. "Well, I'm gonna be needing some steady work. Can't be a husband who sits around all day while my wife sews and stitches her little fingers right down to the bone."

Jackson studied the stain in his can as he pushed it around with the stick. Not saying anything, he waited, sure Sam wasn't finished.

He wasn't.

"What I was thinking is," he said eagerly, "you and me could go into business together."

"What?"

"Now hear me out," he waved one hand at Jackson. "Stillwater's growing. And Seattle's not much more than a spit or two away. Good carpenters are hard to come by, you know."

"Sam . . ." He didn't want to hear the other man's plans. It would only make it harder to tell him no. But Sam wasn't slowing down, let alone stopping.

"Listen, Jackson. It would work out fine. The two of us would have more work than we could handle. There's new shops going up every day in Seattle. With the amount of folks arriving all the time, they're gonna need lots of new houses.

"We'd have to expand, hire some men to work for us. With the lumber mills around here, Lord knows there's plenty of supplies!" His dark eyes gleamed with opportunity. "The Territory's growing, Jackson, and we could be a part of it. A big part."

"Sam, I—"

"Don't say no yet. Think about it." Sam picked up his can and headed for the far side of the floor. He sat down there and yanked off his boots. They'd have to work in their socks to avoid dirtying the floor. They would each start in the middle on either side and stain their way across and down the dance floor.

"It would work out, Jackson. I know it would." Sam grinned again. "Hale and Tate, Carpenters." He shrugged and chuckled. "Or, if you'd rather, Tate and Hale. It doesn't matter to me one way or the other."

"Sam, look—"

"Think about it, Jackson. Just think about it. That's all I ask."

Sighing, Jackson tugged his boots off, then picked up the stain and brush and walked to his side of the floor. He glanced at the other man, who whistled happily under his breath.

Just what he needed.

One more thing to think about for the rest of eternity.

Chapter ☆ Fourteen

By early the next morning, Jackson knew that working himself to death wasn't going to cure him of wanting Rachel.

He lay wide awake in bed and listened to her moving around in her room, next to his. Her footsteps sounded quick and light on the plank floor, and he knew by the muffled tone whenever she stepped onto a throw rug. His mind drew images of what she must look like in her nightgown. No doubt, it was a prim, high-necked white cotton thing that covered her from throat to toes. It probably billowed out around her like a tent, hiding any sense of the figure beneath.

That vision should have helped. Instead, his mind toyed with the idea of undressing her with all the joy of a kid unwrapping a Christmas present.

But what would he know about that? Growing up as he had, Christmas had been just another day. One year, he'd actually sneaked over to his friend's house and peered in through the window to watch the holiday goings on. He could remember the ache he'd felt to be able to tear into the pretty wrappings—just once. But he'd known even then that none of that finery was meant for him.

This thinking about Rachel was that same ache all over

again. Only the pain went deeper. Hit harder.

Her hair was most likely messy and rumpled from sleep—unless she wore it in one long braid for nighttime. In which case, he told himself, when it was undone and combed through, there would be rippling waves of honey laying across the white fabric shielding her shoulders and breasts.

Jackson winced, ground his teeth together, and yanked the flat pillow out from beneath his head to slam it down over his face. He flung his arms across it, pinning the goose feather thing down over his ears. If he could shut out the sound of her, perhaps it would shut off the thought of her.

Several minutes passed before he admitted defeat.

Grumbling under his breath, he sat up abruptly, tossed the pillow to the end of the bed, and got to his feet. Apparently, he didn't *have* to hear her for his brain to torture him with images of her.

Jackson grabbed up his clothes from the chair near the bed and tugged them on. Shirt hanging open over his bare chest, he pulled his jeans on and cursed in a vicious whisper when he was forced to tug his button fly closed across his aching erection.

Blast it, this was no way for anybody to have to live— man *or* ghost.

Next door, Rachel's voice drifted to him as she sang softly to herself.

His body throbbed in response.

"Enough's enough," he grumbled and hopped on first one foot, then the other, to pull his boots on. Then, not even bothering to button his shirt, he stomped out of the room, down the hall to the stairs, which he took at a run.

Work wasn't going to make him forget about Rachel and his need for her. That wasn't the kind of activity he needed. Today, he would prove that by quitting work early, leaving Sam on his own. What Jackson needed was a willing woman with a warm body.

He'd been celibate, too long, obviously. An hour or two with a practiced whore would take care of what ailed him. Then he could keep his mind on the job at hand.

By the time he reached the street and started toward the new house, he already felt better.

At lunch recess, Hester Sutton sat at her desk, going over her students' papers. From outside came the muted sounds of the children playing. Laughter, shouts, and a nonsensical song to jump rope by drifted in through the open windows. But she only half heard them. In truth, she wasn't really concentrating on her work, either.

A soft smile crossed her face briefly as she remembered the night before.

For more than two hours, she and Charlie Miller had sat together in the porch swing in front of her house for all the world to see. Of course, they'd both been perfectly proper. Hester had made sure there was at least five inches of space between them on the swing. Charlie had held her hand gently, as if she were made of some fine, fragile china, and Hester had never known such magic.

If she closed her eyes, she could almost feel the gentle swaying motion of the swing. She could hear Charlie's deep voice as he talked about work and his plans for the future.

She sighed and laid her pencil on the desktop. It had been a nearly perfect evening. The only thing that could have made it better would have been a kiss. Surprised at her own forwardness, Hester sat up straight and flushed guiltily.

"Miss Sutton?"

A thin, young voice shattered her daydream, and Hester reluctantly let it go to focus on the little girl standing in front of her desk.

She hadn't even heard the child come inside.

Molly Beaker, ten years old with knobby knees, red

braids, and a splash of freckles across her tiny nose, waited patiently.

"Yes Molly," Hester said with a smile. "What is it?"

The girl ducked her head and a flush of deep scarlet rushed up her neck to her cheeks. "My ma says to tell you that we can't get no more paper for school 'till next month, maybe."

"Any more paper," Hester corrected quietly.

"Yes ma'am, *any* more."

The girl was still looking at her shoes and so missed the sadness that briefly tinged Hester's smile. Molly's mother, a widow, was the cook at a lumber camp outside of town. With three children, the woman did the very best she could, but money was a hard thing to stretch.

Her heart ached for the little girl. Hester remembered quite clearly the sharp sting of humiliation and knew from experience that children suffered more greatly with such things than adults. She could still recall being the only girl in school who didn't have shoes until she was nearly twelve.

Old pain bubbled up, simmered, then slipped into memory where it belonged. Her parents had done what they could. There simply hadn't been enough money to care for ten kids.

Reaching into the deep, bottom desk drawer, Rachel pulled out three Indian Chief paper tablets from the supply she kept for just such emergencies. Quietly, she'd made it her business to see that no child did without if she could help it. When she offered the tablets to Molly, though, the girl glanced up, shook her head, and took a step back.

"Oh, no, ma'am," she whispered. "We couldn't be taking charity. That wouldn't sit well with ma at all. But I thank you anyhow."

Pride.

A wonderful thing, especially in a child.

"Why Molly," Hester drew her head back and affected

a look of utter surprise. "I wouldn't *dream* of offering you charity."

"You wouldn't?" Two wide, blue eyes grew even wider.

"Of course not." Hester set the tablets on the edge of the desk, within reach of the girl who could barely take her eyes off them. "I was going to ask you to do me a great favor."

"You were?"

"You see," Hester explained gently, "I'm not sure at all if I prefer these tablets or another kind for schoolwork. I was hoping that perhaps you and your little sisters wouldn't mind using these and letting me know what you think."

Molly reached up and chewed at one small fingertip. Hester knew that feeling well. In times of worry, she had been known to gnaw at her own fingers until they bled. Although, she admitted silently, she hadn't been chewing them at all, lately.

"Then," she added, "when these tablets are used up, I'd like to give you each one of the other tablets. So you could compare the two and tell me which is best."

By the time the girls finished with the second tablet, school would be out for the summer break.

"So we would kind of be working for you, huh?"

"Oh yes," Hester said softly. "This is a very important study."

"We could do that," the girl said softly and reached one hand for the precious paper. "I think ma would understand."

"Thank you so much, Molly," Hester said. "It will be a great help to me."

The girl's fingers curled around the stack of tablets, and she tucked them carefully to her chest. "We'll pay real good attention, Miss Sutton, and tell you honest which one's better."

"I know I can count on you, Molly." She nodded solemnly. "And be sure to tell your mother how much I appreciate your help."

"Oh I will, ma'am." Molly gave her teacher a wide grin and backed away. "She'll be proud that you asked us."

Hester nodded again. "Good. Now, you had better go and eat your lunch, Molly. Recess will be over shortly."

"Yes ma'am." The child scuttled down the aisle, ducked behind the cloakroom door, and disappeared from sight.

Hester stood up, stepped off the raised platform where her desk sat, and walked to one of the bank of windows lining each side of the small building. Leaning against the window sash, Hester watched the children playing, her mind drifting with the soft spring breeze that slipped into the room.

"That was a kind thing," a deep, familiar voice said, causing Hester's heartbeat to race wildly.

Slowly, she turned around to watch Charlie Miller walk up the center aisle of the schoolhouse toward her. His hair neatly combed, he held his hat in one hand, while the other hand he kept hidden behind his back. He wore a freshly washed red and black checked shirt, black pants, and his knee-high leather boots had been polished to a high sheen.

He looked wonderful.

Immediately, Hester took note of her own appearance. Something she hadn't even bothered with much until the last few days. Inwardly groaning, she wished she had worn her soft blue dress to school today. Instead, she wore a serviceable gray gown that was now liberally coated with chalk dust. Her fingers were inkstained and her hair was scraped back into her usual no-nonsense topknot.

She must look an absolute vision.

What a disheartening thing it was to know that the man you were sweet on was so much better looking than yourself.

Charlie's heart swelled inside his barrel chest until he thought it might burst. She was such a fine lady, he told himself. So kind. Gentle. Just looking into her pale blue eyes made him wish and hope for things that he knew were well beyond his reach. Why would a lovely woman—with more book learning than he could imagine—be interested in someone like him?

The fistful of wildflowers and apple blossoms he held behind his back now seemed silly. Not nearly good enough.

Not for her.

"I'm sorry," Hester said softly. "What did you say?"

He cleared his throat because it felt like his collar was strangling him. "I said, that was a kind thing you did, for the girl."

"Oh." She flushed and a deep rose color flooded her cheeks, making her even more beautiful to him. "I didn't know there was anyone else here."

He took one step closer, forcing his big clumsy feet to move. "That's part of what made it so kind." Scowling at himself for being as awkward with words as he was with his feet, he went on. "I mean, you done something nice for her. Kind. And you didn't do it so everybody would think well of you."

"I would never do that," she said, stunned.

Damn, he had known he would make a mess of this. Now he'd gone and offended her. He took another step, kicked a desk, and knocked it into the one beside it. Some child's papers slid off the tilted surface and spilled onto the floor.

"Ah . . ." Miserable, he shook his head, then bent down to grab them up at the same time she hurried forward to help. He smacked his forehead into hers, and they both straightened abruptly.

Tears welled up in her eyes as she rubbed her forehead gingerly. Charlie felt like a fool. He'd only come to . . . hell, he wasn't even sure now why he'd come. But it was for sure that he'd do better to leave quick before he did something else humiliating.

"I'm sure sorry, Miss Hester," he said and started backing up. "I didn't meant tò make a mess, or," he waved one huge hand at her, "to hurt you."

Hester closed the space separating them, the growing knot on her head forgotten. He was leaving. Already.

"It was my fault," she said quickly. "I stepped right into your way without thinking."

"Oh, no, ma'am," Charlie answered. "You didn't do nothing. It was me. Always is. Just clumsy, is all." He tossed a look over his shoulder, then glanced back at her. "I better be going, Miss Hester. I've got to get back to work, and you got school and all . . ."

His voice trailed away and Hester didn't even stop to wonder why it was that around him she didn't feel shy at all. Instead, she only asked, "Why did you stop by, Charlie? Was there something you wanted?"

He winced as if in pain.

Immediately, Hester worried. Something must be dreadfully wrong. He looked so out of sorts. Stepping in close, she touched his arm and looked up into his eyes. She saw him glance down at her hand, then held her breath as he looked into her eyes.

"Might as well say what I come to say, I guess." From behind his back, he pulled out a huge bouquet of snow white apple blossoms and clusters of blue and pink wildflowers. She didn't know why she hadn't detected their delightful scent before this. Now, it seemed to fill the tiny schoolhouse.

"Oh my," she whispered as she took the flowers from him. Almost to herself, she said softly, "I've never received flowers from a gentleman before."

Fools, he told himself. Most men were fools. But he wasn't, by thunder. The word *gentleman* echoed in his brain. He straightened a bit in response. Did she really think him a gentleman? And if she did, would she maybe be willing to think of him as something more? Something maybe permanent?

Taking heart from her words and the way she kept touching the fragile blossoms she held to her breasts, he blurted out the reason for his visit.

"Miss Hester," he said the words he'd practiced for hours the night before. "Would you do me the honor of going with me to the town social?"

Silence dropped over them like an old, familiar blanket. Soft and warm and comforting, this silence held no threat, no reproach.

She stared up at him and slowly, a smile curved her lips. "I would like that very much."

Practiced speeches and worries forgotten, Charlie took his cue from the look in her pale eyes and spoke from his heart.

"I think real highly of you, Miss Hester."

She gasped, and her eyes widened.

"Would you be interested . . . I mean, do you think maybe someday you might . . ." Charlie reached up and shoved one hand through his hair. A terrible thing to be so tongue-tied over something as important as this.

"Yes, Charlie?" she asked and again as he looked into those eyes of hers. The eyes that had haunted his dreams and touched his soul.

He made one more try at sounding more intelligent than a stump.

"Do you think you might want to someday . . . I mean, I would be honored if you might one day let me be your . . . beau?"

She inhaled sharply, and he waited to find out if that meant yes or no. Thankfully, he didn't have long to wait.

"I would be honored, Charlie."

Pleasure, richer and deeper than any he had ever known before, welled up inside him. It filled his chest and made him stand even taller than usual.

Slowly, carefully, he bent his head down toward hers. Hester leaned in, still clutching her bouquet to her chest. The heady scent of apple blossoms surrounded them as their lips met in a brief, chaste kiss that tasted of promises.

When he straightened up again, he smiled down at her, then reached out to gently cradle her cheek in his palm. The warmth of his touch speared into her, and Hester felt it dissolve the shadow of loneliness that she'd lived with most of her life.

"Will you take a walk with me this evening, *Hester?*"

"Yes, Charlie."

He smiled again, this time grinning.

"And would you take supper with me at the restaurant?"

"I'd like that," she said. "Thank you for the flowers, too. They're so beautiful."

His thumb lovingly traced the curve of her cheekbone as he vowed, "I will always give you flowers, Hester. And they will never be as beautiful as you."

A film of tears shimmered in her eyes as she stepped into the circle of his arms. Charlie rested his chin on the top of her head and held her carefully, his big hands moving lightly up and down her back. For the first time in a long time, he didn't feel awkward and he knew just what to say.

"I love you, Hester."

By the time Jackson reached the saloon, it was late afternoon and he was fit to be tied. Rachel's image refused to leave his mind, and his body refused to quit responding.

On his way down the street, he'd had to pass the Mercantile. He'd kept his gaze locked straight ahead of him, yet somehow he'd sensed Rachel watching him as he strode past the windows. A flash of guilt had lanced through him, as if she had known exactly where he was headed and why.

Guilt, for God's sake.

Why should he feel guilty for going to visit one of the

fancy women? He didn't *owe* Rachel anything. She wasn't his wife.

His steps staggered a bit at that thought, then he determinedly kept on. Wife. Soon enough, she would be a wife. Though someone else's. He didn't even want to think about why he didn't like the sound of *that.*

Jackson paused outside the batwing doors for a moment and stared over their tops into the darkened saloon. A whiff of tobacco drifted out to him on the wings of cheap perfume and stale whiskey. As he stood there, the piano player started up, and it sounded to Jackson like the man was playing with his elbows.

But he hadn't gone to the saloon to listen to the music.

He swiveled his head and looked back up the street toward the Mercantile. And Rachel. The fact that he would rather be there with her was enough to spur him on. Giving one of the half doors a shove, he stepped into a room that was all too familiar.

Oh, it wasn't The Black Hound. But most western saloons, but for the rare, elegant types, were pretty much the same. Dark, a little on the scroungy side, with loud music, strong whiskey, and willing women.

Of course, he thought as he paused inside the door to let his gaze adjust to the dimness, this place also had Noble Lynch.

His guts twisted, and he welcomed it. Anything was better than the sick pup feeling he'd been having about Rachel the last couple of days. With any luck, he could have himself a woman and later, prod Noble into a fight where he, Jackson, could beat the crap out of the gambler.

Shadows took shape, the piano player started sounding better, and the bartender looked up at him with a hopeful nod.

"What'll it be, mister?"

To reach the bar, Jackson had to thread his way through the scarred, shaky tables sprinkled around the room. Once there, he slapped his palm onto the bar top and ordered, "Whiskey."

As the other man picked up a bottle and poured him a drink, Jackson dipped into his pants pocket. He pulled out a handful of change and one of the gold coins. The bartender's sharp eye landed on it like an eagle picking out a fat rabbit in the middle of a meadow.

"Here now," he sighed and made as if to grab it up. "What's this?"

Jackson shook his head, picked up the coin, and dropped it into his shirt pocket for the moment. "None of your business," he said and laid a fifty-cent piece down on the water-stained bar top. Grabbing up his drink, he tossed it down his throat, slammed the empty glass back down, and ordered, "Fill it."

While he waited, Jackson looked around the room. Just a sprinkling of customers sat at the tables scattered around the building.

And not one of the men was Noble Lynch.

Like most predators, though, he probably preferred to show himself at night. Still, this visit wasn't a waste, Jackson thought as his gaze landed on a bosomy woman with thick black hair, milky white calves, and a red rouged mouth just ripe for kissing.

Kitty wore a white chemise, a red corset, and tight white pantaloons. He gestured to her, and she hurried over. Jackson watched her full, heavy breasts sway with each step as she approached him and waited for a surge of desire to swamp him.

Nothing.

What the hell was wrong with him?

Grumbling to himself, he draped one arm around Kitty's shoulders and pulled her tight against him. Her practiced hands moved over his chest and belly with a bored disinterest that wasn't helping at all.

Still, he was determined to do this. To take this woman

to bed and bury himself so deeply inside her that he wouldn't be able to see Rachel's face in his mind anymore.

Picking up his drink, he swallowed it quickly, tossed a dollar onto the bar, and grabbed the half empty bottle. Then, with one hand laying casually on the woman's breast, he said, "All right honey, let's go upstairs."

Rachel stood on the boardwalk for several long moments, hoping to see Jackson come right back out of that saloon. When he didn't, she finally gave up and went into the store.

Why did he go there? To see Lynch? To get drunk again?

She closed the door and leaned against it. It didn't matter that she told herself not to care why he'd gone to the Golden Garter.

She did.

"No use," Jackson muttered and stomped, pacing around Kitty's cluttered bedroom. He threw her a glance and shook his head solemnly. Definitely something wrong with him, he told himself as his gaze moved over the bored, nearly naked woman lying in bed filing her nails.

The rasp of her nail file irritated him, but he couldn't blame her.

She'd been willing.

Ready.

The problem was *him*.

He'd looked at those full breasts and imagined them to be smaller, firmer. He'd run his fingers through her long curly black hair and pictured it silky straight and the color of honey. He'd looked into her chocolate brown eyes and saw blue eyes, filled with reproach, looking back at him.

Disgusted, he dropped down into the nearest chair, braced his elbows on his knees, and cupped his head in his hands.

Not only didn't he want to crawl into bed with Kitty, he

didn't even feel like getting drunk. What the hell was the world coming to, anyway?

As he stared blindly into the darkness of his cupped palms, he heard the bedsprings shriek, then footsteps behind him. One corner of his brain asked: *When did Kitty put on a pair of boots?*

But then pain exploded in the back of his head, stars shot through the darkness, and he was tumbling forward onto the floor.

"He put it in his shirt pocket, honey," Kitty whispered. "I saw him do it."

Noble Lynch tucked the polished toe of his elegant boot beneath Jackson's ribs and flipped the insensible man over onto his back. "Where would someone like him get a gold coin?"

"I don't know, honey," Kitty shrugged her shoulders, and her heavy breasts shifted and swayed with the movement. "Is he the one says he knows you?"

"Yes." Noble studied the man's features for several seconds, then shook his head. "But from where?" he muttered, more to himself than to the woman.

"You really don't remember?"

One eyebrow arched high on his forehead. Wryly, he said, "May lightning strike me dead if I'm lying."

She nodded solemnly, and Noble wanted to laugh at her obvious adoration. But he didn't. Kitty wasn't his dream woman by any means, but even *she* was better than sleeping alone.

"Noble, honey, you want me to get the coin for you?"

He nodded. "Get it."

Kitty dropped to her hands and knees, stuffed her fingers into Jackson's shirt pocket, and pulled out the golden coin she'd noticed earlier. She turned it over and over in her hands, admiring the dull gleam of gold and the intricate drawings on the coin itself. "Sure is pretty," she whispered.

"Yes, it is," Noble said with a look at the fallen man.

Glancing up at the man she still couldn't believe wanted to spend every night in her well used bed, Kitty watched him study the coin carefully before tucking it into his vest pocket.

"An unusual piece," he said. "I believe I'll make a watch fob of it. Keep it for luck."

"You want me to go through the rest of his pockets?"

Noble leaned down and helped her to her feet. "Let's not be greedy, Kitty my love," he said. Then he shot a quick, thoughtful look at the man lying on the floor, arms outstretched. "Besides, how much more could he have?

Idly, he traced his fingertips across her rigid nipples. When she shuddered, he felt a flutter of interest leap into life inside him. "Kitty dear," he said and dropped one hand to her crotch. "This hour of your time is already paid for, let us not waste it, eh?"

Her head lolled back on her neck as his nimble fingers found the slit in her drawers. Moaning softly, she asked, "What about him?"

Noble chuckled and dipped one finger into her warmth. Her surprisingly strong inner muscles clamped down on him and beads of sweat broke out on his upper lip as he bent to draw his tongue across one nipple. Her hands clutched at his shoulders, and her hips rocked against his hand.

Need rose up in him and as it did, he forgot about Rachel's troublemaking cousin.

"He won't be waking up any time soon," Noble said and steered his companion backward toward the rumpled bed. "We can toss him out when we've finished."

"Anything you say, honey," she murmured and flopped back onto the mattress, spreading her thighs in open invitation.

Hurriedly, Noble fumbled with the fly of his pants, freed himself, then drove into her. The unconscious man on the floor receded from his mind as Kitty's body squeezed him dry.

Chapter ☆ Fifteen

Water sloshed over his face, and Jackson sat up, sputtering.

Pain blossomed behind his eyes, and he groaned aloud.

"What are you doing sitting in my alley?"

A female voice, indignant.

Carefully, he turned his head to look at her. A tall woman, too thin for her size, with medium brown hair and raw, red hands fisted on her narrow hips stood in an open doorway glaring at him. Her face was flushed and wisps of damp hair clung to her forehead and cheeks. Steam rushed out of the room behind her like smoke from the fires of Hell.

"Who are you?" he asked.

She reached up and wiped her sweaty brow with the back of one hand. "I'd say that's *my* question to be asking you."

He squirmed uncomfortably in his soggy clothes and pulled his hands free of the muck beneath him. "Jackson Tate," he muttered. "You the one who threw water on me?"

"Yeah," she said and leaned one shoulder against the doorjamb. "But I didn't know you were there. Just tossing out the dirty wash water."

"Wonderful," he grumbled under his breath.

"Jackson, huh?" she asked. "Then you'd be Rachel's cousin?"

"That's right." The lie seemed easy now. "Who are you?"

"Sally Wiley."

Information about the woman poured into his mind and seemed to increase the painful throbbing. Friend of Rachel's. A member of the Spinster Society. No family. Stubborn. Independent.

A woman too much like Rachel for comfort.

Where were all the weepy, weak women he'd known when he was alive?

"Sorry I about drowned you," she said. "But why were you taking a nap in my alley?"

He glanced at the sky, surprised to see twilight gathering. How long had he been lying in the dirt, unconscious? And who had dumped him in the alley?

Reaching up, he felt a hard, sizable knot on the back of his skull. Wincing as his fingers explored it, Jackson tried to think. What was the last thing he remembered?

Then it came to him.

In a blinding flash of humiliation.

He'd been with one of the fancy women and hadn't been able to do a damned thing. His eyes slid shut on another groan. For the first time ever, his equipment had failed him. But it wasn't really a failure, he thought. Everything would have been fine if he had been with Rachel.

Jesus, he was in serious trouble.

"So," Sally asked, a laugh in her voice. "You planning on getting up any time soon, or are you just gonna sit in the muck for a while yet?"

He slanted her a look, then pushed himself to his feet. As he did, he kept thinking. Kitty hadn't hit him over the head. He vaguely remembered her stretched out on the unused bed filing her nails.

Footsteps.

His gaze narrowed as he stared blankly at the muddy ground. He'd heard footsteps. Someone in boots. A man.

Lynch.

A vicious, churning anger swelled in the pit of his stomach, and Jackson had to bite back the urge to howl in fury. He didn't know why he was so sure of his assailant. But he was.

He could feel it.

"You all right?"

Jackson shifted his gaze to the woman in the doorway. Her expression altered slightly, and he knew she was reacting to the anger that was no doubt etched into his features. Deliberately, he forced his still building temper into a dark corner inside him and somehow managed a smile.

She relaxed visibly.

"I'm fine," he said with a shrug. "Just wet."

"Well," Sally offered, "come on inside. Maybe I can find you something to wear."

"Don't bother. I'll just go home."

He caught himself, and his jaw snapped shut.

The word had slipped out. He hadn't even thought about it.

The Mercantile.

Rachel.

Home.

Oh Lord.

"Come on in anyway," Sally insisted. "I can at least give you a cup of coffee."

He accepted. Not so much because he wanted the coffee, but because it would put off, for a little while at least, having to face Rachel.

Sally's coffee would put hair on a newborn's chest, he told himself later. But it had been just what he'd needed. The ache in his head had faded to a livable, but uncomfortable, roar and even his clothes had dried a bit. He only half listened to the woman's conversation, as he studied her place of business.

Stacks of clean, folded laundry lined one wall. A bare counter stood at the front of the shop, and behind it were several barrels, sawn in half to make tubs that were full of clothes, in various stages of completion. Some were soaking in cold water, others sat in tubs with steam lifting off the water to cloud the still air.

Jackson plucked at the front of his shirt and wiped his forehead with his sleeve. He looked at Sally, bent over a cast-iron kettle that sat atop one of two stoves in the rear of the shop, with her face beet red from the hot steam rising. She used a stick to stir the clothes churning in the boiling water.

How the devil did she stand it?

The damp heat in the laundry made him want to tear his shirt off and run into the cool of the evening. Yet there she was, moving from kettle to tub and back again. As she reached into one of the barrels, he noticed her hands again.

Cracked and raw, they looked painful, yet she didn't seem affected. While she talked—about the town, Rachel and her friends—Sally's poor hands scrubbed, twisted, and wrung the clothes before turning to hang them on a series of ropes strung across the opposite wall.

Jackson's eyebrows lifted. At least in this heat, the wet clothes would dry fast.

Someone stepped into the laundry, and Jackson turned to look at the big, red-headed man with an armful of dirty laundry clutched to his chest.

"O'Hara?" Sally said loudly and dropped a shirt back into the water before stomping her way to the front counter. "What are you doin' back here already?"

Mike O'Hara sent a quick look in Jackson's direction, then obviously decided to ignore him. "Ah, Sally darlin'," the rolling brogue of an Irishman smoothed through the room. "I've only stopped by to drop off a few more of me things."

"Great God Almighty," she said. "You mean to tell me you have *more* dirty laundry?"

"It's a rough life on my ranch, Sally love," the man said quickly, then added, "but a good one."

"You're either the cleanest or the dirtiest man I ever met, O'Hara," she snapped.

Jackson hid a smile as he watched the dark-haired woman glare up at the tall man in front of her. His grin slipped a bit, though, as knowledge about the redhead flooded his mind.

Damn. He still hadn't gotten used to it, that instant sense of *knowing* someone he'd never seen before. Struggling to sift through the information, he kept one eye on the oblivious pair and tried to listen.

"Y'know, Sally," the man said, "I've often thought of maybe having you out to the ranch for supper one night."

The too thin woman grabbed up the dirty clothes he'd dropped onto the counter. Both arms full of his latest offering, she glared at him over the top of the heap. "And just when would I have time to be doing that?"

"Even you have to eat," the big man snapped impatiently. "Though from the look of ya," he went on, raking his gaze up and down her form, "ya don't do it often enough."

She drew herself up and sniffed at him. "I don't have to eat with a man so dirty he can't go two days without dragging in a load of clothes to my laundry!"

"Dirty, is it?" Mike jerked his head back to glare at her and planted two ham-like fists on his hips. "If I was dirty, I wouldn't be wantin' my clothes washed, now would I?"

"And if you were clean, I wouldn't be lookin' at your Irish face three and more times a week, would I?"

Jackson shook his head. He hadn't seen this side of the woman until Mike O'Hara stopped by. Was she this way with all of her customers? Instantly, the answer reared up in his mind. No. Just with O'Hara. A good thing too, he thought. If she talked to all of the people who came to her shop as she did the redhead, she wouldn't have *had* a business.

"Now go on, O'Hara," she told the man, waving the tips of her dry, cracked fingers at him. "Get about your business, and let me tend to mine."

Muttering under his breath, the man turned and stomped out of the laundry, slapping his hat against his jean-covered thigh as he went.

"Thanks for the coffee, Sally," Jackson said and set his cup down on the counter. "I'll be going, now."

She didn't even look up. Grumbling to herself, she dropped the new load of laundry onto the floor, gave it a kick, and said, "Goodbye Jackson. Say hello to Rachel."

Outside, he stopped to watch the big man standing in the street. With his head tipped back, he stared at the darkening sky and muttered something unintelligible.

"What was that?" Jackson asked.

The man turned, startled, then glowered at him. "Nothin'."

"Couldn't quite make it out."

"T'was Gaelic," he said, then shrugged. "Irish."

"Ah," Jackson nodded slowly, "Cursing her, were you?"

O'Hara took a single, long step toward him, shook his hat at the laundry, and complained. "That woman has a tongue like a viper!"

"I heard."

"She's a temper on her that makes a man want to run for the hills."

Jackson folded his arms across his chest, leaned back against a porch railing, and observed, "I don't see you running anywhere."

"Aye well," the rusty-haired man slammed his hat onto his head. "I'm a glutton for punishment."

"Or for the punisher."

O'Hara's gaze shot to his. His affable features suddenly looked harder. "And if that's so, what's it to you?" He stepped even closer, looking Jackson up and down as if judging how well he'd do in a fight. "I warn ya now. If you've ideas about Sally, you best let them go. I'm going to have that woman as me own."

Holding up both hands in mock surrender, Jackson laughed. "I'm not your problem, O'Hara. It looked to me like the lady doesn't want to be had by you."

"Don't I know it," the man grumbled and tossed another look into the laundry.

"Would you mind a little advice?"

"It couldn't hurt to listen."

"Quit dragging in laundry."

" 'Tis me only excuse to see her, man." O'Hara frowned at him. "You've no idea just what hard work it is to dirty enough clothes to warrant three or four trips to town a week."

Jackson rubbed his eyes and shook his head. "You're trying to court her by working her to death?"

"You think I *like* knowing that I'm forcing her poor, hurt hands back into hot water and lye soap?" O'Hara's mouth tightened at the thought.

"Then why do you do it?"

"Blast you to the devil and back, you heard me offer her supper. She won't have me."

That last statement had cost him, Jackson saw. The man had pride. Just no sense about women.

Too bad, he thought, that his problem with Rachel couldn't be solved as easily as this one. "Instead of bringing her work, bring her gifts."

Mike O'Hara scowled more fiercely, stared off down the street, and muttered, "Like what? I've no idea how to court a girl like Sally.'' He risked a quick look at Jackson, then added, ''I've been too busy workin' most of me life to do any wooin'.''

''You've come to the right man.'' Jackson slapped the other man on the shoulder. If anyone knew how to avoid work and flirt with the ladies, it was him. Maybe having been a wastrel when alive would finally be a help to him. ''Bring her flowers you picked yourself,'' he offered. ''Go to the Mercantile and buy her chocolates, or some sweet smelling perfume, or some lotion for her hands. There's ladies hats or a pretty shawl, a nice pair of gloves . . .''

The list went on and on. As Jackson talked, O'Hara nodded thoughtfully, already making plans. There was no way he could know it, of course, but Jackson knew very well that O'Hara had a good chance of success. Sally might bicker and bellow, but there was a soft spot inside her for the big Irishman.

''I'll do it,'' Mike said softly. ''By Saint Patrick's staff, I'll convince that hardheaded, sharp-tongued female that she belongs with me, or I'll die tryin'.''

Still muttering to himself, he swung aboard his horse and only then did he say, ''My thanks, friend. If all goes well, I'll invite you to the weddin'.''

Jackson nodded and watched him ride away with a new sense of determination. Envy streaked through him. Mike. Sam. Hell, even Noble Lynch had what Jackson didn't.

Life.

She was sweeping the boardwalk in front of the store when he stopped just a foot or two from her. Slowly, Rachel lifted her eyes from his muddy boots to his dirt-splattered jeans, over his still damp shirt to his face. Her gaze locked with his, and something in her chest turned over.

She suspected it was her heart.

''What happened to you?'' she asked and silently congratulated herself on keeping her voice steady.

"It's a long story."

"Does this story involve Noble Lynch?"

His eyes narrowed slightly. "What makes you say that?"

"I saw you go into the saloon earlier."

He looked away from her. "I didn't go there to see him."

Small consolation, she told herself. There were only two other reasons he would have gone to the saloon. To get drunk or to find a woman.

He reached up and rubbed the back of his head, wincing slightly.

"What happened?" she asked, concern momentarily erasing her other worries.

"Somebody hit me over the head and tossed me in the alley," he grumbled, obviously ashamed to admit it. "Then your friend, Sally, emptied her wash water on me."

"Are you all right?" she asked. "Who did it? Why?"

"Yes. I don't know. And again, I don't know." He scowled fiercely and pushed one hand through his hair. "Damn, I'm getting tired of saying that."

"Were you robbed?" Rachel demanded, leaning her broom against the wall and stepping closer.

Jackson snorted a short laugh. "I don't have anything worth . . ." His eyes widened, and he shoved one hand into his pants pocket. Quickly, he drew it out again and looked down at the handful of change on his palm. One golden coin gleamed dully.

"You had two left, didn't you?"

"Yeah." Worry tightened his features, then he sighed, in relief as memory flooded back to him. He'd slipped the other coin into his shirt pocket just before going upstairs with Kitty. Quickly, he reached into that pocket. His face fell. "It's gone."

"What do you mean?"

Her voice sounded far away as he swallowed a groan of disgust. Christ, was nothing going to go right for him?

Jackson remembered clearly the greedy look in the bartender's eyes when he'd spotted that coin. The man had seen Jackson stick the coin in his shirt pocket. So had Kitty. He rubbed his eyes tiredly and told her, "I stuck one of the coins in this pocket, and now it's gone."

"Maybe it fell out when you were thrown into the alley."

"Yeah, maybe." But he didn't think so. The way his luck was running, he figured the chances were slim. Still, it was worth a look. Grumbling, he spun about and headed down the boardwalk with Rachel hot on his heels.

Jumbled thoughts cartwheeled through his mind, one on top of the other. How could he have been stupid enough to lose one of his last two coins? And what would happen to him once Lesley found out? That notion reared up in his brain and almost stopped him cold. No doubt, Lesley already knew about it.

What was it he'd told Rachel not long ago? That he'd always run from the messes he'd made? He'd never stuck around to clean them up . . . to right wrongs . . . well damn it, maybe it was time he started.

When they reached the alleyway between the saloon and the laundry, they separated, each of them searching one side of the narrow passage. Jackson kicked at rubbish as he stalked up and down the alley, his gaze moving over the ground relentlessly. Rachel moved the toes of her shoes across the dirt, straining to see the tell tale gleam of gold.

But there was nothing.

A short, sharp wind whipped down the alley, lifting trash and sending it tumbling along the ground. The door to the laundry was closed, and the silence surrounding them grew until it was suffocating. Shadows crept closer, twilight deepened, and the first stars appeared overhead.

Finally, Jackson faced her.

"It's not here." Shaking his head gingerly, he added, "Whoever hit me's probably got the coin."

"And you think it was Noble."

"Damn right I do."

"If it was, don't we have to try to get the coin back?" Rachel took a step toward him. "What if he says the wrong thing while holding it? Anything could happen."

"I guess it's too much to hope for that he'd wish himself to Hell."

"Jackson,"

"I know. I'll think of something." He took her elbow and guided her back to the mouth of the alley. "I can't go and say, 'You know that coin you stole from me is magic, so be careful.' "

"But—"

"But nothing," he snapped. "Whatever I do, you're out of it. I don't want you anywhere near Lynch."

Rachel pulled her arm free and looked up at him. "That's not for you to say, Jackson."

"This isn't something I'm going to fight about with you." He sucked in an impatient breath and said, more calmly this time, "I know Lynch. You don't."

"But—"

"Blast it, Rachel, *I'm* the ghost, here. He can't hurt me any more than he already has."

"He wouldn't hurt me," she argued. "He wouldn't dare."

"You don't have any idea what he would dare."

A long, tense moment passed before she nodded slowly. "All right, Jackson. I'll stay out of it. For now."

"If that's as good a promise as I'm likely to get," he muttered, taking her arm again and heading them toward the street, "then I'll take it."

Close beside him, Rachel thought she caught a whiff of the lingering traces of perfume. She shot him a look from the corner of her eye. Had he been with a woman at the saloon? An ache settled in her chest and pulsed in time with her heartbeat. Had she been so wrong about his interest in her? Hadn't the kiss they'd shared meant anything to him?

As they stepped onto the boardwalk in the deep, lavender haze of twilight, they heard a man's voice shouting over the thunder of a horse galloping at a dead run.

Up and down the street, doors were opened, curtains were drawn back, and windows were lifted. Slashes of lamplight made broad strokes in the dirt, and people called questions to each other.

"What on earth?" Rachel whispered.

Finally, the rider drew his lathered horse to a rearing stop. He jumped off the animal, stood in a splash of golden light, and shouted. "I did it! Hellfire, if I didn't do it!"

"Do what, you fool?" a voice yelled.

The man turned in a slow circle, looking from face to face in the growing dusk. As his gaze swept across Rachel and Jackson, she heard her companion groan.

Before she could ask what was wrong, the stranger shouted again. "I found the damned mother lode, that's what!" He threw his arms wide, let his head drop back on his neck, and crowed to the deep purple sky, "I'm *rich!*"

Jackson's grip on her elbow tightened, and he drew her away from the crowd of people spilling out of their houses to hear the man's story.

"Where are we going?" she asked, looking back over her shoulder.

"Home."

"But why? This is exciting. Don't you want to hear how he did it?"

Jackson shot her a quick look. "I *know* how he did it."

She dug her heels in and yanked back on her arm until he was forced to stop. He rubbed the back of his neck viciously.

"How did he do it, Jackson?"

He looked at her, then let his gaze slide to one side. "He's the one."

"The one what?"

"The drunk I traded that coin to on the first night I was here."

She gasped, glanced back, and peered into the growing darkness at the man surrounded by well wishers. "You mean—"

"Yeah. He found the mother lode because of that gold coin."

"Oh my."

Jackson inhaled sharply, then blew it out in a rush. When she turned around to look at him, he was staring at the sky, scowling in disgust.

"Thanks for your help," he snapped. "Those coins work on the prospector. On Sam. Hell, they even made *me* disappear when Rachel wished it. Would you mind letting one of 'em work *for* me?"

"Who are you complaining to? Lesley?"

His scowl didn't lift when he glanced at her. "At this point," he snarled, "I'm complaining to anybody who'll listen."

"But the coins *did* work for you. On Sam and Mavis."

"The wrong woman."

"She was the right woman. For Sam."

His eyebrows lifted. "You've changed your tune."

"I've talked to her." Then something else occurred to Rachel and she asked, "Did you use a coin I don't know about on Hester?"

Jackson shook his head. "Didn't have to."

"What do you mean? I spoke to her this afternoon, and she's all aflutter over Charlie Miller." Rachel folded her arms over her chest. "She never was before. So when she told me that she had spoken to you, I assumed—"

"You assumed wrong."

"But how?"

"She was half in love with the man already and Charlie,

poor devil, took a hard fall when she looked at him through those big blue eyes.''

''Hester?'' she murmured. ''In love?''

''Yeah.''

His simple, one word answer rattled, around inside her head for a moment or two. This was yet another example of how little she had really known the people she'd thought she was closest to. First Mavis, then Hester. Her thoughts stopped dead. She sent him a sharp, questioning look.

''What about Sally?''

''A big Irishman's got his eye on her.''

''O'Hara?'' Rachel laughed shortly. How many times over the last few months had she listened to her friend complain about O'Hara? She'd never said a kind word about him.

''No,'' she said, ''this time, I'm sure. Sally isn't interested in him. Why, just the sound of the man's name makes her shudder.''

He shook his head and shrugged. ''We'll see . . .''

She didn't like this. Any of it. Everything was changing. Everyone she loved was slowly leaving her behind. Mavis and Sam would marry and have children. Then Hester. And very probably, Sally would too. If not to O'Hara, then to someone else. They would all be busy with their new lives and families. They wouldn't have time for her anymore. Oh, the friendships would still survive, but they'd be different.

So different.

Ridiculously enough, the image of her new house leaped into mind. That huge place. The home she'd built her dreams around. Dreams of a family of friends, living together, caring for each other.

Now, she would live in it alone. She would sit there in the evenings listening to the quiet. She would lie awake at night, straining to hear the sound of another voice. Empty years stretched out ahead of her, and Rachel rubbed her upper arms briskly, hoping to get rid of the chill creeping up on her.

There wouldn't be any magic for her. She knew it deep in her bones. The others could find love and have families.

She couldn't.

Because the man she loved had died fifteen long years ago.

Chapter ☆ *Sixteen*

Days passed quickly and by the night of the social, Rachel's nerves were drawn as tight as the strings on a finely tuned fiddle.

Walking out of the Mercantile into the brightly lit night, she shivered as cool, damp air settled on skin rarely exposed. Maybe wearing the new dress was a mistake, she thought, and glanced down helplessly at the alarmingly low neckline.

Just as quickly, though, she told herself that whether it was a mistake or not, she wasn't going to change. She had a plan and a feeling that wearing this dress just might help it along. Still, she drew her black lace shawl up higher to cover bare arms displayed by the off-the-shoulder sleeves.

Someone called "Hello" to her and Rachel smiled, her gaze already darting over the crowd wandering about under the glow of colorful Japanese lanterns. Puddles of light shifted and danced over the faces as the gentle breeze rocked the lanterns hanging from wires strung across Main Street.

Too many people, she thought, and for a moment, she felt her confidence slip. To combat the thread of cowardice beginning to unwind inside her, Rachel determinedly stepped off the boardwalk into the mob.

Voices surrounded her. Happy, relaxed. Laughter and whispers, giggles and hushed promises rattled in her wake as she moved through the crowd, looking for Jackson.

They'd hardly seen each other in days. He usually left the store before dawn and stayed late working on the new house. In fact, the past few days had given her a taste of what life would be like for her when he left.

And she didn't much care for it.

"Evening, Miss Rachel," a deep, male voice interrupted her thoughts.

"Hello, Mister Wilde," she nodded to the rancher surrounded by his brood of children.

"You're looking mighty fine tonight, if you don't mind my saying so," he told her and ignored the little girl tugging on his coat sleeve.

"Thank you." She pulled the shawl tighter. It was common knowledge that Homer Wilde was in search of a new wife to replace the one who had so thoughtlessly died giving birth to her sixth child.

"Would you like to dance?"

She saw hopeful interest in his eyes and quickly moved to dash it. "Thank you no," she said politely and started walking, skirting a wide circle around the children.

"I'll see you later," he called after her.

Rachel hurried deeper into the throng of people.

Music swelled into the night, lifted up, and drifted down over the heads of the crowd, drawing them closer to its source.

Two lively fiddles, a guitar, two harmonicas, and the piano borrowed from the saloon for the night made enough noise to be heard clearly over the babble of voices. As Rachel drew nearer, she also heard the sound of dancing feet tapping against a wooden floor.

Jackson's dance floor.

With his clever design, he'd even managed to make

Tessa Horn speechless—an occurrence so rare that it had everyone in town talking about it.

Rachel hugged her shawl more tightly around her. Did he see how well he fit in in Stillwater? Did it bother him that he couldn't stay? Did he *want* to stay? With her?

She inhaled sharply and slipped between the last cluster of people separating her from the dance floor. There, she stood and watched, while at the same time, searching the people around her for one face in particular.

Jackson saw her the moment she arrived.

It felt like years since he'd been close enough to look into those blue eyes of hers. To smell the faint scent of flowers that clung to her.

He curled his fingers into his palms until the nails dug into his flesh painfully. It didn't help. He still wanted to rush across the dance floor, grab her up into his arms, and whirl the night away with her.

"Is that her?"

"Huh?" He shook his head and glanced at the man beside him. About forty, the lumberman looked clean and seemed a sober sort. Once again, Jackson sifted through the information he'd received about the man and reassured himself that he was doing the right thing.

"Yeah," Jackson said, his voice tight. "That's Rachel."

"She's a looker." The man grinned. "Hadn't expected a pretty woman."

Jackson frowned, then told himself he was being ridiculous. The man would have to be blind not to notice that Rachel was pretty.

"Looks to have a fine figure, too. Like a woman who can fill out a dress."

Jackson's teeth ground together as his gaze swept over her. Damn it, he should have remembered that she'd be wearing that new dress that he'd ordered for her. The deep, sky blue color suited her, and the soft fabric caressed her figure. When she let her shawl dip, though, Jackson's jaw dropped. He knew he was staring, but he couldn't seem to help himself.

He didn't recall that neckline being so blasted low.

"Oh my," the man beside him whispered eagerly.

A knot of—*something* in his throat threatened to choke him. Glaring at the other man, he said, "You just mind your manners, mister."

"Uh-huh." Without another word, the man began to move through the crowd toward his goal.

Jackson watched, despite his desire to turn away. When the man approached her, he held his breath. He was doing the right thing. She needed a husband. He needed to get out of Stillwater.

This was the reason he'd been sent here, for God's sake. To see Rachel married. Happy. Pregnant.

He scowled to himself at the thought of that big lumberman claiming Rachel's body. He tried desperately to shove away mental images of Rachel, naked, opening her arms to another man.

Pain gripped him, and he wondered why it was that a dead man had to suffer such agony.

The lumberman invited her to dance, and Rachel shook her head, refusing. Swallowing his urge to applaud, Jackson whispered, "It's just a dance, Rachel. Go ahead."

The man kept talking, all the while holding her elbow and trying to pull her onto the floor.

Jackson's teeth ground together. There was no need for the fella to get pushy.

Rachel looked mad. Then, for some reason, she stopped fighting the man and followed him into the center of the dancing couples.

Jackson craned his neck to watch. A woman with a feather in her hair waltzed past him, and he had an instant's clear view of Rachel and her partner. A grim smile crossed his face quickly. She was holding the man at arm's length despite his protests. "Good girl," he murmured, then caught himself.

It wasn't good. She'd never get married if she kept possible suitors at bay with a steely look and a stiff arm.

Surprisingly light on his feet, the big lumberman started guiding Rachel around the crowded floor, and Jackson was forced to shift from side to side to keep an eye on them. Rachel didn't look any happier than he felt, but he hadn't expected her to. At least, not at first. Eventually, she would see that this was all for the best.

He only hoped *he* would.

The lumberman pulled her closer, wrapping his thick, muscled arm around her waist. His open hand drifted slowly downward.

"Here now," Jackson muttered and took a half step forward.

Rachel pushed at her dance partner, but couldn't break away.

"What the hell is he up to?" Jackson grumbled thickly as he stepped up onto the edge of the dance floor to see over the crowd.

The lumberman pulled her tightly to him and looked straight down the front of her dress.

"Just wait a damned minute, here," Jackson said aloud and the youngster beside him said, "Huh?"

Rage rushed through Jackson's bloodstream like a sky-rocket with a short fuse. The man's gaze seemed locked on Rachel's breasts, and just the thought of his eyes feasting on her was enough to stir Jackson's temper to the boiling point.

"Who the hell does he think he is?" he asked no one in particular as Rachel gasped and shoved at the man holding her. "Damn his eyes, I told him to mind his manners."

Before he'd finished speaking, Jackson was moving through the crowd, pushing his way toward the couple. It was like trying to run underwater. No matter how hard he tried, he seemed to make little progress.

When he was close enough, he heard the man say, "Come on honey, just a little kiss."

"Let go of me," she demanded.

"What're you being so fussy about?" The lumberman dipped his head, trying for that kiss. She avoided him neatly. "It ain't like you're some sweet young thing sittin' in her mama's parlor."

Close, Jackson thought. So close. Then a couple swung in front of him, and he was cut off.

When the path was clear again, he hurried forward, in time to see Rachel lift one foot and bring it down hard on the big man's instep. The big lumberman howled in pain, and Rachel pushed away from him.

Fury still pounding through him, Jackson rushed the taller man. He didn't even hear the voices calling to him, questioning him. All he could see was the man who had dared to touch Rachel. Fisting one hand, he slammed it into the lumberman's jaw and felt the jarring, satisfying thud all the way up his arm. The man staggered, then fell to the floor, unfortunately taking one of the other couples down with him.

The music droned to a stop and around them, the dancers formed a curious circle. But Jackson didn't see them. He didn't hear the stunned silence. All he heard was the thunderous roar in his ears.

Standing over the fallen man, feet planted wide, fists ready, he said, "Get up you sonofabitch so I can knock you down again."

The lumberman rubbed his aching jaw, then said, "You're crazy, you know that?"

"Maybe so," he snarled. "But you touch her again and I'll kill you."

"Jackson—" Rachel grabbed his arm, but he shook her off.

"You stay the hell away from her, you understand me?"

The man on the floor shook his head and started scooting backward, moving right over the couple he'd knocked down. The outraged woman took a swing at him and missed.

"What'd he do, Jackson?" Sam called as he pushed his way through the crowd to stand beside his friend. "He get fresh?"

"Never mind," Jackson told him, only now becoming aware of the people surrounding him.

A few more men stepped forward to take up positions behind Sam and Jackson. Rachel watched the battle lines forming and knew she had to stop this before it went any further. She wasn't going to stand still and watch a brawl in her honor. Tugging on his arm again, she said, "Jackson, would you take me home?"

Several long seconds ticked by before she was sure he heard her. Then she felt the hard muscles in his arm relax slowly. Never taking his eyes off his opponent, Jackson covered her hand with one of his own, then glanced at Sam. "Get him out of here," he said quietly.

"You heard the man," Sam said to the men behind him and as one, they moved forward to scoop the lumberman off the floor. The crowd parted for them, and while everyone watched their progress, Jackson led Rachel from the dance floor to an isolated, shadowy corner near the schoolhouse.

"Are you all right?" he demanded and just managed to keep from running his hands up and down her form to reassure himself.

"I'm fine."

"Damn him anyway," he muttered, then took her hand firmly in his. "Come on, I'll take you home."

She pulled her hand back and stood her ground. "I don't want to go home yet."

"But you said—"

"I wanted to get off that dance floor before it turned into a battlefield."

"Oh." He sucked in a gulp of cool, night air, hoping that the chill would take care of the last of his temper.

"I wonder who he was?" Rachel said with a quick glance over her shoulder. "I don't think I've ever seen him before."

"He works at some lumber camp outside town."

Slowly, thoughtfully, she turned back to look up at him. It was too dark to read his expression. "How do you know that?"

"Shit."

"Jackson." A horrible notion leaped up in her brain. She didn't want to think it of him, but why else would a perfect stranger take such liberties in front of a town full of witnesses? "*You* sent him to me?"

"Rachel . . ."

"You did." She shook her head and mumbled, "I can't believe this."

"I didn't know he was going to act like that."

"So that makes it all right?" She drew her shawl up high on her shoulders, fisted her hands in it, and paced back and forth in front of him. "You didn't know he would try to maul me, so it's all right that you sent him after me?"

"That's why I'm here, Rachel," he reminded her, but she cut him off before he could go on.

"I know. To find me a husband." She stopped a foot away from him and stared at him. "Apparently, just any man will do. So long as he's breathing, is that right, Jackson?"

"No," he snapped and sounded every bit as angry as she felt.

"Well, your requirements can't be too harsh, if *he* passed muster."

"That one slipped by me, I admit," Jackson muttered. "Next time, it'll be different."

"There won't be a next time."

"Rachel we've been over this a hundred times."

"And nothing's changed."

"That's right. Nothing's changed. You *still* have to have a husband."

"Fine." Rachel inhaled sharply and in the darkness didn't see Jackson's gaze lock onto the swell of her breasts. "Then I believe I've come up with the solution to both our problems."

Wariness tinged his voice as he asked, "Yeah? What is it?"

She swallowed heavily. The completely logical idea—that had occurred to her only the day before—now seemed, well, less than logical. Rachel knew he wouldn't like it. But as far as she could see, this was the only way they could both be happy.

At least for a while.

Battling back the swarms of butterflies chasing each other around the pit of her stomach, Rachel drew a deep breath and blurted it out.

"*You* marry me, Jackson."

Charlie walked slowly through the crowd, distinctly aware of the small hand resting on his arm. He covered those tiny fingers with his own hand and felt a rush of delight race through him.

He could hardly believe it. Miss Hester Sutton stepping out with *him*. The people they passed smiled and nodded, apparently not surprised in the least to see a big dumb lumberjack walking arm in arm with a schoolteacher.

But Charlie knew the truth. He knew how lucky he'd gotten all of a sudden and he was determined to go on being lucky.

At the edge of the dance floor, he stopped, looked down at her, and apologized ahead of time.

"I'm not much of a dancer, Hester."

She smiled shyly and dipped her head. "I'm afraid I haven't had much practice myself, Charlie."

His chest swelled with pride. He loved to hear her say his name. "If you're willin' to take a chance," he said, "I'll try not to step on your toes."

"I'd love to."

He grinned again, despite the fact that he knew he must look like an idiot. It seemed all he did these days was walk around with a big smile on his face. Stepping onto the raised platform, he paused to help her up.

"Hey, Miss Sutton," a young voice popped up out of nowhere, and Charlie glanced down to see a young boy with strawberry blond hair hanging down into his eyes.

"Good evening, Billy," Hester said, still holding onto Charlie's hand.

The boy tilted his head up and looked from his teacher to the big man beside her and back again. He pushed his hair out of his eyes, squinted at his teacher and asked, "This your beau?"

Charlie held his breath.

Hester turned to look up at him. A soft, slow smile curved her lips. "Yes, Billy. This is my beau, Charlie Miller."

Pent-up breath rushed out of his lungs, and he felt himself grinning again as he held out one hand toward the boy. When the child slipped his fingers into Charlie's huge grip, he looked at his teacher again. "He's a big one, ain't he?"

"Isn't he," Hester corrected instinctively. Then, surprising herself as well as her student, she bent down to meet his gaze and gave him a wide, happy smile. "Yes," she agreed. "He surely is. See you Monday, Billy. Have a good time."

"Yes'm," the boy muttered and watched as his teacher sailed off across the dance floor in the arms of man as big as the mountains. He'd never seen Miss Sutton really smile before. She almost looked . . . *pretty*. Billy straightened up and looked around guiltily as if afraid of being caught thinking nice things about a *teacher,* of all people. Then he raced off to get more lemonade, dismissing all thoughts of teachers and school until Monday.

One second passed. Then another.

Muted sounds of music and chatter drifted to them, but weren't strong enough to break the silence stretching out between them.

Rachel waited impatiently for his reaction. Even though she was fairly certain just what it would be. At first, anyway. Then Jackson spoke and confirmed it.

"That fella was wrong," he said quietly. *"I'm* not crazy. *You* are."

"I knew you would say something like that."

"Jesus Rachel," he said, taking a step away from her, as if a little distance would help, then immediately he came back again. Reaching for her, he held her shoulders firmly, but gently, and gave her a little shake. "Why are you doing this?"

"It would work, Jackson. It would."

"How in the hell could it work, woman? I'm a *ghost!"*

She shivered, and he felt the tremors ripple through her.

Belying her nervousness, her voice was quiet, but steady. "You may be a ghost, but you're as alive as any other man now. You breathe. You eat. You sleep. You . . . *kiss,"* she finished softly.

That kiss. Damn, he'd known that was a mistake the moment their lips had met. Yet, even now when he could see how much pain that kiss would continue to cause, he couldn't regret it.

Just the memory of those few stolen moments would help make eternity bearable. Now, he thought, he would also have this. The fact that she wanted to marry *him.* God Almighty, why hadn't any of this happened to him when he could have done something about it? Why did it all have to come now when the pain was as sharp as the pleasure?

"Rachel, I'm only as alive as Lesley lets me be. It won't last forever."

"But you're here now." Her voice broke. "With me."

"Don't do this," he said, his voice thick with emotion. "Don't do it to either one of us."

"I have to try, Jackson."

"Ah dammit, Rachel," he groaned and pulled her to him.

She leaned into him, and his arms closed around her. For one brief moment, he allowed himself to believe that her idea would work. In his mind's eye, he saw it all. Working with Sam, coming home to Rachel every evening, and even being a father to those four kids that Lesley had talked about. He imagined waking up beside her in the morning and kissing her good morning. He envisioned lazy afternoons and long, quiet nights.

For one shining moment, it was so real he could almost hear their children laughing. And for that one moment, he was happy.

Really happy, for the first time.

He held her tight, reveling in the feel of her arms wrapped about his waist. He felt her heartbeat quicken against his chest and her legs press along his. His hands smoothed up and down her back, his fingertips dusting across the dozens of buttons along her spine. The urge to undo those buttons and feel her naked flesh beneath his hands came swift and hard. His body responded instantly, and Jackson bit back another groan.

Reality came crashing down on him, and he pulled back slightly before tipping her chin up with his fingertips. "It's not right, Rachel. Even if we could, it wouldn't be right."

"Why not?" she asked. "Why do Mavis and Hester get to love the men they choose and not me?"

He let his head fall back on his neck and for a moment or two, he simply stared up at the clouds rushing in to hide the stars. "Rachel, we'll find the right man for you."

"I already found him. Fifteen years ago."

"Don't." He straightened and looked at her, silently cursing the darkness that kept him from seeing her eyes.

"It's true. *You* are the one I was meant to be with," she said in a rush of words. "I knew that then and I feel it now."

"Rachel." Couldn't she see how hard this was? Didn't she know that every word she spoke only drove fresh knives into his soul? What kind of punishment is this, Lesley? He demanded silently, without really expecting an answer. Was this a new kind of Hell? Did Lesley and his boss send him here only to be tortured?

Well, whatever crimes he had committed in life, he figured he'd been punished enough. Besides, they didn't have to torture Rachel, too. She hadn't done a damn thing to earn the pain he'd brought her.

"Jackson," she whispered and reached up, cupping his face between her palms. Her touch sent spears of warmth into the deep, dark shadows of his soul, and he had to fight to concentrate on her voice. "When they sent you here, they only told you I had to be married, isn't that right?"

"Yeah."

"They never said to *who*."

"No." They hadn't. In fact, he'd had the impression that as long as she became a mother, they didn't much care one way or the other just *how* it happened.

"Then why can't it be you?"

Speechless, he stared down at her, wondering if it was possible. Was there even the slightest chance of making some of his imaginings come true? Did he have the right to snatch at some kind of happiness before returning to the prison The Black Hound saloon had become?

"I don't know for sure how long I'll be here, Rachel," he said sadly. They'd only told him she had to be married before the end of six weeks. He'd assumed that the moment his mission was completed, he would disappear. But then, the one thing he'd found out since dying was that he couldn't be sure of anything. "It might be a few days or a few weeks. The only thing I know is, I can't stay forever."

"I know." She licked dry lips, pulled in a deep breath, and said, "But no one is together forever, Jackson. Everyone dies."

He winced.

"You could marry me off to that lumberjack you foisted on me, and a tree could fall on him tomorrow."

He wouldn't have minded that one little bit.

"Don't you see," she went on quickly, "we could spend whatever time you *do* have here—together. Instead of you working so hard to hand me off to someone else, you and I could have this time together."

He closed his eyes when she dipped her head to press a kiss to the *v* of exposed flesh at his collar. Fires burst into life in his blood, and Jackson tightened his hold on her.

Obviously sensing that he was obviously weakening, Rachel reminded him, "I told you that I wouldn't marry anyone unless I was in love. I can promise you that I won't love anyone else but you."

Caught by the simple certainty in her voice, Jackson was lost. How was he supposed to fight that? When he'd been alive, no one had ever said those words to him. Hell, maybe that's why he'd never valued his life when he had it.

A wry smile touched his face briefly. Why did it seem so logical that the one thing that would have saved his life only came to him after he was dead?

Then Rachel stepped back from him, and he felt empty. Alone.

She looked at him, long and hard, then slowly turned around and walked back toward the crowds and the music. She didn't look back.

She'd left the decision up to him.

Chapter ☆ Seventeen

Rachel kept walking. Slowly, but steadily as she threaded her way through the crowd toward the Mercantile. She didn't look back. Not because she didn't want to, but because if Jackson wasn't following her, she couldn't bear knowing it.

As she crossed in front of the dance floor, she absently noted Hester dancing with her lumberjack. Off to one side, staring at each other over cups of apple cider, were Sam and Mavis. Envy pricked at her. She'd like to have been a better person, but she couldn't help herself. It wasn't that she begrudged her friends their happiness.

She only wanted it, too.

The ground looked blurry. She blinked, but it didn't help, It wasn't until she lifted her hem to step up onto the suddenly wavering boardwalk that she realized it was the tears in her eyes distorting everything. She sniffed, rubbed the end of her nose, then blinked back the tears. She wouldn't cry.

At least, not yet.

Behind her, Rachel thought she heard someone running. Coming closer. Hope leaped into life. She held her breath and waited.

The sharp crack of a gunshot sounded, just over the din

of the crowd. The band crawled to a stop, one of the fiddles screeching like a terrified cat. Startled, she turned in the direction of the shot. Jackson leaped up onto the boardwalk and moved to stand between her and whatever was happening in the street.

She barely had time to enjoy the fact that he had come after her when someone shouted.

Rachel moved to one side, rose up on her toes, and tried to see what was going on. A few of the people crowding the dance floor drifted toward the saloon down the street.

She glanced at Jackson. His gaze locked on a tight cluster of people near the front of the saloon. "Stay here," he muttered, then he started walking.

A heartbeat later, she followed him. Her footsteps rang out in time with his as she matched him step for step. He tossed her a quick glare, but she ignored it. She wouldn't be set carefully in a corner by anyone. Apparently, Jackson accepted that, because he didn't try to turn her back.

Still a good twenty feet from the saloon, he stopped, holding one strong arm out in front of her to make sure she did, too.

"What happened?" he asked a man standing near the boardwalk.

"Not sure, but I think that gambler shot somebody."

"Lynch." A hard, cold knot formed in the pit of Jackson's belly.

"That's the one," the man told him.

"All right folks," a loud, deep voice shouted, "go on back to the social."

"What's goin' on, sheriff?" someone in the crowd called out.

Jackson took a single step forward. He was hardly aware of Rachel, clinging to his right hand with both of hers.

The sheriff's booming voice pealed out again. "Nothin' for you to worry about, Harry."

A sprinkling of chuckles rose up and settled back down.

"There was a shooting, but it's over now. Everything's fine," the sheriff said. Then he waved one arm at the motley band. "Go on boys, play something lively."

The fiddlers struck up a tune, and soon the other musicians joined in. Most of the townsfolk meandered back to the dancing, with only a few of the more curious standing about waiting for details.

"Let's go home, Jackson."

He didn't even look at her. "Not yet."

A minute or two later, a short man with wide, excited eyes set in a lean face bustled up to the man standing in the street before Jackson and Rachel.

"You shoulda seen it, Jim," he wheezed, trying to catch his breath.

"What happened?" Jackson asked, forcing his voice to work despite the tightness in his throat.

The little man looked up at him to answer his question. "Lynch shot a fella who called him a cheat."

That hard, cold knot in his belly iced over. A deep chill shook him as memories rushed through his mind. But the other man went blithely on.

"Lynch went all tight lipped and mean. Though I got to say, he give the fella a chance to back up. Lynch says," and the little man paused to screw his features into an imitation of Noble Lynch's autocratic face, " 'You don't want to be saying something you'll be sorry for.' But that damned fool didn't take the opening Lynch gave him. Just called him a cheat again, then went grabbin' for a gun, and Noble shot him dead. Neatest piece of shooting I've seen in some time. Right through the heart. Kid was cold before he hit the floor."

Tremors wracked him.

His jaw clenched, Jackson turned to stare at the saloon where Noble Lynch had just gotten away with murder.

Again.

"Told the sheriff what I seen," the little man went on,

talking to his friend now, "Sheriff said it was self-defense, pure and simple."

Self-defense.

"Jackson, please." Rachel tugged at his arm. "Let's go. Now."

That's what they'd called it when Lynch had killed him. "Jackson?"

He swiveled his head to look at her, finding her blue eyes wide and appealing. She met his gaze as if she knew what he was thinking. Feeling. But she couldn't. She couldn't possibly know what it was like to stand by helplessly as your murderer went on killing others.

Turning from her, he glanced down at the well lit saloon and wondered if there were a new ghost inside, trying to figure out what had happened to him. Or had the dead man gone straight to whatever rest was being denied Jackson?

"Please?" she repeated.

Dragging great gulps of air into his body, he tore his gaze from the saloon. He looked at her, noting the flush in her cheeks and the rapid rise and fall of her chest. Splashes of colored light, thrown from the lanterns overhead, dappled her. Her eyes glittered as she met his gaze, and he wanted to lose himself in that deep, cool blue.

The bone-deep chill had crept through his body until the only warmth left to him was in the hand Rachel held so tightly. He drew a long, shuddering breath. He wanted that warmth. He wanted to feel alive again. Really alive.

Especially now, when memories of his death were so near.

With his fingers curled around hers, he started walking toward the Mercantile. With every step, he moved a bit faster. Desperately. Urgently. He heard the quick tap of her heels against the boardwalk as she struggled to keep up with his long legged stride. Still, they weren't moving fast enough. The familiar path to the store had never seemed longer. He tightened his grip on her hand. He heard her short, sharp breathing, and the rapid gasps teased him, urging him to hurry.

When they finally reached the Mercantile, Jackson threw the door open, led her inside, and slammed the door closed again. He flicked the latch, then pulled her into his arms.

His mouth came down on hers in a wild, desperate kiss. She parted her lips for him, and his tongue plunged inside her. He groaned in the back of his throat as he tasted her, reveling in the sensations he'd denied them both for too long.

Rachel let her shawl drop to the floor, then encircled his neck with her arms. She held him tightly, determined to keep him with her. This time, there would be no stopping. No questions. No guilt. This time, she would finally know what it was to be loved.

Thoroughly.

Completely.

His tongue moved over hers, and she gasped at the ripples of need racing along her spine. Damp heat centered between her legs, and a deep ache she'd never known before was born.

When he tore his mouth from hers, she moaned and tightened her hold on him. But she needn't have worried. Instead of pulling back, Jackson dipped his head to follow the line of her jaw with his mouth and tongue. She felt the warm traces of his attention as he moved over her flesh with an almost desperate need.

She let her head drop back. His kisses moved down her neck to her chest. Her fingers speared through his hair and held on as he bent farther to taste and explore the naked flesh of her chest. One of his hands slipped from her waist to cup her behind. He caressed her backside through the fabric of her gown, and all she could think of was getting out of that dress so she could feel his touch.

As if reading her mind, Jackson straightened abruptly, then bent again and scooped her into his arms. Cradled close to his chest, she looked into green eyes hazy with passion.

"Rachel," he said, and his rough voice scraped the air. "Here's your chance. I give it to you. You say no now and I'll walk away."

Her breath caught.

"It'll kill me," he added. "But I'll go."

"If you go now," she said, "it would kill *me.*" She leaned up to catch his lips with hers.

A soft moan escaped him, and his teeth nipped at her bottom lip, sending sparks of delight flickering through her.

Then he paused, smiled, and headed for the stairs.

Tucking her head beneath his chin, she kissed his throat, flicking his skin with her tongue. His arms tightened around her.

He took the steps in a hurry then marched down the short hallway to her bedroom. Turning the glass knob, he shoved the door open, stepped inside, and kicked it closed again before striding to the high, wide bed.

With one hand, he tossed back the yellow rose quilt, then set her down on the edge of the mattress.

Apprehension warred with desire.

Wisps of moonlight strayed in through the windows on the far side of the room. Her eyes adjusted to the gloom, and she looked up into Jackson's face. His features tightened as his eyes seemed to glow with a fire she was only beginning to recognize as the same flames burning inside her.

She shifted on the bed, and the old springs squealed into the silence.

"I've wanted to do this for a long time," Jackson whispered and reached for her.

Rachel held her breath. Afraid to do something wrong, something foolish, she did nothing. Whatever she was expecting, he surprised her.

She felt him pull the pins from her hair. Her eyes widened as one by one, he discarded them. She heard them hit the floor and skitter across the polished surface. Her hair, freed of its knot, tumbled down across her shoulders.

"Beautiful," he said in a hushed, reverent tone. His fingers combed through the heavy mass, and she closed her eyes to better concentrate on his touch. "I knew it would be beautiful."

Spearing through the hair at her temples, Jackson pulled her face close and lavished a long, slow, kiss on her lips. He rested one knee on the mattress and eased her backward. The fresh, white sheets felt cool against her flesh. Still kissing her, he invaded her mouth with whispered promises. His right hand sneaked around behind her and began to undo the line of buttons marching down her spine.

Rachel half lifted herself toward him to make his job easier. When she did, her already aching nipples brushed across his chest, and she gasped at the contact. He smiled against her mouth, then as the back of her dress loosened, slipped the dress down, off her shoulders.

He sighed, and she felt his breath dust across her skin. Her stomach churned; her mouth went dry. She wished desperately that she knew what to do. How to act. She wanted this time with him to be special. Yet she feared her own ignorance would ruin everything. Closing her eyes tightly, she lay ramrod stiff, awaiting whatever came next.

"I want to see you," he whispered and moved toward the bedside table. "Let me light the lamp."

"No," she said quickly, her eyes flying open as she reached for him. *This* she was sure of. "No light. Please."

Rachel couldn't bear to watch him look at her. What if he were disappointed? She knew her breasts were too small and her body too thin where there should be curves. In the darkness, maybe he wouldn't notice.

"All right, Rachel," he said softly as he lay back down along her side. "No lights."

As he spoke, he pushed her dress farther down until only

a thin, cotton chemise covered her nakedness. He smiled slowly and in the dim glow of moonlight, she watched him reach for the tiny pink ribbons holding the fragile material over her breasts.

She felt the gentle, insistent tug as he parted the fabric that hid her from him. Gently, he stroked her skin with the flat of his palm and moved the material aside.

Rachel bit down on her bottom lip and squeezed her eyes tightly shut. For several long moments, nothing happened, and she knew he was looking at her. What was he seeing though? Was he pleased? Disappointed? Her heartbeat hammered in her chest and though she wanted the answers to her questions, she didn't want them badly enough to risk opening her eyes.

Then her worries disappeared.

His mouth came down on one hard, distended nipple. Her eyes flew open, and she lifted her head slightly to look at him. At what he was doing to her.

His tongue and teeth moved gently over the sensitive flesh. Her fingers curled into the sheet beneath her and she held on for dear life as her world began to rock.

Jackson's right hand swept down her body and smoothed her dress down, over her hips to fall off the mattress and puddle on the floor.

She heard the whisper of movement, but didn't care. Nothing mattered except the incredible sensations she was experiencing. His mouth closed tight over her nipple. Rachel gasped, her back bowed and arched her breasts toward him. He suckled her, his lips drawing, pulling. She groaned aloud and stared blindly at the ceiling as her body began to hum with an indescribable need.

The ache at her center tripled. His right hand moved up her leg, caressed the curve of her knee, and through the fine cotton lawn of her drawers, explored her inner thighs.

She lifted her hips instinctively. He moved quickly, his

fingers slipping beneath the band at her waist to slide her pantaloons down and off.

Hot. She was hotter than she had ever been. Even lying nearly naked on cool sheets, she felt heat continue to build inside her. Her head moved from side to side. Her fingers curled and uncurled into the sheet. His hands smoothed over her hips, her legs.

He shifted slightly and turned his attention to her other breast. "Perfect," he murmured in between kisses. "So perfect."

She looked at him and wished she'd allowed him to light the lamp. Now she wanted to see him. She wanted to watch him kiss her. Embarrassment rushed up and stained her cheeks. How bold she had become in just a few short minutes.

His fingers trailed along the inside of her thigh and neared her center. Damp heat coursed through her in response to his caresses, and she held her breath, sure she would explode if he touched her . . . *there*.

Then he did.

And she didn't.

Jackson bit back a groan as he smoothed his fingertips gently over her tender flesh. She bucked beneath him, and a low moan sighed from her throat. Lifting his head from the breast he wanted to suckle forever, he lifted himself up on one elbow and looked down into her face. Pale moonlight washed the room in a silvery glow. Her honey-colored hair gleamed against the white sheets. Her porcelain skin seemed to shimmer when he touched her.

His gaze moved over her, slowly, lovingly. He wanted to commit every inch of her to memory. He wanted to know her body so well that all he would have to do is close his eyes and she would be there. With him.

Always.

Her small, perfect breasts with their rosebud nipples called to him, and he dipped his head long enough to sip at them. He smiled to himself when she shivered.

His thumb traced across the nest of blond curls at the joining of her thighs, and his groin hardened beyond the point of pain. Now, there was only a throbbing, insistent ache that clamored to be eased. He turned his head to watch as his hand slipped down between her legs to cup the damp heat he craved more than life itself.

No, he corrected himself as one finger dipped inside her. This *was* life. Being with Rachel. Swallowing her sighs and bathing himself in her warmth was life. The only life he wanted.

Or cared about.

She planted her feet on the mattress and lifted her hips into his hand. Leaning over her, he kissed her gently then pulled his head back to watch her face. He wanted to see completion streak across her features. He wanted to look into her eyes and know that he'd at last done something right.

"Rachel," he whispered. "Look at me."

She shook her head from side to side.

"Open your eyes, sweetheart." Deliberately, he inserted two fingers into her depths and the invasion startled her eyes wide open. She looked up at him, and he stared back into the blue gaze that would follow him through eternity. "I want to watch you as I love you."

"Jackson," she said on a choked moan, "something's happening to me."

"I know, love," he reassured her and leaned down to plant a quick kiss at the corner of her mouth.

She reached for him, her hands grabbing at his shoulders. His thumb stroked the bud of her sex, and she clutched at him desperately.

"Hold on tight, Rachel. I won't let you go." His fingers moved in and out of her heat, slowly at first, then faster, harder. He accommodated his movements to her needs, watching her face for the clues to what she wanted. Craved.

Her hips rocked against his hand, and his body screamed to be a part of hers. His thumb continued to stroke, caress her most sensitive spot until he saw her breath catch. She lifted her hips again, higher this time, straining toward him, reaching for the completion he knew was just beginning.

Her tight, hot sheath convulsed around his hand, squeezing him as the tremors of satisfaction shook her. She cried his name out loud and as the last of her climax rippled through her, he claimed her sighs in a soul searing kiss.

Several moments passed before he lifted his head and looked down into her eyes. She smiled, shivered, and said, "Jackson, that was wonderful. I didn't know it would be so—"

"I know," he cut her off because he *did* know. Never before had he been more interested in a woman's satisfaction than his own. Never once had he put off his own gratification in favor of pleasing the woman in his bed. Now though, even if he left this room with his body as hard and aching as it was at that moment, he wouldn't regret a thing.

"We're not finished," she asked softly. "Are we?"

"Greedy girl," he answered with a chuckle.

But she didn't return his smile. Instead, she nodded. "I do feel greedy, Jackson. I want everything. I want to hold you, feel your skin against mine. I want to know what it is to have you become a part of me."

His chin dropped to his chest. What had he ever done to deserve a woman like this? The answer came rushing back to him. Nothing. He didn't deserve her. And his Hell would be knowing for eternity that he would never have her.

Except for now. For whatever time they could snatch for themselves before he was sent away.

Her fingers reached for his shirt buttons. He watched her for a long moment, then brushed her hands aside and yanked the shirt off, sending buttons flying about the shadowy room.

She smiled and lifted one hand to stroke his chest. Her

touch sent lightning-like jabs of desire streaking through him. He bit back a groan and eased off the bed.

Rachel lay in the center of the mattress, wearing nothing but an opened chemise and a welcoming smile. She watched him, making his movements clumsy. Hurriedly, Jackson yanked off his boots, then stripped, tossing his clothes to the floor.

He saw her gaze drop to the hard, thick length of him. Her eyes widened slightly. "I won't hurt you," he said softly.

"I know that," she answered, opening her arms to him.

He knelt between her parted thighs and leaned over her. Her hands smoothed across his back, and he felt her touch burn through his flesh right down to the bone. Jackson kissed her, long and slow, caressing her tongue with his, darting in and out of her mouth in a tease of things to come.

Her palms slid down his back to his hips and the backs of his thighs. He arched into her, brushing the tip of his shaft against her still sensitive flesh. She groaned, lifting her hips slightly.

Unable to wait another moment, Jackson sat back on his haunches and parted her thighs farther. Gently, his fingertips opened her damp, pink flesh to ease his entry.

As he pushed himself inside, inch by tantalizing inch, he stroked the hard bud of her pleasure. Every soft moan that escaped her fed his own needs and desires. She fanned the flames consuming him until they were both caught in an inferno from which there was only one escape.

Rachel tugged at his thighs, silently urging him closer. Deeper. Jackson surrendered and pushed through the final barrier within. She gasped loudly at the jolt of discomfort, but almost immediately began to writhe and twist beneath him.

Lost in a world of sensation, Jackson rocked his hips against hers. Again and again, he plunged deeper inside her.

She lifted her legs to wrap about his waist and she locked her ankles together, holding him to her.

He reached down, slipping one hand between their bodies to find the core of her. As his body tightened into an almost unbearable tension, he ushered Rachel over the edge of pleasure again. Her body cushioned his as he emptied himself inside her and then together, they drifted through the soft haze of completion.

"Have you seen Rachel?" Mavis looked past Hester to scan the crowd again. But it was no use. She hadn't seen her friend in more than an hour.

"No," Hester said and glanced up at Charlie. "But we've been dancing."

"Gettin' better at it too, I think," he said and took her hand in his.

"I can't imagine where she could have gone," Mavis went on, talking more to Sam now, since Hester and Charlie seemed too involved in each other to notice anyone else.

"Maybe she got tired and went home," Sam offered and draped one arm around her.

"Rachel?" Mavis laughed gently and laid her head down on his shoulder. "Rachel never gets tired, Sam." She straightened up abruptly and looked at him as a new idea occurred to her. "Maybe she's sick. Or hurt."

"Oh my," Hester gasped, "do you think so?"

Sam met Charlie's gaze and shook his head before talking to Mavis. "She's not sick. Or hurt. Or dying. Or even missing."

"But Sam . . ."

"Honey, Rachel's all grown up. She doesn't need you worrying over her like she's a child."

"But—"

"Besides," Sam winked, "I saw her and Jackson slipping away to the shadows after that little fracas on the dance floor."

"You did?" Mavis shot Hester a quick, thoughtful look.

"I sure did, and it didn't look to me like they were wanting company."

"Rachel and Jackson?" she asked.

"Sure." Sam grabbed her hand and turned her toward the dance floor.

"But she never said a word to me," Mavis said, almost pouting.

He tipped her chin up and dropped a quick kiss on her mouth before grinning. "And you never said a word to me in five long, wasted years."

Mavis blushed prettily.

"Hester," Charlie said. "Why don't we go try out that dance floor again?"

Hester looked at him, then to Mavis. "If you think we should go find Rachel, just come and tell me."

Mavis nodded as she watched Hester, a new spring in her step, move off with her beau.

"Let's not go off half-cocked looking for Rachel and Jackson, honey," Sam whispered in her ear and she shivered as his breath teased her skin. "Maybe if they get enough time alone, she'll be able to hog-tie that man into sticking around town."

"That would be nice," Mavis said.

"Sure would," her fianceé agreed. "Him and me could make our fortunes building houses and such."

Sam went on, but Mavis wasn't listening. Instead, she was thinking how perfect everything would be if Rachel fell in love with Jackson.

Then, they would all be happy.

Except Sally, she thought with a pang of guilt.

Even now, Sally was at home alone. She claimed to enjoy the chance to put her feet up more than having her toes stomped on by some man. But Mavis knew her friend had stayed away because she had no escort.

It had been different before.

The four of them had attended socials together. United in their spinsterhood. Yet, Mavis wouldn't trade the miracle of Sam for anything.

Besides, Sally wouldn't be lonely much longer. With three friends looking out for her, the town laundress would probably be married by the end of the year.

Smiling up at the man beside her, Mavis took a quick moment to count her blessings again. How it had happened, she would never know. But she wasn't one to question good fortune.

"So," Sam said with another slow wink, "shall we get out there and show ol' Charlie how real dancing is done?"

She nodded and tucked her hand through the crook of his arm.

"You know, Mavis," he said as he led her through the crowd, "this is the best town social I've ever been to."

"Yes," she agreed. "I just wish Rachel was here, having a good time with the rest of us."

Rachel cuddled in close to Jackson, resting her head on his chest. His arms wrapped tightly around her, his deep, even breathing told her he had fallen asleep.

Muted sounds from the social came to her through the partially opened window and she hoped her friends were enjoying their evening as much as she had. Everything was perfect, she thought. Or, it would have been.

If only Jackson's heart were beating.

Chapter ☆ Eighteen

The first hint of dawn began to lighten the eastern sky, thrusting rose pink fingers up through the clouds. Sally shivered, drew her thick, white shawl higher about her shoulders, and stepped up onto the dance floor. She kicked at a fallen Japanese lantern, and the toe of her shoe pierced its fragile paper skin.

Pulling her foot free, she took a step, then another, more quietly. In the early morning hush, even her own breathing sounded overly loud. A quick glance at the buildings lining each side of Main Street reassured her that the town was still sleeping. No doubt, everyone but her would be getting a late start on their day because of the party the night before.

Quickly, she let her gaze slide over the remnants of the town social. Tables and chairs, still littered with dirty plates and cups, were sprinkled around the outside edge of the dance floor. Paper bunting, limp now with morning dew, sagged like a tired old man. She walked slowly, stepping over another lantern that had fallen from the wire still strung from one side of the street to the other.

Her foot came down on something soft, and she paused to look. A half smile touched her lips briefly as she bent down to pick up the crushed rosebud. A straight pin stuck out from its stem, and Sally knew that the night before, that rose had been pinned to someone's dress. A man's gift to his lady.

She inhaled the still-heady fragrance as she straightened up. Running the tip of one finger over the damaged petals, she couldn't help wondering who had lost it so carelessly. Sally sighed and tucked the bent stem into a button hole at the neck of her plain white shirtwaist, then secured it with the pin. She glanced at the blood red blossom and smiled sadly.

She felt a bit like that damaged flower.

Worn, bruised, and forgotten.

A strangled half-chuckle shot from her throat at the thought. Surely she wasn't feeling *that* sorry for herself? Town social or no, her life hadn't ended because she had spent the evening at home, alone. In fact, nothing really had changed. At least, not for her.

But perhaps that was what was wrong.

Nothing had changed for Sally Wiley.

Mavis and Hester had found good men to love them. Rachel was more and more involved with the cousin who had turned up out of nowhere.

But Sally's life just went slumbering on.

She inhaled sharply, shook her head, and lifted her chin. Enough of that, she told herself sternly. She had never been one to indulge in self-pity and she surely wasn't going to start now.

She glanced around her again, making absolutely sure that no one in town was stirring. Then lifting her arms to an invisible partner, she began to dance.

Lightly, gently, her feet moved on the floorboards, making no more than a whisper of sound. She closed her eyes, leaned her head back and imagined a tall, handsome man smiling down at her. He had dark hair, flashing blue eyes, and she knew if he spoke, his voice would roll with a soft Irish brogue.

Her dance came to a sudden stop. Stunned at the image her mind had painted, her eyes flew open.

"O'Hara?" she whispered.

"I didn't mean to sneak up on ya, darlin'."

She gasped and spun around. If she hadn't known better, she would have sworn she had conjured him out of thin air.

He stepped up onto the dance platform, his arms wrapped around a heavy canvas sack. "You're a good dancer, Sally love."

Her gaze fixed on that sack, she shook her head. "None of your blarney, Mike O'Hara. It won't help you. I'm not taking that laundry from you until next week."

He looked down, then up at her again before giving her a smile. " 'Tis not what you think."

"What I think is, you need a keeper," Sally countered quickly. Turning her back on him, she marched to the edge of the dance floor and stepped off, headed for her shop. "Surely there's *someone* who can see to it you don't go through so many clothes."

As she walked, her skirt snapping around her legs, she heard him following.

"Sally," he said, his voice sounding like a shout in the quiet.

She turned on him and laid one finger against her lips.

"Keep quiet! Would you have the whole town up and listening to you?"

Mike came to a dead stop not three feet from her. Shifting his burden to a more comfortable position, he glared at her, then said even louder, "I don't care who's listenin', woman!"

Sally flinched, tossed a glance at the closest building, then gave him a look that could have frosted a lake. "Don't you take that 'Bull of the Range' tone with *me*, Mike O'Hara," she said in an outraged hush. "I won't stand still for it. Now, like I said, I'm not taking any more of your laundry until next week. So you might as well just ride into Seattle and find yourself some other poor laundress to work half to death.''

''By Saint Patrick's staff, you are the most . . .'' His mouth snapped shut as if he couldn't think of the words needed to describe her.

''Thank you.'' She smiled acidly, then showed him her back as she marched on to her shop.

''I've just come from Seattle, woman,'' he called out after her.

She slowed her pace a bit, but kept walking.

His heavy footsteps pounded against the dirt as he came up behind her. ''Do ya not have the decency to stand still and let me say me piece?''

Apparently, the only way to shut him up was to let him say whatever it was he'd come to say. She stopped suddenly, and he crashed right into her. Sally staggered, caught her balance, then tipped her head back to look up at him.

''Well? I'm waiting. What is it?''

Now that he had her attention, he seemed unsure of himself. Almost worried. But that couldn't be, she told herself. The burly Irishman was nothing if not confident.

Not many men could have come to a strange country and in less than ten years built a ranch to rival anyone's.

''I tried to get back last night,'' he finally said and bent to rest the sack's bottom against the dirt. He shrugged his broad shoulders as if working out the kinks in his body.

Sally deliberately looked away from the shifting muscles hidden beneath his dark blue shirt.

''But,'' he went on, ''me horse threw a shoe, and the bloody blacksmith couldn't get to it until early this morning.''

She glanced at the sky. The rising sun had lightened it to a soft pink. He must have had the blacksmith up and working at four this morning to be able to get back to Stillwater in time for the dawn.

What could have been so important?

"Did ya have a nice time at the social, Sally love?"

She stiffened. "I didn't attend," she said. "But judging by the noise, everyone else had a lovely time."

He frowned slightly. "Well, I'd hoped to escort you to the doings last night, so I'm sorry you missed it. But I must tell ya, I'm not a bit sorry you didn't go with someone else."

"What?" Completely puzzled now, she looked up into eyes the color of his shirt. What did he mean, he had wanted to escort her? He had never asked her. As far as she could remember, he had never even *considered* her as anything more than a cleaning agent for his clothes.

"Aye well," he said and cleared his throat. "I'm ahead of meself, aren't I?"

"I don't know what you're talking about."

"I know, I know." Standing tall and straight, he stared at a point somewhere above her head. " 'Tis me own fault, of course. But I hadn't a notion of how to talk to you about . . . well, about lots of things, Sally love."

"Look, O'Hara."

"Hush a minute will ya!"

Sally winced as his voice boomed out around her. From somewhere close by, she heard a window sash lifted.

"I planned this all out on me ride back from Seattle. If you don't let me say it, I'll make a mosh of it."

Relenting, she nodded. She was sure that at any moment people were going to come streaming from their homes to find out what Mike was yelling about. "Fine. Say it and be done with it, then."

Taking a deep breath, he started by mumbling, "Where was I? Ah yes, no notion of how to talk to ya."

Sally dipped her head to hide a smile.

"So for some time now, I've frequented your laundry."

"Often," she added.

"Aye, as often as possible." He glanced at her fondly.

"But recently, someone pointed out to me the way of things."

"Who?" she asked. "What things?"

He shook his head. "This fella, he told me that workin' ya to death was really not the best way to go about courtin' ya."

"*Courting?*" Sally swallowed heavily and looked up at him. But he had shifted his gaze again to stare at nothing. Mike O'Hara? Courting *her?*

She needed to sit down.

"He suggested that I try somethin' different. So I went to Seattle yesterday to do some shoppin'."

"Shopping?" She knew her voice sounded odd, but she couldn't help it.

"Aye." Opening the heavy sack, he reached inside and pulled out a bouquet of only slightly wilted and bent yellow roses.

She sucked in a breath as he gave them to her. Laying one hand briefly on the damaged, forgotten rosebud she'd affixed to her shirt, Sally took his flowers and held them close to her face. Their scent lifted to swirl about her head, making her feel just a bit dizzy.

"They looked a sight better last night," Mike told her.

She thought they looked wonderful.

He reached into the sack again and came up with a huge box of chocolates. Handing it over to her, Mike grinned.

"You're such a skinny little thing, I'll expect ya to eat every last one of these yourself now, mind."

She nodded blankly, hugging the box to her chest.

Next, he drew a forest green, silk shawl from the sack and moved to drape it about her shoulders.

She looked down, stunned at the contrast between her hand-knitted white wool and the extravagance of silk.

"As I thought," he murmured. " 'Twas made for ya."

She couldn't think. Everything was happening so quickly. Sally looked at him, struck speechless by his thoughtfulness. A soft smile creased his features, and the sparkle in his eyes sent wonder skittering through her.

"Mike, I—"

"Hush now," he warned gently, "I've not finished."

"But—"

In the next few minutes, he presented her with calfskin gloves, silver combs for her hair, and a pair of soft, red dancing slippers.

When the sack lay empty and forgotten on the dirt between them, Mike reached into his breast pocket and pulled out a tiny box. Cupping it in one hand, he looked at her, inhaled deeply, and said, "Sally love, this last gift I brought with me from Ireland."

"I don't understand any of this, Mike."

He reached out and stroked her cheek with his knuckles. "Understand this, then, my love. When I came here—to this country—I'd no notion of what I'd find. But I brought this with me in the hope of finding you."

"Me?" Sally's eyes misted, and her arms ached from the burden of offerings she held clutched to her.

"Aye, girl." He opened the box and took out a small, gold ring.

Her breath caught, and the tears in her eyes nearly blinded her.

Holding it out toward her, he said, "I know you'll need some time to think it over, but I was wonderin' if you'd maybe consider marryin' me one day?"

She sat.

Her knees gave out, and she plopped onto the dirt.

He went down on one knee and looked into her face anxiously. "Is the thought of marryin' me so awful, you'd faint just at the thought of it?"

She shook her head. Tears rolled from the corners of her eyes and trailed down her cheeks.

"Ya know," he pointed out, "I'm not nearly so dirty as ya might think. 'Twas harder work than I've ever done,

gettin' enough dirty clothes together to come in and see
ya.''

A low, broken chuckle escaped her.

''I promise ya, love. There'll be no more laundry for you
once we're wed—if you'll have me. Me housekeeper already thinks me a fool for takin' me clothes into town for
a wash.''

Wed.

''Filomena, me housekeeper that is,'' he went on, ''will
be that glad to have you about. She's long been tellin' me
that what I need is a strong woman.'' Mike grinned and
shrugged his broad shoulders. ''That woman is you, Sally
love.''

Sally's brain was spinning. Just a half an hour ago, she
had thought she would spend the rest of her life alone.
Now, she was sitting in the middle of Main Street, gifts
piled in her lap while a proud, handsome man knelt in front
of her to propose marriage.

''Do ya think ya could get used to the idea of me as a
husband?''

It wouldn't be difficult at all, she realized. She had always enjoyed arguing with him. And she knew what a kind,
hardworking soul he was. Mike O'Hara would be a good
match for her. Though it was still hard to take in, that this
strong, gentle man wanted her. Soul deep pleasure opened
up in her chest and flowered like a meadow in spring as
she realized with a start that she wanted him, too.

But there was one thing she still needed to hear.

Fresh tears welled up in her eyes as her heart filled to
overflowing. She came up on her knees, spilling her pres-
ents into the dirt. Meeting his gaze squarely, she asked one
very important question. ''Do you love me, O'Hara?''

He stared at her for a long moment.

''Mother of Saint Patrick!'' he shouted and threw his
arms wide. ''Isn't that what I've been sayin'?''

''Not yet, you haven't, O'Hara,'' she shouted right back

at him. It felt good. Right. She would always love arguing with this stubborn, wonderful Irishman. "If you expect to marry me, I'm going to hear the words from you. Often."

Across the street, another window opened and from the corner of her eye, Sally noted Tessa Horn's interested gaze peering at them from behind the curtains.

She didn't care.

"Well, O'Hara?"

"If you aren't the most hardheaded female I've ever met." He let his head fall back on his neck, and in a voice loud enough to carry into the next world he called out, "I love you, Sally Wiley!"

Straightening again, he looked at her and grinned. "Will that do ya?"

"For starters," she told him with a delighted laugh, then threw herself at him, wrapping her arms around his neck.

He gathered her close and this time, he whispered those words she'd waited a lifetime to hear.

By suppertime, the whole town was talking about Mike O'Hara and Sally Wiley. The burly Irishman had purchased every cigar in stock at the Mercantile and had spent his day handing them out to everyone he met: man, woman, and child.

Rachel turned the "Closed" sign in the window and locked the front door. Safe to say, she told herself wryly, that the Spinster Society had come to an abrupt end. Jackson Tate's arrival in Stillwater had affected so much more than just her own life.

Startled, she jumped at a knock on the door behind her. Lifting the edge of the window shade, she peered outside. Her stomach churned when Noble Lynch smiled at her and tipped his hat.

"We're closed," she said.

"Five minutes of your time," he countered. "No more."

If it was anyone else, she wouldn't have thought twice.

But then, a week or two ago, she wouldn't have been bothered by the gambler, either.

It was different, now. She knew him for what he was. Every time she looked at him, she saw Jackson—dying.

Pulling a deep steadying breath into her lungs, Rachel flipped the latch and opened the door. She moved back as he entered, left the door standing open, and crossed the room quickly. Stepping through the gate in the counter, she hurried to keep the questionable safety of that barrier between them.

"What can I get for you, Mister Lynch?" she asked.

He gave her a winning smile that did nothing to warm the coldness in his eyes. "I had hoped that we were close to enjoying a first name friendship, Rachel."

Her stomach tightened, but she forced a smile in return. Easier to be friendly, sell him whatever it was he wanted, and get him out of the store before Jackson arrived.

"Certainly." She paused, swallowed, then added, "Noble."

He dipped his head in acknowledgment.

"Now, what can I do for you?"

"All I need right now is a small can of gun oil," he replied.

"Gun oil?"

"Yes." He smoothed his jacket lapels. "My gun needs cleaning badly."

It would, she thought, remembering the crack of gunfire the night before. She shuddered as she recalled the look in Jackson's eyes when he discovered that his murderer had just killed another man.

Keep breathing, she told herself. She walked along the counter until she reached the section that held gun supplies. Reaching up, Rachel pulled a small tin of gun oil off the shelf and carried it back to the gambler. She set it down on the counter in front of him. "That's one dollar and ten cents."

One dark eyebrow lifted and the corner of his mouth quirked as though he were amused at her stiffness. Dipping into his pants pocket, Noble pulled out a handful of change and began to count out the right amount.

Rachel's breath caught, her throat tightened, and a heavy fist seemed to grab at her heart, squeezing painfully. Her gaze locked on the telltale gleam of gold in Noble's palm.

The missing golden coin.

She lifted her gaze briefly to study Noble Lynch's profile. A small voice in the back of her mind insisted that the gambler could have come upon that coin in any number of ways. He might have won it in a card game. Received it in change for a purchase. Or he could simply have *found* it.

But she didn't believe any of it.

As Jackson had suspected, Noble Lynch had stolen it from him.

"That's an unusual coin," she said, amazed that she had been able to force her voice to work.

"Hmm?" He glanced at her, smiled and shrugged. "Indeed. It's a family heirloom, you might say. A good luck piece."

"Really?"

His dark eyes sharpened slightly, but his smile remained fixed as he handed her the correct amount of money.

"May I see it?" she asked.

A moment's hesitation. "Of course."

He handed her the gold coin, and Rachel's fingers smoothed over the familiar etched wing and star. She hadn't been mistaken. It was a perfect match to the coin Jackson had given her in case of emergency.

Picking up the gun oil, he asked, "Could I interest you in taking supper with me tonight, Rachel?"

"I don't think so." Her words came clipped, stiff. It was all she could do to stand quietly talking to the man who had killed Jackson.

Glancing down at the can in his hand, he said quietly, "This is about last night, isn't it?"

"I don't know what you mean."

"Your rather chilly reception of me," he countered. "I do hope you realize that the *incident* last night was not my doing."

Amazed, she blurted, "Incident? You shot a man, Noble."

He winced as if deeply hurt. "Yes, I did, though it pains me to admit it."

"You killed him." And Jackson, she wanted to shout.

"In self-defense."

"Small consolation to the man's widow."

"I abhor violence, Rachel," he said and reached toward her, intent on patting her hand.

She pulled back, her fingers clenched tightly around the gold coin.

Another small smile curved his lips and left his eyes untouched. "If the man had given me any other choice, I would have taken it." He spoke so calmly, with such quiet assuredness, he might have convinced her . . . *if* she hadn't known Jackson.

Thinking of him and how much pain this gambler had caused to so many people, she asked, "How many others have left you no choice, Noble?"

"Madam," he said, apparently horrified. "You wound me. I can truthfully say that I have never before taken a life over a card table."

Her expression must have mirrored her feelings because he straightened and swore solemnly, "May lightning stike me dead if I'm lying."

She *knew* he was lying and still, she nearly believed him.

"You know, Rachel," he said quietly, "before your cousin's untimely arrival in Stillwater, I had hoped that we could become . . . better acquainted."

"I don't know what to say."

He nodded, as if in complete understanding. "There is no need to say anything, right away. I only ask that you consider the possibility of our . . . *friendship.*"

Rachel had once seen a rabbit, held motionless by the hypnotic stare of a snake. The poor creature had been unable to move, though it must have known its only chance for survival lay in escape. Trapped in place, the rabbit had stared helplessly into the snake's black eyes until it struck, killing the rabbit instantly with a venomous bite.

Horrified at the time, she hadn't understood the power of that snake's gaze.

Until this moment.

Frowning slightly, Noble broke the spell holding her and asked, "My good luck charm?"

She pulled in a deep breath, then reluctantly dropped the golden coin into his open palm. She couldn't very well demand to keep it. To do that, she would have to call him a liar and then prove her point with him. At the moment, she was more interested in getting him out of the store before Jackson arrived.

Glancing out the front windows, she noted that afternoon was quickly fading into twilight. Soon, he would be returning from work on the new house.

"I'm sorry to have troubled you," Noble said, giving her a half bow before turning for the door.

"No trouble," she lied and followed along behind him in an effort to hurry him along.

But it was already too late.

She heard Jackson's steps on the boardwalk. Saw his shadow from the corner of her eye. Then he was there. Standing in the open doorway, his gaze locked on the man who had killed him.

The air in the room suddenly seemed heavy. Charged with desperation and fury.

Stepping around the gambler, Rachel went to Jackson's side. "Noble was just leaving," she said.

It was as if he didn't see her. Hear her. His voice a hard, grating sound, Jackson demanded, "What are you doing here?"

"Not that it's any of your concern," Noble answered, his tone overly patient. "But I was making a small purchase."

Jackson's gaze flicked to the can of gun oil. "I told you to stay the hell away from Rachel."

"Since hers is the only store in town, I hardly think that a reasonable request."

"Jackson—"

He ignored her. This close to the man who had ruined everything for him, Jackson was beyond her reach. "That was no request, mister."

Noble's entire body stiffened. His cool mask slipped a notch as he reacted to Jackson's insulting manner. "I don't know who you are," he said, his words quiet, deadly. "But if you think to give me orders, you are mistaken."

"You don't remember me, do you?" Jackson asked. Stupid question. Of course he didn't remember. Why should he? Why would one dead carpenter stand out among the others this man had probably left in his wake?

"Please," Rachel whispered.

He heard the worry in her voice, felt the tension shimmering around her. But he couldn't let this go.

"I've never seen you before," the gambler countered, though the expression on his face clearly showed that he was busily sorting through his memories, looking for an explanation for the other man's fury.

"Fifteen years ago," Jackson said, prodding him. "The Black Hound saloon." Even the name of the place made him want to cringe.

"Fifteen years!" Noble snorted a derisive laugh. "You expect me to recall something that happened fifteen years ago?"

The sneer in his voice stabbed at Jackson. "You killed a man in that saloon."

Noble's gaze flicked to Rachel, then back to Jackson. His eyes narrowed into slits. His fingers tightened around the can of oil. "You're mistaken. As I have just assured your cousin, last night was the first time that I've had to do something so unpleasant as take another life."

"You're lying."

The quiet in the room deepened.

A dark scarlet color flooded the gambler's neck and cheeks. His lips thinned into a grim slash across his face. The rigid set of his shoulders and the spasmodic tic in his tightly clenched jaw barely masked the deadly rage coursing through him.

"Who is this person," he whispered, "that I am supposed to have killed?"

"Me—" Jackson caught himself and finished haltingly. "My brother."

Rachel grabbed his forearm, felt the tightness in his muscles, and knew it would be useless to try to stop him. Instead, she turned to Noble.

"Perhaps it would be best if you left now."

Several long moments passed before the man glanced at her and nodded. "Of course. For your sake. Rachel."

Jackson snarled, shrugged off her restraining hand, and took a single step forward. "You do *nothing* for Rachel's sake. You understand me?" Swinging his right arm in a wide circle, he slammed his fist into Noble Lynch's jaw.

It happened so quickly, Rachel hardly saw him move.

The gambler staggered, but kept his feet under him. His right hand shot toward his inside breast pocket before he caught himself. Moving slowly, carefully, he reached into the front pocket of his well tailored suit instead and withdrew a snowy white handkerchief. Gently, he blotted the fabric against his split lip.

Before crumpling the handkerchief, he glanced at the

droplets of blood staining the once pristine material. His eyes lifted to Rachel's face, and she almost took a step back—away from the shining emptiness she saw there.

"If you'll excuse me, Rachel?"

She nodded dumbly.

Lynch stepped around Jackson, keeping one eye on him. Before he left, though, he paused in the doorway. "You and I will meet again, sir."

"Count on it," Jackson snapped.

Chapter ☆ Nineteen

"Damn him," Jackson muttered. "For what he did to me and for not even remembering."

"Jackson, don't."

He stepped back from her. "This isn't any good, Rachel. I can't stay here much longer. Not without—" He left the statement unfinished.

"Noble Lynch won't be here forever," she said quickly in the growing silence. "Gamblers aren't men who put down roots in a town. Sooner or later, he'll move on."

"Yeah." His head bobbed in an angry nod. "He can do that, can't he? Just up and go wherever the hell he wants to. He's *alive.*"

"I'm not worried about him." Rachel laid one hand on his forearm. "I'm thinking about you."

"Don't." He moved back another step and shook his head. "Don't think about me. Don't worry over me. It's long past time where that would do any good."

Pain slashed across her features. But there was nothing he could do to ease it.

His insides still twisted into knots, Jackson left the store a moment later. Rachel called to him, but he didn't stop. He didn't even slow down. Striding down the boardwalk, he didn't hear his friends speaking to him. He didn't feel the growing chill in the spring air. He didn't even notice the sunset.

Staring blankly straight ahead, he marched determinedly toward the meadow behind Rachel's new house.

His brain raced. Frustration rushed through his bloodstream. His boot steps pounded against the rutted dirt road. The mile or so to the house had never seemed so long. With his hands curled into helpless fists, he strode faster, more furiously.

By the time he turned in at the narrow drive, he was almost running.

He passed the unfinished house without a glance. Only an hour ago, he had experienced a wash of pride in the work he had accomplished on the place. Now, there was nothing.

Pride had been swallowed by the rising tide of fury.

Stopping in the center of the meadow, he looked around briefly, then yelled, "Lesley! Show yourself, dammit!"

Almost immediately, the air in front of him shifted, swirled, and became heavier, thicker. He watched silently as the little man appeared before him.

"I thought perhaps I would be hearing from you," Lesley said.

"You know what's been going on?"

"Of course." Lesley lifted his chin and peered along the length of his nose at him. "May I say that quite frankly I am appalled."

"Huh?" Caught off guard, Jackson lost his train of thought momentarily. "What are you talking about?"

"I am disgusted by your misuse of the powers granted to you."

"What powers?" Then a few seconds later, he asked, "The coins? You're still talking about the business with that prospector? And Sam and Mavis?"

"I *meant* what occurred between you and Rachel last night."

Jackson scowled at him. He hadn't given Lesley or the man's bosses a moment's thought the night before. That time with Rachel had been private. Or so he had thought. The realization that last night hadn't been just between the two of them after all only fed his anger.

"Last night's none of your business."

"You are supposed to be finding her a husband."

"I'm trying."

"Are you really?"

"Look, what happens between Rachel and me is none of your concern." Jackson took a step or two away, then spun around to face the smaller man. "But if it makes you feel any better, I didn't use any *powers* on her."

"Ah." Lesley tugged at the lacey cuffs on his sleeves. "Then this was merely another example of your poor judgment."

Poor judgment. Some would call it that, he supposed. But to his way of thinking, the night with Rachel was the only thing he had ever done that he didn't regret. At least, he amended, not for himself. Had it been the right thing for Rachel, though? He didn't know.

"If I made a mistake, I'm sure you'll think of a way for me to pay for it."

Lesley stiffened, and one eyebrow arched high on his forehead.

"This isn't a matter of your mistakes. It *is* a matter of Rachel Morgan's future."

Shoving one hand through his hair, Jackson said, "If it's her future, shouldn't she get a say in it? She doesn't want to get married. Not unless she's in love."

"Then convince her that she *is* in love."

Jackson stared at him. "You don't give a god damn about her at all, do you?"

"I beg your pardon?"

"Rachel. You don't care if she's happy or miserable." He walked back to stand directly in front of Lesley. "All you care about are these kids she's supposed to have. Especially this female doctor. What happens to *Rachel* doesn't matter?''

''I never said that.''

''Sure you did!'' Jackson threw his hands up in the air in disgust. ''You don't care what happens to her so long as your 'plan' for her gets carried out.''

''It is not *my* plan.''

''I don't care whose plan it is!'' he shouted, his voice raw with emotion. ''The plan doesn't matter! Rachel does. Her life. Her happiness, *matters.*''

''No one wants to see her unhappy.''

''You just told me to convince her that she's in love. You want me to lie to her! Do anything I have to in order to get her married.''

Lesley sniffed, clearly insulted.

''It might interest you to know that she *is* in love. With *me.*''

Folding his arms across his ornately clothed chest, Lesley shook his head. ''Therein lies the problem, I think, Jackson.''

''What?''

''You enjoy the fact that she believes herself to be in love with you.''

He couldn't argue with the truth. Blast it all, he *did* like knowing she loved him. He liked knowing that he was finally, at last, important to someone.

''Isn't that so, Jackson? You're failing at your assignment because you don't want to succeed?''

He shifted his gaze to stare blankly at the copse of pine trees beyond the meadow.

Lesley's words rattled around inside his head. True. All true. Just the thought of Rachel giving herself to some man who would never be able to feel for her what Jackson did, was enough to kill him. If he hadn't already been dead.

"All right, yeah," he admitted quietly. "I don't want her to marry somebody else."

"Is it Rachel's happiness or your own that is uppermost in your mind?"

He lifted guilt-stricken eyes to Lesley.

"Your wants aren't important in this, Jackson," the man said.

He knew that. He knew it better even than Lesley did. Every time he touched Rachel, Jackson knew that it might be the last time. Every time he looked at her, he tried to fashion a memory of her. If his wants had mattered in the least, he would be alive right now, begging her to marry him.

"You still have nearly four weeks to complete this assignment," Lesley said softly.

"I can't." How could he be expected to hand the woman he . . . *loved* over to another man?

"You must. Rachel is destined to have four children. And Jackson, she *will* have them."

Kids. He had never wanted kids when he was alive. Had thought them too much trouble. Too much responsibility. Now, what he wouldn't give to be able to father Rachel's children.

"Don't allow yourself to waste time dwelling on things that cannot be," Lesley warned gently. His gaze flicked to one side and a momentary look of surprise colored his features before he turned back to Jackson. "Remember, if you successfully complete this task, there is every chance that your existence will change dramatically."

Jackson took a slow, deep breath, drawing the scent of meadow grass into his lungs.

"You've long wanted to leave the Black Hound," Lesley went on. "This is your chance to go forward, Jackson."

"I know." Not too long ago, that piece of news would have meant everything to him.

"Good." Lesley straightened up and asked, "Was there anything else?"

"Yeah." There was more. The reason he had gone to the meadow in the first place. Jackson looked down at the scraped knuckles on his right hand. In memory, he felt the satisfying smack of his fist meeting the gambler's jaw. He flexed his fingers before asking, "What are you going to do about Lynch?"

Lesley's eyebrows lifted high enough to almost disappear beneath his white wig. "Do? Just what do you propose I do?"

Jackson looked at him. "Send him to Hell."

"A difficult task, as he's still alive."

His eyes narrowed slightly. "I could fix that."

"Don't."

The short, simple word caught Jackson's attention as a long speech wouldn't have. "Why not? I don't have a damn thing to lose. It's not like he can kill me again."

Lesley drifted closer and, for the first time, actually touched him. Laying one hand on Jackson's shoulder, the other man said sternly, "True, Noble Lynch is no longer in a position to do you any damage. Only *you* can do that now."

"What do you mean?" he asked, though he had a feeling he knew where this was going.

"Your soul, Jackson. You have spent fifteen years locked into a prison of your own making." He moved back on a whisper of air and began to fade. "Revenge is a stain that will taint your soul and alter the way in which you spend the rest of eternity."

Words that should have meant something to him. And might have, once. But, if he couldn't be with Rachel, the rest of eternity just wasn't important anymore.

"I don't care," he muttered thickly.

"I know," Lesley told him softly. "But surprisingly enough, I do."

Then he disappeared altogether.

*   *   *

It was several moments before Rachel could move. Her lungs ached for air, and she realized she'd forgotten to breathe. Inhaling slowly, she forced herself to look away from the place where the strangely dressed man had—*disappeared.* Shifting position to watch Jackson, she saw that he had dropped to the ground. Elbows on his knees, his face cupped in his hands, he had no idea she was there. That she had heard everything.

But the other man had known. He had looked directly at her for a split second. Yet he hadn't given her away. Perhaps then, she thought, he had *wanted* her to hear. To know.

Four weeks, Lesley had said. Was that really all the time they had left? Her heartbeat staggered painfully. Nothing else she had heard had made the impact that statement had. Not even knowing that a daughter of hers was destined to become a *doctor.*

Everything faded in importance beside one inescapable fact.

Jackson would be leaving her.

Soon.

And if there was nothing she could do to prevent that, she had to see to it that Jackson received whatever reward he was due. The thought of him having to spend any more time in the saloon where he had died nearly broke her heart.

She wouldn't let him throw eternity away for her sake.

Or for the sake of revenge.

Quietly, she walked across the meadow toward him. When she was close, he looked up, his gaze locking with hers.

"Rachel." He groaned, but didn't seem surprised.

"I followed you," she said lamely.

"How much did you hear?"

"Everything."

"Christ," he muttered and flopped backward into the

grass. Staring up at the lavendar sky, he said, "I didn't want you to know."

"What?" she asked as she dropped down beside him. "That I'm supposed to have four children?" Children who wouldn't have him as their father. A small, sharp pain nestled deep in her chest. She ignored it. "That you're leaving soon? Or that if I marry someone else you'll be able to leave that hellish existence you told me about?"

"Rachel . . ."

"And you didn't want me to know that if you kill Noble Lynch your soul is in jeopardy?"

He turned his head to look at her. "Let me worry about that, all right? It doesn't concern you."

"Don't try to distract me, Jackson," she said. "I want to know. What would happen to you if you—"

"Kill Noble?" he interrupted.

She paled slightly, but kept her voice steady. "Yes."

He glanced at her. "You said you heard everything that Lesley said?"

Rachel nodded.

He shrugged and folded his hands atop his chest. "Then you know as much as I do."

Visions rose up in her mind. Remembered threats from fanatical preachers on Sunday mornings. She could almost smell the scent of sulphur and feel the heat of Hell's fires. In her mind's eye, she saw Jackson, tortured and alone.

Suffering.

For eternity.

Rachel shivered as though a cold wind had raced down her spine. She couldn't let that happen to him.

"You have to stay away from Noble."

His features hardened. "I told you, Rachel. This doesn't concern you."

She flinched, even though she knew his anger wasn't directed at her. She understood all too well the sense of helplessness he had to be feeling. She, too, felt as though

she had been swept up into something she had no control
over. There was a solution to this mess, though. And she
would find it.

But not tonight.

She forced a smile and stretched out beside him, aligning
her body along the length of his. Jackson's arm slipped
around her, pulling her close, and she laid her head on his
chest. "Everything about you concerns me, Jackson," she
said simply. "I love you."

"I know," he whispered, and lifted one hand to smooth
a strand of blond hair back from her face.

Rachel looked up and watched the long, slender blades
of grass dip and sway in the gentle breeze. The first stars
began to appear in the darkening sky.

The world should look different to her, she thought. She
had just eavesdropped on two ghosts discussing what
course her life should take. Yet, everything around her
looked the same as always.

It was Rachel herself who had changed.

"God, I'm sorry, Rachel," he said quietly.

"About what?"

Jackson brushed his hand along her back and committed
one more thing to memory. This evening, with the sky going purple, a gentle wind sighing through the grass, and the
feel of her breath on his neck.

She turned in his grasp and let her hand slide across his
chest. He tensed at her touch, longing to make love to her
again. He remembered how it had felt to slide into her heat.
To feel her hands clutch at him. To hear her soft moans of
pleasure.

"Jackson?" she asked as she propped herself up to look
down at him. "What are you sorry for?"

"So damn much." He was sorry for wasting his life and
dying too young. Sorry to have not found the love of his
life until after he was dead.

But especially sorry for having taken her virtue only to

leave her. He inhaled sharply and went on. "We shouldn't have done what we did last night, Rachel."

She pushed away from him, but he held her fast against his chest, forcing her to look at him.

"I didn't have the right to love you."

"I *gave* you the right."

"Blast it Rachel," he said, "I owed you better. I wanted to do right by you."

She twisted away from him and went up on her knees. "What do you mean, you owe me?"

He sat up and looked directly into her eyes. "Jesus, you told me yourself what a miserable childhood you had! Because of me. Because I didn't care enough to stick around and make sure the Heinz couple were good folks."

"That wasn't your fault," she broke in.

Something inside him ripped painfully. Even now, she was defending him. "Of course it was my fault, Rachel."

"Jackson, it wasn't all bad. You saved my life, remember? Without you, I would have died out there where I lost my family."

He gritted his teeth until he thought his jaw would crack.

"I made wonderful friends in Stillwater," she went on. "I have my own business . . . and now, I have you again, too."

"Rachel, I botched things up so badly, you weren't even able to find somebody to love. You wasted all those years on memories of *me.*"

"Nothing was wasted. Besides, I did find someone to love. You."

He laughed shortly and shook his head. "You deserve a helluvalot better than me, honey."

She reached out to touch his cheek.

He caught her hand and held it to his face, savoring the warmth of her touch. Shaking his head gently, he smiled at her. "You're a hardheaded woman, Rachel Morgan."

"So you've said."

"You know," he said softly, "when I stepped into the Mercantile and saw Lynch standing beside you, I wanted to kill him."

"I know."

He released her, and she pulled her hand back. Standing up, he helped her to her feet and admitted, "Most of that feeling was about what he did to me. But some of it was because he was standing there, next to you. Alive. Able to do all the things I can't."

"Jackson . . ."

"I have a feeling that I'm going to feel pretty much the same way about any man you marry."

"I've already told you—"

"You heard Lesley, Rachel," he interrupted. "So you know about those kids you're supposed to have. Hell! The first one's due to get born early next year."

Her eyes widened, and she glanced down at her flat stomach.

"See, honey? There's just nothin' we can do about this. It's how things are, that's all."

Looking up at him, she reminded him of her suggestion the night before. "You could marry me, Jackson."

"No."

"Why not? For all we know, *you're* the father of that child due next year."

He took one giant step back from her. His gaze swept over her as if expecting to see evidence of a pregnancy he hadn't even considered until that moment. Was it he wondered wildly, even possible? Could he actually have made her pregnant?

"Don't you see, Jackson? You *are* the man I was meant to be with."

"No, this isn't right. It can't be." He didn't want to believe. He didn't want to hope. Because when those hopes eventually died, accepting that would be worse than anything he had survived in the last fifteen years.

"Of course, it can. If you can be here with me now, anything is possible."

He started pacing. Long, jerky steps that took him in a wide circle around her. His brain raced as he tried to figure this out. If he could be the father of her child, why *couldn't* he marry her? Was one idea any more crazy than the other?

"Marry me, Jackson."

He stopped dead and looked at her. If it were only that simple. Lord, he wanted to. He was sorely tempted to risk everything on the chance that it might be possible. But only last night he'd given in to his desires only to feel as guilty as hell today. Then something else occurred to him and he had to shake his head.

"It won't work," he told her.

"Why not?" She went to him, wrapping her arms around his middle.

"Because I was sent here to get you married. Once you are, I'll disappear."

"You don't know that for sure."

"Yeah, I do." He felt the truth of it clean down to his bones.

"Then," she countered quickly, "if I *never* marry, you could stay."

"Rachel . . ."

"No." Stubbornly, she shook her head, then suddenly looked up and asked, "Where's that gold coin you have?"

Puzzled, he reached into his pocket for the last coin.

She grabbed it. "I'll just wish it so. It's magic, Jackson. We can be together."

He pulled the coin from her hand and held it tight in a closed fist. "Rachel, stop. This isn't going to change anything." Sadly, he smiled down at her. "Magic can't help you and me. It's too late for us. It always was."

Her breath caught as she fell against him. His arms closed around her, and he rested his chin on top of her head. The sound of her tears tore at his insides. He felt each tremor as it rippled through her slender body. Sighing, he told himself that it would have been better for her if he had never been sent to her so many years before.

But then he would have gone through eternity an empty man.

Knowing Rachel, loving her, was the only worthwhile thing in his whole miserable existence.

Closing his eyes, he whispered soothing words as his hands stroked up and down her back. The coin he still held tingled with subtle warmth.

When her tears subsided, he looked down at her and waited for her to meet his gaze. "I probably shouldn't say anything more," he said softly. "Guess it's really too late for this, too. But I want you to know."

"What is it?"

His gaze moved over her features slowly, lovingly. Her lovely blue eyes were awash with tears and her bottom lip continued to quiver despite her obvious efforts at control. She had never looked more beautiful, and his silent heart ached.

"I love you," he whispered, in awe of what he had found with her.

She blinked back another surge of tears and fought to smile at him. "I know that."

"I'm glad. It means a lot to me to get to say those words." He bent to kiss her forehead and paused before adding, "I've never said them before. Not to anyone."

She bit into her bottom lip, but still managed to keep that tiny smile on her face. "Jackson," she whispered. "What are we going to do?"

"Ah Rachel," he said with a sigh. "There's nothing we *can* do, honey. I just wish we were back at your house. In bed. Happy, like we were last night."

The coin in his hand began to hum and burn.

His eyes widened.

''Shit!''

A moment later, they lay naked, entwined together in Rachel's bed.

And Jackson's last coin was gone.

Chapter ☆ *Twenty*

"Maybe you should take back the coin you gave me for safekeeping," Rachel said as she watched Jackson getting dressed.

"No." He turned to face her.

His fingers did up the buttons on his dark blue shirt, but she wanted to tell him to stop. To come back to bed. With her.

"I want you to keep that coin," he said, stuffing the tails of his shirt into his pants. "When I'm gone, if Lynch is still around, I want to make damn sure you have a way to protect yourself if you have to."

She heard everything he said, but her mind seemed to snatch at one particular phrase. "What do you mean 'if Lynch is still around?' "

He shifted his gaze from hers, then sat down on the bed to pull his boots on. "I didn't mean anything."

Rachel tucked the sheet around her and scooted to the edge of her bed. The bed she would never be able to sleep in again without remembering these two nights with Jackson.

"Yes, you did," she said and bent to one side until he was forced to look at her. "You're planning something."

"Leave it alone, Rachel."

"I won't. You heard Lesley. Is taking revenge on Noble Lynch worth damning yourself for eternity?"

His eyes met hers briefly, hauntingly. "Revenge is all I've got left."

Rachel's heart ached for him. For them. But she wasn't as willing to give up hope as he seemed to be. "Jackson, we could still find a way."

"Quit torturing yourself, Rachel." He stood up and looked down at her. In the soft glow of the bedside lamp, his green eyes shone with an emotion that she couldn't quite identify. "Quit torturing both of us."

The night was over. The hours granted them by the golden coin had come to an end. Only a short time ago, they'd been wrapped together in a cocoon of love, separate from the world, belonging only to each other. Now, Rachel looked at him and knew that in his mind, their brief idyll was finished. He was already distancing himself from her. Pulling back to make their final parting less painful. She hugged the sheet to her and glanced out the window, dismayed to find the first streaks of dawn blushing the sky.

Jackson dropped to one knee in front of her and took both of her hands in his. "Whatever else happens, I want you to know, it's all right not to get married, Rachel."

"What?"

"You don't want to marry anybody," he said as he ducked his head. And when he looked up again, a wry smile touched his face. "And I've got to say, I don't really care for the idea myself."

"But what about you?" she asked, her fingers tightening around his. "If I don't marry, you'll go back to that saloon. You might be there forever."

"What happens to me is not important." He stared into her eyes. "I had my chance at life. I fouled it up. But I won't throw your life away just to save my miserable soul."

"Jackson—"

"The way I see it," he went on, smoothly cutting her

off, "I'll probably get to stick around here for the next four weeks. They'll expect me to keep trying to get you hitched." Releasing her hands, he stood up. "Then I'll be gone, and you can go back to the way things were."

She came up onto her knees and leaned into him, wrapping her arms about his neck. Laying her head against his chest, she listened for a heartbeat that wasn't there. "Nothing will ever be the same again," she whispered.

"For me, either." He dipped his head and kissed her shoulder. Smoothing his hands up and down her bare back one last time, he said, "Who knows, though? Maybe we'll see each other again, sometime. Somewhere."

Her breath caught on a choked sob as he stepped back from her, turning his face away. "I'm going down to the new house. I want to see how much work I can get out of Sam in the next few weeks."

"Jackson?"

He stopped at the door and looked back at her.

"There's still a chance I might be pregnant." Please God, she added silently.

A wistful smile crossed his face briefly, then he left the room, closing the door gently behind him.

Two weeks gone.

And two weeks left.

The four weeks Lesley had promised Jackson were nearly finished. She couldn't afford to wait any longer.

Rachel tapped her foot against the dirt as she glanced over her shoulder quickly at the bustle of people on Main Street. She shouldn't have come in broad daylight. She should have sent Noble a message, asking him to come to her. Then, at least, she wouldn't feel as if half the town were watching her.

But she hadn't wanted to risk Jackson coming back from the new house early. She didn't want him to know about her plan until it was too late for him to do anything to stop her.

"What's taking that man so long?" she muttered under her breath. A wagon creaked and rolled along the street, and she stepped up onto the boardwalk to get out of the way. Clouds of dust rose up, swirled over her, then settled back down again.

Rachel coughed, waved one hand in front of her face, then smoothed the front of her deep rose-colored dress. She was doing the right thing, she told herself for the twentieth time. The only thing she *could* do to protect Jackson against himself.

Tossing a quick glance at the saloon in front of her, she remembered all the nights Jackson had spent inside that building lately. It was as if he were silently daring the gambler to challenge him.

She reached up and rubbed her eyes tiredly. The argument she'd had with Jackson only the night before rang in her ears again.

"Leave Lynch alone," she had pleaded with him.

"Noble Lynch is my problem, Rachel. I'll handle him my way."

"Despite Lesley's warning?" She had moved toward him, but he stepped back, out of her reach. As he had ever since that last lovely night they'd spent in each other's arms.

"What happens to me doesn't matter now," he had told her just before storming out of the Mercantile toward the saloon.

She knew what he meant. Since she wouldn't marry without love, he would be trapped in The Black Hound saloon. He wanted her happiness at any cost, but at the same time, he no longer worried about the welfare of his soul. To Jackson, *anything* would be preferable to an eternity spent in that saloon.

Even Hell.

"I won't let you do it, Jackson," she whispered and didn't notice the startled look a passing stranger gave her. "I won't let you throw away your chance at Heaven."

A low rumble of thunder rolled across the sky, and she shivered.

" 'Morning, Rachel," Sally called.

She jumped and half turned to look at her friend, standing in the open doorway of the laundry. Blast it, she thought. She should have waited for Noble somewhere else. Somewhere away from prying eyes and well meaning friends. "Hello, Sally."

"What are you all dressed up for?"

"How's Mike?" she countered, trying to avoid Sally's question altogether.

The other woman grinned. "I'm pleased to say that the man isn't nearly as dirty as I thought he was. Now that I've promised to marry him, you'd be surprised how clean he can stay."

"I'm glad for you," Rachel said. She was glad. For Sally. Hester. Mavis. Glad for all of them.

Terrified for herself.

"Rachel?" Sally took a step closer. "Are you all right?"

"I'm fine." At least, she would be once her task was completed and Jackson was on his way to whatever reward awaited him.

"Miss Rachel?"

She turned toward the saloon and looked at the short, round man she'd sent inside with her message to Lynch. "Yes?"

"Noble says he's proud to talk to ya." His bald head bobbed like a cork on a string. "He'll be along directly."

"Thank you," she whispered.

As the man scuttled back into the dark interior of the saloon, Sally moved up behind her.

"Noble Lynch?" she asked. "What do you want with him?"

"I can't talk now, Sally." Rachel threw her a quick look. "I'll explain everything later."

"Explain what?" she demanded, her voice rising slightly. "Rachel, what's going on?"

Noble stepped out of the saloon, a welcoming smile on his lips. He wore a finely cut gray suit over a crisp white shirt. His black string tie was precisely knotted, his graying hair trimmed neatly, and the hat he carried, dust free.

Rachel inhaled deeply. Handsome, well mannered, and a cold killer. She shuddered and told herself to avoid looking into his eyes. This was going to be hard enough as it was.

"Rachel, what a surprise," he said as he came forward one hand outstretched.

"A pleasant one, I hope," she answered and took the hand he offered.

"Undeniably."

Plastering a smile onto her face, she said in a voice that was none too steady, "If you have the time, I'd like to speak with you about something important."

"Rachel . . ." her friend cut in.

Noble flicked a disinterested glance at the laundress.

"Sally, I'll see you later, all right?" Rachel turned and looked at her friend for a long moment.

Sally's worried gaze shot from Rachel to Noble and back again. Her lips thinned in displeasure as she crossed her arms over her chest. "I'll be right here," she finally said with a stabbing glare at the gambler. "Waiting."

Rachel's eyes slid shut momentarily in relief. "Thanks."

"Shall we go somewhere more . . . *private?*" the gambler asked solicitously.

"Yes," Rachel agreed. "That would probably be best."

He tucked her hand into the crook of his arm, set his hat on his head, then escorted her down the boardwalk, past the saloon.

Uneasily, Sally watched them go. In a few short minutes,

they had reached the end of the boardwalk and had disappeared into the crowd.

Something was wrong.

Normally, Rachel would no more seek out Noble Lynch than she would caper down Main Street in her bloomers. A twist of worry gripped her.

She had to find Jackson.

" 'Mornin', Sally me love!"

Spinning around, she grinned. Her big Irishman was just swinging down off his stallion.

Surely it was a sign.

"O'Hara," she yelled as she ran to him, "don't get off that horse!"

Jackson stepped back, giving the newly installed bannister a careful look. Reaching out, he grabbed hold of the newel post and gave it a shake.

"Solid as stone," Sam crowed from behind him.

A flush of pleasure rose up inside him. Damn, it felt good building something strong. Permanent. His practiced eye followed the line of the oak bannister to the second story where Rachel's bedroom would be.

She would be living here long after he was gone. A good, well built house was the last gift he could give her. Wherever he ended up, he would at least know that some part of him remained behind. With her.

"I tell you, Jackson," Sam said, clapping him on the shoulder. "I wish you'd think about my business idea. We could be rich men, my friend."

Indeed, they probably could have been.

He shook his head, picked up a hammer and moved across the completely enclosed room to work on the mantle above the stone fireplace. "Sorry Sam," he said quietly. "But I'll be moving on in a couple of weeks."

"You're crazy, Jackson."

"Huh?" He moved a level from one end of the mantle

to the other, checking the bubble in the glass. "Just because I won't go into business with you?"

"Hell no. For walking away from Rachel."

"It's better for her if I leave," he said quietly.

"That's foolishness. She loves you. And you love her."

Jackson shot his friend a glare. "You don't know what's going on, Sam. So back off."

The other man looked as though he might argue with him, but a shout from outside distracted both of them.

"Jackson!"

The sound of a horse's hooves, thundering along the drive, brought him running to the front door in time to see Mike O'Hara swing Sally to the ground. The woman's feet had barely touched the dirt before she was sprinting for the house.

Fear charged through him, slashing at his insides.

"What's wrong?" Jackson jumped down the three steps from the porch and grabbed her shoulders. "Is it Rachel? Is she hurt? Dammit Sally, talk!"

She yanked free of him and pushed her hair out of her eyes. "Rachel went to see Noble Lynch. At the saloon. She sent him some kind of message and then she went off with him." Sally shook her head and looked up into cold green eyes. "She didn't look right, Jackson. She looked . . . scared."

He started for Mike's horse. As the bigger man stepped down, Jackson snatched at the reins. "I'll need to borrow your animal, Mike."

"Jackson," Sally shouted as he wheeled the stallion around and spurred it into a gallop, "they walked off toward the pines behind the school!"

His reply, if there was one, was lost in a clap of thunder.

"Surely you'd rather finish our discussion back at the Mercantile," Noble said, yanking his hat off before the wind could steal it. "Get out of this storm?"

"No." Rachel shook her head firmly. "I think we've said it all, anyway. If you agree, we can meet at the church in an hour."

Noble smiled, and she saw her own reflection in the dark jet of his eyes. It was no consolation to know she looked as terrible as she felt.

"Of course I agree, my dear," the gambler said, lifting one of her hands to his lips. Rachel forced herself to hold still. "I can't tell you how honored I am that you have come to me like this. It's more than I ever dared hope for."

She nodded stiffly, like a puppet with one broken string. It was settled. In one hour, she would meet Noble at the church and marry him.

By the time Jackson returned from work, it would be over. He wouldn't be able to stop her. Of course, he would be furious, but she was willing to face that. In fact, she was willing to do anything to keep him from spending eternity as he had the last fifteen years.

By marrying Noble Lynch, she could save Jackson from his own need for revenge. He wouldn't kill her husband— as much as he might want to. He loved her too much to deny her the chance of having those four children. Even if their father *was* Noble Lynch.

She shuddered, and her stomach lurched as she realized for the one hundredth time that Jackson's love for her gave her the one chance she had to save his soul.

"Shall I speak to the minister?" Noble asked. "Make the arrangements?"

"No thank you," she said above the howling wind. "I'll do that and meet you there as planned." She needed some time by herself. Time to get used to the idea of being married to a man like Lynch.

The gambler swallowed back a shout of triumph and called on his best manners. They weren't married yet; she might still change her mind. And he wasn't willing to risk her backing out. Surprising as her proposal had been, he was no fool. A rich, lonely wife with a profitable business besides was not a gift horse to be ignored.

"At least allow me to escort you home," he insisted, taking her arm firmly.

Thunder roared, lightning flashed across the dark morning sky. Trees bent low as if in prayer, and Rachel's dress snapped around her legs like a hungry dog.

Jackson rode like a madman, skirting Main Street in favor of avoiding the crowds that might have slowed him down. Wind pulled at him. Thunder shouted overhead, and each bolt of lightning earned a screech of terror from the horse beneath him.

Oblivious to everything around him, Jackson held onto the reins tightly and let his fury race free. His head pounded in time with the drum of the horse's hoofbeats.

A red haze of anger clouded his vision as the first heavy drops of rain pelted him. When the row of pines behind the school came into view, he narrowed his eyes against the rain, straining to find the woman who meant everything to him.

He spotted them as they hurried across the open field toward town. Jackson spurred the stallion on, finally drawing it to a rearing stop directly in front of them.

Jumping down from the saddle, he smacked the horse's rump, sending it running for town. Then Jackson went to Rachel.

"Are you all right?" he shouted, letting his gaze sweep over her.

"I'm fine, Jackson," she cried and pushed wet strands of hair back from her face. "What are you doing here?"

"That's what I want to know from you."

Noble grabbed Rachel's elbow and pulled her close to his side. "Keep your hands off my fianceé."

"What?" Jackson's voice, raw with pain, carried over a clap of thunder, and he didn't wait for her answer before demanding, "What are you doing? Why? Why, Rachel?"

Her eyes stung with tears she refused to shed.

"Get back," Noble snarled.

"I'll see to *you* in a minute," Jackson snapped and grabbed Rachel, pulling her to him, away from the gambler. "What happened to you? What happened to all your fine talk about not marrying unless you were in love?"

"I am in love," she retorted, pushing her hair out of her eyes to look directly into his.

"With *him?*" Sneering laughter colored his voice.

"No." Wind tore at her voice, but still he heard the words that slashed at him. "I'm in love with you. So I'm going to marry Noble."

"That's enough," Lynch shouted and pulled Rachel to his side; at the same time, he gave Jackson a strong shove.

Jackson staggered, tore his wounded gaze from Rachel's face, and lunged at the gambler. Knocking the elegantly dressed man to the dirt, Jackson slammed his fist into the other man's jaw just before the gambler shifted, braced himself, and heaved Jackson off into the grassy dirt.

Gaining his feet quickly, Jackson circled the other man warily, ready for anything. "You're not going to marry her, Lynch. I'll kill you first and send you straight to Hell!"

"Jackson, no!" Rachel yelled at him. "Let me marry him. It will all be over, then."

"You're doing this for me?" He threw her a quick look, then turned back to his opponent.

"Of course," she screamed over a peal of thunder. "Blast you, Jackson, I won't have you spend eternity in misery!"

Dumbfounded, he stopped and stared at her. She had been willing to sacrifice herself for his sake. Rain slapped at him. Jagged spears of lightning shot across the sky, and the resulting roll of thunder shook the ground.

"No, Rachel. I won't let you do it." Tearing his gaze from hers, he looked at Noble Lynch, who was staring at the two of them as though they were insane. "You're *not* going to marry her."

"You can't stop me," the gambler shouted back.

"We settle this between you and me, here. Now."

The gambler jerked him a nod. "Fine with me." His eyes narrowed thoughtfully. "You're like a bad tooth, *cousin*. The only way to cure the ache is to pull the tooth and be done with it."

"Jackson," Rachel rushed to him, looked up into his eyes, and pleaded, "Don't. Don't risk this."

He set her to one side and took a step toward Lynch. "I'll need a gun. Or a knife."

Lynch's eyebrows lifted; he laughed out loud. "Either one, eh? This should be diverting." He pointed to a small rise just twenty feet or so away. "Over there. Away from the *lady*." He gave her a deep bow, then turned and started walking.

"Stay here."

"Jackson—"

"Dammit Rachel," he growled at her. "Stay put. *Please*."

She nodded stiffly. Fear glittered in her blue eyes. Fear for him. But he couldn't let that stop him. He bent, pressed a quick kiss to her lips, then followed Lynch.

"If it's all right with you, I'll flip a coin to decide which weapons we use." The gambler dug into his pants pocket and drew out a handful of change.

"Why should I trust you? It's probably a two-headed coin."

Noble laughed at him and pushed his wind-blown, soaking wet hair back from his forehead. "All right then, how about if I use one of *yours?*" he asked and held up the golden coin he'd stolen.

"A liar, a murderer, *and* a thief."

Noble inclined his head with a smile. "What do you say? If it's a moon, we use guns. Stars, knives?" Without waiting for a reply, he flipped the coin high into the wind-tossed air.

Jackson followed the shining, spinning golden piece until the gambler snatched at it, then slapped it down onto his other hand. He glanced down at it before looking at Jackson. "It's a star, boy! We use knives."

"How do I know it's a star?" Jackson hollered back over the moaning wind. "Maybe you're just better with a knife than a gun."

The gambler threw his head back and laughed. "You can trust me! May lightning strike me dead if I'm lying!"

A white hot streak of lightning pierced the clouds overhead. Brilliant light exploded all around them. Then the jagged bolt stabbed Noble Lynch, slamming him into the earth.

Rachel screamed over the roar of thunder.

And Jackson disappeared.

The Black Hound saloon looked the same as it had the day he had left it for Stillwater.

Stunned by the abrupt shift in his surroundings, Jackson rubbed the back of his neck. His hair was dry. As were his clothes. Only a moment ago, he had been in a storm like none he'd ever seen. Facing his enemy, he had watched the man die, killed by his own black nature. Now, he did a slow turn, noting the same old faces, the same falling down chairs and tables. He was back, in his own private little Hell.

His gaze swept the rest of the room and stopped when he spotted Lesley.

"If you've come to preach at me, don't bother," he said and walked through the rickety wall to the porch outside. He didn't care what happened to him now. The important thing to remember was, Rachel was safe from Noble Lynch. And she would live her life the way *she* wanted to. Maybe, someday, she'd even be happy again.

Lesley floated through the wall and drifted to his side. Annoying, Jackson thought, that he hadn't been able to figure out how to float in the last fifteen years. But then, he told himself grimly, he had the rest of eternity to work on it.

He flicked a quick glance at the small man beside him. No doubt, there was big trouble headed his way.

"Before you say anything," Jackson started, "if this is about Noble Lynch, I didn't kill him. He killed himself by stealing that coin in the first place."

Lesley scowled thoughtfully. "We know all about Mister Lynch. He has been taken care of."

"What happened to him?"

The strange little man cocked his head at him as if to ask, "Do you really want to know?"

No, he didn't. He didn't care enough one way or the other anymore. It was enough to know that the bastard wouldn't be killing anybody else.

"Never mind," he said.

"I've been sent—" Lesley began.

"Let me guess. It's not about Lynch, so you're probably here to show me the road to Hell." Jackson laughed shortly. "Don't worry about it. Left to myself, I'm sure I'll find it."

"If you wouldn't mind allowing me to speak," Lesley replied with a delicate sniff. "I was about to say that the Powers That Be have decided to surrender."

"What do you mean, surrender?"

"Only that They have despaired of your ever learning a lesson while trapped in this world of neither life nor death."

A flash of hope shimmered through him.

"It has been decided that you are to return to a life on Earth." He reached up and adjusted the fit of his wig. "It is to be hoped that you will do a better job at life this time."

Life.

Stunned, he stared at the other man for several long moments, then walked out into the middle of the street. A weary looking cowhand trotted his horse right through him. Jackson didn't care.

He was going to live again.

This time, he swore it would be different.

He could go back to Rachel. Live out his life with her, making love and babies and building houses with Sam and going to town socials and . . .

"I'm afraid not," Lesley interrupted his thoughts sternly.

Jackson swiveled his head to look at him.

"The life we are offering you cannot be spent with Rachel Morgan."

"Why not?" His voice scratched past his tightly closed throat.

"Because she knows who you are." Lesley shrugged his narrow shoulders. "This is to be a new life. Starting fresh. You can't do that in Stillwater."

His dreams and hopes died in an instant. Pain, sharper and more all consuming than he had ever known, crushed him. These people were good at making troublesome souls suffer. Hold out a carrot in front of a starving man, then yank it back just before he can touch it. Taste it.

For less than a minute, Rachel and all they could have had together had been within his grasp. But it had been like grabbing at smoke.

Now there was nothing. He was back where he had started, staring at an eternity of loneliness.

"You will finally be able to leave this place," Lesley said quietly.

No. Even *this* was preferable to being alive and not with Rachel.

"Forget it, Les," he said wearily. "Life without Rachel isn't life. I don't want your damned offer. I'll stay right here, in this piss poor excuse for a town." His gaze swept over the old, weathered buildings, the uneven boardwalks, and the sun-baked, dusty street. Turning to Lesley again, he said tightly, ''Better yet, send me to Hell. But don't expect me to live without Rachel.''

Thoughtfully, Lesley watched him as Jackson stomped past him into The Black Hound.

Rachel pulled her hem out of the mud and raced up the slight incline. Noble Lynch lay where he had fallen, staring up at the sky through surprised, sightless eyes. She turned away quickly, letting her gaze sweep across the area.

Jackson was gone. As if he had never been there. As if the last few weeks had been a strange dream from which she was only now waking.

Tilting her head back, she glared up at the churning black clouds and squinted against the driving rain.

''This isn't finished,'' she swore under her breath, then turned and headed for town.

On Main Street, she hurried blindly past the people scurrying for shelter from the storm. Rain slashed at her. Thick mud grabbed at her feet, making each step an effort. The wind pushed at her as if deliberately trying to slow her down.

Outside the Mercantile, she slipped in the muck, going to her knees. A sob tore from her throat. She dragged herself free, crawled up the three steps to the boardwalk, then staggered to the door.

Once inside, she paused only long enough to close and lock the front door behind her. A heartbeat later, she raced across the floor to a certain shelf behind the counter. Dropping to her knees, she pushed the neatly stacked cans out of her way, sending them tumbling to the floor. Grabbing the small tin box from its hiding place, she tore it open and snatched up the golden coin Jackson had given her and smiled down at it. Its tingling warmth spread up the length of her arm, bringing strength to her limbs and hope into her heart.

Closing her fist around the coin, Rachel stood up and walked to the very center of the store. Her sodden skirt clung to her legs, making each step a trial. She reached up to push lank, muddy hair out of her eyes, then squeezed the gold piece in her other hand tightly. Tight enough that she felt the engraved images on the coin pressing into her flesh.

Taking a long, deep breath, Rachel cleared her throat and in a quiet, but firm, voice announced plainly, "I want Jackson Tate here. Alive. He is the man I choose as my husband."

She waited. One moment. Two.

But nothing happened.

Rachel choked back a rising tide of fear, opened her palm and looked at the coin she still held. It hadn't disappeared as the others had after creating magic.

The dull gleam of gold taunted her silently.

"I'm afraid," a familiar male voice said softly, "it doesn't work that way."

Chapter ☆ Twenty-one

Her heart in her throat. Rachel spun around, coming face to face with Lesley. Immediately, she looked past the fussy little ghost, her gaze scanning the empty store, futilely searching for Jackson.

But he wasn't there.

"Where is he?" she demanded.

Lesley tugged at the ends of his sleeves. His fingertips fluffed the fall of lace draping across his small, dainty hands. "Jackson has returned from whence he came."

"The saloon?" Rachel shouted and took a step closer. Lesley floated backward in response. "He's back at The Black Hound?" she asked.

"He told you?" The little man shook his head slowly and clucked his tongue in disapproval. "Really, the man simply has no regard whatever for the rules."

Rachel didn't care about rules either. All she cared about was Jackson. "Send him back to me," she said.

"I can't, my dear. It is not in my power."

She saw the sympathy in his eyes, but it brought no comfort. Rachel doubted very much if anything would comfort her again. Glancing down at the gold piece in her hand, she whispered, "But the coin. I said what I wanted . . ."

"That coin cannot be used to wish a dead man back to life."

"Then what can I do?" she asked.

"Nothing, I'm afraid."

"He's gone?" Rachel whispered. "Forever?"

Lesley gave her a tired, patient smile. "My dear, one day you'll see that—"

"No."

He blinked at her interruption.

"Don't tell me that one day the pain will pass. Don't expect me to stop loving him."

"I knew it was a mistake to send him here," Lesley muttered.

"No," Rachel countered quickly. "The mistake was in taking him away."

"He was never supposed to stay."

The cold of her sopping wet dress seeped into her bones. She shivered and wrapped her arms tight about her waist. The truth only deepened the cold, shrouding her heart and soul in ice.

"My dear," Lesley said quietly as he hesitantly moved a bit closer, "I understand the upset you've experienced."

"Upset?" She lifted her head to glare at him. Her life lay in splinters around her. Jackson was out of her reach, and the long, lonely years ahead of her suddenly seemed no more than a prison sentence from which there was no escape.

Hope had died as surely as Noble Lynch. For too long, she had deluded herself into the belief that there was a chance for Jackson and her to find a lifetime together. Now there was nothing left. Not even the contentment she had found before Jackson's arrival in Stillwater.

Rage, fear, and emptiness swamped her soul. "Upset?" she repeated, advancing on the horrified ghost.

Lesley scuttled back a safe distance again.

"The man I love has been torn from me without so much

as a goodbye! Every dream I ever had ended in a flash of lightning. Jackson is trapped in some dingy saloon for eternity, and all I can do is wait to die so *maybe* I'll see him again. And you think that I'm *upset???*''

Lesley cleared his throat and nervously ran one finger around the inside of his collar.

She looked away from him, her mind suddenly racing with ideas. ''I'll go to him,'' she murmured, more to herself than the ghost. ''I'll go to Pine Ridge. To that saloon. Even if I can't see him, at least I can be near him.''

''Don't do that,'' Lesley advised quietly.

''You can't stop me.''

''Perhaps not,'' he agreed, then went on. ''You say you love Jackson Tate?''

''Yes.''

''Then don't go to The Black Hound. Your presence there would only torture him further.''

She swallowed heavily and looked at the short man. Again, she noted the sympathy in his eyes, but this time she saw something else as well. Concern.

''To see you,'' Lesley went on, ''to have you close by and not be able to touch you would, to Jackson, be more of a Hell than any sulphur and brimstone nightmare.''

''You care about him too?'' she asked as the first sting of tears welled up in her eyes.

''Surprisingly enough,'' Lesley said with a soft smile, ''yes, I do.''

He was right. She knew it. Rachel had hoped to spare Jackson's soul any pain by marrying Noble Lynch. She couldn't now do something that would only serve to make his private Hell a worse one.

Her shoulders slumped, and she accepted defeat. She had so many questions. How had this happened? How had she and Jackson come to such a pass? And how would she go on without him? ''You realize,'' she said softly, ''your plans for me are finished. I won't marry anyone else.''

He sighed heavily. "Yes, my dear. I had suspected that would be your reaction."

She glanced at him. "What will happen to Jackson now? I mean, since I'm not going to marry and have those children I was supposed to?"

"I don't know," he admitted. "Perhaps nothing."

And perhaps something. Rachel shivered at the possibilities. "Should I . . ."

"I will do what I can for him," Lesley told her as he began to fade. "Be well, Rachel."

"Wait!" she shouted, even as he disappeared. "Tell Jackson I love him!"

A soft voice, filled with regret, swirled around her. "He knows that, my dear."

FIVE MONTHS LATER

"Rachel." Mavis huffed as she tugged the edges of her friend's carpetbag together, "this is foolishness."

"She's right," Sally said as she picked up Rachel's coat and draped it over her arm. "This is no time to be taking a train trip for heaven's sake."

Rachel ignored both of them and concentrated instead on situating her hat properly. Once finished, she gave her mirror image a satisfied nod, then glanced at Hester. "Do you think I'm foolish, too?"

The others stared at her, waiting for the schoolteacher to agree with them. Hester, though, surprised them all. Stepping up close to Rachel, she laid one hand on her friend's arm and shook her head. "No, I don't."

"Hester!" the other two women in the room gasped.

She didn't spare them a glance, but kept her gaze locked with Rachel's. "I think you have to do what you feel is important. And if going to see Jackson's relatives is what you need to do, then you should go."

"Honestly," Mavis sputtered.

"They're both crazy," Sally said.

"But," Hester went on, "you should also be very careful, Rachel. Take time to rest. And come home soon."

Rachel smiled at her friend. Since marrying Charlie Miller, Hester had truly come into her own. Her self-confidence had grown until she was no longer the shy little thing hiding in a corner, but a thoughtful, soft-spoken, happy woman.

"Thank you for understanding, Hester."

"Yeah," Sally's tone dripped sarcasm. "Thanks."

Hester smiled at her. "Sally, you know you wouldn't want any of us telling you what to do just because you're expecting a baby."

"True," she said with a loving pat over her still flat tummy. She lifted her eyes to meet Rachel's. "But then the father of my baby didn't run off and leave me to face a town alone."

Rachel stiffened slightly, then forced herself to relax again. Despite what she said in private, publicly, Sally had defended Rachel, standing up to the town of Stillwater alongside Hester and Mavis.

"I told you, Sally. Jackson *had* to leave."

"Yeah, you told us. But I still don't see what could have been more important than you . . . and his baby."

"Sally!" Mavis hissed at her.

"Fine, fine. I won't say another word." She shook her head and turned to help Mavis close the carpetbag.

Rachel couldn't help wondering what they would say if they only knew that she wasn't going to visit Jackson's family—but Jackson himself. She had done as Lesley had suggested. She had stayed away from The Black Hound, despite the cost. But now she had to go. Jackson had the right to know that he was going to be a father.

Rubbing her palm over the growing mound of her unborn child, Rachel smiled softly. It hadn't been easy, those first few weeks after Jackson's disappearance. Loneliness had almost killed her, until she had discovered that through some miracle, she was carrying Jackson's child.

Then the world had opened to her again. And despite the wagging tongues of the gossips in town, she carried herself proudly, refusing to be ashamed of the child she and Jackson had created. Thank heaven, though, for her friends. Without their support, she would have had to face Stillwater alone. But with Sally, Mavis, Hester, and their husbands defending her to anyone who dared speak their nasty little thoughts, the town had quietly settled into aggrieved acceptance.

Of course, the fact that she owned and operated the only general store in town might have had something to do with that. Though some people may have wanted to shun her, the fact that they needed to shop at her place of business kept them civil at least.

"Rachel?" Mavis asked as she stepped in close, "Are you all right?"

"Hmmm? Oh, yes. I'm fine." She smiled at each of the three women in turn. "I was just thinking how fortunate I am to have such good friends. Without you, I might have had to leave Stillwater."

Mavis teared up and reached for the hanky tucked up her sleeve.

"It wouldn't have come to that, Rachel," Hester said.

"Oh, I don't know," Sally grumbled, then sat down on the edge of Rachel's bed. "Most folks are always ready to believe the worst. Look at Sprague, the banker. Why when he started telling everyone that he wasn't a bit surprised to find you a 'fallen woman'—because you had used your wiles on him to try to get a loan—people started talking."

"Sprague," Mavis sniffed and stuffed her hanky back into place. "As if Rachel would use wiles on that puffed-up old toad."

Sally laughed and winked at Rachel. "The best part was Tessa Horn. Who would have thought that gossipy hen would take a stand for you? I expected her to be the one carrying the tar and feathers.''

Rachel smiled softly and reached up to hold the golden coin hanging from a delicate chain around her neck. ''Tessa liked Jackson very much.''

''We all did,'' Hester told her and gave her a quick hug.

''Yes we did,'' Mavis added. ''Why Sam is still hoping he'll come back and go into business with him . . . ,'' her voice faded off and her eyes welled up with guilty tears as she looked at Rachel. ''Oh, I'm so sorry, honey.''

''It's all right, Mavis. If Jackson *could* come back. He would. I know it.''

''Well,'' Sally said solemnly, ''if he ever does, I've got a few things to say to him before I forgive him.''

A long moment of silence dropped on the four friends before Rachel checked the mantle clock. ''I have to go. The stage will be leaving shortly, and I can't miss it if I want to make my train in Seattle.''

PINE RIDGE, WASHINGTON TERRITORY,
THREE DAYS LATER

Jackson stomped through the center of the poker game and watched as cards and chips scattered to the floor in his wake.

The disgusted grumblings of the players as they reached to gather everything up again brought a tight smile to his face. At least he had finally figured out how to make himself felt in the real world. All it had taken was a surplus of anger, of emotion.

Clearly, being murdered hadn't made him nearly as angry as being snatched away from Rachel without so much as a chance to tell her one last time how much he loved her.

Rachel. He wondered about her. What was she doing that very minute? Was she hard at work in the store? Or maybe

she was at the new house, touching the wood he had
touched. Or lying in the bed where they had come together
those two miraculous times.

Disgusted with himself and the persistent torturous visions of Rachel, Jackson took long strides to the bar. Whiskey, rye, Scotch, and bourbon lined the shelf beneath the
wide bar mirror. His gaze moved over the bottles hungrily
as he wished again that he might get drunk enough to find
oblivion for a while.

But he wasn't allowed even that much. Not only was
oblivion denied him, but Jackson had discovered that he
was once more trapped inside the saloon. Since making a
mess of things with Rachel, he couldn't even go outside
any longer.

Once again, walls of ice stopped him whenever he at-
tempted to leave The Black Hound. Hell, even Lesley
hadn't visited him in months. Apparently, he had fouled his
last assignment up so badly that he wasn't going to be given
another.

But it didn't really matter. Nothing mattered now.

"Well," someone nearby muttered. "Will you look at
that?"

"What in the hell is she doing?"

Jackson lifted his head and stared into the bar mirror. He
felt his jaw drop. Reflected in the grimy, silvered surface?
Rachel had entered The Black Hound and stopped dead in
the doorway. Hungrily, his gaze moved over her. Silhou-
etted in the sunlight streaming in from behind her, her face
lay in shadow, but he would have recognized her anywhere.
Something inside him had leapt to attention the moment
she had came inside.

Slowly, he turned around, afraid to move too quickly,
lest she disappear as all his other dreams of her had.

He needn't have worried. Rachel stepped farther into the
room, letting the batwing doors swish shut behind her. She
shifted her gaze from side to side, glancing over the stunned

faces of the people watching her. She was looking for him.

He started toward her at the same moment that she turned for a table in the darkened corner of the room. Jackson stopped in his tracks. With his gaze locked on her swollen belly, he watched her move slowly to a chair and sit down.

Pregnant. Rachel was pregnant.

New, indescribable, unendurable pain welled up within him. Had she gone ahead and married someone, still trying to save Jackson's soul? Or had she fallen in love with another man? Immediately, images of Rachel in someone else's arms rose up in his mind, and he had to swallow back a howl of misery.

The bartender hurried to Rachel's table and after a brief, quiet conversation, scuttled back to the bar. Jackson forced himself to move toward her, skirting the poker tables. Before he reached her side, the bartender had returned to set a glass of sarsaparilla in front of her. As the man went back to work, Jackson went down on one knee beside the woman he loved.

"Jackson?" she whispered, and the piano player neatly covered her voice. "Jackson, are you here?"

"Yes, Rachel," he said, *even knowing that she wouldn't hear him.*

"I hope you can hear me, Jackson," she went on, her gaze drifting around the room. "I came to tell you something."

Oh, God. Why hadn't she stayed away? Why did she think she had to come to him with the news of her pregnancy? Couldn't she see it would have been kinder to let him go on thinking that she still loved him?

Rachel's palm slid across her heavy middle with a lovingly slow caress. Jackson followed the motion with his eyes and felt his heart break.

"I wanted you to know that you're going to be a father," she whispered.

Jackson jumped up and away from the table. His baby?

She carried *his* child? He looked down to where the baby lay nestled safely inside her. A part of him lived. A part of *them*—he and Rachel—*lived*. He rubbed one hand across the back of his neck and forced himself to listen as she went on.

"I know you're here, Jackson. Lesley came to see me the day you . . . left."

Lesley? Why the hell would Lesley go to see Rachel?

"I tried to wish you alive again with the last coin," she went on, and Jackson dropped to his knees again. Sorrow crushed his chest, and he wondered why it was that such pain could still be felt so long after death.

"Ah, Rachel," he said and reached up to brush one hand across her cheek.

She inhaled sharply and smiled. "Was that you, Jackson?"

A rush of hope filled him. If she could feel him, maybe she could hear him too, if he spoke louder, and directly to her heart.

"I love you so, darlin'," he said. "I wish I could be with you. Care for you."

She blinked back a sheen of tears, but not before a solitary drop spilled from the corner of her eye and rolled down across her cheek.

"Who's she talking to?" someone else whispered a bit too loudly.

"Don't know," another voice piped up. "But you leave her be. Sometimes a woman who's carryin' takes on strange notions."

Jackson frowned at the men and their curiosity.

Rachel smiled sadly. "Strange notions," she repeated quietly. "Like coming to a strange saloon to tell a ghost he's going to be a father." She inhaled deeply, then said, "I have to leave now, Jackson. I can't stay. It's not good for either of us . . . *or* the baby."

He knew that. Hell, he didn't want her in that damned

saloon a moment longer himself. But Lord God, what he wouldn't do to leave with her. His gaze dropped to his child again. Would this baby grow up to be the female doctor Lesley had told him about? What would she look like? Please God, he thought, let her look like Rachel, not him.

"I love you, Jackson," she said softly. "I always will."

His chin hit his chest. How would he survive eternity, knowing that Rachel and his child were denied him? How much Hell was one man expected to endure?

He looked at her beloved face again and noted that her eyes were closed as if she were trying to *feel* his presence. Concentrating all his efforts on making himself known to her, Jackson leaned over and gently kissed the swell of her abdomen.

She gasped sharply and their child kicked as if recognizing its father's touch.

Smiling sadly, Rachel stood up, and Jackson rose to stand beside her.

"You're a brave, strong woman, Rachel," he said, *knowing that raising an illegitimate child would be harder than she knew. For Rachel and the baby. A new emptiness, darker than anything he had ever known before, yawned open inside him.*

"I'll tell the baby about you every day," Rachel said. "And she'll love you as much as I do. I promise."

He knew he should tell her not to waste her life on memories of him. But God forgive him, he couldn't. Even if she *could* hear him, he didn't have the strength to tell her to forget him.

She turned for the door, and Jackson followed her, not ready yet to see her go. Her hurried steps carried her through the half doors and into the afternoon sunshine. He raced after her, rushing headlong into the icy barrier that kept him trapped from everything he held dear.

"Dammit," he yelled. *"No!"*

Helplessly, Jackson stared after her retreating figure until she was lost from sight. Then his head fell back on his neck, and an anguished groan, torn from the depths of his soul, rose up and settled down on the astonished patrons of The Black Hound.

STILLWATER, FIVE MONTHS LATER

Rachel smiled down at her daughter. Angela Tate. Named for the angels who had surely seen to her conception and safe delivery. Angela's little fists swiped the air, and her tiny legs kicked with a building anger. Chuckling, Rachel opened her shirtwaist. Pulling the edge of her chemise aside, she bared her breast and offered a distended nipple to her hungry baby.

As the infant's small mouth fastened tightly to her flesh, Rachel sighed and leaned back against the headboard of her bed. Moonlight filtered in through the lace curtains, which danced slightly in the soft breeze. Outside. Stillwater slept. The silence was broken only by Angela's frantic nursing and the occasional call of a night bird.

This was Rachel's favorite time. This hour before dawn when she and her daughter seemed to be the only two people in the world. The solid feel of the infant at her breast brought a deep ripple of contentment that was marred only by the knowledge that Jackson would never share that contentment.

Smiling sadly, she lifted her head and looked down at the baby. Softly, Rachel stroked her fingertip across her daughter's silky cheek. "How he would love you," she whispered, and the baby slapped one small palm against her mother's chest.

Rachel grinned and lifted the gold coin on its chain from the valley between her breasts. Dangling it near the baby's grasping hand, she watched her daughter snatch at it valiantly, all the while continuing to suckle.

"You're such a good eater, you'll be able to grab

daddy's coin in no time at all,'' Rachel assured her. The baby grinned suddenly, a tiny, milky smile that tugged at her mother's heart. More than anything. Rachel wanted to shout, ''Jackson! Come look at your daughter! See her smile at the mention of your name!''

But she would never be able to share these things with him. Tears pooled in her eyes, but she fought them back. If she couldn't share Angela with Jackson, then she would share Jackson with Angela. Once again, as she had every night since the baby's birth, Rachel told Angela about her father.

Talking about him eased the pain of missing him and somehow, she thought, Angela understood everything she said.

The baby smiled again and smacked her lips against her mother's breast.

''You know,'' Rachel said, ''my mother used to say that whenever a baby smiled, it was because the angels were talking to it.'' Angela swung her little arm wide, opened her fist, and grabbed her father's coin in a tight grasp.

''What a big girl,'' Rachel congratulated her and covered the baby's hand with her own. She looked down into green eyes so like Jackson's and said, ''Angels talk to you, sweetheart. And maybe, because you're still close to Heaven, maybe you could actually *see* your daddy if you really try.''

Angela squirmed in her arms, and Rachel went on.

''Try, baby girl. Try very hard.'' She closed her eyes before saying, ''He's very tall and he has dark hair, like you. You have his eyes, and that hint of a dimple in your cheek is from him, too.''

Beneath the baby's fingers, the golden coin began to shimmer with warmth. A gentle heat, soothing to the touch and stirring to the soul. Angela gurgled, and Rachel smiled absently, lost in her memories. Another moment or two passed in silence, then the baby sneezed, breaking the spell.

"God bless you," a deep male voice spoke from the shadows.

Rachel's eyes flew open. She held perfectly still, almost afraid to breathe. If this was a dream, she didn't want to wake up.

"Rachel?"

That voice. So familiar. So dear.

Slowly, she turned toward him and watched, breath held, as he stepped into a puddle of moonlight. Angela squirmed in her arms, assuring Rachel that she was indeed awake. But Jackson's image was so blurry. So indistinct. Surely, this was just a dream.

Then she blinked, and the tears blurring her vision spilled over onto her cheeks. He was real and whole and there, with her. Speechless, she could only stare at him as he came closer, then dropped to one knee beside the bed.

He touched her face with hesitant fingers. She gasped at the warmth of his touch.

"Jackson?" she finally whispered brokenly, then smoothed one hand through his hair. Tears streaked down her face as he reached for her, and she leaned into his embrace. His arms closed around both her and their daughter, and Rachel knew peace for the first time in nearly a year.

"How?" she asked, her voice hushed reverently. "How did you get here?"

"I don't know," he laughed shortly, kissed her cheek, then released her and stared down at his daughter. "One minute I was at The Black Hound . . . the next, I was here."

"For how long?" she demanded, fighting back new tears that threatened to choke her.

"I don't know that either," he said and looked up, into her eyes, smiling wryly. "Nothing much has changed, Rachel. I still don't have the answers to your questions."

"It doesn't matter." She met his gaze squarely and told herself to remember every moment of this blessed time with him. "Nothing matters now that you're here. With me. With us."

He reached for her again and in wonder, stroked her cheek with his fingertips. She turned her face into his touch and kissed his hand. Unmindful of the tears raining down her face, Rachel smiled and said, "I'd like you to meet your daughter."

"My daughter," he repeated, his tone awed. Hesitantly, he touched her little hand, still clasped tightly around her mother's golden necklace. "She's so beautiful. Like her mama."

"And strong, too," Rachel told him, wanting him to know everything about his child before some cruel Fate snatched him away. "I wear your gold coin on this chain," she said. "And a moment ago, she grabbed it all by herself for the first time."

He dropped a gentle kiss on the baby's forehead, then chuckled gently. "She's got quite a grip on it too," he said. Then he shifted his gaze to stare at Rachel, like a man stumbling out of the desert and finding a lake full of cool, clear water.

The coin. Rachel's breath caught. Angela had grabbed the coin. She had held her baby's small hand, and the two of them together had clasped that golden coin while Rachel spoke of Jackson.

Magic. It had to be. Rachel glanced down at Angela's tiny fist and carefully pried the little fingers free of the gold chain. She sucked in a breath of air; her head spun. Glancing at Jackson, she whispered brokenly, "The coin. It's . . . gone."

"What?"

"Angela and I were holding the coin together while I told her about you. It was there. Now it's not."

He jumped to his feet, paced off a couple of steps, then came back again. Anxiously, he shoved one hand through his hair. "But you told me in the saloon that you had already tried wishing me back."

"I did. Lesley said I couldn't do it."

"If you didn't do it, then . . . Angela?" Jackson's gaze shifted to the smiling baby.

"Is it possible?" Rachel stood up on suddenly shaky legs and moved in close to the man she had never thought to be with again.

"How could she have wished for me?" he asked, smoothing his palm gently across his daughter's small head.

"Maybe," Rachel said softly, "maybe she wished with her heart. Maybe this happened because a baby is so pure. So innocent. Her soul is so new, she's still close to Heaven."

"No closer than I am, right now," Jackson whispered.

But would they stay this way?

Tears blurred Rachel's vision again, and still he looked wonderful. But she had to know if he was here to stay or not. There was only one way to be sure. Cradling their daughter between them, Rachel held her breath and leaned her head against his chest.

He held himself stiffly, waiting.

Rachel felt his desperation as her own. She closed her eyes, murmured a quick, heartfelt prayer, and listened.

Long, silent moments passed, the only sounds in the room that of the impatient baby, fretting to finish her meal.

"Rachel?" he asked and his voice rumbled in his chest. "Dammit, woman, tell me what you hear. Or *don't* hear."

A strangled laugh squeezed past her throat. She lifted her head and grinned at him through a new, heavier sheen of tears. "It's beating, Jackson. Your heart is beating!"

He released a pent-up breath and slapped one hand to his own chest. After a long minute, he returned her grin with one of his own.

"Looks like I'm home," he said softly, unbelievingly

and threw one grateful glance toward Heaven. "Thanks, Les."

Angela chose just that moment to remind her parents of her presence with a squall loud enough to shatter glass.

Her father laughed, took her into his arms, and promised, "You cry all you want to, sweet pea. It is the prettiest music your daddy's ever heard."

Rachel's forehead dropped to his chest, and when he wrapped one arm around her shoulders to pull her tight against him, she smiled in the darkness. "You won't think so when she wakes you up out of a sound sleep."

"Honey," he assured her, "I'll always think it's a beautiful sound. Besides," he paused for a quick, hard kiss, "I don't plan on you and me getting a helluva lot of sleep anyway. Not for a *long* time."

Grinning like a fool, Rachel settled herself back on the bed, took the baby from Jackson, and began nursing her again.

But now, there were three of them together in the moonlit darkness. And Rachel knew that this hour before dawn would always be special to her. This time when they were all still close to Heaven.

Epilogue

Even the sun had made a rare springtime appearance, showering the gathering with light and warmth. The entire town of Stillwater had turned out for the ceremony. Rachel Tate glanced over the familiar faces.

Sam and Mavis and their three children. Hester and Charlie with the twins. She smiled and smothered a chuckle as she spotted Sally and Mike O'Hara sitting in the midst of their six rowdy sons.

"What are you laughing at?" Jackson whispered and bent his head close to hers.

"Nothing," she answered, letting her gaze move over him with a wonder that hadn't faded in the slightest over the years. His dark hair, still a bit too long, was sprinkled with gray now, but those green eyes of his had lost none of their magic. Impulsively, she leaned in and planted a quick kiss on his cheek.

He wiggled his eyebrows at her, mouthed the word *"Later,"* then turned back to listen to whatever their youngest daughter was saying. At eight, little Christine had opinions on everything and didn't hesitate to share them.

Rachel leaned forward to sneak a peek at her other children, dressed in their finest clothes for the occasion. Twelve-year-old Sam, named for his father's business partner, was perched on the edge of his seat. He had always had enough energy for two or three healthy boys, she

thought, smiling to herself. Next to him was Davis. At six-
teen, he was already as handsome and as tall as his father.
Like his father, he had a fine talent for working with wood.
The boy had big plans for the Tate-Hale construction firm.

And then there was Angela. Her firstborn. The child con-
ceived on one of those two stolen nights she and Jackson
had claimed so many years before. The child she had been
carrying when they were married.

The child Destiny had demanded be born.

Rachel sighed and leaned back in her chair, her gaze
shifting to the hastily erected stage in front of her.

From somewhere off to the side, a small band, costumed
in matching blue and red uniforms, struck up a tune. The
crowd quieted as a lone man climbed the steps to the stage
and moved to its very center.

"My friends," he said in a practiced tone that reached
the far edges of his audience. "We're here today to honor
one of Stillwater's citizens."

"Come on, Governor," someone in the back shouted.
"No need to be so blamed formal. Get Angie out here!"

Pockets of applause greeted that statement.

Jackson grinned at Rachel and grabbed her hand to hold
in both of his.

"You're right, friend," the governor shouted back with
a laugh. He turned to one of his aides and took the scroll
being handed to him. Then he looked to the edge of the
stage and waved one hand. "Angela, come on out here and
say hello to your friends."

Hoots and hollers rose up over the thunderous applause
that followed Dr. Angela Tate as she took the steps and
walked with a long, easy stride to the governor's side.

Jackson squeezed Rachel's hand tightly.

Holding out the red ribboned scroll, the politician announced, "This commendation is awarded to Dr. Angela
Tate in gratitude for her service to the Territory of Washington. Almost single handedly, Dr. Tate stopped a cholera

epidemic that—without her—would have cost hundreds of lives.''

Angela grinned, took the scroll, and held it tightly.

"You are a credit to your community, doctor," the governor went on, clapping his hands and beaming the smile of a politician in an election year, "We thank you."

"Atta girl, Angie," a deep voice, sounding suspiciously like Sally's oldest son, Mike Jr., yelled.

As the crowed came to its feet in a roar of approval, Jackson pulled Rachel into his arms. He bent his head to claim a kiss that left her breathless.

Unseen by the cheering mob, someone else beamed a proud smile. Lesley pulled his lace hanky from his sleeve and carefully dabbed at his eyes. As he tucked it back into place, he spared a glance for the couple who had overcome so much to be together. "All is as it should be. They've done well," he said to himself.

Another voice, one that carried the roar of thunder in a whisper, said with a chuckle, "Didn't I tell you it would be so, Lesley?"

"Yes, Sir," the little man replied, coming to attention.

"Surely you didn't doubt Me?"

"Not for a moment, Sir," Lesley assured the voice before giving his former charge one last satisfied nod. Then he faded away into the sunlight.

Jackson and Rachel, holding on to each other, as always, smiled proudly at their daughter—a blessing born of a love stronger than time, stronger than Fate.

On her remote Colorado ranch, Rebecca Hale struggled to raise her small son alone. The last thing she needed was a drifter on her land—a drifter with no horse, no gear and no memory. But Zacariah was even more mysterious than he seemed. He was a spirit whose task it was to usher the souls of the departed into the afterlife. Zack had angered the Heavenly powers and they banished him to earth, where he was to live one month as a human.

Stranded on the Hale ranch, Zack vowed to keep his distance from the desperate, disordered affairs of humankind. But he had a duty that had to be carried out, no matter what the cost to Rebecca and those she loved. And when Rebecca's gentle kiss awakened a new hunger in him, it forced him to choose between Heaven and the little piece of paradise known only by the human heart...

KATHLEEN KANE

A POCKETFUL OF PARADISE

"Nobody can capture the essence of Americana heart and soul quite as well as Kathleen Kane."
—*Affaire de Coeur*

Three breathtaking novellas by these acclaimed authors celebrate the warmth of family, the challenges of the frontier and the power of love...

ROSANNE BITTNER
DENISE DOMNING
VIVIAN VAUGHAN

CHERISHED LOVE
Rosanne Bittner, Denise Domning, Vivian Vaughan
_____ 96171-5 $5.99 U.S./$7.99 CAN.

Against the backdrop of an elegant Cornwall mansion before World War II and a vast continent-spanning canvas during the turbulent war years, Rosamunde Pilcher's most eagerly-awaited novel is the story of an extraordinary young woman's coming of age, coming to grips with love and sadness, and in every sense of the term, coming home...

Rosamunde Pilcher

The #1 *New York Times* Bestselling Author of *The Shell Seekers* and *September*

COMING HOME

"Rosamunde Pilcher's most satisfying story since *The Shell Seekers*."

—*Chicago Tribune*

"Captivating...The best sort of book to come home to...Readers will undoubtedly hope Pilcher comes home to the typewriter again soon."

—*New York Daily News*

No one believes in ghosts anymore, not even in Salem, Massachusetts. And especially not sensible Helen Evett, a widow who lives for her two teenaged kids and who runs the best preschool in town. But when little Katie Byrne enters her school, strange things begin to happen. Katie's widowed father, Nat, begins to awaken feelings in Helen that she had counted as dead. But why does Helen get the feeling that Linda, Katie's mother, is reaching beyond the grave to tell her something?

As Helen and Nat each explore the pain of their losses and the joy of their newfound love, Linda Byrne's ghost plays a bold hand, beseeching Helen to uncover the mystery of her death. But what Helen finds could make her the target of a jealous killer and a modern Salem witch-hunt that threatens her, her family...and the magical second-time-around love that's taking her and Nat by storm.

BESTSELLING, AWARD-WINNING AUTHOR

ANTOINETTE STOCKENBERG

Beyond Midnight